FRANCO'S MAP

Franco's Map

Published by The Conrad Press in the United Kingdom 2020

Tel: +44(0)1227 472 874
www.theconradpress.com
info@theconradpress.com

ISBN 978-1-913567-07-1

Copyright © Walter Ellis, 2020

The moral right of Walter Ellis to be identified as author of this work has been asserted in accordance with the Copyright, Designs and Patents Act 1988.

All rights reserved.

Typesetting and Cover Design by: Charlotte Mouncey, www.bookstyle.co.uk
The Conrad Press logo was designed by Maria Priestley.

Printed and bound in Great Britain by Clays Ltd, Elcograf S.p.A.

FRANCO'S MAP

WALTER ELLIS

Extracts from interviews given in 1945 by Reichsmarschall Hermann Göring to his American interrogators in Nuremberg

'In 1940 we had a plan to seize all North Africa from Dakar to Alexandria, and with it the Atlantic islands for U-boat bases. This would have cut off many of Britain's shipping lanes. At the same time, any resistance movement in North Africa could be crushed. [Afterwards], nobody could have interfered in the Mediterranean.'

'The attack on Gibraltar was so methodically prepared by the Luftwaffe that, according to all human expectations, there could be no failure ... There was only one unprotected airfield on the Rock. In twenty-four hours the Royal Air Force would have been forced off ... and we could have battered it to pieces. This was a real task and we were eager to accomplish it.'

'I urged [Hitler] to put these decisive considerations into the foreground and only after the conclusion of [the Gibraltar] undertaking to examine further the military and political situation with regard to Russia. For, if these conditions were brought about, we would be in a favourable position in the event of an intervention by the United States ... Failure to carry out the plan was one of the major mistakes of the war.'

PROLOGUE

Carabanchel Prison, Madrid,
July 26 1940

The vast prison complex, which Franco boasted would be the largest in Europe, was still not finished and smelled of concrete and lime. On the way from his cell to the execution chamber, Romero passed squads of inmates skimming cement onto bare walls. They averted their eyes as he shuffled by, the jangling of his shackles echoing down the dusty corridors. One old man who mumbled a prayer was rewarded with a sharp prod in the back from a guard's baton that made him wince. Another whispered, 'Don't be afraid, comrade – the people are with you.'

He had nodded at this, wishing it to be true. But now, strapped to the garrotte post, there was no one. Only in the past could he find freedom, or hope. Think back, he told himself. *Concentrate!*

He had been nine years old. It was high summer, 1915 and he was with his father Alonso and his mother Molly at the funeral in Dublin of the exiled firebrand Jeremiah O'Donovan Rossa, whose body had been brought home from America for burial. The rain that day hung in the air like mist and many of the thousands of mourners who lined the route from City Hall to Glasnevin Cemetery carried umbrellas. Among the gaudy memorials, the men wore dark suits and hats, or else the uniforms of the Citizen Army, the Irish Republican Brotherhood or the Irish Volunteers. Sweat ran down his father's face. No one spoke. The word was that this would be no ordinary funeral and the sense of anticipation was extraordinary. The coffin was lowered. The priest in his cassock made the sign of the cross and led a recital of the rosary.

What followed marked the day in history. First a volley of shots rang out, then a young man wearing the peaked cap of an officer in the volunteers stepped forward. Drawing a paper from his pocket, he surveyed those present with a look of almost mystical authority. Padraic Pearse did not have to call for silence. He spoke at first in Irish, which few among his audience understood. Then he switched to English. Ireland's foes, he warned, were strong and wise and wary. But they could not undo the miracles of God who ripened in the hearts of young men the seeds sown by the dead generations.

The voice was compelling. 'Life springs from death; and from the graves of patriot men and women spring living nations. The defenders of this realm have worked well in secret and in the open. They think that they have pacified Ireland. They think that they have purchased half of us and intimidated the other half. They think that they have foreseen everything, think that they have provided against everything; but the fools, the fools, the fools! – they have left us our Fenian dead, and while Ireland holds these graves, Ireland unfree shall never be at peace.'

The speaker was half-mad, half-visionary. But Romero had believed him. He believed him still. The Easter Rising, when it came, would be a blood sacrifice, not a feat of arms, but from it would spring a living nation. A half-Spanish boy, with his dark eyes and sallow skin, Romero remembered how his father placed both hands on his shoulders as Pearse spoke. He remembered the hypnotic impact of the words and how hard his father gripped, the pressure of each finger on his small bones. So long ago and it seemed like the beginning and the end of everything. He had thought nothing as important would happen again in the whole of his life.

But the years, full to the brim with evil, had rolled past like clouds on a windy day. Now, as he faced his own death in this bleak and awful prison, he tried not to let his hands shake. They mustn't know the fear he felt. He prayed for the souls of his father and his mother; for his dead comrades, their bodies heaped into mass graves across Spain, with neither cross nor winding sheet nor a friend's lament; for his new-made companions in the fight against Hitler. And for one in particular. There was no one else. He looked up, twisting his head so that he could focus on the group of officials gathered to legitimise his death.

He had been refused the Last Rites of the church. The priest stood against the wall, reading from the Bible, not daring to meet his gaze, pretending that he couldn't see that the condemned man had not only lost an eye at the hands of his captors, but all of his fingernails. A prison guard circled the garrotte, checking that everything was in order. The man tested the straps and the collar – a technician, nothing more. Then, without warning, a second guard drew a leather hood over his head and the world grew dark. He wished that his last sight had been of the woman he loved. The door to the execution chamber opened, emitting a draft of ice-cold air before it shut again with a distant click. There was a rattle of keys, followed by the footsteps of the executioner. Through the metal, he felt the man's hands grip the lever.

The prison's deputy governor stepped forward. 'Edward Alonso Maria Romero: in the name of the Spanish people and in accordance with the requirements of the Penal Code, you have been convicted of wilful murder and are sentenced to death for your crime. The sentence will now be carried out. Have you anything to say?' Romero straightened himself, feeling the steel of the collar against his skin. 'Long live the republic!' he shouted.

The official nodded. Romero's last words, heard only by himself, were the closing lines of the centuries-old Catholic prayer known as the Confiteor. 'May Almighty God have mercy on me, forgive me my sins, and bring me to everlasting life. May the Almighty and merciful Lord grant me pardon, absolution, and remission of all my sins. Amen.' The executioner began to twist the lever. The collar tightened. After a few seconds, he couldn't breathe. His body began to shake in the wooden chair. His arms and legs pushed against the straps that held him. Then his eyes began to roll. He had no control over them. He felt them bulge and twist. His tongue protruded from his open mouth. It was at this point that the metal screw positioned at the back of his head penetrated his neck and severed his spinal column. His head fell forward, the convulsions stopped, and his life gave out with a sigh.

'Remove the prisoner,' the deputy governor said. 'Bring in the next one.'

1

British Crown Colony of Gibraltar:
six weeks earlier

The Rock divided the light from the darkness. East of the ridge, the colours of the morning were clear and vivid. The Mediterranean reached out, past Oran, past Sicily, past Tobruk and Crete, all the way to Egypt and Palestine. To the west, the town and its dockyards remained in shadow and the colder, deeper waters of the Atlantic pressed against the harbour, where the aircraft carrier *Ark Royal* sat at anchor.

At half-past five, the great lamp of the lighthouse at Europa Point dimmed and went out. A marine sentry finishing his watch in the forward observation post raised his field glasses and swept the narrow Strait from west to east. It was the clearest time of the day and, to the south, Morocco's Mount Jebel Musa stood out in sharp relief against the ochre haze of Africa.

Two miles to the north, in a stone-walled villa overlooking the Spanish border town of La Linea de la Concepción, an agent of German military intelligence, the *Abwehr*, observed the colony through a similar, but superior, pair of high-powered binoculars. He was logging details of the continued extension of the colony's airstrip and focused for several seconds on the face of a heavily moustachioed Canadian Army engineer about to end his shift, who stood for a moment facing east, feeling the warmth of the sun on his face.

The runway, with its support facilities, was the colony's biggest single project in years. Built on rubble left over from a network of supply and communication tunnels, it stretched 200 metres into the bay beyond the Western Beach, continuing across the northern littoral as far as the Eastern Beach, where it looked across to the modest market town of Marbella.

By six o'clock, the streets and alleys of the town echoed to the sound of Reveille as the main garrison came grudgingly to life. Steam rose from the kitchens as ten thousand breakfasts got underway. A destroyer in the harbour, about to embark on a patrol of the Strait, emitted its distinctive high-pitched whoop-whoop and drew rapidly away from its berth on the South Mole, creating a swell that caused even the Ark Royal to bob gently at its moorings.

Lieutenant General Sir Clive Gerard Liddell, Gibraltar's governor and commander-in-chief, glanced up through the open windows of his office towards the limestone peak that reared some 1,300 feet above his head. A battery of naval guns was testing elevation and trajectory, watched by a group of Barbary apes who looked to have interrupted their grooming for the occasion.

Everything seemed to be in order. The Rock, seized from Spain in 1704 and granted to Britain 'for ever' under the terms of the Treaty of Utrecht, was to all outward appearances as unassailable as ever. Liddell knew differently. He had read the reports. Which was why he was about to sit down with a trio of senior representatives newly arrived from London.

Two of the visitors, one from the Treasury, the other from the War Office, were much as he would have expected. He didn't doubt their abilities. Having worked in Whitehall for a number of years, he had come to respect the so-called mandarin class. It was the MI6 man who was a surprise. The name hadn't registered at first, but as soon as he walked into his office, there was no doubting who it was. Older, of course, but the same imperturbable schoolmasterly demeanour, even, quite possibly, the same suit. Tom Strickland was a Yorkshireman of the old school, with a mind like a filing cabinet. They had first met at the Imperial Defence College. As the storm clouds gathered, it was reassuring to know he was on the team.

'Strickland,' he said, 'It's been a long time.'

'Governor. You've come up in the world since we last met.'

'Oh,' said Liddell. 'You know how it is – always openings for bureaucrats. What about you?'

'They've given me Iberia and the Maghreb. Challenge enough at my age.'

'Understood. The years don't get any kinder, do they?' Liddell, born in 1883, was coming up on fifty-eight. Strickland was two years older. Both men would have been facing retirement if it hadn't been for the war. 'Anyway, good to see you. We'll have a chance to catch up later. But we should probably get on. I've asked Admiral Cunningham to join us. He should be here at any moment.' Liddell moved towards a polished oak table, set with blotters and pens and glasses of water.

At this point, as if on cue, the admiral walked in. Sir Andrew Cunningham, commander of Britain's Mediterranean fleet, was tall and grey-haired, with hands that might have belonged to a farmer or a sculptor. In his late fifties, he looked fit and spry, with keen, darting eyes. The governor made the introductions before taking a seat at the head of the table, next to his adjutant. The naval chief, in his summer whites, sat on his own at the opposite end.

Liddell's initial presentation lasted just over five minutes and dealt with the progress he had made since taking over in 1939. The two mandarins, facing the window, treated his account like an audit. His proposals for additional support were mentally scrutinised and costed and set against earlier projections.

Strickland, with his back to the wall, knew only too well that any increase in outlay would have to be met out of the contingency reserve – a ruinous, but largely fictitious fund, as elastic in its scope as the duration of the war. He could only guess what Cunningham was thinking, but was unsurprised when the naval chief cleared his throat theatrically and glanced up at the clock on the wall.

'Gentlemen,' he began. 'I hate to interrupt your calculations, but I'm due to fly to Alexandria in an hour's time and there are a couple of points I'd like to make before I go.'

Liddell gestured his assent. The mandarins nodded obediently, pens poised.

Cunningham's demeanour was weary, yet resolute. 'The governor has presented you with details of the strengths and weaknesses of Gibraltar itself, and I strongly endorse each one of his conclusions. My concern, however, is to drive home the absolute, overriding military necessity of keeping it out of German hands.'

He glared at the civil servants, with their clipboards. 'London has no idea. They look upon this place as a fixed asset, like a house on which the mortgage is fully paid up. They forget that though the Rock itself is fixed, we are not. We could be driven off at any time. And if we are, God help us. The plain fact of the matter is, if Franco ever decides to throw in his lot with Hitler and Gibraltar falls, the chain that holds the empire together will be broken.'

Twisting round in his chair, he pointed out the window towards the impressive array of naval vessels moored in the harbour. 'British sea power in the Mediterranean is already under threat. The Italians have a formidable navy. A number of their ships are modern and their officers and men know what they're doing. Worse, every one of our bases is within easy reach of their air force. That's one thing. We can deal with that. But imagine the ships that you see moored in front of you gone.' He swept his hand across the civil servants' line of vision. 'Aircraft carriers, battleships, cruisers, destroyers, submarines – the lot. *Vanished!* Imagine now what would replace them. The Bismarck and the Tirpitz, both of them coming up for completion, bigger and more powerful than anything we've got right now – together with heavy cruisers, escorts and a squadron of U-Boats. Italy would control the Mediterranean. At the same time, the *Kriegsmarine*, hugely emboldened, could hope to achieve total domination of the Atlantic and the western approaches.'

He paused. No one spoke. 'And where would *we* be?'

It was a rhetorical question and Cunningham did not wait for an answer.

'What remained of Force H would be a thousand miles away, in Egypt, bottled up, unable to get out of the Med without getting into the scrap of our lives. At the same time, the oil and other raw materials on which our country depends for its survival would have to be sent via the Cape – an additional eight *thousand* miles – subject to enemy attack at every turn.'

He paused, taking in the silence that greeted his monologue. 'It's a truly awful prospect, gentlemen – worse than anything in our lifetimes.'

'We're all on the same side, Admiral,' one of the mandarins said.

Cunningham looked sceptical. 'In that case, with your permission, Governor, gentlemen, I'll leave you to it.' He rose from his chair and placed his cap on his head, straightening the peak so that there was no sign of his rapidly receding hairline. Before he left, he tapped the MI6 man on the elbow. 'I don't know what your lot get up to in Madrid, Tom,' he said. 'But it's time for a re-think.'

'Depend on it,' said Strickland.

Cunningham nodded, then turned on his heels and left.

For a moment, nobody spoke. The governor turned away from the grey-faced officials, who seemed suddenly to depress him, and gazed out towards the harbour and the more distant prospect of Africa. 'The hell with Whitehall!' he said finally, wheeling round to stare straight at Strickland. 'I want you to go straight to the PM. Tell him that if he wants to win this war, or at any rate to survive it, he must do everything possible to forestall an attack on Gibraltar. There is simply no time to lose.'

London: Roland Gardens, South Kensington, June 10 1940

The only thing Charles Bramall noticed that was different when he returned to his London flat after a ten-week absence was the smell. He'd forgotten to empty the bin in the kitchen and the bottle of milk in his tiny refrigerator resembled a school science experiment gone terribly wrong. A bunch of flowers his mother had given him from the garden of the family home in Northamptonshire was little more than straw bleached white by the sun. Atrophy and death, it seemed, were life's natural accompaniment.

Aged 31, he had been home for less than a week when the order came through instructing him to rejoin his regiment, the First battalion Irish Guards, in Glasgow the following Monday. Glasgow? That made no sense. How were they supposed to get to France from Glasgow? You had to hope that the brass knew their business, but the signs were not encouraging.

Before making it back to London, he had spent several days with his parents at their cottage in Northamptonshire, listening to his father as the old man huffed and puffed, torn between paternal pride, anxiety, and political despair.

Major General Sir Frederick Bramall had served with the Dublin Fusiliers on the Western Front throughout the Great War, rising to the rank of Brigadier. His final months of active service, in the autumn of 1918, had witnessed the greatest feat of British arms since Waterloo. His son, living at their home in County Monaghan, had followed the exploits of the Irish regiments with particular pride. Each day, Billy McKenna, the family's long-serving head 'keeper, a veteran of the Battle of Omdurman and the second Boer War, would read him the accounts in the Irish Times of how the British Army outfought the Germans until they brought the war to a triumphant conclusion.

'Would you have me read it you all the way to the end, Charlie?' McKenna would invariably ask, barely suppressing the pride he shared with the young fellow sitting opposite him at the kitchen table. 'You know my eyes aren't what they were.'

'Yes, please, Billy,' Bramall would reply. 'I'll make you a cup of tea afterwards, I promise.' And McKenna would smile and resume, his Ulster vowels struggling with the names of faraway places, like Amiens and Ypres. To a nine-year-old boy, the reports were an epic, like something out of Homer.

The years that followed were unforgiving. Homecomings for Irish regiments were muted. The 1916 Easter Rising, and its bloody aftermath, had transformed the public mood, and instead of being greeted as heroes, they were scorned as occupiers. Soldiers in uniform were spat on in the street. The political settlement that followed, giving the Twenty-Six Counties their independence, sounded the death knell of the Anglo-Irish. Emboldened by their own success and embittered by the tactics of the British irregulars, the Black and Tans, rebels drove Protestants off the land they had worked for centuries, claiming it in the name of the Irish people.

The loss of Dreenagh was both profound and shocking. The house itself, built in 1796, was a storehouse of memories. It was burned to the ground as if it were the palace of the Tsar. Worst of all, Billy McKenna – more of a father to him than the general had ever been – had been murdered in front of him and his mother, shot in the belly, left to die like a stuck pig.

His mother was traumatised by the experience, which had turned her hair white and left her with a fear of strangers. For his part, Sir Frederick could not believe that such an injustice could go unpunished. His first and only principal became that governments should stand firm against Socialism, thuggery and petty nationalism. From his family's new home in England, where they lived in reduced circumstances, he watched, appalled, as the same Bolshevik attitudes spread across Europe. He saw the General Strike of 1926 as an assault on the natural order. Unable to use cavalry to break the protest, he had mobilised a force of undergraduates from Oxford and Cambridge alongside young fellows from the City, using them to force a path through picket lines. The 'Bramall Boys' made quite a splash and few in the Government cared to object.

Bramall, raised with an awareness of exile, was proud of his father, as he might have been proud of a distinguished ancestor. But it was hard to listen to him sometimes.

Over dinner in Aynho, his father was convinced that Churchill would once more lead England to disaster, just as he had at the Dardanelles.' We should be fighting the bloody Communists, not each other,' he announced, stabbing the air with his fork.

'You took on the Germans soon enough in the last lot,' Bramall replied. 'Didn't seem to bother you then.'

The general shrank back. 'Different thing altogether. The Kaiser getting above himself. Hitler admires England. Sees it as a force for stability in the world.'

'And the invasion of Poland?'

'Only claiming back what's rightfully his.'

'Like DeValera?'

A scowl. 'That bastard was half-Spanish, born in New York. Ireland was our home for centuries. We belong there. He stole our birthright.'

'You don't have to tell me, father. It was my home, too.'

As it turned out, the First Irish were never going to France.

Their war would be fought among the ice floes a thousand miles to the north. Churchill, as First Lord of the Admiralty, had sought to implement his long-standing plan to occupy Norway, thus denying the Germans the sea lanes essential to their imports of iron ore from Sweden. It never happened. Hitler struck first, obliging the British and their allies to take on an enemy already in place and confident of reinforcement. The Navy responded as best it could. It sank a number of German ships, including a whole squadron of destroyers. But ultimately it was forced to withdraw under a relentless air assault. Bramall's hastily cobbled-together invasion force fought with distinction at Narvik, 150 miles inside the Arctic Circle. The port was taken and held against a determined counter-attack. But it was too little too late and a general retreat was ordered. By June 7, all allied forces had been evacuated to the UK to lick their wounds. The entire Norwegian campaign, mismanaged from start to finish, had lasted exactly a month.

Back in London, Bramall shut his eyes against the memory and the shame. Someone at Brigade headquarters said he'd been mentioned in dispatches. There was even talk of a medal. He wasn't displeased by this. It would be something to show Pa. But he didn't care that much either. He simply wanted to enjoy his remaining week's leave and then return to his regiment.

Apart from the smell and the flowers, the flat was just as he had left it. The difference was that familiar things were now strange to him as if he were removed, or dislocated, from the ordinary world. It wasn't the first time this had happened to him. He had had the same experience after his return from Spain. He remembered, too, the day he and his parents fled Ireland in 1921, travelling through a countryside that was suddenly, heartbreakingly alien. At the railway station, his mother had shielded him from the mockery of local youths while his father shook his fist at them. On the train, they were mocked for their accent. One fellow, stinking of beer, with spittle in his beard, shouted out that they weren't wanted and get the hell back to England. It was as if their lives had been turned inside out. That's what it felt like now, except that this time he was needed. It was time to call home. He dialled the operator and gave her the number. Then he waited and pressed the phone to his ear.

It was his mother who answered. She sounded old – and Irish. 'Aynho 54.'

'It's me, mother. I'm in London.'

All he could hear at the other end was silence.

London: Roland Gardens, four days later

The sergeant from Special Branch. closed the front door and replaced his warrant card in the inside pocket of his tweed jacket. 'I really am sorry about this, sir,' he said. 'I know you're you're supposed to be on leave, but I've been asked to give you this and wait for a response.'

'Quite all right,' said Bramall. 'I was getting bored anyway.' Motioning to the officer to follow him into the living room, he continued over to the sideboard and switched off the wireless. Then he opened the letter. It said Secret Intelligence Service at the top and 'Most Confidential.' Its message was terse and to the point.

You are ordered to report to the Hatton Court Hotel, Hanslope, Bucks, tomorrow [June 15], there to await further instructions. You are to tell no one, family included, where you are going. When you have read this letter, hand it to the officer who gave it to you and he will provide you with tickets and cash sufficient for the undertaking. A room has been booked for you at the hotel in the name of Mr Chris Germaine.

There was no signature.

Bramall folded the letter and handed it back to the sergeant, who exchanged it for a larger white envelope.

'Your rail pass and hotel details,' he said. 'I'll tell them to expect you then, shall I?'

'Do I have a choice?'

They both smiled at that.

When the Branch man had gone, Bramall switched the wireless back on and boiled a kettle. He wanted to catch the news on the Home Service. He'd assumed he'd be reassigned to France to join the BEF, but the retreat from Dunkirk had put paid to that. He remembered talking to a major on the troopship home from Narvik. If the Germans took France, he said, the country wouldn't have the men or equipment to go in a second time. It would be back door stuff: sabotage and espionage. All the attention would be on forming an armed resistance.

So maybe that was it. Maybe they wanted him to go behind enemy lines and help set up some form of militia. But if so, they had got the wrong man. He knew as much about organising armed resistance as he did about the theory of relativity.

The sudden whistling of the kettle brought him back to the present with a start and he made himself a pot of tea. At three o'clock, the news came on. A special bulletin, it said. It could hardly have been worse. It was like an announcement of the end of civilisation, and he wondered how the newsreader, seated in his studio in Broadcasting House, managed to keep his voice from cracking. German troops had entered Paris. The Swastika was flying over the Arc de Triomphe. The Government of Prime Minister Reynaud, operating from its provisional headquarters in Bordeaux, had declared the capital an 'open city' three days before and the resistance offered to the *Wehrmacht* had been minimal. To the east, the Maginot Line was breached. France's much vaunted frontier defences had been reduced to an irrelevance. In Brest, Canadian troops under the command of General Alanbrooke were being evacuated after destroying most of their heavy equipment.

Bramall sat still for several minutes. Then he drained the remains of his tea and stepped outside to clear his head.

Madrid: Puerta del Sol, June 14

They made an odd couple. As Colonel Raúl Ortega walked up the ornate marble stairway of Spain's Interior Ministry next to his boss Ramón Serrano Suñer, the comparison to Don Quixote and Sancho Panza made by his wife did not seem out of place The pencil-thin Serrano gesturing, his head held high, looked to be lost in some higher realm. Ortega, bobbing and weaving, taking two steps forward for each one of his master's, gave the impression that he would rather be at lunch. But if either man found the situation comic, he did not betray the fact. Their conversation was deadly serious. It was as if the fate of all Spain depended on their deliberations, which in fact, arguably, it did.

The colonel briefly accelerated on the landing so that he reached Serrano's office in time to throw open the double doors. He could scarcely contain his glee. 'The news is even better than we hoped,' he announced as the minister swept past his secretary and made his way into his inner sanctum.

Minister Serrano didn't reply. Instead, he closed his eyes and offered a silent prayer. There was relief mixed with exultation in the expression that creased the pale parchment of his face as Ortega reeled off the headlines: *Wehrmacht enters Paris; Maginot Line breached; Canadians scuttling from Brest*. 'After all its boasting,' the aide concluded, 'France is finished.'

It was an *annus mirabilis*. Serrano Suñer, just 39 years-old, his shock of prematurely white hair swept back from his forehead, stood by his desk and struck a heroic pose. 'I detect the hand of God, Raúl,' he said at last. 'Who would have thought, after all we endured, that we should ever see this day?'

Ortega nodded contentedly. A police wagon outside in the square was bringing in a fresh batch of leftists to be interrogated and shot. As the vehicle passed into the combined ministerial and police headquarters, he could hear the double doors slam shut. The noose was continuing to tighten. More enemies of the state under lock and key, soon to learn their fate. Everything was as it should be.

The minister, whose appearance could switch in an instant from suave international statesman to a child in adult's clothing, was not only the most important member of the Government after Franco, he was also the *Caudillo's* brother-in-law and Inspector-General of the Falange. Tall and gangling, obsessed with his health, he had only recently transferred his primary allegiance from Fascist Italy to Nazi Germany and was still coming to terms with the consequences. Instead of wishing to consolidate Spain, as Mussolini had urged, he was now infused, like his master, with a new imperial vision. Just that very day, as he had urged for months, Spanish forces had occupied the international zone of Tangier, putting the League of Nations in its place and demonstrating in the clearest possible fashion Spain's disdain for the old world order. Berlin, meanwhile, had been informed that Madrid was adjusting its status in the European war from 'neutral' to 'non-belligerent.' All that remained before Spain entered the war was the negotiation of a treaty of economic cooperation with Germany. But the march on Tangier demonstrated good faith. The *Führer* would be pleased.

The minister breathed in deeply. 'The New Order has been blessed by Providence,' he said, addressing his aide as if he were a public meeting. 'This is a great day for Spain, where the first battle was fought. France – vainglorious France – has been crushed by the forces of Fascism. Germany and Italy are on the march. Soon, I promise you, Spain will join them. Today is not the end, my friend, it is only the beginning.'

In the cells below, someone screamed.

2

England: SIS Headquarters, Hanslope Park, June 16 1940

The name on the office door read *Strickland*. Inside, across from a ground floor window that gave on to the park, a man of about sixty was seated at a strictly functional, civil service-issue desk. He was engrossed in a file and indicated with a wave of his hand that Bramall should take the seat opposite.

He did so and waited impatiently, pulling at threads on the armrest of his chair. Three minutes later, he stood up and wandered across to the window. The sun shone overhead with peculiar vehemence and a Tortoiseshell butterfly seemed briefly to return his stare as it fluttered, dazed and confused, against the glass. In the distance, behind a line of trees, a parade ground sergeant shouted commands, while closer by a bright red Post Office van sped up the central driveway. Bramall shifted his gaze towards a group of young women making their way towards a group of prefabs. One of them, with ebony hair down to her shoulders, was laughing, but when she saw him framed in the window she fell silent and stared straight into his eyes.

He turned away but not in time to halt a familiar memory, like a migraine, from rising unbidden in his mind. He was in Spain, on the banks of the Ebro, west of Tarragona. It was midnight, July 23, 1938. The battered Republican Army, desperately short of air cover and artillery, was shuffling forward onto the boats that would take them over the river towards the enemy dug in on the opposite side. If they could drive Franco's eastern Army back from the Mediterranean and link up with the embattled defenders of Catalonia, victory might yet be theirs. If not, they were finished. As a journalist, Bramall could only look on as the exhausted lines of soldiers, ill-fed and sickening after two years of war, waited their turn to board the assault craft.

It was a hot, unforgiving night and the bitter-sweet smells of summer drifted across the water. Overhead, the faint drone of an aircraft could be heard – probably a spotter. He ignored it. He had other thoughts on his mind. Twenty-one-year-old Manuela Valdés, the daughter of a union organiser from Salamanca, stood with him, one arm around his neck, the other clutching her rifle. Against all logic, she was convinced that with this final push the Left could at last regain the initiative. During the month-long build-up to this latest offensive, they had become lovers and he found their affair, conducted on the edge of destruction, impossibly romantic. He kissed her fiercely, pressing himself hard against her.

The old moon had only just risen above the trees and the principal light, save for a faint glow off the river and the luminescence of fireflies underfoot, was from a series of torches used to direct the soldiers to the boats. He felt in his pocket for his lighter, an American-made Zippo he had taken from the body of a dead Irish *brigadista*. Flicking open the brass lid, he ran his thumb against the flint wheel. The flame that jumped into life illuminated Manuela's face, sending deep shadows down the hollows of her cheeks and reflecting itself in the coal-black pupils of her eyes. '*Te amo* – I love you,' he told her impulsively. Nothing else would have fitted the moment.

'*Te amo también*,' she replied, stroking his cheek. 'But now you must let me go.'

No sooner had she spoken than everything changed. Two-thousand feet above their heads, the pilot of a Messerschmitt 109, one of scores that virtually wiped out the Republic's antiquated Air Force, throttled back his engine and turned into a steep dive. The drone they had heard a minute earlier was the sound of a night-fighter, not a spotter. Attracted by the flickering torches, the *Condor* veteran, with his battle-trained 20:20 vision, focused his eyes on the shifting scene below and selected his target, the assault boats pulling away from the river's eastern shore. His twin cannons and machine guns ripped into the bedraggled column so quickly that there was no time to react. It was as if all the terror and capriciousness of war had been concentrated into a single moment.

Two years later, Bramall gripped the windowsill of Strickland's office so tightly that the ends of his fingers hurt. His mouth was dry and, just as he always did, he shut his eyes against the memory. Another ten seconds went by before he relaxed again and turned back into the room, doing his best to appear normal.

'Look,' he said, swallowing hard, 'I don't wish to be rude, but could we possibly make a start on whatever it is you want to talk to me about? Because I really think I should be getting back to my regiment.'

No response. Strickland waved him silent and carried on reading.

Bramall groaned and clasped his hands together behind

his neck. The man was deliberately ignoring him, which was bloody rude. After a further prolonged pause he said: 'Look, you're obviously busy, but shouldn't I be on my way to France by now? Isn't that where the war is?'

There was a slight snort from the far side of the desk, either of amusement or derision, it was impossible to say which. Strickland pushed the centre link of his spectacles up the bridge of his nose with the end of his middle finger and leaned forward in his chair. 'Oh do grow up, Bramall,' he said, squinting. 'That particular war is over. France has fallen.'

'They're still fighting.'

'Are they? You could have fooled me.'

'So that's it, is it? We got our chaps back from Dunkirk. Most of them, anyway. The French are ready to surrender. Everything's hunky-dory. That it?'

'Oh, do grow up, Bramall,' came the withering reply.

Strickland, small and balding, with sprigs of hair over his ears, removed his glasses, breathed on the lenses one at a time and polished them vigorously, using a large white handkerchief that appeared in his hand, as if by magic. He was a Yorkshireman – one of many thousands of Britons up and down the country for whom the coming of the war had provided a fresh lease on life – and was clearly not lacking in self-assurance. 'Mr Bramall,' he began, 'are you familiar with what the prime minister says in the House when he is asked variants of the same question over and over again.'

'I'm sorry, I don't see...'

' – He says, 'I refer the honourable gentleman to the answer I gave earlier."

'What?'

'That's what I think I'm going to have to do with you. Whenever you ask damn-fool questions, I shall refer you to the answer – or at any rate, the comment – I made earlier.'

'Which was …?'

' – "Oh, do grow up, Bramall."'

Christ al-fucking-mighty!

The intelligence man coiled the stems of his glasses back over his ears and peered for several seconds at the tall, elegant figure sat opposite him. It was like someone had just slapped his face and he wasn't quite sure how to respond. His hair was thick and sun-bleached; his skin was a light olive colour, as if he had spent years in the tropics.

As Bramall looked on, Strickland, removed a briar pipe from his top pocket and began to nibble at the stem with his front teeth. 'So what do you think of this place?' he said at last. 'Bit of a change from Narvik.'

'You could say that.'

'I suppose you think we should be in Whitehall.'

'It'd be closer to the action.'

Strickland cast his eyes up to his office's ornate ceiling. 'Too close, quite possibly. Meanwhile, I get to enjoy the open spaces of Buckinghamshire. A chequered history this place, or so they tell me. Murder and intrigue. Appropriate, really. Sir John French used to visit quite a bit before the war – the last one, I mean. Squire's wife were his niece.' He paused. 'But then, I expect he and your father knew each other.'

'French? Absolutely. Pa fought under him at Ypres. Came to stay with us once when he was Lord Lieutenant of Ireland. But I was only a child at the time. I don't really remember. You know how it is.'

'Not really,' said Strickland stiffly. His memories of Ireland were very different. 'But let's get to the business in hand. Spain is what you know best, Mr Bramall.' He looked up, spreading his hands flat on the desk in front of him. They were very pink. 'You don't mind my calling you "mister," do you? You're not in uniform now. So, like I say ... Spain. You studied there, reported the war, speak the lingo, and, as we both know, you've got a history of – what shall we say? – "co-operating" with the authorities.'

Bramall sighed. So that was it. So much for organising a Resistance group in France. He was a bloody fool. He should have realised what was coming the second the Special Branch sergeant turned up on his doorstep. 'Look,' he said, speaking slowly and with emphasis, 'what I did back then – it's over. Finished. Dues paid. A closed book. When I put on uniform, it was to fight the Germans, not to re-live my past. So let's not waste each other's time, shall we?' He rose from his chair to indicate that the interview was over.

Strickland shook his head, but didn't look particularly put out. 'Oh my, you do get yourself in a lather, don't you? We'll have to watch that. But never mind, there's work to be done and it's time you came down off your high horse.' He rested his arms on his belly. His hair, or what little remained of it, bore the unmistakable sheen of Brylcreem. 'It may have escaped your notice, but the war has not been organised for your personal convenience.'

Bramall looked as if he was about to say something, but all that emerged was a stifled sigh.

'Look,' said Strickland. 'We could go on like this for the rest of the day, but what's the point? My business is matching good people to bad situations. You're part of that, like it or not. I've been reading your file. You're a lost soul, Mr Bramall – not quite sure what you're about, restless and rootless, looking for a chance to do something worthwhile in the big, bad world. It could go on like that, believe you me. You could end up my age, asking yourself what the hell was it all about. But, like they used to say in church on Sunday, there's good news.'

Running a hand up his cheek, Bramall realised he should have shaved more closely that morning. Perhaps he'd been hoping to make the wrong sort of impression. 'You'll forgive me,' he said, 'if I don't throw my hat in the air.'

'Cheeky bugger,' Strickland said. 'But I'll allow you that. Fact of the matter is, you fit a very specific profile, Mr Bramall. A star-shaped peg in a star-shaped hole. If you were an actor, you'd say this was the role you were born to play.'

'But since I'm not …'

'Not yet.' Strickland tapped the side of his head. 'But the script is right here, just waiting to be sent off to the printer's. So here's the thing. You're a linguist. You've been a soldier – a pretty decent one at that – and a diplomat. More to the point, you spent two years as a war correspondent in Spain, moving with admirable ease, I'd have to say, among the bigwigs of the Falange.'

He stopped for a second and stared across to the opposite side of the desk, as if wondering what response his deliberately chosen words would provoke. Bramall's eyes narrowed, but he said nothing.

'At the same time, your father, as I'm sure you're only too aware, is one of the most right wing men this side of the parade ground at Nuremberg. His reputation goes before him.'

'Oh, for God's sake!' Bramall didn't approve of his father's politics, but he was no Nazi.

Strickland wiggled his fingers to indicate that he wasn't in a mood for nit-picking. 'Such tomfoolery, it seems, runs in the family. You not only spent time, as we know, with Sir Oswald Mosley, you travelled with him as far as Berlin, where you met none other than Adolf Hitler, the *Führer*, Chancellor of the Third Reich, your country's greatest enemy, and passed some fifteen minutes contentedly in his company. There's not many as can say that. In fact, you've been all over, haven't you? Austria, Argentina, Burma, Spain, Norway. Quite the travelling man.'

Bramall felt weary all of a sudden. 'Go on,' he said.

'Oh, I will, ' said Strickland. 'You seem to ricochet through life, looking for a cause you can believe in. Have you ever seen a pinball machine?'

'No.'

'An American game. Most diverting. You pull back a knob on a spring. It shoots forward and knocks a metal ball into play. You try and guide it to the opening at the far end, via a series of obstacles, with a set of nudges. That's what you put me in mind of. *Ping!* You're dining with Mosley, hobnobbing with Hitler. *Ping!* You're disgusted with them. Now you're informing on the BUF to MI5. *Ping!* You're in Spain, reporting on the agonies of Republican troops as they struggle against the odds to avert catastrophe. *Ping!* You're stood next to your old college pal Kim Philby as he picks up a gong from Franco. *Ping!* You're in Norway, defending democracy from the Nazis. I could go on, but do you see what I'm driving at?'

'I'm just waiting for you to ram it home.'

'My point is, Mr Bramall, that you are a man of proven courage, skill and resource, not to say duplicity, and once again your country needs you.'

'Bugger!'

The spymaster looked pained. 'It was a colleague in Five drew you to my attention. You were right about that. I'd never heard of you. But he'd worked with you back in '36, said you knew what you were about, even if you were a bit bolshy.'

'Am I supposed to be grateful?'

'Only if you think he was right. When I heard you were in Norway, I thought, oh, here we go, now he's going to turn up dead. But I was wrong. Not only did you get through, you were mentioned in dispatches. Kept your head. Seems as if you lead a bit of a charmed life.'

'Is that what you're looking for?'

'It's handy in our game. Remember what Napoleon said: "Give me a general who's lucky".' Strickland turned to the file of papers in front of him. 'Speaking of which, you will be aware that General Franco has been thinking of joining the Axis powers?'

'You don't have to be a brain surgeon to work that out.'

Strickland ignored the crack. 'No. But what do you suppose would happen if he did?'

'I expect they'd have to double the guard at Gibraltar.'

'A bit more than that, I'm afraid. But the right track. First thing to happen, probably just days after the announcement, is that Gibraltar will come under a combined assault. The *Luftwaffe* will go in, then the *Wehrmacht*, backed by Spanish troops. We may, just, survive the onslaught – though I rather think not – but the Fleet would have to put to sea or else be blown out of the water. Gib would no longer be a stronghold. It'd be a bloody liability, vulnerable to a takeover at any time.'

He paused for a second to see how all this was going down.

'What's more, Spanish entry into the war on the German side would mean U-boat bases at Cadiz and Vigo. The Canaries, too, if we let them. There could even be a Spanish threat to our forces in North Africa – to say nothing of the example set to Dr Salazar in Portugal. Do I make myself plain?'

'All except the bit about how I'm supposed to put a stop to it.'

Strickland laughed – a deep-throated, derisive chuckle that seemed at odds with his faintly music hall appearance. 'Oh yes, Mr Bramall. They told me you were a particular sort of chap, but they didn't say you were a card.'

Part of Bramall wanted to wring Strickland's dewlapped neck. But at the same time he was intrigued. 'All right,' he said, 'so I'm not your principal weapon in this war, but I do have some part to play, right?'

'Exactly. But before we go any further, let's have some tea, shall we?' He rose from his chair, drew open his office door and called out. 'Two teas, please, Ethel – quick as you like, there's a good girl.' Shutting the door again, he spun round, surprisingly nimble for a man of his age. 'What we want from you is information, Mr Bramall. Information about what the Spanish are thinking, what they're talking about at party gatherings, what sort of pressures and inducements are coming from Berlin.'

'You mean I'd be a spy?'

Strickland pursed his lips and leaned forward once more. 'That is one description. The fact is, our embassy in Madrid has not exactly been on best of terms with Franco and his people.

They're suspicious of us – understandably enough. They don't like the fact we're at war with Hitler and could at any moment take the fight to Mussolini as well. They think we're soft on the Left and unwilling to make an accommodation with what they regard as the New Order.'

Bramall massaged the backs of his hands. 'Shouldn't you put someone in who would better suit the mood?'

'Ah, but we have, Mr Bramall. It may have escaped your notice, but Sir Samuel Hoare has just been appointed His Majesty's ambassador to Madrid.'

Bramall snorted. Hoare was a former foreign secretary, best known for the Hoare-Laval Pact in 1935, concluded with the French, which gave Mussolini a free hand in Abyssinia and ended up scuppering the League of Nations. 'Man's an appeaser,' he said.

Strickland rubbed the side of his nose. 'Can you think of a better man for the job?'

'*Touché.* So what do you need me for?'

'You can pour the tea, for a start.' Strickland looked up as his secretary came in with a pot of tea and two mugs on a tray. 'Thanks Ethel,' he said. 'No biscuits, I see.'

'You've had two already this morning,' she replied.

The Yorkshireman frowned and turned to Bramall. 'See what I have to contend with. Have to watch my weight, she says.'

As Bramall poured the tea, Strickland continued his monologue. 'You do realise,' he said, 'that what I'm about to tell you must go no further than this room?'

Bramall nodded, adding milk to both teas.

'We're talking about a sensitive aspect of national security.'

'Say when.'

'When! Don't drown it.' Bramall harrumphed and placed a steaming mug on Strickland's desk. Reaching into a side drawer, the spymaster withdrew a cup of sugar, a spoonful of which he ladled into his tea before stirring briskly. He did not offer his guest the opportunity to indulge any sweet tooth he may have had, but replaced the cup in the drawer, complete with spoon. Sugar was a prized wartime commodity and rationing made misers out of the most unexpected people.

Strickland raised his mug. 'Cheers!' he said. 'Thing is, Hoare's already got his work cut out for him. Just getting into flaming embassy each morning is half a day's work. Has to shove past hordes of bloody Falangists shouting out, *'Gibraltar Español!'* Bloody cheek! He's under direct orders from Downing Street, and he'll be working at the highest level.'

'So who do I report to, then?'

'Good question.'

Bramall raised an eyebrow. He was puzzled. 'I'm guessing I won't be working on my own?'

What seemed to the young officer a logical assumption evoked a pained expression from Strickland 'That's where you're wrong,' he said. 'Franco has made it crystal clear that he won't tolerate British Intelligence operating inside Spain. He doesn't object to Jerry. Positively relishes having the *Sicherheitsdienst* around. You might even say the *Gestapo* runs the bloody place. But MI6? Nothing doing. Anyone from our side gets caught is on his own, and that means instant expulsion, or a firing squad at dawn. That's the reason you're tailor-made for the job.'

'Oh, please! ... You're not serious.'

'Never more so. Mr Bramall. You are to be our eyes and ears in Spain's dark corners. I have this on the authority of no less than the prime minister.'

'Churchill?'

'Who else? He has asked that you should keep open channels that might otherwise close.' Strickland took another slurp of tea. 'You may also, as the occasion arises, be required to perform certain ... services.'

'Such as ...?'

'Well now, let me think ... liaison, negotiation, bag-carrying.'

'Assassination?'

'I hardly think it will come to that.'

'But it might?'

Strickland halted, an almost imperceptible smile crossing his features. 'It might,' he said at last.

'And Sir Samuel in that event would naturally deny me his protection?'

'Naturally.'

'Well, I'm flattered that the PM has confidence in my abilities, but what makes you think the Spanish wouldn't rumble me?'

Strickland offered a thin smile. 'There are few certainties in this world, Mr Bramall. It's a calculated risk. Before you left for Spain, you were thick as thieves with Mosley and the BUF. They'll know that. During the fighting, you met several of the top people in the Falange and got on well with them by all accounts. That'll be in the file. Photographs, too, I shouldn't wonder. Your father's reputation goes before you, of course. They'll know who's side he was on during the fighting. Finally, there's the small matter of your meeting the *Führer* in Berlin., complete with your picture, bold as brass, in the *Völkischer Beobachter*. It all adds up. I won't pretend it's cut and dried. Not yet, any road. But if anyone has a better *c.v.* for this business than you, I've yet to meet him.'

A resigned look crept over Bramall's face. 'You've obviously done your homework,' he said. 'I feel like a trussed chicken about to be popped in the oven. But if I'm to do this I'm going to need help. There has to be someone I can turn to.'

Strickland sniffed noisily and pinched the end of his nose. 'Your main port of call will be our man in Lisbon. He'll brief you. Then there's the SIS station in Gibraltar, – assuming, that is, that you ever make it across. The *Abwehr* has the place surrounded and they don't miss a trick. And I'm afraid to say, that's it.'

Bramall sat back in his chair, exhaled deeply and crossed his legs at the ankles. He knew when he was beaten. 'So when do I start?'

Strickland purred with satisfaction. 'This afternoon,' he replied, taking his pipe out of his pocket. 'It'll take a fortnight or so to bring you up to speed. I take it your Spanish still cuts the mustard.'

Bramall looked faintly surprised, as if he'd been asked if he knew how to tie his shoelaces. '*Mostaza, Senf, moutarde* … I cut all three.'

The Yorkshireman sucked air through his pipe, then made a face as a sliver of tar shot into his mouth. He swallowed hard and grimaced before regaining his composure. 'And arrogant with it,' he said. 'Just like it says here.' He tapped the dossier in front of him. 'Your life in one slim volume. Still … welcome aboard. Let's just hope you live up to your billing.'

Madrid: Malasaña Quarter, June 20

The old woman's eyes looked infinitely sad. She was dressed entirely in black. Her woollen dress, stretched tight across her ample belly and buttocks, was black. Her stockings were black and torn and the soles of her black shoes had worn through, exposing black, calloused feet. Her headscarf was black. Even her teeth were black, matching her eyes. She looked up from the steps on which she was squatting and glanced across at the young woman opposite. If she was curious about the good shoes of the Señorita – made from the finest Spanish leather, like the pair she herself had owned on the day of her wedding – she didn't register the fact. Nor did she look to be interested in the sheen and obvious good condition of the stranger's hair, or in the radiant whiteness of her teeth. Such details might have aroused her suspicions a year or two ago, when her family was still alive and spies were a constant threat. But now? What did she care? Everyone she had ever loved was gone from her and there was no more 'they' could do to her. She would have got up and shuffled away, but her legs buckled when she put her weight on them. It was her hips. Like the rest of her, they had given up. She turned away, losing herself in the ache of memory.

So far as her mother knew, Isabel Ortega, twenty-one years-old, her eyes as green as the Asturian countryside in which she had been raised, was in Malasaña to distribute food to the poor and dispossessed, watched over by Father Rojas from the church of Santa María de Real de Montserrat.

Cardinal Isidro Gomá, the Archbishop of Toledo and Primate of Spain, had been one of Franco's strongest supporters during the War, which he saw as a crusade against wickedness and the godlessness of Russia. But after the fighting stopped, he had called on the victors to show compassion for the people, who had suffered much and needed to be guided back to righteous living by the example of a Christian administration and priesthood. Gomá, now seventy years-old and unwell, knew that he would never win Franco over to his point of view. That was why, having previously endorsed public masses, often held on street corners, at which the people of Madrid were implored to seek forgiveness for their sins, he had ordered his priests to demonstrate greater pastoral care and to work with charitable institutions in the relief of poverty. The rich were as baffled as the *Caudillo*. Their preference was for forced labour. All over the country, 'penal detachments,' made up of former Republican combatants and their families, were worked almost to death in the construction of bridges, dams and irrigation channels. Isolated buildings throughout the country had been turned into makeshift prisons in which the inmates were subject to torture, starvation and the firing squad. The bodies of these fallen were buried without honour in mass graves, covered with quick lime and left to rot,

Father Rojas, thirty-three years-old and so pinched he looked perpetually surprised, was no Republican sympathiser. From good family in Seville, he saw Church and State working hand in hand as the proper instruments of God's purpose. But he dared not defy the Cardinal and thus, working mainly with women of the better class, he reluctantly distributed alms each week to the mothers, wives and children of the vanquished. That morning, Isabel had arrived at his presbytery at Santa Maria to offer her services. It was the first time in her life she had set foot in Malasaña, a tightly knit quarter north of the

Gran Via. Known to her mother's generation as the *barrio de maravillas*, or district of wonders, it was one of the most deprived in the city, and also one of the most dangerous.

Isabel looked pale and anxious as she handed out small portions of stale bread and olive oil, plus a few onions and tomatoes that her mother considered unfit for the table. Though she was pleased to help the destitute, the real reason for her presence in Malasaña was one that she could never mention to Father Rojas, let alone her mother. Her childhood friend, Teresa Alvarez, was in desperate need of her help and, to her shame, she was a day late in responding. Teresa's father, Colonel Eduardo Alvarez, was a wanted man, one of those who had organised resistance to Franco in the capital in 1936. He had later served as an adviser to the Socialist prime minister, Juan Negrín. Every member of the *Guardia Civil* carried his picture in his breast pocket. It was said that Franco, irritated beyond measure by the capital's Republican leaning, blamed it on Alvarez and would tighten the garrotte himself.

The colonel and Isabel's own father had once been close. They had gone through the military academy together and served as brother officers during some hard times in Morocco. Later, when they were both majors, serving under the regime of the dictator Miguel Primo de Rivera, their daughters attended the same school in Oviedo. Both girls were bright, with a flair for languages, but Isabel was the sporty one, captaining the netball team in her final year and winning medals for swimming.

It was on July 17, 1936 that news came in of a rising by troops in Morocco. Franco had been the leading light then, as he was now, and both girls had been horrified by tales of rapes and mutilations carried out by his Moorish troops. Isabel had protested to her father that Franco was a brute and a tyrant. He told her not to listen to rumours and insisted everything would be fine. Six months later, he had sent her out of Spain into the care of his brother Rafael in Argentina. Teresa had stayed on in Spain with her parents.

It was not yet nine o'clock in the morning in Malasaña, but the summer heat was building and the streets stank. Refuse piled up on the pavements, spilling over onto the roads. The sewers had not worked properly in years. A dog, its ribs showing through its wizened flanks, snuffled in the gutter among the debris, searching for a rat that suddenly emerged and sped across the street before disappearing into a drain. The dog looked disappointed, then sat down wearily and buried its nose in its rear end. A number of the shops and houses, dating mainly from the Enlightenment, 150 years earlier, were marked by shell holes, patched up with sheets of sacking. Most of the windows were cracked or shattered. There were few young men left in the barrio. Mothers and children made up the majority of those who crowded the narrow streets, and old women, like the one who had just averted her eyes. They looked hungry. The eyes of the children, as they waited next to their mothers for their handouts from the rich, were ravenous, causing Isabel, as she distributed her small parcels, to feel a brief, unseasonable chill and to pull her cheap shawl, borrowed from a housemaid, closer about her shoulders.

Two days before, she had met Teresa in the Arco de Cuchilleros, a bar carved into the rock beneath the Plaza Mayor. Her friend had called her from the local telephone office, the *locutorio*. Isabel had been shocked to hear her voice. She had assumed that Alvarez had got his family out at the end of the war, probably to France or England. She had no idea they were still in Spain. Now it turned out that the colonel had been badly hurt in the fighting around Madrid in the last days and forced into hiding. Would she meet her? Teresa wanted to know. She *must*. It was a matter of life and death.

Isabel didn't know what to say. It was late, and her parents had forbidden her to venture out alone in the daytime, nevermind the early hours of the morning. But in the end she had agreed. She felt she had no choice. She told one of the serving girls who was about to go to bed that the police officer guarding their villa looked cold and hungry. 'You should take him out some bread and olives,' she said, 'and maybe a glass of wine.' The girl had looked startled, but Isabel had noticed them talking on several occasions in the course of the day. It was obvious the girl was attracted to the handsome young officer and she did as she was asked. As the two flirted innocently at the front of the house, Isabel made her way out the back gate and down the steps of the alleyway behind, towards the Calle Yeseros, ten minutes from the city centre.

Once in the Arco de Cuchilleros, she had only minutes to wait. Teresa looked terrible, causing Isabel to gasp when she saw her. Her skin was yellow, almost jaundiced, and her cheeks and eye sockets sunken, as if she hadn't had a proper meal in weeks. Her hair, once lustrous, hung in dark hanks. It was in the end the clothes Teresa wore that alarmed her most. She had always been a fastidious dresser; now she was virtually in rags. Isabel hugged her friend, averting her nose to the smell, and undertook to return the following day with money, medical supplies and bandages.

'We need money to buy food and clothes. – and to pay a

doctor if we can find one who will dare to treat my father. Then we must find a counterfeiter to forge documents for us so that we can leave Madrid and make it across the border with Portugal. After that – who knows?'

The situation was getting worse by the day, Teresa said. They had no money and her father's condition was deteriorating. Luisa, her mother, had been driven practically mad with worry. Worst of all, the nightly patrols of the secret police, fronted by the *Guardia Civil*, were sweeping Malasaña and closing in on their location and it was certain they would be discovered soon. That was when Isabel had burst into tears. Giving her friend the few banknotes and the small change she had in her purse, she promised to bring more next day, as well as whatever medical supplies and bandages she could lay hold of. Teresa took the money without a word. Then she wrote out her address on a piece of paper and fled into the night.

But Isabel had not kept her promise. The next morning, having got back to the Calle Beatriz Galindo a little after two, she was awakened early by her mother, who informed her that they were due at a special mass in the cathedral at ten to solemnise the Government's proposal of a permanent memorial to the Fallen, *El Valle do los Caídos*, in the mountains north of the capital. The mass, which would last two hours, would be followed by a reception at the Escorial Palace and dinner at the Pardo with Franco and his ministers.

There was no way to avoid it. It was simply too big an occasion. But the Alvarezes had survived this long, she told herself. What real difference could another twenty-four hours make? The important thing was that her help, when it came, would get them out of Spain before they could be arrested.

The *barrio* was a sprawling, ugly place. Her two companions – daughters of a university professor and a lawyer – were obviously nervous and stayed close to Father Rojas and the two *Guardia Civil* officers who accompanied them on their mission. Only by carefully choosing her moment did Isabel managed to break free from the group.

She had with her a little over 200 pesetas in cash that she had kept as savings in a tin box in her bedroom, as well as the entire contents of her mother's medicine cabinet. Having consulted a pre-war street plan, she thought she knew where she was going, but ever since the siege few roads and alleyway in the quarter were marked and within minutes she was lost. A boy, aged about twelve or thirteen, sidled towards her. Thrusting a handful of *céntimos* into his mud-caked palm, she told him the name of the street she was looking for and said there would be more if he could take her there. He nodded sullenly and indicated with a movement of his head that she should follow him.

Minutes later, he stopped outside the ruins of what had once been a bakery

'Is this it?' she asked. 'Are you sure?'

'That's the address you gave me. Now where's my money?'

She handed him a few *pesetas*, He spat on the coins, gripped them in his fist and turned away.

An open gate next to the bakery's front door led into a stinking alleyway. Flies were swarming around something unidentifiable lying on the ground, causing her to look away. A mouse scuttled past and disappeared into a crack in the wall. Isabel felt a lump rise in her throat. At the end of the alley was a set of stone steps leading down into a cellar. Ignoring the stench of urine and rotting flesh, she made her way to the top of the steps and looked down.

That was when a man's voice called out to her.

'You looking for the old fellow with the broken leg?' he said. 'Him and his wife and the girl?'

'That's right.' The speaker was bent over and bronchial – seventy if he was a day. He was standing with the sun behind him and she had to squint to return his gaze.'

'You're too late,' he said. 'The police came for them last night. Turns out the father was something high up in the old government. They'll have shot him by now – garrotted him more likely. His wife, she was screaming at them. The daughter, too. Didn't do no good. Even if they're not dead, they'll be on their way to a labour camp, which is the same thing, only slower. There's nothing you can do – nothing anybody can do. Light a candle for them if you're that way inclined. Otherwise, go home and forget about them.'

For the second time in less than a day, Isabel burst into tears.

The old man stared at her for several seconds without saying anything. Then he began to cough convulsively, sounding as if his chest was full of soot. Each paroxysm was worse than the last. Eventually, he hawked something dark green onto the earth floor of the alley and turned away, fighting for breath. 'Take my advice,' he said, holding both hands to his chest. 'Leave well alone. The dead and the dying are beyond our help. It's the living you have to watch out for.'

Isabel stood up and wiped her eyes with the back of her hand. She couldn't believe it. She had failed them and now they were dead. It was all her fault. If only she had told her mother that she was too unwell to attend Franco's celebrations. If only she had managed to get back to Madrid in time to do what she had promised. But she hadn't. Instead, she had sat within ten metres of the man responsible for their deaths and looked on in silence as her father drank a toast to the Fallen. Now it was too late. She threw her head back so that the sun, as pitiless as Franco's mercy, shone directly into her eyes. For a second she let the searing light burn into her retina. Never again would she believe anything that came out of the mouths of the Falange and its agents. From this moment on, she was at war.

Madrid: German Legation, June 21

The German ambassador to Spain, His Excellency Baron Eberhard von Stohrer, tugged at the front of his frockcoat as he waited to receive the visit of Foreign Minister Juan Beigbeder and Interior Minister Ramón Serrano Suñer. The ebullient, six-feet four-inch Stohrer was a practical man. Like many whose families were recent additions to the pages of the *Almanach de Gotha*, Germany's Debrett's, he believed in class and privilege and civilised warfare. The louche Beigbeder was a man after his own heart. Serrano was something else. There was about the *Caudillo's* brother-in-law a smell of greasepaint, as if he was made up for the occasion. He was clever – brilliant even. There was no doubt about that. And he was ruthless. Yet there was, as well, a certain archness about him, reminiscent of Göbbels, that made the Bavarian in Stohrer wonder what really drove him.

Normally, the ambassador would have reported to Serrano at the interior ministry in the Puerta del Sol. But Beigbeder wasn't happy with that. After all, he was supposed to be in charge of foreign policy. Besides, today's three-way get-together gave Stohrer the chance to show off his magnificent new premises – Germany's largest overseas representation, big enough to dwarf most Spanish ministries.

Franco had indicated three days ago that he was finally prepared to come off the fence and join the armed struggle. The problem was how to get on the stage while the play was still running. Stohrer knew this, just as he knew that all dreams of empire were an illusion. As he continued to muse, there was a discreet knock at the door of his office, which swung open to reveal the nervous face of his private secretary, Klausener, who glanced across at him, every hair in place, eyes shining. *'Herr Botschafter,'* he announced, as if springing a surprise on his boss. 'The ministers' cars are about to arrive.'

'Ja, ja, Franz. I will be straight down.'

A minute later, the ambassador stood, somewhat stiffly, in the Legation's ornate entrance hall beneath a large, bronze Swastika and two gaudy portraits of Hitler and Ribbentrop. Beigbeder's limousine was first. The foreign minister, it seemed to Stohrer, was a wily fellow, whose sympathies veered between support for the Reich and an older, almost atavistic loyalty to the British. If his trust were to be retained in the face of Hitler's indifference towards Spanish participation in the war effort, then he, as Hitler's messenger, would have to come up with something fast.

Beigbeder struggled out of his car seat and adjusted his uniform. Tall and swarthy, his dark eyes hidden behind thick-lenses, he could have arrived at the embassy either from an assignation with his mistress or from Friday prayers at the mosque. Both were passions, vigorously pursued. Stohrer, also something of a lothario, but lacking religious conviction, stepped forward. 'Good afternoon, Minister. I am delighted you have honoured our embassy with your visit.'

'My dear baron, always a pleasure. And let me say at once what a splendid refurbishment and expansion you have achieved in so short a time.'

Then it was the turn of Serrano Suñer, whose car, though second to arrive, swished to a halt in front of that of the foreign minister. Serrano, who always reminded the ambassador of an American matinee idol, was on his feet in an instant and gliding towards his host.

'Mr Ambassador, I come straight from the Pardo, where the *Caudillo*, my brother-in-law, continues to enthuse over Germany's miraculous feats of arms. As your new embassy so clearly reflects, we live in a time fit for heroes.'

Stohrer offered a slight bow, no more than five degrees from the perpendicular. 'Your sentiments are much appreciated. And now, gentlemen, if you would care to step inside, we have much to discuss.'

The meeting took place in Stohrer's private suite, with no one else in attendance. Down the hall, however, in the office of SD Major Klaus Hasselfeldt, a veteran of the Polish campaign, recently arrived to head the embassy's security section, everything that was said was captured on an ingenious reel-to-reel recording device that Hasselfeldt had brought with him personally from Berlin. The machine, big as a suitcase, was known as a Magnetophon and had been developed by AEG and BASF in Germany using technology unique to the Reich. It would never have occurred to the ambassador, who had only recently come to terms with the wireless, that his rooms might be bugged. It was the sort of thing that he would have found ill mannered in the extreme. Hasselfeldt, as it happened, bore no particular ill-will towards his head of mission, whom he regarded as an idle functionary, typical of his type. He merely wished to assure himself – and Berlin – that the Reich's best interests were not being compromised.

Serrano chose an upright chair facing Stohrer's work desk. Beigbeder preferred the sofa. Often on these occasions, especially if the proceedings dragged on, as they often did when Stohrer was in control, the Spaniard would fantasize about his mistress. But not today.

'I must say, Stohrer, I am at a loss,' Serrano began. 'We offer you our cooperation in the European enterprise, and, after more than three days, we have yet to have a response.'

'I can understand your vexation,' Stohrer began, hoping to minimise the impact of the news that he knew would shortly arrive from Berlin. 'The *Führer* is grateful for your offer of assistance in the war. Please be assured, however, that, as far as Berlin is concerned, the place of Spain in the New Order is already guaranteed.'

'And what place would that be, exactly?' The cold-edged calculation of Serrano's voice appeared to Stohrer to go perfectly with his theatrical appearance. 'Will we have Berlin's support in the restoration of our empire in North Africa? Or are we to hold our troops in eternal readiness, without reward, lest the Reich should fail and we must rush to your aid?'

Stohrer couldn't help but admire the fellow. 'You will understand,' he said, 'that these are questions to be decided elsewhere, at the highest level – most obviously by the *Führer* and the *Caudillo*.'

Serrano bent his head back, twisted in his chair and stared fixedly out of the window. 'I see,' he said at last. 'I understand perfectly. Come, Beigbeder,' he continued. 'There is nothing to detain us here.'

The foreign minister started and looked pleadingly at Stohrer. 'Let us not be too hasty,' he said. 'We are old comrades, are we not? Strategies change, plans alter. But interests remain constant.'

Beigbeder could always be depended on to come up with the most emollient cliché, and Stohrer was grateful. 'The foreign minister,' he said, 'is absolutely right. We in Germany know who our friends are. We know on whom we can rely. While the world awaits the longer-term consequences of our great victory in France, there is a service Spain can yet render that would win for the *Caudillo* – as if he did not have it already – the *Führer's* undying gratitude.'

Serrano, an opera lover, felt cheated of his exit, but he could not possibly leave without hearing what the German had to offer.

'Continue,' he said.

In his office down the hall, Hasselfeldt stopped fidgeting with the knobs on his recorder. He adjusted the headset in which the ambassador's words were playing.

'As you will know,' said Stohrer, 'the Duke of Windsor is expected shortly in Madrid.'

'Ah, yes,' said Beigbeder. 'Fleeing from France. The Duchess, too – a most intriguing woman. They were reported in Barcelona this morning. Apparently some French officer requisitioned the hotel they were staying at in Perpignan.'

Stohrer smiled indulgently. Beigbeder would have made a

splendid diary writer for one of the more lurid pre-war magazines. 'Just so, Minister,' he said. 'Churchill wants him back in England, but His Royal Highness, it appears, has a mind of his own. Which provides us with a unique opportunity.'

Serrano's eyes narrowed. 'What are you suggesting, Ambassador?'

'Simply, my dear minister, that if Spain were to prevail upon the Duke to take a more, shall we say, *conciliatory* view of relations with the Reich than is currently in evidence from the clique surrounding Churchill, perhaps a way could be found to amplify his voice and to invest it with the kind of authority that could yet make an invasion of England unnecessary.'

Now the Spaniard's eyebrows arched. 'So you wish us to offer to the Duke the prospect of his restoration to the throne of England in return for his support for the *Führer* and a negotiated peace.'

'As ever, you cut to the heart of the matter,' said Stohrer, steepling his fingers.

Beigbeder looked shocked. 'The Duke would never agree to such a thing. He may be attracted to the New Order, but you misread him, Ambassador if you think he would betray his country.'

Serrano was no less dismissive. 'Oh dear, Stohrer,' he began. 'Has it come to this? We are men of the world, are we not? We should not waste our time indulging in fantasies.'

The ambassador shrugged his heavy shoulders. 'Gentlemen, gentlemen. We are on the same side here. You believe this business to be a nonsense, and, confidentially, so do I. But not everyone in Berlin is as hard-headed as we. There is room for fantasy, even in the Reich.' He looked down the length of his nose directly at Serrano. 'In my experience, it is the dreamer, not the dream that is important. If we each of us assist in this matter, the quid pro quo could prove considerable. We may even find that our own dreams come true.'

There was a moment's silence before Serrano spoke again. 'My dear baron,' he said, 'you are a master of your profession – and, of course, if we can, we should be delighted to help.'

Stohrer raised his hands in blessing. 'Gentlemen,' he began, 'already our interests are converging. You see – is it not exactly as I said?'

In his office, hovering intently over the slowly turning reels of the *Magnetophon*, Hasselfeldt allowed a sly smile to play about his features. He had no idea who was right and who was wrong in the matter of the Duke of Windsor. But he knew disloyalty when he saw it. Stohrer was not loyal. He was a careerist, doing his job without believing in it. If not a crime, it was at the least a misdemeanour – and one for which the ambassador should be made to answer. More than that, the idea that the key to the ultimate success of the Reich in its war with England could reside right here in Madrid, within minutes of where he sat, was to Hasselfeldt irresistible. It was time to contact his SD superiors in the Prinz Albrechtstrasse.

SIS Headquarters, Hanslope Park, June 22

Strickland was standing with his pink hands joined behind his back staring out his office window when Bramall knocked and walked in. The Yorkshireman wore a brown suit which looked as if it hadn't been dry-cleaned in months. Sharp concertina creases in the backs of the knees drew the turn-ups of the trousers above the tops of his shoes. 'It's a matter of record now' he said, not even turning round. 'France has accepted occupation and Pétain's in charge of a new puppet regime.'

'So I heard. I wouldn't have thought giving in – giving up, more like – was quite Pétain's style.'

'Probably not. But needs must. What choice did he have? According to Berlin, the instrument of capitulation – sorry, the armistice – was signed in same railway carriage used by the French to take the German surrender in 1918.'

'That must have hurt.'

'Intended to.'

There was a pause as both men once again took in the implications of France's formal withdrawal from the war.

'So it's official, we're on our own,' said Bramall, breaking the uncomfortable silence.

Strickland turned to face him, unfastening his waistcoat as he did so and breathing out. 'Not exactly a surprise, but a shock all the same.'

'And my little jaunt?'

'No change. In fact, we're moving it forward. Had a stroke of luck. How's your training coming along?'

Bramall smiled to himself. He was in pretty good shape. He could run, he could box, he was proficient with a handgun. But it was still a hard, bloody slog. 'I'm above average on the physical side,' he said. 'But the 'tradecraft' stuff – dead letter boxes, radio codes, how to get beaten up without saying anything: All that bollocks tends to pass me by.'

The air seemed to drain from Strickland's chest. 'I see. Well, we want you in position as soon as possible. Next few days if we can manage it.'

'Just like that. Doesn't give me much time. Still via Portugal, I suppose?'

'Embassy'll sort you out. And while you're there, you can meet your opposite number in Lisbon.'

'What's he like?'

'Dependable. He'll give you a few pointers before he sends you on your way.'

'No doubt. But that still leaves the small matter of how I suddenly materialise in Spanish high society, trusted by Spain and Germany, with links to Britain that go high enough to get me past just about any front door.'

The look he received in reply to his ostensibly reasonable question was suffused with a mellow, long-suffering superiority. Bramall, for some reason, was put in mind of a ripe stilton in port.

'Did you think we were just going to move you in and leave you to get on with it?'

'Like in Norway, you mean? Or France, come to that.'

Strickland strode round to his desk with little short steps, gaining in authority as he did so. Reaching into his drawer, next to his secret sugar cache, he drew out a slim, grey folder, which he proceeded to hand across. 'Problem solved,' he said. 'Couldn't have worked out nicer. Read this, memorise it, then hand it back.'

'What's the gist?'

'The gist is, Mr Bramall, that His Royal Highness the Duke of Windsor, and *Mrs* Simpson' – he lingered on the Duchess's former status – 'have turned up in Spain. You probably know the Duke served as a senior military liaison officer in Paris.

Well, contrary to orders, he didn't attempt to make it back to England with Lord Gort's forces. Too much like hard work, I'd imagine. Instead, he and his entourage jumped into an official limousine and headed full-tilt to Biarritz, then on to Barcelona.'

'Is that where he is now?'

'About to arrive in Madrid, apparently.'

'Then what happens?'

Strickland stretched out a podgy finger and tapped the folder. 'It's all in the file. Answer to a maiden's prayer, if I say so myself. Neat as a Duchess's knicker drawer.'

'Right.'

Taking a seat by the window, he began to read.

<u>Top Secret</u>
Most Confidential
For the attention of Mr Thomas Strickland, SIS; Mr Charles Bramall, SIS
cc The prime minister; the foreign secretary; Sir Samuel Hoare, HM ambassador to Madrid; Mr Walford Selby, HM ambassador to Lisbon

Following the German attack on France and the subsequent enemy occupation, HRH the Duke of Windsor, accompanied by the Duchess, last week left his home in Paris and drove south to Madrid by way of Perpignan. His Royal Highness, who chose not to be evacuated with the BEF from Dunkirk, is still considering the request issued to him by the prime minister that he should return to England for reassignment. In the meantime, it is likely that he and the Duchess, together with their household, will divide their time between Madrid and Lisbon. Sir Samuel Hoare, as HM ambassador to Spain, will shortly issue invitations to a party at the embassy on June 29 at which HRH and the Duchess will be introduced to Spanish society.

For the purpose of inserting SIS agent Charles Bramall successfully into Madrid, it has been decided that he should be named as an equerry to HRH, separate from the embassy, to be available throughout the period of the Duke's stay in Spain as principal liaison between him and the Spanish authorities.

Upon the Duke's expected return to the UK, Bramall will remain in situ in Spain, with official, but unspecified, duties related to HRH. It should be suggested during this time that he has the ear of Lord Halifax, as well as of imprisoned BUF leader Sir Oswald Mosley. The usefulness of this royal appointment to Bramall's true purpose in Madrid need hardly be emphasised. In anticipation, he should familiarise himself with the circumstances of HRH in Spain, the Duke and Duchess's history and elements of court etiquette.

The document was signed by the deputy chief of operations MI6 and in green ink by an unknown official, apparently in overall charge, known simply as 'C.' Bramall read through it several times. Strickland was right. The Duke's unexpected emergence on the Spanish scene was a godsend. Added to the BUF stuff, it gave him all the entrée he could possibly want, confirming that his sympathies, if not exactly anti-British, were certainly less than antagonistic to the German and Fascist cause. It was brilliant, if a little troubling.

A more detailed document, included in the same folder, laid out the career of the former king, his character (and that of his wife), and what was known of his political beliefs, including who shared them in the British Establishment. Apparently, he was a firm believer in Irish unity and an opponent of the Northern Ireland state. He believed, like DeValera, that it was possible for a free Ireland to retain Dominion status and thereby keep a connection with the monarchy. Bramall wondered what his father would think about that. Finally, there was a briefing on royal procedure, advising on how the Palace functioned and the correct form of address for the Duke and Duchess – the latter, he noted, was Ma'am ('rhymes with ham') or Your Grace, not Your Royal Highness – together with potted biographies of the Royal Family and various specifics relating to the secretariat and its links to Downing Street. There was even a synopsis of the more pro-German, pre-war utterances of Halifax and Sir Samuel Hoare. What a bloody collection!

Strickland had been observing him as he read. Now the Yorkshireman reached out a podgy hand.

'All clear, I take it?'

'More or less,' Bramall replied

'Good. Any questions?'

'Only one. Why is the Duke such an absolute arse?'

This evoked the faintest of smiles. 'Maybe you should ask him.'

Madrid: villa of Colonel Raúl Ortega, Calle Beatriz Galindo, June 23

'What do you mean, you can't stand him? He is your fiancé.'

'Father: Felipe Luder is not my fiancé. I've told you before,

I hardly know him, and what I do know I detest.'

'But you agreed to marry him!'

'*You* agreed. I had no say in the matter.'

'You were seventeen.'

'Exactly. And how dare you sell me to the highest bidder this way? This is 1940, not 1490. Am I a *houri*, to be traded in the market place? Are you my pimp, offering me as a plaything to whichever man offers you the most lucrative business deal?'

Colonel Raúl Ortega looked at his daughter and bit his tongue. Late of the Army of Africa, he was not a large man, but stocky, with a bull neck. He had begun to put on weight in his fifties, which for some reason that he could not understand appeared to amuse his wife. Doña Vittoria would pat his stomach playfully and joke that he was Sancho Panza to the Don Quixote of his superior, the interior minister Ramón Serrano Suñer.

'If your mother should hear you say such things!' he said at last. 'The matter is settled. It was settled four years ago between Felipe and myself, with the full approval of his family and your mother.'

Isabel Ortega pulled at the ringlets of her distinctive blonde hair. She felt ready to shriek with fury. 'I will not do it,' she hissed. 'I will not go along with your filthy scheme. All you want is that the Luder fortune – earned God knows how in Argentina – should be joined to our family, to add to the profits that you have already made from the war.'

Colonel Ortega's eyes burned darkly. He could feel the vein in the middle of his forehead begin to rise. 'That is enough! I forbid you to speak to me in this way.'

'You will forbid me nothing,' Isabel retorted. 'Luder is not only a Fascist, he is a Nazi. He adds the last piece to the mosaic of your life that you have been so busily constructing these last five years. Do not think that I do not see what you are up to? Your closeness to Serrano Suñer gives you power. Next, you will expect a title – Barón Ortega de las Huelgas – which Don Ramón will one day secure for you if you do his bidding for long enough. Then will come the Luder dowry and admission to the highest echelons of Nazi society. We are to become one of the leading families of the New Europe. Is it not so, father? Do I not read you like a book?'

The blow when it came was not unexpected. Indeed, Isabel welcomed it. It was her father who felt the pain. He stood, aghast, looking at his daughter as she ran her hand down the stinging flesh of her cheek.

'You were a good man,' she told him quietly. 'You loved mother and you loved me and you believed in the honour of your calling. What happened to you?'

Colonel Ortega did his best to respond, but he had lost his voice. What he said came out in an anguished whisper. 'I have always tried to do what is best. What I have done, I have done for you and your mother and the good name of our family.'

'If you believe that, father, you will believe anything.'

During the silence that followed, Ortega struggled to reinflate himself. He drew air into his chest and felt his voice return. 'We did what we had to do, in times that were hard beyond all reason. You are too young to know what Spain was like in the years before the *Caudillo* took control. The country was riven by factions. There were the Basques, the Catalans and the Galicians. There were the landowners and aristocrats, believing themselves gods in their own estates. Then there were the

Communists, who would have swept away all tradition and handed us over to the Soviet Union. Have I mentioned the Anarchists, who believed in no law, just the destruction of the family and the abolition of property? We had the monarchists – medievalists – who believed that the king was anointed by God and could do no wrong. There was the Church, seething with corruption, supporting every reactionary impulse, every call for Spain to be locked down tight, as if it were a military barracks.'

Ortega paused, exhausted by the sheer force of his narrative. 'And then, of course, there were the people. Let us not forget the people – those who were not members of any of the other groups. What did the people want? They wanted better lives. They wanted education for their children and the promise of a future that was not based on everyone else sucking the blood from their veins. But the people did not know their own mind. They voted for every kind of party and every madman who came among them. As soon as one government was formed, those excluded would cry 'treason' and mobilise the mob to abandon every principal on which it was elected.'

The embers of a once hot fire still burned in the colonel's eyes, as if he were reliving the proudest moment of his past..

'The *Caudillo*,' he resumed, smashing his right fist into the palm of his left hand, 'broke through all of this. The past, he told us, would not be a model for the future. *He* would be that model – he and the Falange. There would be no more argument, no more division. From now on, there would be unity in Spain and one single movement that would express the national will, taking the decisions that would allow us to live in peace and prosperity.'

'But, father,' said Isabel. 'You know better than most what

happened in Asturias – our own family's home! How many ordinary Spaniards – boys I went to school with, sheep farmers, mineworkers – died to ensure that the *Generalísimo* could sleep easy in his bed? And what is the difference between the Spain you described a moment ago and the Spain we have today? Where is the harmony? Where is the peace and prosperity? Where is the reconciliation? Would you ask us to forget these things – to pretend that it did not happen, so that our future as a people is built upon a lie? The people are starving. Children are dying. Hundreds of government opponents are murdered every night by uniformed mobs or garrotted each morning in our prisons.'

She glared at him. 'There are labour camps in every town and city, where the opponents of the regime are worked to death as slaves. Franco believes that he *is* the State. Criticism of him is the worst treason, punishable by death. Generals grovel before him; they queue up to do his bidding. Even Don Ramón, your own boss, only occupies his position at the discretion of the *Caudillo*, who just happens to be his brother-in-law. If this is an improvement, then I am glad I am too young to have known anything worse.'

Ortega turned away, not daring to look at his daughter as he spoke. 'Mistakes have been made,' he said. 'Mistakes will always be made. But we have authority once more in our country. If the laws are sometimes harsh, they are at least understood. They give a shape to our lives. They give each man his place – and each woman, too. Duty is no longer scorned. Anarchy has given way to obedience. This is a good thing. It allows us to progress. If the price of peace is a pact of forgetting, then us make that pact and honour it in the years that lie ahead of us. I have learned my place in the New Spain. And so will you. Today, you distributed alms to the poor. That was a duty. You should learn from it. You will not defy me over Felipe. You will honour your word and you will offer him your vows. If you do not do this, you will no longer be my daughter.'

Ortega drew himself up to his full height. 'Did you hear what I said, Isabel?'

'I heard you father. I missed nothing.'

'That is good. Then we understand each other.'

Isabel breathed in deeply. 'We understand each other perfectly,' she said.

3

England, Southampton Water, June 24, 1940

Bramall had expected to be trussed up in the belly of a bomber for the run to Lisbon. In fact, he was to leave from the Solent, off Southampton, in a Sunderland flying boat, made in Belfast. The flight began in a mad, flapping dash that put him in mind of an overfed swan desperate to be airborne. The Isle of Wight, off to the right, looked heartbreakingly green and intimate, with its network of neat fields and tidy villages. England remained England, he decided, even in its remotest corners. The aircraft, its four Pegasus engines generating maximum thrust, veered east a minute or so after, hugging the Hampshire and Dorset coasts, so that the resort town of Bournemouth came into view and, just beyond, the curious spit of land known as Portland Bill. The only thing left to focus on as they reached cruising altitude was the drone of the engines, and Bramall settled down and accepted a mug of tea from a polite, but efficient steward. Two RAF fighters accompanied them as far as the Scilly Isles; after that, they were on their own. Bramall and the four other passengers on board looked on somewhat wistfully as their escort peeled off, waggling their wings. By then the huge seaplane was flying high, well out to sea, and everyone on board felt alone with their thoughts.

The idea that he might end up in espionage had never occurred to Bramall. At school, just the notion of it would have been risible, while at Cambridge those who were sounded out over sherry tended to be drunks, homosexuals or failed priests. His entire previous knowledge of the subject was confined to *The Thirty Nine Steps* and *The Riddle of the Sands*, which he had read and enjoyed when he was about sixteen, never dreaming that he might one day star in a sequel. It was his father, as usual, who was to blame. Sir Frederick and Oswald Mosley had held opposing views during the General Strike, when Mosley was a Labour MP, but in the years after, as the BUF had declared itself opposed to Communism and the 'World Jewish Conspiracy,' the two men became friends.

It was over lunch at the Savoy, not long after his return from Buenos Aires, that Bramall was introduced to the Blackshirt leader. 'Thought you might knock some sense into my boy here,' his father said, pouring Mosley a glass of hock. 'Give him a dose of reality before it's too late.' Mosley, with his jet black moustache and darting eyes, had smiled and said he would do what he could.

What troubled Bramall, now as he looked back on it, was the fact that he was not instantly repelled. Rather, he was intrigued. He was impressed by the fact that Mosley espoused not Communism, but something he called Communalism – a form of society, apparently, in which industry, unions and consumers worked together to ensure order and prosperity for all. He also noted the fact that, in spite of all the propaganda used against him by his enemies, Mosley had appointed Jews to several key positions, as well as ex-soldiers and union men, and that the party was specifically opposed to the exploitation of native peoples.

It was only when the brutal, tawdry nature of the enterprise was finally exposed that disillusionment set in. A protest in London's East end, led by Mosley himself, had started out in the usual way, with demands for an end to the foreign domination of capital and greater rights for Britain's 'native' people. But the 7,000 or so Blackshirts quickly realised that they had walked into a trap. They were outnumbered by counter-demonstrators, many of them Communists directed by Moscow, who had massed in the East End to put a stop to the Fascist threat once and for all. Within an hour the first stones were thrown and the BUF heavies, goaded into action, began to press forward, screaming out their detestation of Marxism, Socialism and the Jews.

Mosley always said 'we don't start fights, we finish them.' That night, he had made good on his boast. Bramall wasn't there as a reporter. The Post, though it tapped him from time to time for diary items on Mosley, kept him at arms' length from the story. The reason he tagged along was that he had received a tip-off from a friend that something out of the ordinary was in prospect – a confrontation in Cable Street, a Jewish neighbourhood, 'that will make Westminster sit up and take notice.' He was curious to know what this meant, only to end up shocked by what he saw. Jews and other counter-demonstrators were beaten with cudgels. Shop windows were smashed and anti-Semitic slogans daubed on walls. 'Come on, Bramall,' William Joyce, one of Mosley's principal lieutenants, from Galway, called out to him, 'this is no time for choking – there's work to be done!'

Mosley scoffed at him afterwards for his naivety. 'If you

can't stand the heat, stay out of the kitchen,' he joked, noticing how Bramall's hands were shaking. His father, excited as ever by conflict – which he saw as the essential building block of progress – advised him to 'grow up' and accept what needed to be done.

Sickened by what he had seen, and appalled even more by what he had almost become, he thought of moving to Canada, where they were crying out for teachers. But then one night in the pub, his pal on the news desk suggested to him that he could do worse than approach a contact of his in Special Branch. At first, Bramall had objected. 'Wouldn't that be like jumping from the frying pan into the fire?' he asked.

'Lord, no,' came the reply. 'Absolutely not. Tell you what, I'll give him a call soon as we get back to the office, let him put your mind at rest. He's a good bloke. Knows what's what. All you have to do is talk to him. Can't do any harm, can it?'

And that was how his undercover career began. Overnight, the Post, put him onto hard news – giving him free rein to go wherever he wanted, the only proviso being that none of it should compromise the newspaper. Suddenly, editorial 'independence' was out the window. The police and the Home Office, previously happy to tolerate the BUF, had come to realise their mistake and wanted inside dirt on what was going on, 'just in case.' He'd been cautious to begin with, but soon got into the swing of it, supplying details of where trouble could be expected and who was fomenting the violence, first to Special Branch, later to MI5. He even managed to photograph several pages of the party's accounts, using a special camera provided by the intelligence service.

His big moment came that autumn. On October 6, 1936, Mosley married Diana Mitford, one of Hitler's closest confidantes, at a secret ceremony in Joseph Göbbels's drawing room in Berlin. Diana and her sister Unity, two of the fabled Mitford Girls, had made a big impression on the Nazi hierarchy and were often photographed at rallies and party gatherings. Hitler was one of the invited guests at the wedding and, with Bramall as interpreter, spent several minutes in private talks with the BUF leader.

Bramall found the experience disturbing, but also fascinating. Speaking in his thick Austrian dialect, the Chancellor stressed the urgency of Germany's drive for territorial expansion and the need for the BUF to adopt a more openly anti-Semitic stance. 'The time for compromise is past,' he said, slicing through the air with his right hand. 'It is time to act.'

Mosley nodded vigorously. Hitler then emphasised his admiration for the British Empire and his conviction that the two Anglo-Saxon European powers, once reconciled, could dominate the world for centuries to come. As soon as he could get a word in, Mosley made a discrete plea for financial support so that the anti-Jewish crusade should not be confined to Italy and Germany. Hitler tapped his arm and said he would see what could be done. He then turned to Bramall, taking in his fair hair, blue eyes and broad shoulders. 'This young man is one of us,' he said to Mosley, shaking Bramall's hand. 'He knows I am right.' Then he laughed. 'We speak the same language.'

The Sunderland's engines continued to throb. They rounded the Brittany peninsula, a good hundred miles offshore, and eventually made landfall above the medieval city of La Coruña.

Bramall had never been there and knew of it only from the famous poem, The Burial of Sir John Moore, by Charles Wolfe, telling of the death of an English general during the Peninsular War.

> *Slowly and sadly we laid him down,*
> *From the field of his fame fresh and gory;*
> *We carved not a line, and we raised not a stone,*
> *But we left him alone with his glory.*

Would that be his fate? he wondered – except for the 'glory,' of course. He didn't reckon there would be much of that. Spies were not recognised; they were denied, like ghosts. The realisation caused him to shift uncomfortably in his seat.

By the time they arrived at their destination, night had closed in and the lights of Lisbon trailed like a necklace across the suburbs, from Estoril in the north to Cabo Espichel in the south. The Sunderland's passengers, used to the wartime blackout that rendered British cities so dismal after dark, appeared enchanted by the show. Bramall hardly noticed.

The landing was spectacular. The great flying boat, its engines throttling back with a throaty cough, descended in a shallow arc towards the water, steering between two lines of illuminated buoys, until, with a slap, its floats struck the waves, sending spray up against the windows so that they ran white with foam.

Minutes later, as they sat bobbing gently in the water, a tender approached from the harbour and squeezed up next to their starboard door. The steward dropped the handle, admitting a cool sea breeze, and a tall Portuguese customs officer appeared, rising and falling in the swell. 'Welcome to Lisbon,' he said, beaming broadly.

Lisbon: British Embassy, Rua São Domingos à Lapa, June 25

Bramall had expected him to be bigger. He was supposed to be one of MI6's most effective agents, but he couldn't have been more that five feet eight. In his mid–to-late forties, with sagging jaw muscles and red-rimmed eyes, he wore a pale, slightly ill-fitting linen suit of the type favoured by the English middle classes on holiday in Nice. His tie, a startling concoction, looked as if it had been pressed onto an artist's still-wet canvas. The room itself was dull to the point of paralysis. A view of the Tagus River would have been possible through the dormer window if the desk had been arranged differently. As it was, it faced inwards, towards filing cabinets and shelves packed solid with documents.

'Sorry about the stairs,' a man's voice said. 'The Nazis give their intelligence people large offices with brass plaques on the door, next to the ambassador. Mussolini's lot go for comfortable settees and coffee tables strewn with the latest magazines. If one of their secretaries pauses on her way out to adjust the seams of her stockings, the Italians regard it as time well spent – which I suspect is why they'll never make it as full-blown Fascists. This, however, is the standard British model: an attic room in what used to be the servants' quarters. I've got a desk with an inkwell and there's a gas ring in the corner so that any time I get fed up with the diplomats stealing the credit for the work I do, I can always make myself a nice cup of tea.'

Bramall felt immediately at home. 'Charles Bramall,' he said.

'Douglas Croft.'

They shook hands.

'Pull up a chair and we'll talk,' Croft said.

Bramall sat down. It was odd, he realised. Here, in this peculiar environment, in which diplomacy was replaced by a lethal variant of chess, he could feel anxiety creeping up on him like shadows on a September evening.

'You smoke?' Croft asked, reaching for an open packet of Player's on his desk. His accent was London of some kind, or maybe Essex, but not cockney, which would have been a real surprise.

'I wouldn't mind, actually,' Bramall replied.

Croft passed the Player's. 'Helps keep the flies off.' He struck a match and lit both their cigarettes. Then he leaned back in his chair. 'There are two things you have to bear in mind about what lies ahead of you. The first is not to let anything get past you. Watch, listen and learn. The second is, don't get killed.'

As he drew smoke gratefully into his lungs, Bramall couldn't help observing how tired Croft looked. It was not the welcome exhaustion that concluded a period of intense activity, in which a good night's sleep sent the body clock back to zero. It was the deeper-seated kind, built over time out of effort expended without reward. Others on the embassy staff, he imagined, came and went, progressing their careers and moving on, being careful not to dirty their hands. Not Croft. He would have bet his life on that. Croft had dirt beneath his fingernails. Blood, too, he shouldn't wonder.

'How long have you been stationed here?' he asked.

Croft fiddled with the front of his collar, struggling to release the stud. 'Too long,' he said. 'I'm not sure I can remember what England looks like.'

Bramall nodded. 'At least you don't have the Germans on

your tail.'

The look Croft gave him in response to this was not one of contempt, more of mild bewilderment. 'I don't know where you got that idea from, and I won't ask. Just take it from me, the fucking Nazis are everywhere. I go to meet someone in a bar, ten to one an SD agent will be seated at the next table. We've had a couple of our people disappear. Just last month, a mining engineer from Birmingham got his brains blown out in Vila Real. I'm told some poor sod's just come out to take his place – you have to wonder what the job description was. And then there was a local lad that smuggled documents for me. Antonio. Found him face down in a drain, his throat slit. And of course now that the French are run from Vichy, we don't know what the Germans know and what they don't about our past operations. Yesterday's trusted friends turn out to be today's enemies. Not an easy number, Charlie. Got to watch your back.'

A large, fat fly flew in the open window. Croft picked up a fly swat from his desktop and scythed the air with it, to no effect. 'Like walking into the lions' den,' he said. 'I'm betting you'll be dead inside of a month.'

'How reassuring. What odds did you get?'

'I'm not joking. Have you any idea just how many SD and *Abwehr* agents there are in Spain today?'

'They told me quite a few.'

'Two thousand. And the number's going up all the time. Some of them even wear their uniforms. Strut around like they own the place. You'll be watched everywhere you go. If they think you're getting too close to them or look like you might stumble on something interesting, they'll be perfectly happy to put a bullet in your brain. We've complained, of course – even sent the police and foreign ministry lists of known operatives. But it's done us no good.'

The fly landed on his knee. He swiped at it with his hand, again without result.

'And how does our side compare?' Bramall asked. 'Strickland gave me to understand I'd be pretty much on my own.'

'How many? Well, there's five – or is it six? – working in the iron ore and wolfram trade, who send us reports from time to time of anything unusual goes on. For the most part, they're up North, miles from anywhere. Then there's an SIS security squad – bodyguards really – attached to the embassy. You'll meet them when you catch up with the Duke. What else? Well, there's a strictly unofficial network of expats and Spanish sympathisers. But you can never put your faith in them. Some of them'd give you away to the Germans for an envelope stuffed with Swiss francs.'

Croft paused for a second, then clipped the edge of one of his curtains with the fly swat, so that the unfortunate bluebottle fell dead at his feet. A look of satisfaction came over his features. 'And then, of course, there's you – the sole full-time agent of His Majesty's Secret Intelligence Service, MI6 division.'

The lines around Bramall's face tightened. 'Sounds like I'd better brush up on my Solitaire.'

'Patience more like it. Given that you're a complete novice, I wouldn't go taking too many chances. Never forget, you're not supposed to be there. Here, in Lisbon, they know I'm a British agent. Turn a blind eye – oldest ally and all that. Bloody Madrid, they find out you're MI6, you'll be on the first plane out of the country – either that or strapped to a hospital trolley with electrodes fixed to your nuts.'

Whatever modicum of optimism he had retained drained out of Bramall like air from a collapsed bellows. But Croft hadn't finished. He sniffed the air and scratched the underside of his chin, where he hadn't shaved properly.

'Here's the fact of the matter,' he said. 'If Strickland had asked my advice, I'd have said, 'either send me someone who knows what he's doing, or don't bother sending anyone.' But, of course, he didn't ask me, so now I'm stuck with you.'

'Is this supposed to be my pep-talk?'

'No. It's your stop feeling sorry for yourself and get off your arse and go and learn something talk. I'm a busy man. I don't have time to nursemaid you or anyone else. In case you hadn't noticed, there's a war on and what we're engaged in is called 'active service.' So my advice to you is, get active.'

'Any chance you could be more specific?'

Croft rubbed his eyes, which were red-rimmed. He looked as if he'd been up all night, reading.

'Okay,' he said, 'try this. Espionage is like a lot of other high-risk activities: long periods of boredom punctuated by moments of fear and excitement. You've got to listen out for things, just like they told you, and keep your eyes peeled for likely contacts, just like they said. There are always people a couple of notches down from the top who are liable to say a little bit more than they should over a drink. Do them a favour if you can. Slip them a few pesetas if they're short, lie to their wives about where they were that night they were out screwing their mistress. Nothing fancy, mind, just enough to make them feel they can trust you and they owe you something.

The Londoner sat back and drew on his cigarette.

'And if you ever do get five minutes to yourself in the office of a general or a cabinet minister, don't waste it. Take a look at his desk diary, or, more likely, his secretary's. Read any letters you see lying around. Open a filing cabinet if you get the chance. Why not? Only, try to pick the right drawer. Remember the alphabet – and don't leave prints. Most important, never forget you need luck at both ends – to get the stuff in the first place and to live long enough to tell the tale. Other than that, do what the dips do: assess, interpret, put two and two together. If you've got time, it'll start to add up.'

Croft ran his hand through his hair and bared his teeth. 'Oh, and one more thing. Don't make me have to clean up your mess. I'm head of station, Iberia, not a dish rag.'

Bramall felt as if he had just been kicked around the room by the school bully. "Well,' he said. 'Strickland said you were – what was it? – *crusty*. He didn't mention you were a sadist.'

'How is the old sod anyway?'

'He's well.'

'Don't suppose he mentioned his time in Russia?'

'No.'

'And you didn't ask?'

'No.'

'Pity. Never let good manners stand in the way of finding out what you need to know. That's where your sort usually fuck up. The point is, Strickland's forgotten more about this business than either of us will ever know. Don't make them like him any more. Russia was the big one. Sidney Reilly tried to get the Bolsheviks to stay in the war. Damn near succeeded. Strickland worked the other side. Knew Kerensky, tried to nudge him towards a deal with General Kornilov and the Whites. Hairy stuff and no medals. But somebody's got to do it.'

'Right.'

'Of course, in 1916 he was in Ireland.'

'Was he?'

'Where he didn't exactly endear himself to the rebel cause.'

'I would imagine not.'

'But then, the rebel cause didn't exactly endear itself to you, did it?'

'No.'

'So you have that much in common.'

The heat was suffocating. Croft blew out a thick cloud of smoke in the direction of a small electric fan, which re-directed it towards the open window. Bramall would never have guessed that the podgy figure of Strickland had had a ringside seat at some of the most momentous events of the century. It didn't seem to go with his waistcoats and his hidden sugar supply. But then, he realised, we all grew older and became pastiches of ourselves. It was the way of the world, which contrived to turn high drama into light comedy. As for Croft, he seemed to him the epitome of a good man resigned to his fate. If he ended up like him, it wouldn't be the worst thing he'd done.

'Is Strickland married?' he suddenly asked. He didn't know why.

Croft looked puzzled. 'Married? Strickland? Shouldn't think so.'

'He never said?'

'No.'

'And you didn't ask?'

'No. And before you ask, the first Mrs Croft ran off with a salesman from Penge. The second died in childbirth. That was ten years ago.'

'I'm sorry. Did the child make it?'

'No. Poor little bleeder was the wrong way round. Tried to come out feet first, got strangled by his own umbilical.'

Croft stubbed out his cigarette into a saucer already crammed with butts. 'One thing I need to get straight. Turns out, you and the Nazis weren't always at daggers drawn. Even met the *Führer*, so I'm told.'

'I was young then.'

'Painful subject, is it? I'm not surprised. Point is, you were tempted. We all were. Same when you were in Spain during the war. Some would call your reporting fair, others would say it didn't give Franco's censors too much trouble.'

Bramall could feel his hackles rise. 'Look,' he began, 'I've been through all this with Strickland. I was young. I was naïve – stupid, if you prefer. But I wasn't to know how things would develop. When I saw for myself what lay under the stone, I tried to put things right. But you know that.'

Croft fixed him with a icy glare. 'What about now? Can we trust you?'

'Yes.'

'Not that you'd lie to me.'

'Exactly.'

This induced a weary smile. 'Right, then. I think we should get started. Pay attention. The Duke's been in Madrid the best part of two days already and the embassy do's coming up on Saturday. If you're not careful, you'll miss it. So concentrate. The man you've got to watch out for is Javier Bermejillo – strictly speaking the Marqués de Bermejillo, known to his friends as 'Tiger.' Picked HRH up at the border and escorted him to

Madrid. A diplomat, smooth as silk, arrogant as bedamned, and Beigbeder has assigned him to the Duke so that anything that's said goes straight to Franco. Then there's Miguel Primo de Rivera, brother of the late, unlamented Falange leader, José Antonio. Miguel's the civil governor of Madrid, so he's got clout. A bit of a playboy on the side, but he's also pretty thick with the Generalísimo, if you get my drift – so tread carefully.'

So many names. But Croft wasn't done yet.

'And then, of course, there's the Germans. Paul Winzer is the police attaché. *Gestapo* – a right devious bastard. But you might also want to keep an eye on Klaus Hasselfeldt, an SD major, newly arrived from Berlin, hard as nails, said to be a personal protégé of Schellenberg's.'

'The counter-intelligence wallah?'

'The very same. Said to be on his way up, with the scalps to prove it. Ruthless – and devious. If Hasselfeldt's his man, you can be sure he's trouble.'

Bramall was struggling to take all this in. 'You do realise,' he said, 'that I'm only using the Duke as cover. I couldn't actually give a stuff what he's up to in Madrid. Good God! The man's an idiot.'

'Do me a favour,' said Croft.

'What do you mean?'

'Listen to what I'm telling you. Before he became King, he and the Duchess went to see Hitler, who, you may recall, took quite a shine to him. Bit like yourself in that respect. He's also spent a fair bit of time in the company of your pal Mosley and he's not above coming out with pro-German sentiments when he thinks he's in safe company. Even speaks German! Probably doesn't know which side he's on. As for her…' Croft emitted a low whistle. 'You know she had an affair with Ribbentrop in '36?'

Despite himself, Bramall was shocked.

'He was ambassador in London at the time and she was the King's mistress, but that didn't put her off – not until after they got engaged. Dirty sod used to send her seventeen red roses every day. I heard that from Special Branch. Seventeen! Why not a dozen, or two dozen? You might well ask. Because seventeen's the number of times they slept together. I tell you what, if Ribbentrop's got the Duchess wrapped round his little finger and she goes on to convince the Duke he's the once and future king, who's to say where it's all going to end?'

Bramall made a face. 'That's ridiculous. I don't know about her, but he's not a traitor.'

'For Christ's sake, how would you know? Wouldn't be the first time we'd got a king over the water. Just remember … how many times do I have to repeat this before it gets through your thick skull? Keep your ears open, as well as your eyes. Look a right 'Charlie,' wouldn't you, if you turned up in Spain as the Duke's minder and him and the Duchess wound up in Berlin giving an interview to Lord Haw Haw?'

Bramall stuck out his jaw. He was beginning to resent the impression Croft had formed of him. 'You won't win that bet,' he said. 'When I get back from Madrid, you're going to take me to dinner, with champagne – Veuve Cliquot – to celebrate my accomplishments. What do you say?'

Croft rolled his eyes, exposing a faint network of veins, like an electrical circuit map. 'You're on,' he said. 'Only you'll pardon me if I don't put the order in just yet. For here's the thing: we don't fix the timetables, the timetables fix us. Same with priorities: we don't choose, we get chosen. Once you get the Duke safely out of your hair and into mine, you'll have all the time you need to sort out Gibraltar – which ain't going to be easy, I promise you. Until then, snap to it. Know what I'm saying?'

'Go on.'

'Looking after the Duke will give you the sort of entrée into Falange and Nazi circles money can't buy. Spaniards are mad for royalty, and as his equerry you'll get more than your share of reflected glory. It'll be a crash course in who's important and who's not in downtown Madrid, and it'll put your face about.'

Croft was sweating pretty badly now, but he sounded like he could go on forever on this topic. Bramall realised that he probably didn't get the chance that often to pass on his experience. Then, all of a sudden, he stopped and stared hard at Bramall. 'Bloody hell! You've got to have worked this out for yourself. I mean, you're not fucking stupid … are you?'

Bramall returned the stare. 'No,' he said, 'I'm not fucking stupid, and I had worked it out. But if the future of this war should happen to turn on whether or not the Duke of fucking Windsor buys his shirts in London or Berlin, then I'm afraid I've missed the bloody point.'

Just for a moment, a smile, or at least the semblance of a smile, crossed Croft's haggard features. 'I can't argue with that. Unfortunately … '

'– I know. Ours not to reason why. So let's just get on, shall we? Any chance of a cup of tea?'

'Yeah, why not? Always time for a cuppa. You fill the kettle, I'll light the gas. When are you off?'

'There's a plane tonight.'

'That soon? Right, then, no time to lose. We'll start with Serrano. What do you know about him? Fuck-all would be par for the course.'

Madrid, the Ritz Hotel, June 25

The flight from Lisbon took nearly two hours. As the aircraft, a De Havilland Dominie, made from plywood, crossed the border at Badajoz, Bramall could make out the peaks of the Sierra de San Pedro, then, the long, fertile valley of the Tajo, stretching as far east as Toledo and Aranjuez, after which the plane veered sharply north for Madrid.

It was sixteen months since he had left Spain, heading for home on the eve of Franco's victory. But his memories of the war's final chapter remained crystal-clear. His last day had been spent in Figueres, close to the border with France. It was bitterly cold and he remembered how his lip had split on contact with a cigarette. He had drawn the blood down into his throat with the smoke. The sky was too clear for snow to fall, but the temperature in the mountains had plummeted ten degrees, halting the streams, weaving icicles into the wool of the few sheep that had not been butchered and eaten.

Roads leading in and out of the town were packed with refugees fleeing Franco's vengeance. Everyone who could get out was on the move. Vans, lorries, motor cars, mule-carts, as well as donkeys laden with sacks, were being used to carry the defeated army of the Republic and their families over the high passes to sanctuary in France.

He remembered the flag of the Republic, with its horizontal

stripes of red, yellow and purple, fluttering limply from the tower of the Castell de Sant Ferran. Once a recruitment centre for the International Brigades, the ancient fortress was staging the last-ever meeting of the Republican parliament, which had fled north in the face of the deepening chaos in Madrid and the fall of Barcelona. Only a handful of deputies had turned up for the wake. The rest were already running for their lives.

He had watched the drama playing out in front of him as if it were a scene from Russian opera. There was Martínez Barrio, leader of the Cortes, his thin grey hair swept back from his forehead, and President Manuel Azaña, a man whose hold on power had long since disappeared. They wore heavy overcoats on top of crumpled suits and ties. Their shoes, of finest Spanish leather, were scuffed and stained. Azaña's dark, sloping eyes, peering out through gold-rimmed spectacles, registered the deep depression into which he had sunk in recent months. Not far behind was Prime Minister Juan Negrín, once the socialist strongman, whose betrayal by Stalin was a blow from which he would never recover.

Bramall had shut his eyes, unable to confront the pathos, as these last, ragged members of the Cortes, their breaths ascending like lost souls, broke into a defiant rendition of the anthem, *Himno de Riego*.

> *Children of El Cid,*
> *The Mother country*
> *calls its soldiers to combat.*
> *Let us swear by her*
> *To win or die.*

A change in the noise from the Sunderland's engines

interrupted his revereie. The plane had begun its final descent into Madrid. The sun streaming through his window was so strong that he had to pull down the shade and look away. The pilot made a perfect three-point landing and taxied the short distance to the terminal. In the makeshift aerodrome, still battered from the war, customs and immigration officials examined his papers and led him straight through to where a car was waiting. The advertisements on the walls were faded and torn, promoting luxury items that hadn't been common currency in Spain for more than five years. The fact that he held a newly issued diplomatic passport embossed inside with the royal crest actually brought one official to attention. No one was interested in his letter of introduction, signed by the King's private secretary in London, which remained unopened in his pocket.

He sank gratefully into the cracked leather seat of the embassy car. The driver, an alert-looking fellow made no attempt to hide the pistol thrust into the waistband of his trousers. The journey into the city was a predictably miserable experience. Spain in the aftermath of three years of fighting was a dustbowl. There were few animals in pasture, and those there were scrawny, with little meat and certainly no fat on the bone. Fields that ought to have been green with maize were brown and dry. It was like the surface of the Moon.

He watched a gang of prisoners with shackles on their ankles digging a ditch between two large, open fields. They looked drugged, as if all resistance had been purged from their systems. Their arms rose and fell mechanically, driving in the entrenching spades, then pulling back. Guards with shotguns, wearing broad-brimmed hats, looked on vacantly, occasionally drinking water from earthenware jars.

The car turned off the airport highway into the outskirts of the capital, halting for several minutes to allow a convoy of lorries to pass by on the sides of which were written the slogan, 'Spain's food surplus for the workers of Germany.' Someone obviously retained a sense of humour. It was still hot in the final hours before nightfall and he wound his window down in a vain search for cooler air. A group of woman, on their knees a little back from the road, were busy washing clothes in a row of identical zinc baths. They looked exhausted. Small children stood naked next to the road, their hair matted, intrigued, he supposed, by the sight of a limousine. Most disconcerting of all, a pair of vultures was busy feeding from a pile of rotting refuse, their claws scrabbling, their beaks tearing at a smear of decomposed offal with a liquid snap.

Madrid had enjoyed an economic boom in the 1920s. Now it was like Madras. Bombs or shellfire had destroyed many of the new housing blocks. In their place were rows of huts, made from corrugated iron. Shallow trenches, gouged out of the mud, drained off water and sewage. A donkey pulling a cart loaded with straw relieved itself on the street, sending up a cloud of steam. Somewhere, a radio played, its crackling report of what sounded like a football match overlaying the monotonous, leaden clamour of an Angelus bell. The prevailing aroma that would once have contained quince and lavender and, here and there, a hint of orange blossom had given way to the stale odour of decay.

As they picked their way through the older suburbs, the lack of trees struck a chord in his memory. Thousands of trees, some of them hundreds of years old, had been cut down for fuel in the terrible winter of 1937-38, when Franco's Army, camped outside the city, refused to let goods in or out. Artillery shells landed every couple of minutes, terrorising the population and denying them sleep. Madrileños that winter had suffered the most appalling hardships. It wasn't only the trees that disappeared: furniture, books, even paintings, were thrown onto fires as people struggled to stay alive in temperatures that each night fell well below freezing. Now, with the siege long-since concluded, he noticed how many doors were missing as well. How cold and desperate did you have to be, he wondered, before you would rip your own front door off its hinges and burn it, knowing that next day there would be no door and no fuel either? He knew the answer, of course. When the Fascists finally shouldered their way in, through the corpses of the Communists and what remained of the Army of the Centre, they were entering a virtual city of the dead.

The car halted at a junction guarded by a set of traffic lights that had probably last worked in 1936. They had reached the broad Avenida de Alfonso XIII and were about to enter the city centre. Downtown Madrid, in spite of some ominous-looking gaps, was a different kind of place, at first glance more like the metropolis he had once known. As they drew up in front of the Ritz hotel, he could feel his spirits start to lift. A bellboy saluted and took his suitcase. At reception, he learned that a suite with private bathroom had been reserved for him on the sixth floor, below the Duke's no doubt palatial quarters. That was a surprise. On being shown into his suite, he found not only that there was a telephone in each room, but a wireless and a gramophone – the latter, he noted, with a selection of pre-war Spanish and American disks. From the windows there were views across the Plaza de la Lealtad towards the Retiro, Madrid's Central Park..

He washed his face and hands and combed his hair before making his way back to the lifts. A note pinned to the landing wall informed him that only one of the four *ascensores* permitted access to the royal suite and that to take that he had first to descend to the lobby. He took the stairs. Back in reception, a uniformed guard stood by the lifts asked him for his papers. He produced his letter of introduction, written in Spanish as well as English, before being frisked and permitted to enter the reserved car, in which a uniformed attendant stood waiting. Moments later, the fellow stepped out on the sixth floor and directed him towards a set of double doors. Once again he showed his papers, this time to a British official.

'Ah, Mr Bramall,' said the man, who couldn't have been more than twenty-five, with an Anthony Eden moustache and startlingly blond hair. 'His Royal Highness is expecting you.'

Inside, sat cross-legged on an ornate chair in the middle of the room was a small, immaculately dressed figure, a gin and tonic in his left hand, an empty cigarette holder in his right. The duke was certainly handsome, in an arthritic, upper-class kind of way, but he seemed to Bramall to have a fatally weak chin. He was talking to someone, evidently a Spaniard, sitting bolt upright on a matching sofa.

Bramall coughed politely and waited for his cue. The Duke looked up and nodded.

'Who are you?'

'Name's Bramall, sir. Newly arrived from London. I'm here as arranged to provide liaison with the Spanish.'

'Of course, of course. They told me to expect you.' The voice of the former monarch, whose interrupted destiny had been to be, by the grace of God, King of Great Britain and Northern Ireland, Emperor of India and Defender of the Faith, was light and reedy. 'To tell you the truth, I'm not quite sure what it is you're supposed to do for me, but I've no doubt you'll do it awfully well.'

Bramall bowed ever so slightly, feeling a fraud as well as a fool. 'Your Royal Highness,' he said, as if that were a statement in itself.

'You're General Bramall's son, are you not?'

'That's right, sir.'

'Irish!'

'Born and bred.'

'But didn't stay on after independence. Fled to England, that it?'

'Not much choice in the matter.'

'Hmm. That's what they all say. But you know Spain, I gather.'

'Yes, sir. I spent a year in Madrid as an undergraduate and covered the war from the Nationalist side for the best part of two years. I speak the language and studied Spanish culture and politics.'

The Duke wiped a speck of lint from the sleeve of his jacket. 'Well, that's something, I suppose. So what do you have in mind for me?'

Out of the corner of his eye, Bramall caught sight of the Duchess, standing in the adjacent bedroom next to a vase of red roses, which immediately made him think of Ribbentrop. He tried to work out how many stems there were. After eleven he got confused and lost count. She was holding a dress up against herself and studying her reflection in a mirror. She had good legs, he would give her that, but her expression, fixed in the glass, was cold as a Narvik winter. He turned away. The Duke, who didn't appear to have noticed the unintended act of voyeurism directed at his American wife by his newly arrived equerry, looked puzzled.

'Bramall! Are you listening?'

'I'm sorry, sir. Just a bit tired, that's all.'

'Well, pay attention, man. I said, what's on the agenda?'

'Oh! Well, the reception at the embassy is just a few days off. There's a lot to do by way of final preparation. Also, I shall be talking with officials in Madrid about issues of security and protocol that may arise during your stay.'

From the bedroom, the Duchess offered a smile of the sort that Bramall imagined a female preying mantis would offer to her mate before eating him, then closed the door with her heel.

The Duke still didn't appear to have noticed anything. 'If you really want to know what's happening, perhaps you should start with my guest, Don Miguel Primo de Rivera, governor of Madrid – an old friend assigned to me by the *Caudillo* to see to it that everything is sweetness and light.'

The Spaniard offered a fractionally raised eyebrow. He reminded Bramall of the maitre d' at an Argentinian nightclub he'd visited once. 'Don Miguel,' he said, once more inclining his head. 'An honour.'

Primo de Rivera, who Croft had assured him was a perfect conduit to Franco but otherwise a waste of space, extended his right hand in such a way as to imply that Bramall should make only the briefest of contact with the ends of his fingers.

'Señor Bramall,' the Spaniard said, withdrawing his hand

like a snake retracting its tongue. 'Be assured that His Royal Highness is in safe hands and will receive the fullest protection of our Government.'

'Of that, sir, I have no doubt.'

The Duke sat back on his chair and drew from his pocket a gold cigarette case, from which he extracted what looked to Bramall like a Dunhill's. A sly smile ran across his features. 'I am informed, Mr Bramall, that you were once an associate of Sir Oswald Mosley and his Blackshirts.'

Primo de Rivera's ears pricked up at this.

'That is true, sir,' Bramall replied. 'But it was several years ago. In my present capacity, I am required to be apolitical.'

'Is that similar to being asexual?' Primo de Rivera asked, adjusting the line of his trousers across his knees. 'Or shouldn't I ask?'

Bramall brought the ends of his fingers together and smiled thinly in a manner that he hoped conveyed his true feelings on the observation. 'I wouldn't presume to say, sir.'

'Nevertheless,' the Duke continued, 'it must be, shall we say, *interesting* for you to be negotiating now with a government that – were he able any longer to express an opinion on the matter – would meet with Sir Oswald's enthusiastic approval.'

'As you say, sir – interesting.'

'You know he came out in support of me during the abdication business?'

'I was abroad at the time, sir – in Burma. But I read about it.'

'Said there should be a referendum. Put it to the people!'

For a second it looked as if the former king was going to say something he shouldn't, but he bit his lip instead. 'All a long time ago now. Different world. And I'm sure we've all got better things to do than reminisce about what might have been. Have you spoken with the ambassador yet?'

'No, sir. I just got in.'

'Excellent fellow. Knew him in the old days, when we were both ... differently employed. We'll meet up with him in the morning. Come to my suite at, shall we say, eleven. We can talk then.'

'Yes, sir.'

'Well, that will be all. Good night to you.'

'Good night, sir ... Don Miguel.' For a split second, Bramall fancied he was supposed to reverse out of the room bent double, but after a hesitant step backwards, he turned smartly around and made his exit in the standard fashion. It was only when he regained the corridor that he realised he was sweating. Time for a drink, he told himself. He made his way to the lift and was conveyed back down to the lobby. The bar, it turned out, was just across the hall.

Draping himself over the counter, he signalled to the waiter, fellow in his sixties wearing a white jacket that was slightly too small for him. '*Buenos días*. Gin & tonic, please. And go easy on the tonic.'

The barman nodded and turned behind him to the optics.

'*G&T!* came a voice from somewhere close by. 'Clearly a man after my own heart.'

Bramall turned slowly round. The man who had spoken to him didn't look like he was a Spaniard. He had brown hair and blue eyes.

'I'm sorry, I ...'

A hand stretched out. 'Klaus Hasselfeldt, from the German

legation, commercial section. And you are … ?'

Bramall did not accept the hand, which then clenched into a fist and withdrew. 'The German legation, you say. Well, that's a bit of a problem. I'm attached to the British embassy, you see, and given the fact your country is planning to invade my country…'

The fellow's face creased into an ironical smile. 'Oh,' he said. '*That!* I'm not here to talk about the war. It is much too hot an evening for that, Mr…?'

' – Bramall.'

His first mistake.

The German raised his glass. 'Also commercial section, I imagine.'

'Royal equerry, actually.'

'An *ekverry*? ' I'm sorry. My English is pretty good, but I don't know that word.'

'Personal assistant. Factotum. Drudge. *Ordonanz*. I'm what you might call a glorified secretary.'

'Really? How unusual. Most embassy types one meets these days are in trade, don't you find? There are so many of us engaged in commerce, I wonder we have any time for war.'

'Indeed. But as I say, I'm not a diplomat.'

'Even so, it is strange I haven't seen you before.' The fellow's accent was Austrian, Bramall decided.

'That's because I wasn't here before. And now, Herr Hasselfeldt, if you'll excuse me, I must attend to my duties.'

'Naturally. His Royal Highness will be waiting.'

The man was grinning. Fucking nerve! Not in the country five minutes and already the SD was on to him. He'd planned to get his bearings first, find his way around. They'd said he would be approached after a week or so at a foreign ministry reception or other public gathering, or else that he'd get a discreet invitation through a third party to lunch at the legation. But this Hasselfeldt fellow must have been given a different message. He obviously intended to wind him up, put him on the defensive. And the worst thing was, it worked. Clearly he had underestimated Croft. How the hell had the man managed to survive all these years?

He drained his drink and made his way to the lifts. Back in his room, he lay down on the bed suddenly aware of how tired and confused he was. Only now was the significance of being in Spain under the New Order getting through to him. It wasn't so long since Franco was regarded as little more than a war criminal. Today, if the same man appeared in front of him, he would have to bow and call him Your Excellency. Then again, he had toadied to both sides during his time as a correspondent. Hadn't liked either gang, if the truth were told. His life, it sometimes seemed, was a series of role reversals designed to mock him. Nothing except memory was constant. But what use was memory? Memory was like a faulty time bomb that preserved pain and detonated it when it would cause most hurt.

There was a knock at the door – not Hasselfeldt, thank God, but an embassy security guard with the guest list for Saturday's gala reception. Included with the four sheets of fullscap was a note that said simply, 'Let me know what you think – Hoare.'

Half an hour later, in the hotel restaurant, where he had hoped he would be left alone to peruse the list, he was joined by the same young fellow who had inspected his papers outside the Duke's suite. He introduced himself as Anthony Buchanan-Smith and it turned out that he, too, was an equerry, except that he was the real thing, appointed by Buckingham Palace, not the Foreign Office. When the Duke left for Lisbon, thence, it was assumed, to London, he would go with him, fated to spend the war arranging dinner parties, gazing out at high society across the rim of a champagne glass.

'If you need me to show you the ropes, you've only to say the word,' Buchanan-Smith enthused. He looked as if he was not merely supercilious, but supercilious for England. 'Dealing with royalty is no easy matter. I can imagine how awkward it must be for a Foreign Office type like you to be thrown in at the deep end like this.'

'I think I can manage,' Bramall said quietly.

'The party's all arranged.'

'Is that right?'

His uninvited guest, who had been consulting the menu, looked up, irritated. 'What's that supposed to mean?'

Bramall ran his eye down the list of *hors d'ouevres*. They looked extremely good. 'Just that the list will not be final until it has my approval.'

'Really? Does His Royal Highness know that?'

Cocky young bastard! 'He will. My instructions come directly from Downing Street. From the prime minister himself.'

The smirk that had lurked on the younger man's face faded at once. 'Ah.' he said. 'I see. That puts rather a different complexion on things.'

'I should imagine it does.' It had been a while since Bramall had found himself in the superior position dealing with British officials – or indeed, anyone at all – and he had to admit he found it refreshing. 'But there is no reason for us to quarrel,' he continued grandly. 'We are both, after all, doing our duty.'

Buchanan-Smith ran his hand down his moustache, which he had presumably cultivated to add gravitas to his youthful bearing. 'We can do no more.'

'So we're agreed, then. Now what about starters? I rather fancy the calamari.'

Madrid: German Legation, Avenida del Generalísimo Franco, June 26

Hasselfeldt was first in to the embassy, long before the ambassador and his team of diplomats, even before his secretary, which was why he had to make his own coffee. As he sat at his desk, stirring in some powdered milk, he decided to run a check on Charles Bramall. He might be exactly what he said he was. Where there was royalty there were flunkies. But Bramall had looked too fit, too sharp, to be just another royal lackey. He would ask Berlin if they'd heard of him. They'd need a picture, of course. Bramall might well not be his real name. The best thing to do would be to get the hotel photographer to snap the Duke in the foyer of the hotel and capture Bramall at the same time. It was probably nothing. In all likelihood he was exactly what he said he was. But it made sense to check.

Madrid: British embassy, Calle del Fernando el Santo, June 26

Sir Samuel Hoare, so dull of temperament he was rumoured to be descended from a long line of maiden aunts, was not a man given easily to levity. He had been in Madrid for less than a month, charged with ensuring that Spain did not throw in its lot with the Axis powers. Yet, this week, with everything hanging in the balance, inordinate amounts of his time had been given up to the organisation of a gigantic party. He could not bear it. The Duke of Windsor, freed from what he regarded as the intolerable pressures of Palace life, was exerting himself in exile and had turned out, predictably, to be a right royal pain in the neck. It was tedious, as well as achingly unproductive.

'Your Royal Highness,' he began. 'How good to see you again – and after so short an interval. What can I do for you this time?'

The Duke stood with his hands clasped in the side pockets of his jacket, the thumbs pointing towards the creases of his trousers as if they were a pair of concealed Derringers. 'It's not what you can do for me, Hoare, it's what I can do for you.'

'I am intrigued.'

The Duke beckoned Bramall forward. 'I don't think you've met Mr Bramall, my newest equerry, appointed by a lethal combination of the Palace and Downing Street.' The two men shook hands. 'He's been taking a look at our list of invitations for Saturday's party, and you'll be pleased to know that he has decided not to exercise his power of veto.'

'That is good news, sir. So it will be one thousand for canapés and drinks?'

'Absolutely. He agrees with you, though, that it might be unwise to invite the Germans in present circumstances.'

The ambassador gave Bramall the curtest of nods. 'I really do think that would be best,' he said.

'Can't see the problem myself. Here, in Madrid, on neutral

soil, who's to say that we might not do some good and set the tone for some kind of longer-term rapprochement?'

Hoare, shocked beyond words, decided to leave the Duke's argument where it lay. 'And might I assume that the Duchess is happy with the list, as presented?'

'Her Royal Highness? She was the one drew it up in the first place. With your people, of course.'

'Excellent. I trust she continues to find her stay in Madrid satisfactory.'

'As far as anything can be in the circumstances in which we find ourselves.'

'With respect, sir, you would need to talk to Downing Street about that.' The ambassador turned fractionally in the direction of Bramall. 'And what about you, Mr Bramall? You come with the personal imprimatur of the PM. What should I make of that exactly?'

'That it is a measure, presumably, of the importance he attaches to my mission.' The preposterousness of his response hit him like the punch line of a joke. It was as if he was speaking a different language in which he'd suddenly become fluent. You had to laugh.

Hoare drew himself up to his full height, looking as if he was about to deliver a magisterial rebuke. Instead, he forced his patrician features to soften and resolve themselves into something like indulgence. 'And in relation to that,' he said, 'it is my solemn duty to remind you that the safety of His Royal Highness is your first and paramount responsibility. I must therefore ask you to check and double-check on everything in relation to his stay and to keep my staff informed of any concerns you might have that could conceivably be eased by my attention.'

Just for a moment, the Duke looked mildly alarmed. 'I say, Hoare, what are you implying? I'm not in any danger, am I?'

The ambassador threw up his hands. 'Not that I am aware of, sir. But it is our duty to be sure.'

'Ah. Right. Well, I'll leave you two to get on with it then. The Duchess and I plan to do a bit of shopping this morning – if we can find anything, that is – and I don't like to keep her waiting.'

'Your Royal Highness,' said Hoare and Bramall in almost perfect unison.

Once the Duke had gone, Hoare invited Bramall to join him on the terrace outside his window.

'What's your first impression?' he asked.

Bramall thought for a second. 'Bit early to say. The Spanish press was hanging around the hotel lobby this morning, looking for quotes. The Duke was a model of decorum. The only thing that went off was a flashbulb.'

'Man's a nightmare,' Hoare said suddenly, with what struck Bramall as admirable candour. 'But of course I didn't say that. I didn't say it either when he was soliciting my advice during the abdication crisis. There are those who argue that the sudden appearance in Madrid of His Royal Highness is a godsend and that it gives us a perfect excuse to entertain *le tout Madrid*. They may even be right. We shall see. But frankly, Bramall, between you and me, the sooner he's out of our hair the sooner we can each get down to business.'

'I'm inclined to agree with you, sir.' He wondered how much Hoare knew about his mission and how free he should feel in his company.

'You're probably wondering if I know what you're up to and

how much you can divulge to me of your activities.'

'Not at all.'

'So let me make it easy for you. We are both men who, shall we say, did not instinctively favour war with Germany.' Bramall started at this. Hoare had obviously done his homework. 'Like you,' the ambassador continued, 'I am here at the request of the prime minister, whom I have known for the best part of 20 years. My task is to persuade the Spanish Government that it is in their best interests to remain neutral in the war and, in particular, that they should avoid any tomfoolery over Gibraltar. But whereas I will perform my role for the most part in the light of day, employing negotiation and legitimate diplomatic stratagems, you, Mr Bramall, will perforce spend much of your time in the shadows, often among people with whom it would be impolitic, not to say impractical, for me to converse. We are to be like two pieces in an invisible jigsaw puzzle. No one will see how well we fit. Once the embassy function is out of the way, we shall not be seen together. The only reason we are talking now is that you arrived with His Royal Highness, in whose service you are ostensibly engaged. You should not trade heavily on your connection with me. If things go wrong, if you find yourself in hot water, I shall deny all knowledge of you. You will be, so far as I am concerned, a royal factotum of doubtful provenance. Do I make myself clear?'

Not for the first time in recent days, Bramall was overcome by the sensation of doors closing all about him. 'Don't worry,' he said. 'I know exactly where I stand.'

'Very good. A difficult task lies ahead of you. How you are supposed to uncover Franco's war plans and the likelihood, or not, of a German attack on Gibraltar is, frankly, beyond me, but no doubt you have your methods. Should you have urgent cause to contact the embassy, you will do so through the consular section. A Mr. Burns there will act as middleman. There is little else that I can say to you, save that, in spite of all, you carry with you my best wishes.'

'Thank you, sir. If nothing else, you have been more than straight with me.'

'Goodbye, Mr Bramall.'

Two minutes later, Bramall found himself back in the street, where the summer heat was already approaching thirty-five degrees Celsius. He'd forgotten how hot it could get in Madrid – worse even than Barcelona. A group of Falangists, still chanting their *Gibraltar Español* mantra, surged towards him, a couple waving their fists and shouting obscenities. A solitary member of the *Guardia Civil*, stationed at the embassy front door, shrugged his shoulders as if to say that it was nothing to do with him.

Back at the Ritz, he was handed a note at reception inviting him to cocktails that evening, beginning at 18.30, at the home on Calle Beatriz Galindo of Colonel Raúl Ortega, principal adviser to interior minister Serrano Suñer. Dress, lounge suit. That was quick, he thought. The embassy had obviously put the word around of a newly arrived member of the Duke's party. The question was, would he be watching them or would they be watching him?

Madrid, German Legation, June 26

The pictures of Bramall taken at the Ritz were wired to the

Prinz-Albrechtstrasse less than an hour after they were taken. Researchers in Berlin had no difficulty in producing a match. Hasselfeldt was surprised, to say the least, when two photographs were in turn transmitted back to his office in Madrid. One showed the former King's equerry in conversation with the *Führer* and the British Fascist leader Oswald Mosley. The other, taken from a newspaper, showed Bramall, again next to Mosley, at an anti-Jewish demonstration in London's East End. There had been violence, apparently, and he was shown standing on the front line between the two opposing groups. The cable that came with the photographs advised that the subject was the son of a retired British Army general and a long-standing member of the British Union of Fascists. Before entering royal service, it added, he had been a diplomat in Buenos Aires and Vienna. Later, he had spent time in the colonial service in Burma.

Hasselfeldt sat back in his chair and studied the images in front of him. In the two pictures taken with Hitler, the *Führer* seemed to be listening intently to what Bramall had to say. In the second of the two, there was even a hint of a smile on his face. Where had this conversation taken place anyway? He consulted the cable: home of Dr Josef Göbbels, Reichs Propaganda Minister, Berlin, October 6, 1936. Fascinating. The new arrival was more interesting than he had given him credit for. Time, perhaps, for him to pay a visit to the Legation. He could prove a useful source in the days ahead. Alternatively, of course, he could be an agent, planted by the British, perfectly positioned to play a dual role. He would have to see. The SD major silently congratulated himself on his initiative and reached onto the shelf behind his desk for an invitation card.

Madrid, Villa Ortega, June 26. Evening

It had been years since Bramall had attended a society reception. He had almost forgotten the form. The last time was in Madrid, immediately after its occupation by Franco's forces in March, 1939, when the mood of the conquerors had not been conducive to social exchange. Revenge was the order of the day. Franco took the view that combat missions were over but the struggle continued, and the country was left in no doubt that he would hunt down every last opponent of the regime, no matter how long it took. Bramall had witnessed several street executions. Once, in a commandeered football field, filled to capacity with 'the enemies of Spain,' he had looked on, dumbstruck, as uniformed officers, flanked by firing squads, read out lists of those to be put to death that morning. Sometimes they would read out just the first name, then pause, grinning, as all those of that name felt their stomachs turn to liquid. It was state-sponsored sadism, nothing less. Interviewing the officer in charge, he had been invited into the 'special' execution chamber – formerly the visiting teams' changing room – to witness the garrotting of a man who three years earlier had issued pamphlets urging his fellow citizens to defend the elected Government against the rising. Bramall left the room as soon as he realised what was happening, but the sight of the victim's bulging eyes and open mouth, as he fought desperately for breath, had caused him to throw up into an open drain already flowing with blood.

'Have you met our esteemed foreign minister, Señor Bramall?'

The question, jarring him back to present-day concerns, was put by his amply proportioned hostess, Doña Vittoria, seated next to him on an ornate metal chair in the shadow of a potted palm. 'I'm afraid not, Señora,' he told her. 'I still hope to have the honour.'

Doña Vittoria fluttered her fan and smiled. On the far side of the sunlit *terraza*, a German officer was talking to an attractive young woman of twenty or so, dressed up to the nines and clearly enjoying the opportunity to shine in adult company. In other circumstances, Bramall might have gone out of his way to impress her. She was really quite exceptional. But not today. Today he was on his best behaviour. Instead, to distract himself, he concentrated on the German, a *Gestapo* officer he thought, to judge by the uniform. For a moment, their eyes met. The sensation of a cold intelligence sent a shiver down his spine.

Meanwhile, the Señora was still talking. 'The minister,' she said, as though addressing a public meeting, 'is a great man. A man of destiny. The fact that he and my husband enjoy such a close association is, I must confess, a matter of some pride to me.'

Re-engaging his mind a second time, Bramall struggled to find a suitable response. 'Indeed, Señora,' he said, the words tumbling from his mouth. 'The minister has the ear of the *Caudillo* and the colonel has the ear of the minister.'

For a moment, he feared that his remark, which struck him as particularly asinine, might cause offence. A picture sprang into in his mind of the ears of a particularly feisty bull being presented to the matador at the end of a contest in the *Plaza de Toros*. But he need not have worried. The Señora was clearly in a benign mood and enjoying her terrace, with its distinguished assortment of guests, on what was undeniably a fine summer evening.

'My husband informs me,' she said, swatting at a fly, 'that you are an English Fascist.'

Bramall swallowed hard, though her comment, like his own, was intended to be approving. 'That is not precisely true, Señora,' he said at last. 'As a public servant, I am required to observe strict neutrality in matters of politics. But as to English Fascists, there are more than you might think.'

She fixed him with a triumphant look. 'But not yet quite enough, it seems. For your country opposes Hitler and is presently at war with Germany.'

'That is true. But with honour accruing to both sides, we must hope that an accommodation can yet be reached.'

He felt his face flush with embarrassment. Was there to be no respite from this new language?

'You are equerry to the Duke of Windsor, are you not?'

'Just so. And I assure you, the Duke would never countenance …'

The hostess giggled – the sound surprisingly girlish, Bramall thought, for one so … substantial. 'Oh dear, Señor Bramall,' she said from behind her fan. 'Now you sound like one of the *Caudillo's* speech-writers.' She laughed a second time and sat back in her chair, evidently well pleased with her performance.

Bramall never had been much of a one for small talk. He felt trapped. It was becoming difficult to breathe. As he considered his next step – which hopefully would be in the direction of one of the Army officers on the other side of the courtyard – he was aware of a sudden movement to his left.

A female voice, young, clear and confident. 'Good evening, Señor…?'

Bramall looked up. The sun was in his eyes, blinding him.

'This is Señor Bramall, dear,' said Señora Ortega. 'He is here with the Duke of Windsor.' By now the mistress of the household was enjoying herself thoroughly. She surveyed the stranger across the top of her spectacle frames. 'And, this, Señor, is my daughter, Isabel.'

Bramall stood up. It was the girl he'd noticed just seconds before. 'Señorita Ortega,' he said. 'A great pleasure.' She was certainly a more inviting prospect than her mother. In fact, she was stunning.

She fixed him with a cool, detached stare. 'I'm glad to hear it, Mr Bramall. One always likes to give pleasure. But please, tell me, what is it you do for His Royal Highness?'

It was not an easy question to answer. The girl's hair was a golden honey-blonde. Her skin glowed with vitality. It was all he could do not to reach out and touch her arm. He swallowed hard. 'The Duke ... ' he began.

'What about him?'

'The Duke ... he, er, has arrived unexpectedly in Madrid ... and it is my task, as his equerry, to ensure that no difficulties attend his progress.' He hoped this sounded less absurd to her than it sounded to him.

'I see. So you work at the embassy.'

'No, dear,' said her mother, admirably deadpan. 'Señor Bramall is a Fascist.'

'Oh.' Isabel's voice at once turned cold. 'One of them.'

'What do you mean, dear, one of *them*?'

'I assure you,' said Bramall, interposing himself hurriedly between mother and daughter, 'that, for all practical purposes, my politics are strictly neutral.'

'As Spain is 'neutral' in the present war?'

The daughter was implacable. 'Well ...'

'Such flexibility is admirable.'

Bramall attempted to register a smile and turned away, running his finger round the edge of his shirt collar. Away from the jacaranda tree, a faint tang of urine drifted upwards into the evening air. The stone balustrade of the courtyard, just a metre or so from where he stood, gave onto a steeply angled alleyway below. Even with the sun still beating down, the steps of the alley were undisturbed and bathed in shadow. Beyond was the Viaduct Segovia, or Bridge of Suicides, linking the Palace across a steep ravine to the domed church of San Francisco El Grande: the aristos above, the plebs below. He wished he was on the steps of the church right now, observing the gathering from afar, removed from its sharp-edged conventions. But then again ...

The Ortega girl, who, to judge from her well-bred sneer, viewed his discomfiture with contempt, allowed him only a brief respite before resuming her interrogation. 'What will you do, do you suppose, when the Germans invade your country? The fight, from what I'm told, will be bloody, but short-lived. Will you join the Resistance, do you think, or will you accept a position in the English equivalent of Vichy ... in Cheltenham, perhaps?'

Bramall seized, rather desperately, on the mention of his country's leading spa resort. 'You know Cheltenham?' he enquired.

'No. I don't know Baden-Baden either. But I've heard of it. It's called education, Mr Bramall. Did you have time for education in England, or were you too busy beating up Jews in the streets?'

'That's enough, Isabel.' Señora Ortega had risen to her feet, a look of cold disapproval on her patrician features. 'You must forgive my daughter, Senor Bramall,' she said. 'She learned this week that the father of one of her oldest friends – a man who chose to follow the wrong path during the recent conflict – was arrested this week and suffered the ultimate penalty for his treason. She is upset. We all are.'

'Please do not concern yourself, Señora,' Bramall said. 'Terrible things happen in war. In a civil war, with brother against brother, the results can be especially cruel. May I ask what happened to your daughter's friend?'

The Señora's face flushed with emotion. 'The mother died of a thrombosis brought on by the news that her husband had been ... executed. Her daughter – Isabel's friend – was sent to a labour camp on the *Caudillo's* express instructions. My husband tried to intervene, but there was nothing he could do.'

At this, Isabel spun on her heels and disappeared in the direction of the kitchen.

Bramall watched her go before turning back to his host. 'Please convey my sympathy to your daughter,' he began. 'It has clearly not been an easy time for her.'

Señora Ortega frowned. 'In Spain today, sympathy is considered a sign of weakness. We are all so sure of the rightness of our cause. I have to believe that better times lie ahead. But now, if you will excuse me ...'

'Of course.'

'Enjoy your stay. And please come again.'

Bramall realised he was sweating. He stood under the shade of a tree for the best part of a minute, sipping from a glass of champagne, then allowed himself to move towards the unmistakable sound of argument. Groups of important looking persons, mainly men, some in uniform, were obviously engaged in sorting out the issues of the day. One group in particular was speaking in French, which intrigued him. Two of them, to judge from their appearance, were Spanish, though entirely at ease in the language of international diplomacy. The others were French. He waited until one of the Frenchmen noticed him before extending his hand. 'Excuse me,' he said. 'But I don't believe we've met.'

The man was in his late fifties, short and stocky, with a pock-marked face, but he was immaculately tailored and stood with the command of someone six inches taller. Given that he enjoyed no obvious physical advantage, his appearance was, to Bramall, a triumph of self-possession.

'Charles Bramall, equerry to the Duke of Windsor.'

'Philippe le Maitre, chargé at the embassy of France.'

They shook hands crisply as the Frenchman, somewhat improbably, examined the much taller Bramall down the length of his nose – a manoeuvre that required him to bend his head back almost to an angle of ninety degrees. 'A piquant situation, is it not?' he said. 'The old certainties banished. Phone links cut. The ferries to Dover tied up in the harbour at Calais. Are we allies or enemies? I really don't know.'

'Allies, surely,' Bramall replied. 'I mean, the fortunes of war are one thing, but we continue on the same side of the argument, do we not?'

Le Maitre raised his eyebrows and smiled. He looked weary. 'I should need to have notice of that question. But permit me to introduce you to the Marqués de Bermejillo and Don Angel Alcázar de Velasco, both diplomats in the service of Spain. Also my countryman, Monsieur Henri Ardant, managing director of the Société Générale de Banque, visiting from Paris.'

'Gentlemen,' said Bramall.

The two Spaniards and the Frenchman nodded.

'So you are here to advise the Duke?' Bermejillo began. He was a florid man, with crinkly hair and a hint of mischief about his eyes. 'Did you know that he and I were acquainted?'

'But of course, sir. Indeed, I am informed that you and his Royal Highness have been friends for some time. No doubt we shall be seeing you at the embassy on Saturday.'

'Wild horses could not prevent me from attending. Is that not what you say in English?' Le Maitre laughed. Ardant simply looked blank.

'I met your former King once in Paris,' Ardant said, as if suddenly remembering something important. 'His views on the European situation were close to my own.'

Bramall made a passable attempt at insouciance. 'You have the advantage of me, Monsieur. I wouldn't presume to know what opinions you hold on the present ... situation.'

The banker leaned in, as though imparting a confidence. 'France has been humbled, Monsieur. England's resistance, though understandable, will end soon. I am sure of it. Then we will all have to learn to make the best of things ... together. That is why I am here, on a brief visit. I am exploring the creation in Europe of a single economic area, with a common currency. It could work wonders for our Continent, you know.'

Ardant had an austere, patrician look to him, like an aristocratic monsignor. Bramall would not wish to have been one of his servants. All he could think of, by way of reply was: 'An interesting outlook, Monsieur, but, with respect, as yet a little premature.'

'We shall see, Monsieur Bramall. We shall see. The New Order has arrived. The beach does not reject the arriving tide.'

'Nor,' said Bramall, 'does it accompany it upon its withdrawal.'

That wasn't bad, he thought.

Ardant's head drew back, like a tortoise's into its shell.

'Touché, Monsieur,' said Velasco, a small, dark figure, impeccably dressed. 'But you will need more than a gift for *repartée* when the *Wehrmacht* arrives on the beaches of Sussex.'

'That is why we have an army, Monsieur.' *Or what is left of one.*

As he spoke, Bramall realised with a start that he had met Velasco once before. It was in Salamanca, in 1937. The Spaniard had been one of those who defeated an attempt by rivals loyal to the memory of Primo de Rivera to keep the Falange out of Franco's control. The 'Old Shirts,' as they were known, had been beaten into submission. One at least had been shot. He was a dangerous man – a Galician like his boss – and best avoided. But the question was, would he remember him? Their encounter had been brief: a snatched interview for the Post, conducted after yet another outrage involving the Condor Legion. But those who lived in the secret world rarely forgot a face. That's what Strickland had told him. He made an instant decision.

'Don Angel, I don't know whether you recall our last meeting.'

'But of course,' the Galician said matter-of-factly. 'Salamanca, July, 1937. 'You asked me if it was our intention to bomb civilians in Republican villages *pour encourager les autres*.'

Bramall laughed to cover his embarrassment.

'I told you that it was.'

'Quite so.'

There was a brief silence. 'Yes. Well, I must be going,' Bermejillo said. 'Work to be done, people to bribe.' He laughed slyly, showing a full set of blackened teeth. 'I will see you at the embassy party, Señor Bramall. Please tell His Royal Highness that I am looking forward to it.'

The departure of the Marqués was a signal for the impromptu gathering to disperse. Bramall nodded once more to Le Maitre and stood back as the Frenchman ploughed purposefully towards an Italian Army Officer smoking a pipe. He craned his neck to search out a waiter but instead saw the burly figure of his host, Colonel Ortega, bounding towards him, his face suffused with importance. Immediately behind, radiating a cool, professional indifference, stood the second-most important man in Spain.

'Señor Bramall,' the colonel began sonorously, 'I should like to introduce you to our interior Minister, Don Ramón Serrano Suñer. I know you and he will have much to say to each other.'

'Minister,' said Bramall, hardly able to bear the unexpected weight of the moment. 'An honour.'

A thin, incredibly sleek hand emerged from an immaculately turned sleeve. 'I have heard of you, Mr Bramall,' the Spaniard said in slightly accented English. 'You are, I understand, a confidant of Sir Oswald Mosley and the son of Sir Frederick Bramall.'

Bramall took the hand, which was surprisingly firm. After barely half a second, it withdrew. 'That is correct, sir.'

'A tragedy about Sir Oswald. One that I trust will be corrected in time.' Serrano's voice was like honey poured across hot buttered toast. His face was that of an ascetic – thin and clear, with cheekbones like a Russian. Its only failing was that it looked slightly too small for his body. Almost imperceptibly, his head turned around, picking up a remark from the corner opposite. 'I trust,' he resumed, 'that all goes well with His Royal Highness?'

'Indeed, sir. He finds Madrid and its society most congenial.'

'Does he, though? We in Spain have been through a most debilitating time for our economy and culture, but I hope we have not lost our sense of hospitality.'

Bramall smiled, but said nothing.

Serrano looked at his watch. 'You have been circulating, I hope. *Mingling*, I believe, is the word. That is as it should be. But occasions such as this, though agreeable, are not necessarily conducive to statecraft. One can never be quite sure who is listening. That being so, I should be obliged if you were to visit me at my office. There are matters of mutual concern that we might usefully discuss.'

'Of course, Minister. You should know that I am at your service.'

'I don't doubt it for a second. Very well, then. Colonel Ortega will arrange it.'

There was to be no goodbye. The minister simply turned on his elegantly shod heels and disappeared in the direction of the Cardinal Archbishop of Toledo, the colonel trotting behind.

Perhaps the scent of urine had got to him.

'Well,' said Isabel Ortega, appearing suddenly from behind where Bramall was standing, 'that seemed to go well. But then Don Ramón always did respond to flattery.'

'So good to see you again, Señorita Ortega.'

The look she shot back at him was pure vitriol. He couldn't

work out what he had done to deserve it. 'Look,' he said, trying to keep his eyes off her cleavage, 'we don't seem to have got off to a good start, which is rather a pity, I think. I'd like to put that right – start afresh. So do you suppose I might interest you in lunch one of these days? Give us a chance to clear up whatever misunderstanding there might be.'

As a romantic ploy, Bramall thought it almost perfect, and he was taken aback when it fell flat. 'Is that really all you're interested in?' she demanded. 'Lunch with the first pretty girl you meet? And then what? An invitation to visit you at your hotel?'

'At least I know what I want.'

'And you think I don't, is that it? You think I am just some privileged plaything to wile away an idle hour.' She glared at him, flashing the emerald in her eyes. 'There are people in my country who are starving. Others are being hunted down like dogs, to be hanged or garrotted, or else worked to death in labour camps. Is that the sort of world you want?'

This was intolerable. Bramall groped for a suitable reply, but before he could open his mouth, she was gone.

4

Madrid: Ritz Hotel, June 27, 1940

Bramall was taking breakfast in his room – a luxury that would have seemed both comic and preposterous only six weeks before as he and his men prepared for the final assault on Narvik. He virtually spooned the butter onto his tostadas and lifted whole forkfuls of tortilla into his mouth. The egg and potato mix was soft and delicious and he washed it down with hot, dark coffee. Exquisite. In the midst of the horror that he knew was the reality of life for most Madrileños, this was how life ought to be.

When he had first arrived in Spain as a journalist, he had expected to find nobility in the midst of suffering. Instead, he had seen Communist mobs baying for the deaths of landowners and their families, as if the excesses of the French and Russian revolutions had been templates, not warnings from history. He saw anarchist groups calling on enemy forces to surrender before shooting them down like dogs, to general approval. In the midst of such carnage, the more decent sorts of Spaniards – democrats, liberals, libertarians – were left floundering. Their small kindnesses and everyday civility got lost in the fog of war, where only the grandest or most grotesque of gestures stood out.

A shaft of sunlight fell across his face, awakening in an instant the image of Isabel Ortega at the previous day's reception. She was infuriating – so full of herself, so arrogant, so unwilling to see how the world might look to him through non-Spanish eyes. And yet she was absolutely intoxicating.

He stood at his bedroom window and looked down towards the Plaza de la Lealtad. The surviving trees were in leaf; couples walked arm-in-arm in the park; vehicles sputtered by – all under the supervision of the city police and the *Guardia Civil*. He had read the recent reports of Francoist excess: mass arrests, executions, beatings. He had seen for himself what the historians liked to call the 'distressful conditions' of the peasantry on his way in from the airport. There would be much else in the days ahead that would turn his stomach, he had no doubt of that. But was it really worse than when the Left had been in power in 1936?

He turned back into the room and refilled his coffee cup. It was getting late. Time to get the day underway. He still had the invitation list for Saturday's reception. If someone turned up who shouldn't, he knew who would get the blame. After all, he had boasted to Buchanan-Smith that he had the final power of veto. Scooping the file off his bedside table, he began flicking through. At the list of O's, he paused. There she was, buried in among the diplomats, Falange officials, government placemen, generals, members of the nobility, minor poets and secret policemen: Col. Raúl Ortega, accompanied by Doña Vittoria and their daughter, Señorita Isabel.

So she was coming to the party after all. Perhaps the colonel had put his foot down – either that or, against all the evidence, she couldn't resist the chance to meet him again. He almost laughed. The idea was so absurd. But then, without warning, his mood darkened. There hadn't been a woman in his life, in any sense, since Manuela Valdés, and two years on the thought of her still weighed heavily upon his mind. He was not a religious man – never had been – but there were times he envied the Catholics, who with a simple act of penance could put the past behind them and move on.

It happened so suddenly, there had been no time to think. He had felt literally rooted to the spot. Ahead of the main body of Republican troops, a hundred metres or so out from the Ebro, one of the assault boats took the first salvo from the Messerschmitt. A dozen men died in an instant, their helmeted heads falling in sequence. The roar of the raider's engine and the cacophonous thunder of its guns drowned out the screams of the dying. What happened next was a blank. He could remember nothing. All he knew was that when the 109 broke off its attack and banked left towards its own lines he was no longer exposed in the open but crouched behind a line of trees. He was alive and uninjured But there was no sign of Manuela. Jumping up, aware abruptly of the sounds of suffering all around him, he had called out her name. *'Manuela! Manuela!'* Where was she? Was she injured? It was inconceivable to him that someone so young, so passionate, so full of life, could have died. And then he saw her and for a moment his whole world stopped. She was lying, face down, in a clearing just beyond the trees. Her entire upper body was covered in blood. One arm stretched out ahead of her, the forefinger of the hand unnaturally extended; the other hand, by her side, still held on to her rifle. Bodies were strewn in a line from the river's edge far up into the tree line. But it was hers that stood out. A young survivor of the attack, no more than eighteen, was staring at her, tears streaming down his face. She was pointing, he said, to the far bank of the river, indicating the direction in which they still needed to go. An Army captain, wounded in the neck, the collar of his tunic turned to scarlet, had looked at him with contempt. She had shown the true fighting spirit, he said. She was their *Pasionaria* and they would not forget her.

Staring down at the Plaza de la Lealtad, Bramall wiped the sweat from his forehead. He looked at his hands. They were trembling. To steady his nerves, he fetched a glass of water, took several sips and forced himself to concentrate on the business in hand. Serrano Suñer had asked him to arrange a meeting via Colonel Ortega. He should attend to that straight away. After that, he would brief the Duke on the final guest list for his party and remind him of the need for diplomatic propriety. Looking ahead, there was the small matter of Gibraltar and how to thwart its planned capture by the *Wehrmacht*. More than enough work, in short, to keep his mind focused and hold the past at bay – a place where there was only misery.

He picked up the telephone receiver and rang through to the switchboard. 'I wish to speak with Colonel Raúl Ortega at the interior ministry in the Puerta del Sol. He is expecting me.'

'Si, Señor Bramall. I will call you back directly.'

Fifteen minutes later, having fixed an appointment to see Serrano, Bramall was making his way through the hotel lobby towards the Duke's private lift when one of the clerks at reception called out to him. A letter had just arrived, hand-delivered and personally addressed. He tore open the envelope and gasped in astonishment. It was from Klaus Hasselfeldt at the German Legation – the fellow from the bar the previous evening. He peered at the ornate gothic script, intrigued and repelled at the same time. Would Bramall do Hasselfeldt the distinct honour of attending lunch with him at the German embassy the following day, June 28, at one o'clock? 'Just turn up', it added in English. 'No *r.s.v.p.* required.'

He stared at the elegant cream-coloured notepaper, with its embossed Swastika. He was being invited into the heart of enemy intelligence where the rules that applied were those written in Berlin by men with Death's Head badges on their collars. The German – or Austrian, or whatever he was – was clearly no slouch. The question was, what did he know about him? Had he been tipped off to expect a potential traitor or a possible double agent? It was impossible to say. He shut his eyes and tried to concentrate his thoughts. Just minutes before, he had thought dealing with the Duke or Serrano was challenge enough for one day. Now he realised how naïve he was. This was when the game truly began. It was as if his head had been pushed beneath an ice-cold shower and when he came up he was cleared-headed and shaking.

Vichy: capital of the French Unoccupied Zone, June 27

Pierre Laval, deputy prime minister of what now passed for the French Government, did not cut a heroic figure, even to himself. A day short of his fifty-eighth birthday, squat and hunched, with lank hair, a drooping moustache and teeth that were black and worn, he had survived in politics through will power and perseverance. Other *capitulards* drew strength from his example.

Vichy, the town from which he operated, had been declared capital of the unoccupied zone partly because of its insignificance – it had no resonance in French history beyond its links with the leisure pursuits of Louis Napoléon – and partly because of its improbably efficient telephone service. Laval felt no attachment to the place. He was a committed *boulevardier*. But at least it was a base from which to rebuild his shattered career.

He bore, he felt, a heavy burden. His boss, the eighty-four-year-old *Maréchal* Pétain, though perfectly happy to work with the Nazis, and even to follow their example in such matters as the isolation of the Jews, had largely lost interest in the present. His preoccupation was with redemption. He did not favour war with England, which Laval had hoped to present to Hitler as a gift. So far as Pétain was concerned, the British could engineer their own downfall. For him, the exercise of civil authority in the Zone and of military as well as civil power in the Empire was both the limit of his ambition and the focus of his honour. France, he believed, had to expiate its sins, and central to the process was sufferance of German domination.

Not all were so sanguine. Major Alain Delacroix, a combatant of sorts from the recent war with Germany, was now a senior aide to Laval and one of those most keen on war with England. Laval found him exasperating, but also loyal. During the Battle of France, he had been a junior staff officer under the newly-recalled Commander-in-Chief, General Maxime Weygand. The general had recommended the young captain, whose experience of actual warfare was even more deficient than his own, as 'somewhat dense, but dependable – the sort of fellow you can rely on to do your worst' – which was exactly what Laval required in the new circumstances in which he found himself.

During the Great War, the reluctance of Field Marshal Haig to accept the authority of France's High Command had instilled in Weygand a disregard, amounting almost to contempt, for the English, which he had clearly passed on to Delacroix. But there had also been talk of a bungled protestation of love made to an English nurse during the fighting in Saint Valery that had ended, he was told, with the girl slapping his face in a ward full of wounded men who had roared their approval of his humiliation. Who knew? War brought nations togther, but it also drove them apart.

'The English hope to add us to their dominions,' was Delacroix's latest interpretation of events, vouchsafed as Laval returned to his office after a frustrating meeting with Pétain. 'Surely the *Maréchal* must see that. If we rouse the empire and launch a strike against them, we can repay them in kind. We will be able to raise our heads again and show the world that France is still master in its own house. The English will run from us in shame.'

'My dear Alain,' said Laval, running his fingers through his hair, showering the shoulders of his suit with dandruff, 'I do not disagree with you. Though it would be a painful decision, war with England would certainly restore balance to our affairs. The problem is, the Old Man is not focused on revenge. He seeks survival. To the *Maréchal*, our continued governance of the empire and the existence of the French fleet are our only realistic guarantors of honour.'

'In that case, are we not just a puppet state?'

'A non-belligerent power is, I think, the correct term.'

'Like Spain, you mean?'

'Exactly.' Laval inserted the nail of his little finger into the gap between two of his bottom teeth and drew out the husk of a sunflower seed. 'And while we are on the subject, tell me, what is your view of Franco's position?'

Delacroix thought for a moment. 'He would take everything if he could. He will see the war as an opportunity to scavenge.'

The minister nodded. 'But facts are what count in matters such as this. Speculation is for diplomatic receptions and the mess hall. It cuts no ice with Hitler. That is why I want you to discover for me what exactly is going on in Madrid. I need to be appraised each week of any plans that are being hatched there.'

Once again, Delacroix looked alarmed. 'You want me to go to Madrid? As a *spy*?'

Laval smiled to himself, as if he found the very idea of Delacroix as a spy risible. 'No, no, my dear fellow. I want you to find someone who knows what they're about and see to it that he reports to you each day on what is being said, not only in the Pardo, but in the Falange. He must be your eyes and ears, as you are mine.'

Relief passed across Delacroix's pale amber eyes. But then a thought occurred to him. 'What if the British attack us first? What if De Gaulle should seek to prize the empire from our grasp? What then? You heard his broadcast from London. He said that the French Empire stood behind France and that the British Empire stood behind both. It is obvious he believes himself to have all rightful authority.'

'To the *Maréchal*,' said Laval, 'our colonies are the very touchstone of honour. That is why I have asked you to perform this service for me. Should De Gaulle and the British attack, we will defend. Should Franco try to arrange some back door deal, we will defend. Berlin must know that we are not a subject people, but true allies of the Reich.'

Delacroix considered the world of villainy that surrounded his country. 'I have no doubt we will be tested,' he said. 'But when the time comes, we will not fail.'

Madrid: Ritz Hotel, Royal Suite, June 27

Bramall was fuming. He had hurried back from the interior ministry, where he had requested an interview with Serrano, to present himself outside the Duke's door at exactly eleven o'clock, as instructed. But it was a good fifteen minutes before he was admitted.

'I'm awfully sorry,' said Buchanan-Smith, clearly enjoying every moment of his brief exercise of power, 'but His Royal Highness and the Duchess were out until late with friends and aren't ready to receive visitors. I'm afraid you're going to have to wait.'

When the door finally opened and he was allowed in, his patience had snapped and he shoved an indignant Buchanan-Smith out of his path.

'It really is a bit much, sir,' he began.

The Duke wheeled round from the salon mirror in which he had been putting the finishing touches to his famed Windsor knot. 'What? What is? What are you talking about?'

Bramall pulled himself up short, aware that he had only just entered the room and already he had blown it. His public role, he had only begun to appreciate, had to be convincing not only to the Germans and Spanish, but to the Duke as well. He took a deep breath. 'I'm sorry, sir, I don't mean to be rude. It's just that I've been sitting in the corridor outside for the last quarter of an hour.'

'Really? Sounds like a waste of time to me. Why didn't you wait in here? Plenty of room.'

'Your equerry felt that ...'

' – Oh, don't listen to him. Fellow's an arse – aren't you, Smith?'

Buchanan-Smith looked as if he might explode with frustration and rage, but said nothing. Bramall fixed him with a glare.

The Duke turned his attention back to his tie, looking pleased as the characteristic dimple appeared in the centre of the knot. 'So what have we got today?' he asked brightly.

'Well, sir ...'

At this point, the Duchess entered the salon from the main bedroom, giving the new arrival a knowing look. Over her arm was a bathing suit. 'Ah!' she began. 'Our new equerry from London, if I'm not mistaken. Bramall, isn't it?'

'Spot on, my dear,' said the Duke. 'Sent out to make sure we don't make fools of ourselves in Spain.'

'I see. And are we keeping you busy, Mr Bramall?'

Her voice was American, which for some reason surprised him. 'Not overly so, ma'am. Not yet, at any rate.'

'Well, that's a blessing anyhow.' She assessed him with a practised eye. 'So tell me, where do you buy your suits?'

'My suits? Well ... I don't exactly recall. It's been a while. Some place in Saville Row. My father opened the account years ago.'

'I thought so. Have you ever shopped for suits in New York?'

'No ma'am.'

'You should. They do excellent tailoring for the younger man. Now try not to bore His Royal Highness with too much stuff about keeping Spain neutral in the war. I think we've already grasped that particular nettle.'

'With respect, ma'am,' he replied, 'I'm not sure that is entirely accurate.'

'Meaning what exactly?'

He paused. 'Only that there has been talk in London.'

The Duchess shot him an acerbic glance. He was reminded of an expression used by their cook in Dreenagh, a lovely, fat woman from Cavan – *her look would have taken the skin off a rice pudding*. 'Talk!' she said, huskily. 'What sort of talk? I trust you are not referring to the King and Queen?'

That would teach him to jump in without looking. The last thing he wanted was to be drawn into the increasingly bitter family quarrel.

'Not at all. Far from it. Their majesties, to the best of my knowledge, are the very souls of discretion.'

'You could have fooled me.'

Bramall shook his head. 'I doubt that very much.'

At this, the Duchess smiled. 'Very well, then,' she said, in her peculiar, mocking drawl. 'Spit it out. Let's hear it.'

Bramall ran his hand down his mouth. 'How shall I put this? Downing Street, the Foreign Office and the intelligence services are anxious that neither you nor the Duke should at any time give … comfort to the enemy.'

This statement was greeted by the Duchess with a stony-faced glare. 'Go on.'

He drew a breath, then continued. 'It's just that they are aware of the fact that His Royal Highness and yourself may once have harboured – what shall we say? – sympathies for the National Socialist position. You visited Hitler in Bavaria; you had dinner with Himmler. You met with Ribbentrop on a number of occasions when he was ambassador in London. It goes without saying that there is no suggestion – none whatsoever – that this in any way gives rise to any disloyalty ... '

' – I am relieved to hear it.'

'I myself, as you know, have spent time in the company of Sir Oswald Mosley – even attended his wedding in Berlin, where I was photographed with the *Führer*. So it's not that I ...'

He let the unspoken thought hang in the air. He was not proud of his past, of which he now had to boast. 'Anyway, the fear is that you might, however inadvertently, convey to enemy propagandists monitoring your every move the impression that you favour a negotiated peace rather than any continued prosecution of the war.'

The Duchess raised her eyebrows almost to her hairline as if someone had just insinuated that she liked drinking claret with oysters. 'I see,' she said.

'I'm so glad that you do,' stammered Bramall, 'for it means that I don't have to go on like this, embarrassing us both.'

'That's the most sensible thing you've said in the last two minutes.'

'Thank you, ma'am.'

The one-time Mrs Simpson, looking simultaneously radiant and pinched, turned to a fresh vase of roses that had been placed in the royal suite that morning and broke off a single stem, which she then placed in Bramall's buttonhole. 'That's better,' she said, straightening his lapel. 'Please be assured that the Duke and I will bear your concerns very much in mind when we are making chit-chat with our friends.'

Bramall bowed slightly. 'I am obliged to you.'

She gazed at him down the sharply defined ridge of her nose. 'More than you know, Mr Bramall.'

Vichy, Occupied France: Office of Alain Delacroix, June 27

Thirty-two year-old Dominique de Fourneau, said to bear an uncanny resemblance to the Napoleonic beauty Madame de Récamier, might plausibly have presented herself as a heroic figure, or at least the wife of a hero. On April 28, twelve days before the German attack on France, a German assassin had murdered her husband, the Comte de Fourneau, a leading member of French Intelligence. The reason the Comtesse made no claim to heroic status – apart from the fact that such posturing would have struck her as absurd – was that she knew none of this. Her husband, Alexei, had been to the best of her knowledge, a gem specialist, employed by Dresdnerbank, murdered by a Polish Jew in revenge for the fact that his family's diamond business had been taken over by the Nazis.

Delacroix had known Dominique de Fourneau most of his life, ever since their parents had taken summer homes next door to each other in Biarritz. They were never truly friends. She much preferred his brother, now a naval officer based in Dakar, with whom she had once made love in a sentry box. But there was a tense cordiality between them nonetheless, and when Laval had instructed Delacroix to place an agent in

Madrid, Dominique was the name that sprang immediately to mind. She knew Spain and spoke fluent Spanish. She had a flat in a fashionable district of Madrid, left to her by her father's older brother, a former financial adviser to King Alfonso XIII. Not only that, she had at one point been engaged to a prominent Castilian landowner and was on excellent terms with a number of Spanish noblemen and generals. Finally, and most important, she possessed one of the sharpest brains he knew and would, he was sure, relish the opportunity to spy for her country.

'What exactly do you want of me, Alain?' she asked him, refusing to sit down, moving instead across his linoleum-floored office to the metal window at the opposite side, with its view of the gardens. She was wearing a long Chanel skirt that billowed out slightly below the knees. Her blonde hair was up and perched coquettishly on her head was a black pillbox hat with just a hint of a widow's veil. She lit a Black Sobranie cigarette (almost her last one, though she would never tell him that) and twisted round to observe him as he struggled to reply.

'I w-want you to do a service for your country,' Delacroix said after a nervous pause. There was just a hint of a stammer in his voice that he knew she would at once detect. She had always overawed him, causing him to feel inadequate and gauche. Today was no exception.

'And which country would that be, exactly?'

'Dominique, p-please don't be difficult.'

'I'm not sure I approve of the new dispensation,' she continued. 'Vichy is like a sub-branch of the Reich. The Marshal is manager, Laval is his deputy. But where does that leave you?'

'Chief cashier,' said Delacroix, suddenly inspired.

Her eyes opened wide. 'Ah! Interesting. Go on, then, I'm listening.'

It was the card Delacroix had been waiting to play – the only one certain to trump Dominique's overarching contempt for small-town values. The De Fourneau family had once been among the greatest landowners in France. Their estates, on both banks of the Loire, east of Angers, were known for their dairy cattle and their wine. But bad investments at the end of the 1920s resulted in a dramatic fall from grace, so that Dominique's husband was obliged to take a series of jobs in commerce, latterly with Dresdnerbank, commuting each month between Lyon and Zurich. His murder in Bern was a double blow. She had been fond of Émile, even if he was twenty years her senior, and in recent years had made a special effort to be faithful, at least when he was home from Switzerland. But more to the point, his death had robbed her of a handsome income, leaving her with a villa in Lyon and an apartment in the Rue du Bac in Paris, together with her flat in Madrid – and virtually no money to pay for any of them. Dominique would never show it, but she was desperate and ready to jump at almost any offer that came her way.

Delacroix, who in fact already knew the extent of the crisis she faced, sat back in his chair and twisted a pencil round and round between finger and thumb. It felt good at last to be on the dominant side of the argument with his formidable childhood friend. He was not, he assured her, asking her to do anything disagreeable or dangerous. What he wanted was accurate, well-sourced information on Spain's war plans and, in particular, Franco's attitude towards Vichy and its African empire. Surely that would not be too much for her. In return, an amount in Swiss francs would be lodged each quarter in her account in Bern. Expenses in Spain would also be met, including the cost of a cook and personal maid. All she had to do in return was talk to the right people at the right time, reporting each week to him on the latest position as she saw it.

'Tell me, how exactly am I supposed to know what's happening in the innermost circles of th Pardo?' she inquired. 'I am neither a politician nor a mind reader.'

'No,' said Delacroix, 'but you are well-connected and, if it is not impertinent of me to say so, still beautiful and certain to turn heads in Madrid.' He looked at her through hooded eyes. 'I'm sure you will think of something.'

'Just so long, Alain, as you are not expecting payment in kind.'

'I d-don't know what you mean, Dominique.'

'No,' she said, drawing a strand of hair back from her eyes. 'Wasn't that always the problem?'

Delacroix was stung by her reply, but decided not to show it. 'So you will do it?'

'How will I get there?'

'It will be arranged.'

'I will need money straight away.'

'That, too, can be provided.'

She hesitated for a second, then said: 'Very well. Would next week be soon enough?'

'Perfect. I will arrange at once for funds to meet your immediate needs. I presume you would prefer cash …'

'In Swiss francs and pesetas. Future payments should be deposited in Madrid and Bern.'

'Very good. I cannot tell you how pleased I am that you have decided to answer your country's call.'

Dominique rose from her chair and proffered her cheek to Delacroix. 'My dear Alain, how could I possibly refuse?'

Madrid: Restaurant Casa Gallega, June 27

The dining room was full almost to capacity when the cars bringing the royal party and the Spanish Foreign Minister drew up outside. Two beefy-looking men with bulges under their jackets stood by the door. A squad of *Guardia Civil*, with machine pistols, had taken up station on the opposite side of the street. A large table, set into an alcove, had been prepared, surrounded by uniformed waiters. Diners stood up and broke into spontaneous applause as the Duke and Duchess entered, to be greeted by a fawning Maitre d'. The Duke, moved by the warmth of his reception, raised his right hand close to the side of his face in an almost pontifical gesture. The Duchess offered her standard regal smile. Beigbeder, accompanied by his French wife, was simply delighted.

Once the fuss had died down and the seating organised, Bramall – who had been invited to the lunch at the last minute at the request of the Duchess – found himself sat next to Miguel Primo de Rivera, whom he had met in the Duke's suite on the night of his arrival in Madrid. They exchanged polite nods, but it was clear to Bramall that he could expect no conversation from the capital's civil governor, a snob as well as a roué. All eyes were on the Duchess, who was at her sparkling best.

The Duke, too, was in fine form. 'I hope you're all looking forward to my party,' he announced, smiling broadly. 'The ambassador is really pushing the boat out and I should imagine there will be quite a lot for the diary items in the newspapers.'

Beigbeder beamed, amused by the idea of a diary column in *Arriba*. 'Your Royal Highness, he said, 'tomorrow's reception is a fitting symbol of the rebirth of Madrid society after the years of war, and also of the importance attached by Spain to the good company of our British friends.'

Primo de Rivera, rarely seen without a glass in his hand or a girl on his arm, decided to cut straight to the heart of the matter. 'But what about you, my dear Duchess? Are you finding our society terribly limited or do you think there is still a capacity for fun?'

The Duchess leaned across and tapped the younger man's hand. 'There is always fun when you are around, Miguel.'

Beigbeder's moustache twitched. He smiled nervously and exchanged glances with his wife. Fortunately, at this point, chilled champagne was offered around the table. The Foreign Minister stood and announced, apparently to the entire restaurant: 'On behalf of the Government of Spain, it is my honour to welcome to our country His Royal Highness the Duke of Windsor and the Duchess of Windsor. May their time among us be long and may each day bring the promise of a safer world. The Duke and Duchess!'

At this, the entire clientele of the restaurant rose once more to their feet to join in the toast. Bramall felt he had become part of a bizarre historical tableau in which there was no substance, only light shining at different moments on different characters. The meal passed for him in a blur as those present referred constantly to previous parties and gatherings, in Switzerland, on the Riviera, in Monte Carlo, in Rome, wondering aloud when the next Paris fashion week would be held and what on Earth had happened to old so and so, whom no one had seen for years. At least, he thought, the food was good: Gazpacho, fresh fish from Galicia, Jamón Serrano (*well, you had to smile*), even, at one point, roast suckling pig – all matched by some of the best Rioja wine he had ever tasted. If there were shortages in Madrid, clearly they did not apply to the ruling class.

It was only as the coffee was brought that conversation turned at last to the serious issues of the day. Beigbeder leaned towards the Duke. 'We have been talking of former times, when life and its possibilities seemed to stretch out forever. But Your Royal Highness will be more aware than most of how the world has changed and of how much pain there has been in recent years. Do you think it possible that Europe can learn once more to be at peace with itself, or must it simply be conquest, victory and defeat, and to the victor the spoils?'

The Duke appeared to give the question some thought. 'You raise an interesting point, Foreign Minister. Spain has endured more in recent years than any country should reasonably have to expect, even in time of war. I myself have, of course, been through an extended conflict of my own. Now it is the turn of my country. Mutual antagonism, a refusal to see the worth of the other side – the ruthless pursuit of victory at all costs. Europe is bleeding, my friends. Even here, at this table, each of us is bleeding. We have known so much hurt. I don't know how it can all be resolved. But I tell you this much: someone must make an end.'

Bramall's mouth had fallen open half way through the Duke's brief peroration. It was not so much the stab at eloquence; it was the sheer thoughtfulness and sensitivity of his words.

Perhaps he had got the man wrong after all.

Beigbeder's eyes, flickering behind his large, tortoiseshell spectacles, darted from face to face around the table. 'Mr Bramall,' he said suddenly. 'We have not heard from you. I understand you were involved in the fighting in Norway.'

How on Earth did Beigbeder know that? He hadn't told anyone. 'Yes, sir,' he said. 'At Narvik.'

'Wasn't that where the allies won and then withdrew the next day?'

'I'm afraid so.'

'A somewhat disagreeable sensation, I should imagine.'

'Well, yes. We lost a lot of men, but got the job done. The Navy and air force were superb. Problem was that with the rest of Norway gone and France about to fall, there didn't seem much point in hanging on.'

The Duchess accepted a light for her cigarette from a hovering waiter. 'At least it showed that Germany can be beaten. Their armed forces may be formidable, but they are not invincible.'

'Absolutely,' said Bramall, grateful that his earlier strictures had actually had some effect. 'His Royal Highness is, of course, correct to deplore the fact that we are at war. Germany and England have so much in common. Yet, once the fighting starts, every man must know his duty.'

Beigbeder looked from one side of the table to the other. Stohrer would be interested to hear about this. 'And what do you think will happen now? They say the invasion force to be sent against England will be more powerful than anything since the Armada.'

Bramall turned towards the minister, around whom a fug of smoke had gathered. 'An instructive comparison, sir, if I may say so. Only this time it is not only the Navy that is waiting, but the Royal Air Force as well.'

'A bloody business just the same,' said the Duke, leaning forward into the table. 'Thousands would be killed on both sides. Hundreds of thousands. And the destruction! Remember what happened to Rotterdam. London could be next.'

Bramall groaned. The Duchess looked as if she was about to add something, but took a sip of coffee instead. It was Madrid's gadfly governor who characteristically blurted out what most of those around the table were obviously thinking.

'Look,' he said, 'I know I'm not the politician my father was or my late brother was, but I know which way the wind is blowing and I can tell that peace now between England and Germany would be preferable to peace later, when Fascism has triumphed everywhere, from the Atlantic to the Urals.'

'My dear Miguel,' Beigbeder interrupted, 'I am not sure that …'

' – No,' said the Duke. 'Don't mind me. Let him speak.'

Bramall's sense of anticipation was almost painful.

'Well,' said Primo de Rivera, indicating to the waiter that another glass of wine would be in order, 'it's just that we all know the Duke and the Duchess have spent time in the company of the *Führer* at the *Berghof* and that they are not exactly overwhelmed by the way things have turned out.'

'That's certainly true,' said the Duke. 'The whole bally business is a tragedy. To see the *Luftwaffe* and the RAF squaring up to each other – to know that one day soon the Royal Navy might have to defend our shores against a German invasion – well, it sickens me right to my stomach. And I must tell you now that if there were some means available to methat would resolve the situation short of continuing conflict, I would welcome it with open arms.'

A silence descended around the table. Beigbeder looked thoughtful. Primo de Rivera just looked pleased with himself. Bramall coughed and caught the Duchess's eye. She understood his meaning at once and turned, beaming, to their host. 'Minister,' she said, 'it has been a most enjoyable and stimulating lunch – as always when you are involved.' Beigbeder beamed. 'But now, if you will excuse us, the Duke and I have urgent business we simply must attend to.'

'But, of course, my dear Duchess.'

As the Duke and his consort rose to their feet, everyone in the restaurant, as if responding to a hidden signal, followed suit. The Foreign Minister escorted his guests back out to the street where their car was waiting. He bowed to the Duke and kissed the Duchess's hand, whispering something to her that got lost in the general hubbub. Moments later, as the car pulled away from the restaurant, Bramall could contain himself no longer.

'My God, sir. What were you thinking of?'

'What do you mean?'

'To tell the Spanish foreign Minister that you would be ready to sponsor some sort of negotiated peace with Germany.'

'What are you talking about, man? I never said that.'

Bramall's exasperation surfaced, freed of all constraints of protocol.

'But you did, sir. Near as dammit. What else could he have taken from your words? What other possible meaning could there have been?' He paused, picking his words carefully, anxious that what he said next should not be inconsistent with his supposed BUF allegiance. 'With respect, you really must be more careful. It is one thing to wish for rapprochement with Germany, even at this very late stage. You would not be alone in harbouring such sentiments. But even those of us who wish that things were different cannot go around expressing anti-war feelings willy-nilly. People here hang on your every word.'

'Rubbish. It was only conversation, nothing more. We were among friends. You must realize, Bramall, that I would never engage in anything that worked againsst the interests of my country. I learned that much as King, if nothing else.'

Nothing else at all, apparently, Bramall thought. This was self-delusion on a truly regal scale. He tried to catch the Duchess's eye so that she might say something that would convey to her husband the seriousness of the situation he had created. But she turned away. So he sat back instead and looked out the car window. A military truck halted halfway across an intersection to give way to the royal procession. In the back were a score or so of young men, their hands tied, guarded by half a dozen soldiers. Bramall dreaded to think what was going to happen to them.

It was back at the hotel later that afternoon, as he emerged from the shower, that he noticed a pale white envelope lying on the floor. It had obviously been pushed under the door while he was in the bathroom. He picked it up, sniffed it and reached for the letter opener on his desk. Inside was a single sheet of notepaper. The handwriting, in English, was immaculate copperplate.

Charlie,

Who'd have guessed it? I thought I'd seen the last of you for sure. But it looks like I was wrong. Anyway, now that you're here, it'd be a crime if we didn't meet up. What do you think?

If you're interested, (and I can't see how you wouldn't be), be in the Plaza Dos de Mayo tomorrow night after ten. Only do me a favour, don't look for me – I'll find you.

E

He stared at the note and read it again all the way through. Who the hell was 'E'? He had no idea. And then it hit him, like a sockful of coins. Eddy bloody Romero. Fucking Hell! He hadn't seen his fellow Irishman for at least eighteen months. Not since Barcelona. Mad as a snake and twice as deadly, possibly the most violent man he had ever known. He had first run into him during the Ebro campaign, just before the fighting started. An Irish *brigadista*, with a Spanish father, he was a mad bastard who'd stop at nothing in pursuit of his warped vision of justice for all.

How in God's name would Romero know he was in Madrid? He put the note in his pocket and made his way downstairs to the cocktail lounge. There was nothing he could do tonight that would change anything. He surveyed the bar counter. At least bloody Hasselfeldt wasn't there. There was only a young man and woman, in their late twenties by the look of them, sat at a table in the corner, lost in each other's eyes, and a couple of men in suits, one of them a German, arguing about the price of good scotch. He took a stool at the counter and signalled to the barman, a stocky fellow with unusually thick hair, who walked over to him with a dish of pistachio nuts. 'Whiskey!' he said out, dipping his fingers into the pistachios. 'Irish. And make it a double.'

Four hours later, when he got back to his room, he was

barely able to speak. He fell asleep, fully clothed, listening to the Tommy Dorsey Orchestra singing *Marie* on his wind-up gramophone.

Madrid: Ritz Hotel, next morning

Bramall's head was pounding. He sent his breakfast trolley away, all except the coffee, and spent the next half an hour in the bath. He hadn't intended getting drunk; sometimes it just happened that way. Still draped in a towel, he called the Interior Ministry to confirm his appointment with Serrano Suñer. The minister couldn't see him for several days yet, apparently, but Ortega would look out for him at the embassy reception and provide him with the necessary details.

After that he spoke briefly with Buchanan-Smith, and asked about the Duke and Duchess's evening. It turned out that nothing untoward had occurred, which was a relief.

'Went pretty smoothly, from what I hear,' the equerry drawled. 'Pair of 'em didn't get back until two in the morning, all smiles.'

'And today?'

'Lunch with yet another old friend. Portuguese chap, name of Ricardo do Espirito Santo Silva. Doesn't that mean Holy Ghost or something? 'Fraid you're not invited. Strictly tête-a-tête.'

Croft had mentioned Santo Silva. He sounded like a complete creep: a monumental social climber and Nazi sympathiser. Still feeling the worse for wear, he made his way to the Duke's suite to make inquiries, only to be told by a detective on the door that His Royal Highness was under no circumstances to be disturbed before midday. Stymied, he went back to his room where, after placing a Do Not Disturb sign on the door knob, he fell asleep again for the best part of an hour.

His alarm went off at midday and he awoke, still groggy, to prepare himself for the meeting with Hasselfeldt. If dealing with the Duke was problematic, into what category should he place having lunch with a senior officer of the SS? He had only been in Madrid a couple of days. It was all happening too soon. He wasn't ready. He wasn't sure he'd *ever* be ready. One hour later, having satisfied himself that he had not been followed, he walked up the steps of the newly re-opened German Legation on the Avenida del Generalísimo, entering the building beneath a massive bronze Swastika. The scale was gigantic. There was room for a hundred people, maybe more, in the lobby. Two guards clicked to attention, their boots echoing on the polished marble. 'Heil Hitler!' he replied, raising his right arm from the elbow in the half-hearted fashion he associated with party functionaries from newsreels.

Hasselfeldt was waiting for him. Dressed in the field-grey uniform of the SD, with its twin lightning-bolt 'runes' on one lapel and the four pips of a *sturmbannführer* on the other, he was clearly out to impress, and no doubt, as well, to intimidate.

'*Guten Tag, Herr Bramall. Wie geht's?*'

'*Sehr gut. Und Sie?*'

'I also. You were not followed, I hope?'

'Not that I noticed.'

At his throat, Hasselfeldt wore the Iron Cross, awarded, Bramall assumed, during the fighting in Poland, which had proved harder than Nazi propaganda ever admitted. So whatever else he was, he was not a coward. Now he hid a sly smile behind his hand. 'Please,' he said. 'Come upstairs to my office. There is much to discuss.'

'Lead the way.'

As they made their way upstairs, Bramall reminded himself for the umpteenth time to be careful. He mustn't sound too keen or submit too readily. Croft had stressed to him that when he was approached, he should be careful not simply to fall in with whatever proposal was put to him. They'll see through that straight away. It was one thing, he had said, to be an appeaser, even a former acolyte of Mosley. There were plenty enough of those. But he should not offer himself up on a plate as a spy. Espionage was a game with its own rules, played by professionals. It was important that Bramall should appear to be the troubled amateur, desperate to do the right thing. He had to maintain some distance, show a certain defiance . That way, his compliance, when it came, would be all the more convincing. Or so he thought.

The SD chief's office was on the first floor of the embassy, half way along what looked like the executive corridor. The architecture, he noted, was both opulent and austere: like one of those stately homes where the owners couldn't make up their minds whether to go classical or Gothic. He fancied that the giant double doors at the far end were those of the ambassador, Von Stohrer. Stohrer, he calculated, would be a major player in the game on which he was now embarked. How he could ever hope to outmanoeuvre him was a question to which he had no answer.

Hasselfeldt turned the handle of his own, more modest office door and stood to one side to let Bramall walk ahead. The room was light and airy and overlooked a pleasant courtyard, with trees, shrubs and wooden benches.

'Please sit down,' he said, indicating a comfortable fin-de-siècle-style chair, padded with an oversized cushion. 'Would you care to smoke?' Bramall shook his head. Hasselfeldt replaced the silver cigarette case he had taken out of his jacket pocket and made his way round to his desk, which, unlike the chair, was uncompromisingly modern. 'Now tell me,' he said, leaning back in proprietorial fashion, 'are you feeling better after last night?'

'I don't know what you mean.'

'Oh, someone told me you had been hitting it pretty hard in the bar of the hotel. They saw you staggering into the lift in the lobby at two in the morning. But what of it? None of my business.'

'Just out of interest,' said Bramall, irritated almost beyond words, 'do your men watch me the entire time?'

'Not at all.' Hasselfeldt smiled, observing Bramall's upraised eyebrows. 'But we, too, have people at the Ritz, and we like to make sure they are safe. After all, this is a dangerous city in dangerous times.'

'Well, I can look after myself, thank you very much, so do you think we might get to the point? Why am I here?'

This was his show of defiance. It was pathetic really, he felt.

Hasselfeldt waved a hand airily in front of him. 'Oh! Plenty of time for that.' He reached into a drawer of his desk and pulled out a Leica camera. 'Smile, please.' The was a soft click as the shutter opened and shut. The SD man laughed, as if at some private joke, and replaced the camera in the drawer. 'Now,' he said, 'what about some lunch? You must be starving. I don't suppose you managed to eat much by way of breakfast this morning.'

It turned out they were to dine in the embassy. It was the wrong time for lunch in Spain, where everything was two hours behind the rest of the world. They moved from Hasselfeldt's office to a private dining room upstairs, where they were served pea and ham soup, then lamb stew scented with rosemary by a waiter wearing a swastika armband. A signed photograph of Hitler flanked by two half-size German flags dominated one wall of the room. Another wall contained two matched canvases by the Belgian surrealist, Magritte, which surprised Bramall until he realised that their subject was the distinction between appearance and reality – presumably an SD preoccupation.

During lunch, conducted in a mixture of English and German, the two men skated lightly around the royal duties on which Bramall was seemingly engaged in Madrid. Hasselfeldt expressed the hope that he had not embarrassed his guest in any way in the hotel bar on the night of his arrival. 'I'd no idea who you were,' he said, truthfully. 'I was just looking for a little conversation.'

It was then that Bramall noticed, hanging on the wall to the right of the window, next to a series of pictures apparently taken at the Nuremberg rallies, a framed photograph of himself talking with Hitler at Mosley's wedding. The shock made him gasp – much to his host's amusement.

'*Ach so!*' he said. 'You have seen it, then. I was wondering how long it would take. I'm afraid I must apologise again. Just my little joke.'

'Yes, but how on Earth?'

'Oh! Quite simple. I send your picture, together with your name, to Berlin and Berlin sends me this. I have to tell you, it was quite a surprise.'

Bramall remembered the flashbulb going off in the Ritz. So that was it. He had to hand it to the fellow. He must have been trained in the theatre. Still, no real harm done. Given that his cover was never supposed to be a secret, what difference did it make? Might even speed things up.

Hasselfeldt was now smugness personified. It was as if he had set the stage for a parlour game and was enjoying watching it play out. 'But tell me – how did it come about? I'm afraid the information on the back of the photographic print is a little sketchy.'

'Pure chance, I assure you,' Bramall replied, blinking. 'I'd been working closely with Sir Oswald for several years, and the occasion of his wedding, at the home of Dr Göbbels, was the opportunity of a lifetime. Still, I couldn't believe it when I was summoned to meet the *Führer*. It was such a shock – and an honour.' He let his voice trail off. 'Of course that was before the war. It would be a little different today.'

More defiance, but muted. He wondered how he was doing. Hasselfeldt gave no clue He listened politely, then wiped his mouth delicately with his napkin and called for coffee and Schnapps. After a moment, he seemed to make up his mind about something and leaned across the table. 'Herr Bramall,' he said, 'give me your hand.'

'I'm sorry?'

'Your hand. I read palms, you know. The practise is much encouraged by *Reichsführer* Himmler. Astrology, too. We are all of us given indicators of our fate.'

'Oh, I see.' Nervously, he held out his hand.

'Ah yes,' said Hasselfeldt, prodding at his palm with a

fingernail. 'The love line is a bit thin here at the start, with many branches, but clarifies itself later. Here, do you see? And the head line – straight and extending quite far over, but touching your heart line at this point. I wonder if that holds any significance for you. Then the life line. Oh, now this is interesting. So many twists and false trails at the beginning, but then – ha! – a revelation. All becomes clear. Perhaps our meeting was ordained. What do you think?'

'I'm afraid, I know little of such things.'

'No, of course not. You are a rationalist, are you not? But Fate applies to all equally. It is a matter of making the most of what is possible.' He let go of Bramall's hand. 'Come,' he said, 'we should return to my office.'

They took the stairs. As soon as he was seated once more at his desk, Hasselfeldt picked up a pencil and began to roll it between his slender fingers. He stared hard at Bramall. 'You will have gathered by now,' he said at last, 'that my role at the Legation extends some way beyond the mere exigencies of trade.'

The traffic on the street outside seemed all of a sudden to go quiet. 'The thought had occurred to me.'

'Just so. And I have to tell you that your arrival here in Madrid intrigues me. My information is that you are a member in good standing of our British sister-party, the BUF. You are also someone who, as we know, has had the honour of a personal conversation with the *Führer*. In addition, I am hearing reports that you are – what shall we say? – disenchanted with the present state of affairs between our two countries. Given your history and outlook, it comes as no surprise that you should be one of His Royal Highness's chosen advisers.

He would naturally wish to have someone around him whose appointment owes nothing to the warmongering of the Churchill clique. I might even go so far as to conclude that you and I share a particular … *Weltanschauung* – a common outlook. What do you say? Would that be a fair interpretation?'

'You wouldn't necessarily be wrong. But that doesn't mean …'

The Austrian cut off the protest with a wave of his hand. He stared at Bramall, who did his best to maintain a steadfast gaze, though his heart was thumping. 'Of course. It is a fine judgement, is it not? You have consented to meet with me here just days after your arrival in Spain. I did not have to persuade you. You came willingly. What sort of a man, I ask myself, would visit the Legation of his country's bitterest foe in time of war? A naïve man? A fool? Yes. But I don't think you quite fall into either or those categories. A spy, then? A possibility. But one whose tradecraft would appear to be seriously deficient. Could that be you? Perhaps. Or then again, you could be a highly experienced agent, whose apparent lack of guile is in fact the product of the most studied artifice? In that event, your naivety could be a double bluff. So many doors, and only one that leads to the truth. Which is it? I wonder.'

Bramall still said nothing, but let his mouth fall open slightly. There was no point in denying or confirming any of this. The Austrian waited several seconds before he spoke again. 'I am informed that you spent some time the other evening talking to Fraulein Isabel Ortega.'

The Gestapo officer. He must have reported back straight away.

'What if I did? I'm a single man. I can talk to whoever I like.'

Hasselfeldt steepled his fingers so that Bramall could see the fine bones of his wrists. On the third finger of his right hand was a silver signet ring, with a tiny skull and crossbones – the Death's Head. His voice dropped to a steely whisper. 'I doubt Colonel Ortega's daughter revealed much of herself to you during your brief encounter – though not, I think, for want of trying on your part. But here is what is important. The young lady is spoken for. The man she is to marry, Herr Luder, is a prominent Italian banker and a trusted friend of the Reich.'

Bramall could hardly believe it. 'Luder, you say. Felipe Luder?'

Hasselfeldt's eyes narrowed. 'You know him?'

'We ran into each other when I was in Argentina.'

'*Ach!* Small world! But then you will know that he is not a man to be crossed.'

'For God's sake, I only just met her.'

Hasselfeldt smiled thinly. 'I am not blaming you. Truly! We both know what Spanish girls are like. They are so … tempting. But that is not the point. I need to know that you are not playing some kind of ridiculous and futile double game. I shall look upon this as a test – an earnest of your good faith.'

Hasselfeldt purred with satisfaction. 'Do we understand one another?' he asked, once more extending his cigarette case.

This time, Bramall did not refuse. 'I think we do,' he said.

'That is excellent. I am most gratified.' The Austrian adjusted his wire-rimmed glasses and joined his hands together on the blotter on his desk. 'Now let us move on. We could spend all day out-smarting one another, but, frankly, I haven't the time. You were stationed in Vienna, were you not?'

'1934-35. You've obviously done your homework.'

'I dislike surprises. You will learn that.' He ran the length of the pencil back and forth beneath his nose, as if it were a fine cigar. 'An interesting period. An object lesson in the recovery of order from chaos. Did you know, by the way, that your former embassy is now the regional headquarters of the National Socialist Flying Club?'

Hasselfeldt, Bramall decided, was like a surgeon with a scalpel. He knew just where to place the blade for maximum effect. 'No,' he said, 'I hadn't heard.'

'Yes. Apparently they picked it up for a song.'

'The Horst Wessel Song, I should imagine.'

'Very droll.' Hasselfeldt's face fell. He now looked like a doctor giving bad news to his patient. 'You are a very funny man, Herr Bramall. I would be careful, however, if I were you, about where you choose to deploy your English sense of humour. In the New Order, jokes are not high on our list of priorities.'

'No laughing matter, then?'

'But there you go – doing it again. So ... audacious. I trust you found your country's defeat in Norway and France equally amusing.' He took off his glasses and made a minor adjustment to one of the stems. 'Your problem – and I do not envy you – is that you do not know how much I know or what actions I may be about to put in motion. You might suppose that the same is true in the opposite direction. In any event, my advice to you is the same – and you would do well to remember it. When Spain joins the Axis, as it undoubtedly will, you, Herr Bramall, will become at that moment an enemy alien, unprotected by any quasi-diplomatic status you may currently enjoy. Work with us and you will survive the transition. You may even prosper. Make mischief and ... well!'

He twisted the pencil so that it was stretched between his fingers and thumbs and broke it in two with a snap. It was a trick that Bramall presumed must have been taught to him on Day Two of his SD interrogation class and seemed unworthy of him, hinting perhaps at the schoolboy bully concealed inside the suave manipulator. He would have to remember that.

'But there is no need,' Hasselfeldt continued, 'for us to dwell on such negative possibilities. You are, one might say, a free agent, and it is up to you which course you adopt.'

'Well,' said Bramall, 'I am certainly ready to discuss matters of mutual concern. But I will not betray my country. You should know that.'

Hasselfeldt pursed his lips before he spoke and there was a definite twinkle in his eyes. 'Of course not,' he said. 'You are a man of honour, as are we all, I hope. I am not asking you to become a traitor. I am asking you to become the truest kind of patriot: the kind of man who puts country before self. Is that too much for you?'

Bramall made a show of swallowing hard. 'If you put it like that.'

'Well, there we are then. Ours will be a partnership aimed at peace and reconciliation.' Hasselfeldt glanced up at the clock on the wall. 'Oh! But I am forgetting. Before you go – one other thing. Your employer, the Duke of Windsor, lately of the House of *Saxe-Coburg und Gotha* [he lingered on the Royal Family's well-known German family lineage]. An interesting figure, much exercised, as we have said, by the ... *difficulties* that exist between our two countries. It would be useful to know what action he might be willing to consider to help resolve these difficulties. And you, my friend, as a British patriot, are perfectly placed to come up with the answer. In this, as in all things, we should be a team, working together for the new Europe. Do not disappoint me, please.' He smiled an oily smile. 'Let us leave it at that. We are both busy men. If there is anything else I can do for you, please to let me know.' At this, he sat suddenly to attention and his right arm shot out. *'Heil Hitler!'*

As soon as he was alone, Hasselfeldt sat staring once more at the photograph of Bramall in conversation with Hitler. The fellow was so plausible. In the picture, he looked the very soul of solicitude, obviously hanging on the *Führer's* every word – as well he might if he were a true Fascist. But what if he was not what he claimed? Berlin could have got it wrong. And the fellow was Irish, after all. He knew Oswald Mosley alright. Of that there was no doubt. He had also provided sympathetic coverage of the Nationalist position in the Civil War, with only the occasional sideswipe at the excesses of the Condor Legion. The question was, what did it all add up to?

Berlin had sent him several pictures. One showed Bramall at a BUF protest in London. He looked at it now. It was newspaper quality and grainy, but there was something there.

Reaching into one of his desk drawers, he drew out a large magnifying glass. Two minutes later, under the powerful light of his desk lamp, Hasselfeldt poured over an enlarged image of the old Daily Mail photograph taken at the Cable Street riot. Mosley was standing at the head of his men, eyes staring fixedly ahead, arms folded – in unconscious emulation of the *Führer*, perhaps. Several of the men in the BUF front rank were hitting out with clubs. On the other side, a group of Communists – Jews most probably – shook their fists and shouted abuse. Some threw bricks and stones. Hatred and mutual antagonism were what screamed out from the scene as caught by the camera. But then he turned to the figure standing almost isolated to Mosley's left. One of his hands was placed on top of the arm of a Blackshirt lieutenant, as if to restrain him. Bramall was staring, open-mouthed, as if he could not believe what was happening. Hasselfeldt's sense of unease increased. He had seen that stare before. But where? Then it came to him. He had seen it in the eyes of a city policeman in Graz who stepped in to stop a group of SA thugs from beating up a Rabbi on his way into synagogue. It was May, 1933, and what happened had inspired him to become a National Socialist. He was inspired by what he saw. Two of the SA men seized the officer from behind. Another grabbed hold of his hair. Together, they forced him to look at what was happening from close up. The look in the man's eyes as the Rabbi's face became streaked with blood told its own story. It was a look of ... horror.

Madrid: British Embassy, June 28

Sir Samuel Hoare, who had not expected his brief note to Bramall to elicit a personal response, was distinctly put out when its recipient turned up at the embassy asking to see him. 'My message was a warning,' he said.' Nothing more. I thought I had made it clear that you were not to involve me in your schemes.'

'I realise that. But I'm worried that things may be about to get out of hand.'

Hoare was seated at his desk. The room was unostentatious, but comfortable. What interested Bramall was the set of photographs showing Hoare engaged in his two favourite pursuits, ice-dancing and fencing. There was even one showing him at full stretch, lunging with a foil at Oswald Mosley. Now he leaned forward at his desk, fearful of chaos. 'What do you mean?'

'It's the Duke. I'm afraid he's developing a messiah complex.'

'A what?'

'He's starting to believe in the Second Coming – regally speaking, that is. He has been persuaded that if only the right support can be mustered, here and in Germany, he could yet be the salvation of his people.'

'Does he now? Well, we all have our views on what might be agreed with Berlin, but that's most unfortunate.'

The ambassador, who had excused himself from a meeting with the head of the Department of Economic Warfare, in order to hear what Bramall had to say, was fast running out of patience with the Duke. 'Are you telling me that His Royal Highness, after everything that has been said, might actually fall for Berlin's blandishments and make a total arse of himself? Is that it?'

Bramall couldn't help smiling.

'In a nutshell, yes – though I don't think he'd see it quite that way himself. As far as I can tell, he views the war with Germany as a kind of diplomatic cancer that needs to be cut out. It's time, he says, for someone to rise to the occasion and wield the knife, and if London can't see that, then what's a chap to do? And all this before anyone has turned the screws on him. That's the thing. For the moment, from what I can see, the Germans are content to work behind the Spanish, waiting to see what pickings come their way. No, it's the man himself, fuelled by a higher patriotism, love, the Divine Right of Kings – whatever you want to call it. He's convinced the war is lost and he's ready to step in as the British Pétain.' He looked straight at Hoare. 'You've got to muzzle him or else get him out fast. If he won't go back home, what about the empire? We rule a quarter of the globe, for God's sake. There has to be somewhere that needs a high commissioner or a governor general. What about Canada or South Africa? Maybe New Zealand? Couldn't get him further away than that.'

Hoare snorted. 'Taken. Jobs like that don't grow on trees, you know.'

'Don't they? Aren't they in the gift of the Crown, routed via Downing Street? If the PM can appoint the Archbishop of Canterbury and decide who gets to be Master of my Cambridge College, he can surely find a job for the Duke of Windsor. I'm telling you, sir, the man is about to snap. All it needs is the right offer in the right place.'

'What about Portugal?' Already, it seemed to Bramall, Hoare was wondering if he might not profitably export the problem to Lisbon.

'The pressures will continue wherever he goes – unless it's so far away and remote as to be impractical. But Spain is the core of the German operation. If he goes to Lisbon, the pressure will only be on to bring him back.'

The envoy swivelled slowly in his chair and looked out the window of his office. There were builders working on the façade of the building opposite, reconstructing the architraves of a set of eighteenth century windows. 'What about the German Legation? What have they been saying?'

'They tell me only so much, but they've made it clear on

which side they expect to find me. The Duke's not the only one on borrowed time.'

'Quite. Which is precisely why you shouldn't be here now.'

'I realise that. But I didn't feel I had the luxury of choice.'

The ambassador knuckled his eyes, which were red-rimmed with fatigue. His brow when he removed his hands was furrowed with concern. 'Before you go,' he said, 'how are you getting on with the main part of your mission? Any joy?'

'Early days, sir. I've hardly had a chance to turn round.'

Hoare harrumphed. 'Be that as it may, the whole business of Gibraltar and Spanish neutrality is moving rapidly up the Government's agenda. Hitler's too, from what we hear. You know what's at stake. Suffice to say, if we lose Gibraltar we lose everything. Franco knows this. He's made it clear there's an auction in progress, with us and the Germans as the bidders. I'm doing everything I can think of to keep us in play. I won't go into detail, but it's not pretty. The point is, diplomacy and economic warfare, as we've learned to call it, can only achieve so much at a time when everything, greed included, is magnified and appetites grow by what they feed on. Franco's basically a provincial bully – prickly, and cunning as a weasel. He grew up in Galicia and wants to end up master of the Mediterranean. Serrano's worse: twice the brainpower; three times the radicalism; steeped in envy and hatred – a pinchbeck Robespierre who'd stab us in the back quicker than you could say "knife."'

Bramall swallowed. He was not used to this kind of confessional talk from one of His Majesty's ambassadors.

'Ordinarily,' Hoare went on, 'it wouldn't matter. Pair of 'em would be nothing more than piss and wind. But today, with France fallen, Italy climbing on the bandwagon and the future of Europe hanging by a thread, they reckon their hour has come at last. We have to stop 'em, Mr Bramall. We have to stop 'em in their tracks. Time for you to practice your trade.'

Remembering his lunch with Hasselfeldt, Bramall felt like asking what exactly his trade was. Instead, he said: 'I'll do my best, sir. And I'm sorry if I've spoiled your evening.'

The ambassador's face fell. He was like a helium balloon left around after a children's party that had deflated and fallen behind a sofa. 'Oh, *that!*' he said. 'Only doing your job. I presume you can find your own way out.'

Bramall left the embassy by the main door, clutching his passport, hoping to convey the impression to anyone who might be watching that this had been a routine visit and he had nothing to hide. He was chastened by what he had heard. Hoare, after clinging to the upper sections of politics's slippery pole for more than twenty years, looked and sounded as if he was at the end of his tether. Negotiation was supposed to be his principal gift. It was said he could coax blood from a stone. If he felt that something new was needed – something outside of the ordinary – in order to preserve Gibraltar and keep Britain in the war, then the situation must truly be serious. But was he, Charles Bramall, that extraordinary something? It seemed unlikely.

Back out on the street, he checked his watch. It was nearly time for his rendezvous with Romero. To make sure he wasn't being followed, he downed a *caña* at a bar on the Gran Via and made his way to the Plaza Dos de Mayo by the most circuitous route he could think of. Doubling back on himself every two streets or so, he checked reflections in shop windows and one occasion removed his jacket, turning it inside out, so that the lining was what showed, and draping it over his shoulder. Only when he felt well and truly lost in the maze of streets north of the Telefónica did he at last begin to relax.

For more than a century, the Plaza Dos de Mayo was the most atmospheric open space in Madrid, famous as the scene of a heroic stand by two Army officers and their supporters against the French colonial occupiers in 1808. But in the aftermath of the civil war, it presented a sorry spectacle. The once-elegant properties, now strung with washing, that surrounded the square were filled to overflowing with impoverished Madrileños and families of refugees from the countryside. There were beggars on the pavement, ranging from five-year-olds to grandmothers dressed all in black. Groups of men, drinking rough wine ladled into glasses from wooden barrels, ogled the various emaciated and disease-ridden prostitutes who inhabited the shadows, plying for trade. Dogs were everywhere. Flea-ridden mutts that whimpered if approached. But one or two still managed to snarl at anyone who drew too close.

It was intolerably hot and humid when Bramall stepped onto the square. He made to loosen his tie, then realised he had left it off back at the hotel. Something pungent and fetid wafted into his nostrils. The ground was strewn with rotting vegetables and the sewers were obviously blocked. He could see now why aristocrats in past centuries carried bottles of cologne. Picking his way across the cracked and broken flagstones to the monument commemorating the events of 1808, he stood for several minutes beneath a flickering gaslight. To his left, a man pissed against the stone effigy of a *resistente*, who looked as if he was used to it. More minutes ticked by.

Maybe Romero wouldn't come. Maybe something had happened to change his mind.

A Spanish voice, cracked and dry, broke into his reverie. 'Looking for a good time, señor?'

He turned his head wearily. 'No thanks, Señorita, not this evening.' And then he had to catch his breath. It was Romero, large as life, standing behind him mimicking the predictable sales-patter of a Madrid whore.

He was a few years older than Bramall – tall, maybe six feet-two, with thick, slightly unruly hair and just the beginnings of a beard. A tiny gold earring hung from his right lobe, so that he looked like a gypsy, or a dancer. When he spoke again, it was in his own voice, honed in the Quays of Dublin, looking across the Liffey to Guinness's brewery. 'How are you, Charlie? Pleased to see me?'

'Eddy Romero, as I live and breathe.'

'Which up to now, you seem to be managing just fine. So how's it hangin'?'

'Not so bad. And you?'

The Dubliner offered an enigmatic smile. 'Who knows?' he said. 'Fair to middlin', I'd say. Depends who's askin'.'

The two men looked at each other, as if trying to work out what to say or do next. It was Romero who once more broke the silence. 'Come on,' he said. 'Let's get the fuck out of here. There's this bar I know. It'll take but a minute.'

The walk from the square took them away from Madrid's public face. Their destination turned out to be a small, anonymous establishment, of the type known locally as a *tasca*. It had a black porcelain bull in the window. 'Here we go,' said Romero. '*Bienvenido*, Charlie boy. Welcome to your new home from home.'

The interior of the bar was small, dark and smoky. Bramall looked around and took in the half dozen or so customers. Two elderly men played chess by the window. Four other men, in their fifties, talked in low voices over a bottle of cheap wine. The counter, lit by candles, was about six feet long, made from wood worn smooth by generations of elbows and scrubbing cloths.

The barman, a tall, thin fellow, wore a long green apron. He didn't say anything, but offered the visitor a plate of olives and a slice of dried, fatty ham that he cut sideways from a shrivelled haunch on the counter.

Bramall nodded his thanks. He threw some change down on the counter and asked for a packet of cigarettes. What he got back was *Ideales* – roll-ups made from heavy, black Cuban leaves. Extracting what he needed, he pushed the packet towards Romero, who was squinting at him as if trying to take him in piece by piece. The former *brigadista* rolled a cigarette almost without looking, his fingers clearly practised in the technique.

'What were the chances of this?' he asked.

Bramall shrugged. Romero inclined his head in the direction of a table in the corner. They walked over and sat down. The barman brought a bottle of wine – a decent label, Bramall noticed.

'So tell me about it,' Romero said, helping himself to a full glass. 'I thought you were back in London.'

'I was. But I got bored.'

'Bored? With a war goin' on? Why aren't you in the Army anyway, giving Jerry a jolly good thrashing?'

They both smiled at that.

'I was,' said Bramall. 'Not France, though. My particular

shambles was in Norway.'

'Ah! Where you came second in a two-horse race. But at least you lived to run away another day.'

'Well, as you can see, I'm here.'

'True enough,' Romero said, taking everything in, missing nothing. As a Dubliner, he felt he could sum up a person just by looking at them. 'So what happened you? What are you doin' in this neck of the woods? I take it you're not in the newspaper game any longer.'

Bramall nodded. 'Not for the last couple of years. What about you? How did you know I was here?'

A sly smile crossed the older man's sunken features. 'Just keepin' an eye out, Charlie. You're in my territory now. You wouldn't be forgettin' that now, would you?'

'What are you talking about?'

Romero pushed out his lower lip, looking for a split second like Mussolini. 'Don't be gettin' yourself all excited. It's simple enough. I go uptown most days. Talk with old friends, maybe grab a beer at the Café Gijón – you know it?'

'I remember it.'

'Yeah, well on my way there a few days back, I stops by at the British embassy, just to see how the action's goin'. Know what I'm sayin'? And who do I see walkin' out the front door, large as life and twice as ugly, but my old comrade and fellow Irishman, Charlie Bramall.'

Bramall's mind raced as he tried to absorb this sudden glut of information. Could he trust Romero? He wasn't working for the Government side – that much he was sure of. He had killed too many of them – soldiers, *Guardia Civil*, party officials – to be on any list but the death list. The piece he wrote about him had described him as 'bloodthirsty' and 'hell bent on revenge.' But it also labelled him the Republic's Robin Hood, so maybe – if he'd read it – he wouldn't feel too badly done by.

'Well, I have to tell you, Eddy,' he said, 'it's a queer thing finding you here like this. A coincidence. And you know what they say about coincidences – there aren't any. The war ended more than a year ago and, like the Yanks say, the good guys lost. So what could you possibly hope to accomplish by staying on?' He paused as a sudden thought struck him. 'Oh, wait, wait. I get it. You're one of those sharp-shooting fanatics that gets back at the *asaltos* and the secret police.'

Romero's mouth twisted into an amused contempt. 'You must think I'm some kind of eejit, he said.'

'But you *are* an eejit. And didn't you once tell me you were going to Madrid to rip out Fascism's heart?'

'I said a lot of things.'

'Including that Madrid wouldn't be safe for any kind of Government until Franco and his goons were shot by firing squad in the Badajoz bullring.'

Badajoz, where Romero's father was born, was the scene of the one of the worst massacres of the Civil War. More than 1,500 Republican prisoners were machine-gunned to death in the town's bullring, mainly by Moorish auxiliaries. Others were hacked to pieces with knives or blown apart with hand grenades.

'You remember that, do you? Well, changed times. These days I've come to see that one man can't make much of a difference after all. There's just too many of the buggers, Charlie. All the good fellas are dead and gone, or else living in exile a thousand miles from here.'

Bramall felt a distinct twinge of disappointment. He had imagined Romero making a last stand, defying the odds, calling out to the *asaltos* to come and get him as he reloaded his revolver. But he was human after all. 'So you've put revenge on hold, is that it?'

'Given it up, Charlie. Took up booze and religion instead.'

'Religion? Really?'

'It's not so crazy. There has to be some explanation that makes sense of all this.'

'I suppose.'

Romero refilled their glasses and began to roll another cigarette. He smoked quickly, like he was in a hurry. 'Okay,' he began. 'My turn. Where do you fit into all this? First off, what are you playin' at workin' for that prize bollox, the Duke of Windsor?'

Bramall couldn't hide his dismay at this latest evidence of inside information. His reaction seemed to please Romero. 'You sound surprised,' he said. 'Well don't be. I asked at the embassy front desk. Turns out your job isn't exactly a secret. Anyway, I told myself, there has to be a story there. I mean, come on Charlie, you can't just have said to yourself one mornin', 'hey, there's a war on, I think I'll sign up as a royal flunky.' You know what I mean?'

Romero always did have a turn of phrase. Bramall shifted uneasily in his chair. 'The thing is,' he said, running a thoughtful hand down the length of his jaw, 'the crisis isn't about Spain now, it's the whole damn world. And, yes, as you have obviously deduced, there's more to my present role than meets the eye.'

Romero lit his cigarette and drew a lungful of smoke into his throat. 'Go on,' he said, coughing phlegm into his handkerchief. 'I'm listenin'.'

There was a pause as Bramall waited for the other man's chest to settle. He felt uneasy all of a sudden. It was like he was standing above himself, looking down, and he didn't much like what he saw. Turned out you didn't have to torture MI6's Man In Madrid if you wanted to find out what he was up to. All you had to do was offer him a glass of wine. Still, in for a penny, in for a pound. If Romero loathed Franco – which he did – he had to be spitting teeth over Hitler. And there were times when you had to take a chance, go in with both feet. Otherwise you might as well be selling insurance.

He drew a long breath. 'It started when I got back from Narvik.'

Romero leaned back, his chest heaving. His eyes were ringed with black as if he hadn't slept for a week.

Over the next five minutes, Bramall recounted the story of how he'd met Strickland and the brief he'd given him to stop Spain launching an attack on Gibraltar. He told him about Hasselfeldt and the pressure he was under to prove his Fascist credentials. He described his unlikely role of royal equerry and the danger that the Duke could end up defecting to the Germans. It was cathartic, he realised. It felt good to talk about it all to someone who wasn't going to conclude every two minutes that he was letting the side down.

Romero waited all the way to the end, until Bramall was obviously done, before offering any comment. 'Feelin' better now?' he wanted to know.

'I am actually.'

'Good. Only the thing is, I seem to be missin' somethin'. You have to keep in with the Germans, right? Find out what they're up to while arrangin' tea parties for the Duke of Windsor and that Yankee woman he's with – if she is a woman, that is. Don't let her fool you into thinkin' she isn't crazy. I've heard stories about that one that'd make your hair curl. But that's just the start of it. Now you've got to convince Franco to reject a deal with Hitler that would restore Gibraltar to Spanish sovereignty – a key policy aim of every leader of this country, Left, Right and Centre, since whoever it was lost it in the first place. Is that it? Would I be any way close?'

Bramall offered a lame shrug by way of reply.

'Right.' Romero drew deeply on his cigarette. 'And your ace in the hole is what exactly?'

Bramall laughed. He needed this. 'I wish I knew, Eddy.' He reached for the wine bottle. 'I'm waiting for something to break. It's going to be something to do with North Africa. That much I'm sure of. Franco and Serrano are obsessed with getting the French out of Morocco and Oran. The *Generalísimo*, they tell me, even talks about expanding further south and creating new colonies in black Africa. As you can imagine, that kind of talk goes down like a bad oyster with Vichy. If I could get something hard and fast that would set those two at each other's throats, then maybe – just maybe – I could get somewhere.'

Outside, from the direction of the square, there was a distant crackle of gunfire. Romero flicked his cigarette end onto the floor. He closed his eyes and pressed the fingers of his right hand against his forehead.

Just one thing.'

'What's that?'

'Let's assume it all works out like you say. Franco stays neutral, your crowd hold on to Gibraltar and the war goes on. Why should I care? What's it to me? The Brits and their fuckin' empire occupied Ireland for 700 years. Left nothing but blood and poverty in their wake. And what's their record on Spain? When the Fascists staged their coup, what did your precious English do to protect democratic legitimacy? I'll tell you, Charlie, fuck-all is what they did.' He ran a languid hand across his brow as though lamenting the unique depth of British perfidy. 'No,' he resumed. 'Let me correct that. They worked with France from 1936 to 1939 to make sure no arms got through to the constitutionally elected government ... while all the time the Nazis and the Eyeties were stompin' all over the place with their heavy artillery and their bombers and their commando units. Even when they begged for help, London and the empire said no. Just looked on, shakin' their heads.'

His voice was hoarse and he coughed to clear his throat. It sounded like his lungs were full of soot. 'That self-same empire, you're now tellin' me, should be supported just so's the Brits can stop the Nazis doin' to them what they cheerfully watched them do to the Spanish. That it? Have I got it?'

Bramall looked down at his shoes. 'That's about the size of it.'

'Thought as much. They were wrong then, they're right now, so forgive and forget.'

'Exactly.'

'And all those thousands who died at the Ebro – men and women, boys and girls a lot of them – whose lives could have been saved if Britain had just honoured its obligations ...'

Bramall remembered Manuela lying in the mud, her body soaked with blood, and looked away. 'Yesterday's news, Eddy. What happened three years ago was a tragedy, maybe even a crime. We both know that. But that doesn't make what's happening now any less important. It only heightens the urgency. For all its faults, England right now is all there is. France is gone, the Russians are taking every advantage they can from the situation and America looks like it's going to sit this one out. Ireland and its concerns don't come into it. DeValera's decided to stay neutral and play both sides against the middle. But we don't have that option, do we Eddy? I know where I stand. What about you? Seems to me you either back Britain or you back out of the war.'

A despairing look crossed Romero's gaunt features. 'Okay, fair play to you – as far as it goes. But if it's my help you're after, Charlie, I have to tell you I'm not exactly overjoyed by the prospect. The only thing Britain wants in this case is to hang on to Gibraltar – which, begging Franco's pardon, seems a pretty reasonable ambition. What the fuck are they doin' there anyway?'

Bramall's response was emphatic. 'Don't ask me to justify English history. The Empire's a dead duck. It's on borrowed time and the clock's ticking. But that doesn't help us, and it doesn't help Europe either. Hitler has declared war on everything you hold dear – and he's winning. The *Wehrmacht* are less than twenty miles from Dover, with the *Gestapo* and the SS right behind them. Rhetoric doesn't cut it any more. You have to ask yourself, when England's gone, who's left? Time to pick sides, Eddy. It's time to pick sides.'

Romero's rolled his glass between his fingers. 'Well, we know which side your family picked when it came to independence for Ireland.'

Beneath the table, Bramall made fists of his hands. Abandoning the land of their birth had been for his entire family. The home, Dreenagh, was never especially big or grand – not by British or continental standards. Just six bedrooms, if you didn't count the servants' quarters, and the surrounding 500 acres given over mostly to beef production, with a decent shoot, a trout stream and a couple of small lakes on the side. It provided jobs for ten of the local people, and homes for their families, Catholic as well as Protestant. His grandfather had been elected a Member of Parliament; his uncle John was the resident magistrate for close on two decades. The Bramalls had settled in Monaghan in 1692, just after the Williamite wars. His mother's people, the FitzGeralds, were in Kildare even longer, going back on one side to Norman times. It wasn't as if the family had just turned up, built the Big House and sent the natives to Hell or Connaught. But that cut no ice with the new enforcers of gaelic supremacy. Within two years of the treaty, the Anglo-Irish had been all-but eradicated from history. Dreenagh was burned to the ground, Billy McKenna – a good man who never did anyone any harm – was dead and the Bramalls, after centuries of dedication to their country, erased from the nation's story.

He closed his eyes for a moment, remembering the crack of the windows blowing out and the sight of Billy dying in his mother's arms. 'Don't start,' he said quietly. 'That's not a path I want to go down. What's important is the here and now. It's a simple question, Eddy. Do you want to fight Fascism or don't you?'

Romero joined his hands together and bent his fingers back until the knuckles cracked. 'I've been out of the game more than a year now. All I know these days is how to run a bar and maybe get a few things on the black market for children without fathers, wives without husbands – that sort of thing.'

'It's not enough, though, is it?'

The two men stared at each other. It was Romero who blinked first. 'They say that next to our enemies, some of the worst people we ever have to deal with are the ones we call our friends.'

'The human comedy, Eddy.'

'Right. Except, I'm not laughin'.' He stared up at the tobacco-stained ceiling, trying to resolve the bitter debate still raging inside of him. Bramall thought he was the great hero. But *he* knew different. 'Okay, Charlie' he said at last. 'A truce, then, God help us. For the greater good. So what do you want me to do?'

Bramall almost sighed with relief. 'You're forgetting,' he said. 'Up until this afternoon, I didn't even know you were still alive. I thought it was me versus the entire apparatus of the Fascist state. Now I find I'm not the only lunatic in town. You were asking about my ace in the hole. Well, I don't know, but maybe it's you, Eddy.'

Romero choked down his memories. What was happening across Europe was bigger than a couple of renegades, neither of them the full shilling. He grinned and raised his glass. 'I'll drink to that.'

5

Madrid: British embassy, June 29, 1940

The Duke of Windsor paced up and down the length of Sir Samuel Hoare's already threadbare Axminster rug. Suddenly, he spun round. 'Is it going to work, do you think? I mean, there are bound to be those, in present circumstances, who will think it's no more than keeping up appearances.'

'Only those,' said Hoare, using his most soothing diplomatic tones, 'who would think the worst of us no matter what we did. I assure you, sir, that everything is set for a splendid party and I am confident that we shall all derive nothing but good from the experience.'

The Duke stopped pacing. 'Whatever you say, Hoare. You're in charge. But if you've any doubts or suggestions … anything … let me know.'

'Of course. Before you go, sir, have you had any further thoughts about Downing Street's offer to bring you home? There's an aircraft waiting for you, you know. Two, in fact. They've been sitting off Lisbon for the past four days.'

'So I believe. Well you can tell them to take off and start hunting a few U-Boats, or whatever it is they do for a living when they're not following me about the place. You know that my brother, the Duke of Kent, is in Lisbon at the moment…'

'I presumed that you would wish to spend time with His

Royal Highness while you had the opportunity.'

The Duke shook his head. 'No, no. It doesn't work that way, I'm afraid. Can't have two members of the Royal Family in the same place abroad at the same time – not unless they're married, of course. Bad form.'

'I see.'

'But my brother will be returning to London tomorrow – no doubt on one of your damned flying boats – and that gives me the chance to spend a bit of time in Lisbon, catching up on friends, that sort of thing.'

Hoare rubbed his hands together. 'Excellent, sir. The ambassador in Lisbon, sir Walford Selby, will be most gratified.'

The second the Duke left the room, Hoare heaved a sigh of relief. Perhaps he had sailed a bit close to the wind. But who could blame him? He sat back in his chair. It was time to check with the kitchens and with security. The sooner this damned party was out of the way, the sooner the Duke would be gone from Madrid and someone else's responsibility. He had already spoken with Number Ten over his concerns about the Duke's wayward nature and been told the matter would be looked into as a matter of urgency. In the meantime, he did not envy Selby, who had already, on three occasions, endured the company of the Duke while stationed in Vienna. The first time he'd been Prince of Wales; King the time after that. On the third occasion, in the immediate aftermath of his abdication, he and the Duchess had stayed for an unbelievable three months. But Selby's loss was his gain. Once more he picked up the telephone receiver. 'I wish to speak with our ambassador in Lisbon.'

Portbou: Franco-Spanish frontier, June 29

The arrival at the Spanish frontier at the wheel of her lime-green, open-top MG sports car of Dominique de Fourneau caused something of a stir among officials on both sides of the border. She seemed to the Spanish in particular a creature from another world – a type not seen in Catalonia since before the Civil War. The French allowed her to pass upon inspection of her laisser-passer, signed by Pierre Laval himself. They did not bother to search the capacious trunk strapped to the exterior of her vehicle's boot; nor did they ask her to step outside the car. Instead, they were content simply to gather round and ogle her while passing her papers from one to the other.

The Spanish, however, could not resist the opportunity to run their hands through her carefully packed dresses and underwear. Her trunk was lifted from the car and opened for all to see, while the captain of the border unit invited its owner to accompany him into his modest wood and concrete office.

'Would you care for a drink, Condesa? Perhaps a little wine?'

'No thank you, Captain. But I wonder, while your men are going through my things, if I might make just the quickest of calls to Madrid?'

'Madrid?' said the captain, a sly smile playing on his features. 'So you are headed to the capital, is that it?'

'Indeed, Captain. You are most shrewd. But while I'm here, there is someone I really have to talk to. Perhaps then we could have that drink.'

'Very well. Do you have the number? I will speak to the operator myself.'

'Of course. It's right here.'

One minute later, seconds after Dominique revealed her identity to his secretary, Juan Beigbeder's booming baritone voice came on the line. 'My dear Condesa ... Dominique. Is it really you? After all this time.'

'Yes, Juan. I'm on my way to my house in Madrid. But I seem to have got stuck at the border. The captain here wants me to have a drink with him and his men are going through my luggage, taking everything out and inspecting it piece by piece. You can imagine! I fear I could be here for some time.'

The Foreign Minister grasped the situation at once. 'If you could just will put me across to the man responsible for this outrage.'

'Thank you Juan.'

'But how long has it been? Three years?'

'Nearer four.'

'Casablanca was an infinitely duller place after your return to France. I missed you so much.'

'That can still be remedied. You know that my husband is no longer alive.'

Beigbeder gasped. 'Alexei? No. I had no idea.'

'He was shot in Bern.'

'But that is terrible. Oh, my poor Dominique. We must have dinner together and you can tell me all about it.'

'That would be wonderful, Juan. I will call you as soon as I arrive.'

She turned to the Spanish officer, who was leaning against the wall opposite, staring down at her and tweaking his moustache. 'My friend would like a word with you,' she said.

The captain shrugged and took the telephone. 'Vázquez here. Who is that?' he asked, blowing a kiss to the exquisite

Frenchwoman whose presence had so unexpectedly made his day.

Dominique could not hear what Beigbeder was saying. But it sounded like an angry wasp had got stuck in the earpiece. The captain swallowed hard, straightened the jacket of his uniform and stood rigidly to attention. 'Yes, Minister ... Of course, Minister ... My apologies, Minister ... No, sir, that will not be necessary, I like it here just fine ... Yes, sir. I shall see to it myself. The Condesa will be on her way within minutes ... Yes, we will repack everything most carefully. You have my personal assurance. Once again, my apologies. Good afternoon, Minister.'

He replaced the receiver.

Dominique smiled sweetly. 'Did Minister Beigbeder explain everything?' she asked.

The Spaniard was shaking with fright and almost grovelled in front of her. 'Yes, Condesa. A thousand apologies. Now, if you will excuse me.' He bowed, turned around and made his way out of the hut towards the car, where one of his men was holding up an expensive Paris creation against his chest.

'What do you think you are doing, you fool?'

The man looked puzzled. 'I just thought that my wife ...'

'Well, don't think! Pack everything back exactly the way you found it. If you have damaged anything, your next posting will be to Guinea.'

'Yes, captain.'

Five minutes later, Dominique moved swiftly through the gears of the MG as she pulled away from Portbou and headed inland towards Zaragoza and Madrid. She was laughing.

Madrid: British Embassy, June 29

It was the party that all who attended it would talk about for years. Everybody who was anybody was there, from the foreign and trade ministers to ambassadors, bishops, bankers, industrialists, ideologues, party hacks, newspaper correspondents, actors, poets and aristocrats. Sir Samuel Hoare, in spite of himself, was enjoying the occasion hugely, not least because if gave him the opportunity to show the assembled company the quality of his dancing. At one point, when the hastily assembled orchestra struck up a tango, it was His Majesty's ambassador who partnered the Duchess of Windsor, drawing comments from all who saw them as they advanced almost brazenly across the floor.

'I must say, Your Royal Highness,' said Juan Beigbeder, appreciatively, 'I never knew the Duchess was such a dancer.'

'Oh yes,' replied the Duke. 'She is a woman of many accomplishments.'

Among the very few at the reception who did not appear to be enjoying herself was Isabel Ortega. Left to herself she would have shunned such a display of indulgence in the midst of war. But her father had insisted, as had her mother, who, after Spain's years of struggle, had chosen to regard the British party as a kind of ersatz debutantes ball.

'Why is the minister himself not here?' she asked abruptly. The absence of Serrano Suñer from the proceedings was something that several guests had commented upon. 'Is he too busy signing death warrants?'

A mixture of indignation and alarm crossed Colonel Ortega's face. 'Don Ramón takes no pleasure in the loss of any human life ,' he lied. 'He is driven by duty and has little time for parties. His concerns are for the people of Spain.'

This encomium clearly cut no ice with Isabel. 'But I thought you said it was important that we should be here. How can it be frivolous for Don Ramón, but important for us? What does that say about us?'

Ortega could feel himself being steered into dangerous waters – which was frequently the case where his daughter was concerned. 'That is enough, Isabel,' he said testily. 'Affairs of state are not your concern.' He looked around. 'Why don't you speak to Señor Bramall? I saw you with him on the terrace the other evening. Perhaps he can talk some sense into you?'

'If you say so, Father.'

She walked across what was by now a crowded room to where Bramall appeared locked in conversation with a Spanish airforce colonel.

'Buenas tardes, Señor Bramall ... Colonel.'

Both men turned gratefully towards the beautiful young señorita, who was offering them a dazzling smile. The air force officer looked especially pleased,

'Señorita Ortega, is it not?' he said.

'That is correct.'

'I know your father well, of course, but I had not realised his daughter was quite so ... extraordinary.'

'You flatter me, sir.'

'The colonel is right, Señorita,' said Bramall. 'Your presence here enlivens what some might find a rather predictable occasion.'

A flicker of a smile crossed Isabel's features. 'Is it really that bad? I should have thought you would be pleased by such a turnout.'

'One is gratified, naturally, but ...'

' – you are anxious for a diversion!' interposed Isabel.

The colonel looked embarrassed.

'I'm sure Señor Bramall didn't mean to imply ... ' he began.

Isabel's eyes lit up and she flicked the airforce man on the lapel with the lace fan she carried. 'But I am teasing you, Colonel. Can you not tell?'

'Oh, I see.' The Spaniard laughed nervously.

Bramall decided to seize the moment. 'I think the band is about to strike up again. Would you care to dance?'

'If it wouldn't bore you intolerably.'

'There is little danger of that.' He turned to the bewildered military man, still trying to work out if he was privy to a joke or its object. 'Will you excuse us, colonel?'

'Are you always so cruel to your father's colleagues?' Bramall asked as he whisked Isabel towards the centre of the floor. The dance was a waltz, which was fortunate as his tango was rudimentary at best.

'I don't know what you mean.'

He slipped his hand around her waist. 'Oh, I think you do.'

'It's simply that I cannot bear to see the Army and the Air Force, and all the rest, swaggering around Madrid doing nothing while the rest of Europe is at war and the people of Spain are starving.'

'Quite the radical, then.'

They moved in swirls across the dance floor. At one point they found themselves next to the Foreign Minister, Beigbeder, partnering a striking-looking woman who Isabel said was a French countess newly arrived in Madrid.

Bramall heard the name, but forgot it instantly.

'What do you think the Spanish Government *should* be doing?' he asked.

'Staying clear of Hitler and Mussolini. Feeding the people.'

'And what if it joins the Axis instead?'

'That will not happen,' she said. 'If it did, I would have to leave the country.'

Bramall wheeled her round. 'The first thing they'd do is attack Gibraltar, and then things really would be serious.'

'Is that all you care about? Holding on to your empire?'

'It's not the empire, Señorita Ortega. I don't give a fig for the empire. It's the fact that without Gibraltar Britain would lose the war – and then where would we be?'

Isabel thought about this for several seconds, but before she could reply, the waltz ended and the airforce colonel appeared at her side.

'Señorita Ortega,' he began, 'you move so beautifully that I am almost too embarrassed to ask, but may I have the honour of the next dance?'

'But of course, my dear Colonel. I should be delighted.'

The music swelled up. As Bramall looked on, Isabel turned her head towards him. 'Call me,' she said.

Bramall bowed in her direction. This girl was trouble. He knew it. Time for a spot of air, he told himself.

Madrid: German Legation, July 1

Paul Winzer a *Gestapo kriminalkommissar* and the Legation's police attaché, with the SS rank of *hauptsturmführer*, did not wholly approve of his colleague Klaus Hasselfeldt, whom he considered both impulsive and unstable. In spite of being just thirty-two years-old, Winzer had a long history in Madrid. He had helped train Franco's Secret Police, the *Dirección General de Seguridad*, and was adept at kidnapping. He was methodical and cool-headed – a believer in archives and the building up of files of evidence. He did not believe in the current doctrine of jumping in with both feet, which he attributed to a rush to the head brought on by his country's unalloyed military triumphs.

This morning he had arrived early to talk with Hasselfeldt about the Duke of Windsor. He knew from his own contacts among the Spanish that something was brewing. Berlin was reticent about the matter, but he called in a few favours and now felt he had sufficient facts with which to construct a theory. Ribbentrop, he decided, had picked up on the *Führer's* half-baked notion that the Duke could turn England against the war. It was all too predictable. Left with nothing to do now that diplomacy arrived out of the barrel of a gun, the foreign minister was reduced to mischief-making – and fantasy.

The reality of the war with England was difficult enough without such meddling. Göring had promised Hitler that the *Luftwaffe* would sweep the RAF out of the skies and leave England open to invasion. But what if he was wrong? An invasion without mastery of the air would be hazardous in the extreme. In that event, the leadership would be looking for new ways of taking the war forward. One, which he found particularly intriguing, began with a German-led assault on Gibraltar, which had interested both the High Command and elements of the Spanish military. Winzer considered the Gibraltar scheme a sensible proposition, with a high probability of success so long as Franco could be brought on board. It would knock England out of the war at a stroke. The alternative, trying to open a diplomatic second front, using the Duke as honest broker, was the sort of wishful thinking he associated with Ribbentrop. The minister's fingerprints were all over it. Winzer considered it both impractical and mad. The question was, since both approaches required the intervention of the Legation, where did Hasselfeldt stand?

At seven-fifteen, he heard the Austrian's boots on the stairs. He did so love his uniform. 'Good morning, Klaus,' he called out, putting his head round his office door. 'Care for some coffee?'

'Yes, please. But you're up early.'

'Business. The war isn't all about Blitzkrieg. Each of us has our part to play.'

'Indeed.'

Hasselfeldt entered Winzer's well-ordered office and sat down, leaving the *Gestapo* officer to pour the coffee and bring it to him.

'You must be extremely busy these days,' Winzer began.

'Oh, you know …'

'I mean, with Ribbentrop obsessed with the Duke and him about to leave for England.'

The SD officer looked as if someone had slapped his face. 'What makes you say that?'

'I keep in touch.'

'Are you involved in some way?'

'Don't you know?'

'Are you going to tell me?'

Winzer smiled to himself. This was going better than he had

hoped. 'Listen, my friend,' he said, 'the *Wilhelmstrasse* may say now that all it wants is surveillance and 'indications' of the Duke's mood while he is here in Spain. But Ribbentrop, you should realise, is impulsive and volatile. You should take nothing for granted. If you want my advice, have a plan drawn up and ready to go, so that they can't take you by surprise. Don't rule out any option, not even a pre-emptive strike. Face it, the Duke is never going to agree to join us voluntarily. Oh, he may wish things were different. His wife, too. But until they are, he has no choice but to do Churchill's bidding. What are you going to do if Berlin says it wants him set up to negotiate with the *Führer* and then you find out that the Duke has left for London?'

'Are you suggesting we kidnap him?'

'You tell me.'

Hasselfeldt took off his glasses and held them up to the light before rubbing the lenses with a clean white handkerchief. 'What part does the *Gestapo* play in all this?' he asked, thoughtfully.

'I'm afraid we have other preoccupations.'

'Such as?'

'Helping to persuade our Spanish friends that their future lies with us.'

'You mean the Big Picture?'

'The same picture, just a bigger frame.'

Hasselfeldt sipped his coffee. He remembered the confrontation between Stohrer and Serrano Suñer: the degree of resentment on the Spaniard's part. 'I doubt the *Führer* is overly bothered with Spain just now.'

'You're probably right. Our work is riddled with blind alleys.'

'So you think I should recommend an abduction?'

'If I were in your shoes,' said Winzer, glancing down at Hasselfeldt's gleaming jackboots. 'A bird in the hand, isn't that what the English say?'

There was a moment's silence as the two men considered their next move. 'Thank you for the coffee – and the advice. You should know how much I admire your professionalism, Paul.'

'And I yours.'

Madrid: Ritz Hotel, July 1

Bramall had decided on an early night and when he heard the discreet knock at the door assumed it was the waiter bringing his supper.

'Come in!' he called out. There was no response. 'I said, come in.' Still nothing. And then the knock was repeated. Swearing, he levered himself out of bed, threw on his dressing gown and made his way to the door. 'Who's there?' he asked.

'Isabel Ortega.'

The name halted him in his tracks. What if one of Hasselfeldt's goons had followed her? What if her father found out? Or Luder? On the other hand, what if she was here to … well, to seduce him? He allowed himself a sharp intake of breath. If so, he would have to deal with it. He checked his robe and opened the door. 'Señorita Ortega, what in the name of …?'

'I need to see you,' she said.

He looked quickly up and down the corridor to check there was no one else about. It was empty. 'Does anybody know you're here? Did anybody recognise you?'

'What are you talking about?' She looked achingly attractive, dressed in a powder blue frock that barely covered her knees. The neckline of the dress was low, and if her face not been so appealing he would have found it difficult to keep his eyes from her cleavage. But what was she up to? He may not have read all the way through the agent's handbook yet, but he was sure this was the oldest trick in it. He clutched his hand to his head, which was now throbbing. 'Just tell me,' he said. 'Were you followed? Did anyone in the lobby appear to be especially interested in your arrival?'

She looked at him. He was sure she was flirting with him. 'Well, I did notice one or two heads turn in my direction.'

'I didn't mean that.' *Christ!* He had to make a decision. 'You'd better come in,' he said, making way for her, then quickly closing the door and locking it. 'I don't know what you're doing here, but if we're going to talk, we might as well get on with it.'

Isabel placed a tiny clutch bag she was carrying on an occasional table in the centre of the room, beneath a lamp, and then went over to the window, where she stood looking out over the Plaza de la Lealtad. Her hair was tied back with a bright red ribbon. The street lights here were on and she could make out groups of young people and couples arm in arm promenading past on their way to dinner. No starving dogs next to the Ritz. No beggars. No old people robbed of their children. Did Bramall care about such things? She thought she had detected something in his eyes when they spoke before – something plaintive that was missing entirely from the look of the young Spanish men she knew, all of them wary of feeling and only out for what they could get. She turned slowly to face him, tilting her head and pulling a stray batch of hair from in front of her face. He was staring at her.

'I have to tell you, Señorita Ortega, that your presence here shocks me. What would your father think? You're engaged to be married, and in the circumstances I really don't think ...'

'– Nonsense! Who told you I was engaged?'

'I don't know. Someone at the embassy.'

'Well it's not true. My father might think I am engaged. After all, it was he who arranged it when I was just seventeen. And the brute he arranged it with may believe it also. But the fact is, I am not.'

Bramall sighed. 'Listen to me,' he began. She really was stunning.

'No. First, you must listen to me.'

He gave up. 'Very well,' he said.

'I'm not what you think I am,' she said.

'And what might that be?'

'The pampered, empty-headed daughter of a senior government official who contrived to avoid the entire horror of the Civil War by staying with family in Buenos Aires.'

'Actually I had no idea you were in Argentina. That must have been how you met your fiancé.'

Isabel's eyes narrowed. She had considered seducing Bramall, but she did not take well to these constant knowing references to her and Luder. 'He's not my fiancé,' she said. 'We're not lovers and we never will be.' She looked into Bramall's eyes to see how he was taking this piece of frankly intimate news. All she could see was a studied blankness. The whole idea of seducing someone older had appealed to her for years, ever since she turned fourteen and saw the change in the way men regarded her and the looks they gave her when they thought she couldn't see. They undressed her with their eyes. She could read their techniques. Some would start with her skirt. If she parted her legs only slightly, they would fix their eyes on her knees, hoping to see whatever she might reveal next. Others would concentrate on her breasts, which had achieved an early and sustained popularity, having a youthful firmness to them that she knew drove men mad with lust. Only a few – and Bramall, she thought, was one – looked first and foremost at her face, on which this evening she had lavished considerable attention. Now, as she studied his reaction to her surprise arrival in his bedroom, the thought of what must be going through his mind was positively intriguing.

'The point is,' she said, 'that I am not a Fascist, or even a Fascist sympathiser. I am a patriot. And if I'm any judge of character, you are too. 'Friend of the Party' just won't do, Señor Bramall. There's something you're not telling me.'

'I'm afraid you have me at a loss.'

'To begin with, you're not the equerry sort. You're interested in events, politics, the war – not place settings and knowing how to bow backwards out of a room.'

Bramall turned away, remembering Hasselfeldt's warning. 'That may be,' he said. 'But the point is that your arrival here, like this, is not something that my superiors, or your father, would readily understand. There are other factors, too, which I so not propose to discuss. Suffice it to say that it's dangerous for you to be seen with me. Dangerous for both of us – for all sorts of reasons. You have got to leave right now and then you have got to stay away from me. Do you understand?'

Isabel felt a knot of frustration rise in her throat.

Bramall continued his harrangue, though it pained him to

do so. 'You should understand that I have a lot on my mind. Madrid these days is a very serious place. A great deal is happening, and I have things I need to get on with – things that, with respect, are no concern of yours.'

'Such as?'

'Such as dinner and a good night's sleep in my own bed.' He picked up her bag from the table and handed it to her. 'So now, if you will excuse me ...'

He was finding this very hard. It went against his every instinct.

'Aren't you going to invite me to join you?'

'To which? Dinner or my bed?'

'Which would you prefer?'

'Goodnight, Señorita Ortega.' Placing his hand lightly on her waist, he attempted to guide her to the door.

'It's about Gibraltar. That's it, isn't it? That's why you're here.'

Shit! He grabbed her arm and pulled her hard towards him. 'Who told you that?'

'Please! You're hurting me.'

He released her. What she had said was probably no more than a lucky guess, but now he had given the game away.

'I'm right, aren't I?' She was staring at him. He looked away, unable to meet her gaze.

'Tell me,' he said, 'is there any way I can persuade you to go back to your home and get on with your life and never mention any of this to anyone?'

'That depends.'

'On what?'

'On you. I need to know whose side you're on and what it is you hope to achieve. Do you care about Spain, do you care about defeating the Germans, or are you just a Fascist stooge?'

As she spoke, there was a sharp knock at the door. 'Oh fuck,' said Bramall. 'That must be my supper.'

'Do you want me to hide in the bathroom? Like in the films?'

'What? No! Well … yes, I suppose so.'

'Ask him for some champagne.'

As soon as she closed the door behind her, Bramall coughed and called out, 'Enter!'

The waiter tried the handle. It was locked. 'Hold on a second,' Bramall said. Pulling his bathrobe tightly about him, he turned the key and pulled back on the door. The waiter, a grey-haired man in his fifties, entered the room carrying a tray.

'Your supper, Señor. A simple paella, like you ordered, and a bottle of water.'

'Thank you. Just put it over there, would you?'

'*Si, Señor.*' The waiter deposited the tray on a table next to the bed and hovered for a second, waiting for his tip.

Bramall found himself saying, 'Do you think you could bring me a bottle of champagne?'

'Champagne?'

'Yes. Would that be possible?'

'Of course, Señor. A bottle of champagne. For one. It will take a few minutes.'

'Not a problem.' As the waiter left, Bramall wondered if he suspected anything. Well, what if he did? It wouldn't be the first time a gentleman entertained a lady in his room at the Ritz Hotel.

'He's gone!' he called out.

Just for a second, Bramall wondered if Isabel might have taken her clothes off in the bathroom. It would be such a cliché.

Then again, if clichés weren't true, they wouldn't be clichés. But when she emerged, moments later, she was fully clothed. Was he relieved or disappointed? Both, he realised. He was just glad that he was wearing a thick robe. The only thing he could see that was different was that she had untied her hair, which now fell loose about her shoulders. What did it mean? What was she trying to tell him?

'So do we talk now?' she said.

'Sit down.' He decided he would pretend that he hadn't noticed the change in her hair.

There was an armchair by the window, next to a two-seater sofa. 'I'll sit here, you sit there,' she said, indicating the sofa. As she sat back, she curled her legs up beneath her, causing the hem of her skirt to rise up above her knees.

He tried not to look at her legs. 'What do you want to know?'

'The truth. What are you doing here?'

The ensuing pause lasted several seconds.

'I work for the British Government.'

'So your work for the Duke is just a cover?'

'Not exactly. I do, in fact, keep an eye on him. He's a bit of a loose cannon.'

'So I've heard.'

He decided to plunge straight in – apparently his standard *modus operandi*, he realised. Better to be hung for a sheep than a lamb. 'The truth is, I'm here to assess the chances that Spain might join the war. As you can imagine, the arrival of *Wehrmacht* forces here would not exactly be welcomed by the British government. What you said about me and Gibraltar, was that just a guess?'

'Not exactly.'

'What, then?'

'I've heard my father talking. I know that Franco wants it back – and a whole lot more besides. I know that the Germans are interested. And I know that your side are pretty desperate to hold on to it.'

'You're very well informed.'

'I move in the right circles.'

This was true, Bramall realised with a start. 'What's your own opinion?' he asked.

'About Gibraltar?'

'Yes.'

'That it's part of Spain and must be handed back. It's one thing to have captured it during a war two hundred years ago. But to hold on to it against the wishes of the Spanish people after all this time – that is unforgivable.'

'I understand your point of view, of course.'

'But you don't share it?'

'Well … not right now. With the war the way it is, it's one of our few trump cards. Lose it and we might as well say goodbye to any hope of victory. Hitler would shut off the Mediterranean and he and Mussolini would lay siege to Egypt. Before you know it, Britain would be in the same position as France.'

Isabel allowed the hem of her skirt to rise another centimetre or two up her thighs. 'So you're suggesting that Spain should abandon one of its oldest national claims in order to preserve the British Empire? That's asking rather a lot, wouldn't you say?'

'It's about a lot more than preserving the empire,' he said. 'More to the point, it's about stopping Hitler from taking over the whole of Europe, and much of Africa into the bargain. Like it or not, Britain right now is the only defender of freedom still in the game, and Gibraltar is the new front line against tyranny.'

She glared at him, not wanting him to think he had gained the upper hand. 'So why did England not support the Republic? You could have given guns and other supplies to Azaña and Negrín. But you didn't. You and the French did everything you could to make sure that the legitimate Government of Spain was starved of the resources it needed to defend itself against what was a right wing military coup.'

Bramall swept a hand through his hair. She sounded just like bloody Romero. 'I agree with you,' he said. 'You're absolutely right.'

'It was a disgrace.'

'Yes it was.'

'You left it to Hitler and Mussolini to decide the issue.'

'You're right, we did.'

She intensified her glare. 'Is that all you have to say?'

'What do you want me to say? It was indefensible. England was wrong – terribly wrong. France, too. We thought that if we got involved, we would be aiding a Communist takeover on our doorstep.'

'Instead of which you ended up with a Fascist dictatorship.'

Bramall could feel himself starting to become exasperated. 'Well, don't blame me for that,' he said. 'I was a journalist, not a statesman.'

Suddenly, out of nowhere, Isabel saw the face of Teresa Alvarez. She shut her eyes against the image and turned in fury towards Bramall. 'You were here. You saw what happened. You could have done something. You could have warned the British people.'

Bramall shifted uneasily in his chair. 'Don't overestimate

the power of the press. Even when I was in Madrid, I only ever saw a tiny part of the picture – and as far as brutality was concerned, both sides were as bad as each other. What's important now is that England has learned its lesson. We have a new Government, a new Prime Minister – someone who has argued all along that war was coming and it was up to the democracies to prepare themselves. We may have got off to a bit of a bad start, but we're still in the fight.'

Isabel appeared to digest this latest information. 'So what about Gibraltar? If England wins the war and Spain has been helpful, will you hand it back?'

She shifted her legs again.

'That's not for me to say.'

'Ha!'

'Well, I'm sorry, I'm not in the fortune-telling business. But I will hazard this much: if Franco joins the Axis and then Hitler loses the war, hell will freeze over before Churchill agrees to any kind of deal.'

'That would be logical. But what if we end up on the winning side? You have to admit, the Germans are doing rather well just now.'

'In that case, things will be worse than anything you can imagine. It would be the beginning of a new dark age. Ownership of Gibraltar would at that point be the least of all our problems.'

Isabel sat up and pulled her skirt down. She tried to imagine how she would feel if word arrived that England had been invaded and Churchill had been shot. It would spell the end of freedom not just for a generation in Europe, but for generations to come. 'Very well,' she said, the tone suggesting a hard-won concession. 'We have all done things of which we are ashamed. What do you want me to do?'

Bramall felt a frisson of relief course through him. It wasn't so much that he thought Isabel could actually be useful; it was just good to know that she wouldn't be a thorn in his side. 'What can I tell you?' he said. 'Keep me informed. Tell me anything you hear. Other than that, stay out of trouble.'

She looked straight at him. 'When will I see you again?'

Bramall sighed. 'That's going to be a problem, I'm afraid.'

'Why?'

'The thing is, I know Luder.' Isabel's eyes registered her shock. 'Or at least, we've met. I was a diplomat in Buenos Aires and I ran into him a couple of times. We discussed business and his assessment of the situation in Europe. The usual stuff. He's a Nazi, working for Berlin. Most people have good sides and bad sides. Not Luder. All he thinks about is money and power, and he doesn't care who gets hurt in the process. More to the point, people are frightened of him. Women especially. And with good reason.'

This analysis did not appear to take Isabel by surprise. 'I know all about that ... side of him.'

Bramall leaned forward in his chair. A sudden, detestable image had entered his head. 'You don't mean that he ...?'

She blushed. 'No, no. He didn't ... violate me. There were too many people around and, anyway, my uncle would have shot him. But I could tell that he wanted to. I could see it in his eyes. The thought of it excited him, I'm sure of it. And if I don't get away from him, one day he'll do it.'

'Not if I'm around, he won't,' Bramall said hurriedly.

A satisfied expression crossed the young Spaniard's features.

Bramall had lost the initiative and he knew it. Suddenly, though, he didn't care. He watched her as she touched a finger to her lips and studied him for what seemed an eternity. Eventually she spoke. 'So are we friends now?'

Bramall's mind raced. 'Well,' he said, 'it complicates matters. But it looks as if I'm stuck with you.'

'How awful for you. I'll try not be a burden.'

Bramall grinned. 'You could never be that,' he said.

'What do you mean?'

'I mean that I'm glad you decided to come here tonight. Not just because you may be of assistance to me – though that's obviously welcome – but because, well ... it's been a long time since I met a young woman as ... *beguiling* as you.'

She smiled at him through half-closed eyes. 'I think I should go,' she said.

'Yes,' he said. 'I think you should.'

Madrid: British embassy, July 2

The Windsors' car, an elderly Buick, driven by a member of the Intelligence Service, with an armed colleague in the front passenger seat, was drawn up outside the embassy ready for the trip to Lisbon. Behind it was a Citroën, with an embassy security guard at the wheel, for the conveyance of the Windsor's friend and neighbour in Antibes, Captain George Woods, his Viennese wife, Rosa, and two small border terriers, as well as the redoubtable Buchanan-Smith. Hoare had briefly inquired about the appropriateness of an enemy national, Rosa Woods, as part of the entourage but was assured by the Duke that she didn't have a political thought in her head, which he reluctantly accepted. Jeanne-Marguerite Moulichon, the Duchess's *lingère* and maid, was left behind, charged with fetching more of their belongings from Paris. In the absence of the Duke's valet, Fletcher, whom London had returned to front-line duties with the Army, there were no actual servants among the party, which meant a greater reliance on friends and other third parties. Thus, the third car in the convoy, pulling a trailer filled with luggage and personal effects, was driven by a Spanish police officer accompanied by two members of the *Guardia Civil*.

Hoare, who had cabled both Churchill and Halifax with the news that the Duke was on his way to Lisbon, thence to the governorship of the Bahamas, was relieved that his time as chaperon to the royal party was almost at an end. Churchill's decision to provide the renegade royal with an minor imperial role was exactly the response he had been praying for. God knows, the nine days in Madrid had taken their toll on him, bringing on several fits of depression. This morning, however, he was the picture of bonhomie – so much so that he was humming 'The Lady is a Tramp,' by Rodgers & Hart, when the former king came sauntering down the embassy steps wearing a pale grey suit with lemon pinstripes set off by white spats. There was some paperwork to clear up and he had requested a last-minute chat with the PM in London, which meant using a secure line. But now, at long last, everything was in place.

Hoare's voice exhibited a judicious mix of respect and affection. 'Time for the off, sir. Nothing too taxing by the sound of it. The Spanish security services will be close by at all times. A suite has been booked for tonight at the Hotel Nacional in Mérida. Upon your arrival at the frontier in the morning,

Portuguese officials will take over and a representative from the embassy in Lisbon will escort you to the Hotel Palacio in Estoril, which I am sure Your Royal Highness and the Duchess will find most agreeable.'

'We're obliged to you, Hoare,' said the Duke. 'Hope we didn't cause you too much trouble. Know this must be a busy time for you.'

'Not at all, sir. You made many friends, and the reception on Saturday was quite the talk of the town

'Very good. Tell Bramall we look forward to seeing him in Lisbon.'

'Indeed, sir.'

The Duchess, looking pale and drawn, as if she hadn't slept, extended her hand, the back of which Hoare brushed briefly with his lips.

'So, Ambassador,' she said, in the husky accent that seemed to the Englishman a fruity mix of Baltimore and the Home Counties. 'It's goodbye – again. Or should I should say, 'adieu?' We are grateful to you for everything you have done.'

'Thank you, ma'am. I am, as always, at your service.'

And that was it. The last thing His Majesty's principal envoy to Spain heard from the royal party was the yelping of the border terriers. He waved, then turned on his heels, avoiding the temptation to break into a jig. As he mounted the steps of his embassy, he felt like a jaded husband whose wife has just left for a month in the country. He was a free man again. His life was his own and there was nothing he could not accomplish.

Mers-el-Kebir, Bay of Oran, French North Africa: July 3

Vice Admiral Marcel Gensoul, in command of the French fleet in Oran, didn't need to be told that his ships were sitting ducks. At sea, they presented a formidable force. There were the brand-new battleships Dunkerque and Strasbourg, backed up by the more venerable Provence and Bretagne, plus a seaplane carrier, six large destroyers, a dozen torpedo boats, six submarines and a gaggle of oilers and supply ships. But they were at anchor, their boilers unlit. To make things worse, they were clustered together in an unfinished harbour, lacking even the security provided by a concrete outer wall.

As dawn broke, it promised to be another hot African day, airless and stifling. Gensoul, a handsome, upright figure approaching his sixtieth birthday, lamented his situation. At the time of the Armistice he assumed the fleet would sail for British waters, to fight on with De Gaulle. Instead, High Admiral Darlan, the only commander-in-chief of the Marine de Guerre never to have commanded a ship, had thrown in his lot with Pétain and ordered him to Mers to await instructions. Gensoul took a sip of mint tea. The Royal Navy's newly assembled Force H was almost upon him. They would arrive off Oran within the hour and he could only guess at what would follow. He knew that a number of French ships in English ports were already commandeered and that others had volunteered to fight on under British orders. In such cases, French commanders felt able to make their own decisions. But Gensoul was not in charge of a scratch flotilla. He could not sign away half the navy on a whim. What he needed was direction – and fast. Force H, operating out of Gibraltar, was powerful. It comprised two battleships, the Resolution and the Valiant; the battlecruiser Hood and the aircraft carrier Ark Royal; as well as two cruisers and a flotilla of eight destroyers. Gensoul, in order to do the right thing, had to know what was expected of him. But his people, exiled in Bordeaux (or was it Vichy? – he didn't know where his orders came from any more), were silent as the grave. All they had done was confine him to port. He would have given anything to lead his force back into battle alongside his brothers in the Royal Navy. But he would not tolerate naked threats to the safety of his ships. France had been humiliated enough. He cranked the telephone on his desk.

'Give me Signals.'

'Yes, Admiral.'

The voice of the duty officer came through seconds later.

'Cresson.'

'What news?'

'None, Admiral.'

'Then signal them again. We cannot remain indefinitely in a vacuum.'

'Yes, sir. At once.'

At 8.05, as the temperature on board the flagship Dunkerque registered twenty-four degrees Celsius, and rising, a Royal Navy destroyer, the Foxhound, approached the entrance to the harbour at Mers. It paused, not crossing the line. A launch was lowered that slowly puttered across to the central point of the anchorage, where it was met by Gensoul's barge. A fresh-faced lieutenant handed over a note marked: 'Most Confidential. Vice Admiral Somerville RN, Task Force H, to Vice Admiral Gensoul, commander French Squadron, Oran.' Five minutes later, Gensoul opened the envelope and started to read. It was worse than he had feared.

It is impossible for us, your comrades up to now, to allow your fine ships to fall into the power of the German or Italian enemy. 'We are determined to fight on until the end, and if we win, as we think we shall, we will never forget that France was our Ally, that our interests are the same as hers, and that our common enemy is Germany. Should we prevail, we solemnly declare that we shall restore the greatness and territory of France. For this purpose we must make sure that the best ships of the French Navy are not used against us by the common foe. In these circumstances, His Majesty's Government have instructed me to demand that the French Fleet now at Mers el Kebir and Oran shall act in accordance with one of the following alternatives:

The four options were then listed: sail with Somerville and continue the fight; sail with reduced crews to a British port, where the French ships would be immobilised; sail to a French port in the West Indies; scuttle the squadron.

The note concluded:

Failing the above, I have orders from His Majesty's Government to use whatever force may be necessary to prevent your ships from falling into German or Italian hands.

Gensoul sat in stunned silence for more than a minute after reading the ultimatum. It was as if his entire world had collapsed around him. Then he called for a pen and paper.

In no circumstances, he wrote, would his ships be allowed to fall into Axis hands. This would be contrary to French policy and principals. But neither would he, as commander of a French Squadron, act under duress. In the event that the Royal Navy took precipitate action against his ships, force would be met with force.

Handing the note, in an envelope, to his staff officer, marked for the attention of Somerville, Gensoul ordered that a further signal be sent at once to the French admiralty: 'I have been informed that I either surrender my ships or face their immediate destruction. What are your orders?'

To his surprise, a return signal (intercepted by the British) instructed him to open immediate negotiations. At the same time, his ships were to get up steam and await reinforcements. All French ships in the Mediterranean were ordered to proceed to his position. Gensoul was to hold fast, protect his force and await their arrival. It wasn't much of a lifeline, the admiral concluded, especially since the nearest French ships were at best half a day's sailing from Oran. But it was something. It gave him a bargaining counter.

On the bridge of his flagship, Admiral Somerville recalled a dinner he had shared with Gensoul and his senior officers onboard the Dunkerque only six months before. He knew full well that the Frenchman was both a patriot and a defender of democratic freedom. It distressed him beyond words to realise the immense and unfair pressure he was heaping on a friend.

Churchill, who had twice served as First Lord of the Admiralty, was equally aware of the horror his policy was about to unleash, and while reinforcing the importance of the mission did what he could to offer his support. 'You are charged with one of the most disagreeable and difficult tasks that a British admiral has ever been faced with,' he cabled from Downing

Street, 'but we have complete confidence in you and rely on you to carry it out relentlessly.'

Somerville read the signal without comment, knowing that in the end the only two players who mattered were himself and Gensoul. Captain Cedric Holland, commander of the Ark Royal and a fluent French speaker, was theoretically his intermediary. But Holland, now on board the Foxhound, was unable to talk with the French commander face to face. He was negotiating by letter, then signalling Somerville for further instructions. As lunchtime came and went, with the temperature on board the ships of both fleets soaring into the forties, word came that French tugs had begun working to release the Strasbourg and Dunkerque from their moorings.

Somerville ordered the mining of the harbour. 'Instruct Gensoul that if his ships attempt to put to sea, they risk imminent destruction.'

Minutes later, a group of Swordfish light bombers from the Ark Royal flew across the harbour mouth and dropped contact mines in full view of the French. Almost simultaneously, the 13-inch guns of the Strasbourg and the Dunkerque began to rotate.

Signals came and went. London grew increasingly impatient. Sometime after three, Somerville signalled to Holland. 'Does anything you have said prevent me opening fire?'

Holland, in despair, replied: 'Nothing I have said, since terms were not discussed, only handed in and reply received.'

The sun blazed down, glinting off the metal of the Hood's 15-inch guns. Onshore, a group of four French shore batteries were uncovered and made ready for use.

Late in the afternoon, with shadows lengthening, Somerville

sent Gensoul a further, despairing cable:

If one of the British proposals is not accepted by 1730 BSM, I must sink your ships.

Back came the reply from Gensoul, in English:

Do not create the irreparable.

In Vichy, Darlan was under pressure from Laval to strike a blow for French arms. The admiral did not, in fact, need any prompting in this matter. He loathed the British, frequently recalling that his great grandfather had died at Trafalgar. When he ordered his ships into battle, it was in the knowledge that the French squadron at Alexandria was in active discussions with the British and in no position to assist. Only a handful of French ships in the Mediterranean enjoyed freedom of action, and none, apart from a couple of submarines based down the coast in Oran, were within striking distance of Mers. France could only trust to Gensoul and hope for the best.

Madrid: Office of Interior Minister Serrano Suñer, July 3

Bramall was ushered into Serrano's office through double doors that would have admitted a man twice his height. The doors were grandiloquent. They spoke of a man of gigantic stature. In fact, the minister, crouched behind his ormolu encrusted desk, seemed to have shrunk since Bramall saw him last. He was dressed in his Party uniform, a pale imitation of SS garb, minus the jackboots. In place of the oak leaves and braided threads of the Death's Head hierarchy, he sported the traditional Yoke and Arrows badge of the Falange, dating back to the time of the *Reconquista*, and looked more like an airline pilot than a paramilitary chief. His office was both tasteful and efficiently organised. Filling one entire wall were glass panelled bookshelves lined with legal volumes and what looked like party archive material, while prominently displayed on a side table were two copies of *Mein Kampf*, one in the original German, the second translated into Spanish as *Mi Lucha*.

There was a pile of identical-looking documents on his desk. Bramall wondered if they might be death warrants and flinched as several were signed in quick succession.

At length, Serrano looked up, screwing the top back onto his fountain pen. 'Señor Bramall, is it not? Come to nursemaid your former king. I trust you are well?'

'Never better, sir. Spain obviously agrees with me.'

'I'm glad to hear it.' The minister rose to his feet and made his way round his desk. He was tall as well as slender. They did not shake hands. Bramall had been warned that his host was something of a hypocondriac and did not welcome human contact. There were two armchairs set either side of a window overlooking the Puerta del Sol, and Serrano folded himself into one, his long legs exposed like the blades of a penknife. Bramall dutifully sat opposite him.

There was a short pause. *'Muy bien!'* The minister drew the left sleeve of his jacket over the gold watch on his wrist, then sat back and crossed his legs. 'I understand that the Duke will not be returning to England.'

'That's right. He has been appointed Governor of

the Bahamas.'

'What does that suggest to you?'

'That Nassau is a lot further away from London than Madrid.'

Serrano registered silent agreement. 'And his time in Lisbon?'

'Not yet determined. Part of my remit is to remain here in case His Royal Highness should decide to return.'

'You think that likely?'

'I know he enjoyed his time here. He felt he was among friends and more able to express himself. He was also, I think, intrigued by the Foreign Minister's suggestion of a house near Seville.'

'Ah yes. I've no doubt he would find it agreeable.' Serrano leaned forward. 'We are men of the world, Señor Bramall. Just between us, what are the chances he might take Beigbeder up on his offer?'

'I consider it a possibility. I wouldn't put it higher than that.'

'It would be a slap in the face for Churchill.'

'True. But it could be borne. In any case, after all that's happened in recent years, His Royal Highness may well feel that such a blow would not be entirely inappropriate.'

The comment, indicating a break with protocol, was met with a thin smile.

Bramall was not sure whether to go on. Serrano was obviously interested in his opinions. But if he played up the possibility of a royal rumpus and then the ex-king departed meekly for the Bahamas, how would it look?

Serrano twisted in his chair to look out of the window into the square below, where two beggars, a woman and her small daughter, were being moved on by a policeman. 'You will, of course, have heard the news,' he said at length.

'You mean the business at Oran? I'm afraid I know very little, sir. Just what I learned in my hotel before setting out to come here. What information do you have?'

'There is much confusion. But it looks as if the French admiral has been issued with an ultimatum: join the British or see his ships sent to the bottom. It would appear, Señor Bramall, that your Prime Minister is not a sentimental man.'

Bramall looked away. 'What alternative does he have? He couldn't let the French fleet become an instrument of the Axis powers.'

For several long seconds, the Spaniard appeared to reflect on the character of the British war leader. Then he turned back to his guest. 'Like you,' he said, 'I await to see what will happen. But it is by any standard an extraordinary affair.'

'You're right, of course. We can only hope that the two sides will somehow arrive at a peaceful solution.'

Serrano continued to look thoughtful. 'Which brings me to my next point. In the event that Spain should agree not to join the present European conflict, what do you imagine would be the attitude of the United Kingdom towards the future status of Gibraltar?'

Bramall breathed in. It was a question that got right to the heart of his mission. 'That is a matter you should raise with our ambassador,' he said at last. 'How can you trust anything I tell you on so vital a subject?'

'Come, come, Señor Bramall. There is no need to dissemble. I am not asking you to betray your country, I am asking your opinion.'

'Well, Minister, if you press me, I would have to say that there are those in London sympathetic to the Spanish claim.'

'Including Churchill?'

'*In extremis*, yes – and these are extreme times. But Lord Halifax, I am reliably informed, is already willing to consider the issue, providing of course that some arrangements can be made for the re-disposition of the Royal Navy in the western Mediterranean.'

'In Morocco, for example.'

'That would certainly be one possibility. The Ceuta peninsula could conceivably be traded for Gibraltar, allowing both our countries to move forward with dignity.'

Serrano's eyes turned upwards to the ceiling and he clasped his hands behind his neck. 'Suppose, then, that Spain remains neutral. Perhaps we are even helpful to the British position. And at the end of the war, negotiations are opened on Gibraltar. How likely is it, do you suppose, that London would support Spanish claims elsewhere? I'm thinking in particular of Morocco and Oran. We cannot expect Pétain and the French to be in favour, but what of your Mr Churchill?'

Bramall sensed that everything up to that moment had been no more than a gentle probing exercise but that now they were reaching the crux of the matter. Gibraltar and North Africa were clearly not separate issues; they were the same issue. If he was able to convince Serrano that Britain was flexible on both, then he might actually begin to justify his existence in Madrid. 'You raise an interesting prospect, Minister,' he began. 'Should the French fleet be attacked in Oran, it will take a generation at least for France and Britain to become reconciled. Even if he doesn't go to war, Pétain is bound to break off diplomatic links. In such circumstance, always assuming that British interests are not threatened, ours, I feel sure, would be a neutral voice.'

How that had gone down? he wondered. Did it make any sense?

'Fascinating,' said Serrano. 'But what if Spain were to take the alternative route? What if we abandoned "non-belligerence" and joined the war?'

'Then, sir,' said Bramall, feeling tiny beads of sweat break out on his forehead, 'the die would be well and truly cast. Anything could happen. It seems to me that Britain is over the worst militarily and will grow in strength from this point on. And with the United States in the wings, the fighting could go on for years. Even if Spain and Germany succeeded in storming Gibraltar, Churchill would insist on retaliatory strikes – most obviously in Morocco and the Canaries. You could end up losing territory instead of gaining it. Germany would join you, of course, in defending your rights, but what then? Spain and France have claims in Africa. Italy, too, of course – the *Duce* talks almost every day about beefing up his Libyan possessions. But what about Germany? The *Kaiser* objected to Spanish expansionism in Morocco in 1906 and again in 1911. I can't see Hitler joining a protracted war in Africa only to sit back as others divide up the choicest properties among themselves.'

So far, he thought, he had done well against the polished and indefatigable Serrano. But he didn't want to push his luck. Now would be a good moment for the minister to bring an end to the discussion. Instead, the Spaniard uncrossed his legs and with the backs of his fingers brushed several items of imaginary fluff from the trousers of his uniform.

'What you have argued makes sense,' he said, 'even if it is a little self-serving – which is entirely understandable. I note that you take no account of the naval strength of Italy. This seems to me to be a mistake. I spoke yesterday on the telephone to Count Ciano. Have you met him?' Bramall shook his head at mention of the Italian foreign minister. 'A delightful man,' Serrano continued. 'More like Canaris. So much more *obliging* than Ribbentrop. The *Duce*, he tells me, considers the Mediterranean to have been transformed into a prison by the British, who sit as sentinels at either end, controlling who enters and who leaves. But – and on this he was most insistent – Italy will not remain supine forever.'

The minister lolled back in his chair, observing his guest over the tops of his steepled fingers, the nails of which were more perfectly manicured than any society girl's. 'You are a difficult man to read, Señor Bramall,' he said. 'I have the strong feeling that you know more than you are saying. Is this because you are a natural diplomat or it is because you are not telling the whole truth? We have examined your *curriculum vitae* most carefully and have discovered several things. Among these is that you reported fairly and honourably on our cause during the recent war. You were are a friend of the *Times* Correspondent, Philby, who was of course decorated by the *Caudillo* himself. Was there something about you and Philby getting drunk afterwards? Possibly. I don't remember.'

When Bramall only smiled, Serrano pressed on. 'Another thing we learned was that you have an almost astonishing spread of social and political contacts. There is the Duke, obviously, but also Downing Street, the Foreign Office, the British military hierarchy, even the former BUF leader, sir Oswald Mosley. You are young and hold no special rank in society and yet there seems to be no door that is not open to you, my own included. Is it your charm, do you think, or do you know where the bodies are buried?'

Bramall swallowed and affected what he hoped was a puzzled expression. 'You have me at a disadvantage, Don Ramón,' he said. 'But it would be wrong to imagine that I occupy some bizarre, elevated place in my country's inner circles. You mentioned my father. He didn't raise me to be a radical. I have served as a soldier and a diplomat and I hear what people tell me. I am also a lover of Spain – the true Spain. Because of my background, from time to time I learn of things that my Government would rather remained confidential …'

' – But which drive events and policy.'

'On occasion, certainly. But see things from my perspective. I am sitting now with one of the most powerful men in Spain. Does this mean that I direct Spanish policy?'

A mischievous smile played about Serrano's patrician features. 'Just so, just so. Your point is taken. But what about your ambassador, sir Samuel Hoare? He was for some years a senior Minister. Does he enjoy similar … access?'

Bramall gritted his teeth. 'I don't doubt it for a second. I know that his appointment to Madrid was well received in my father's circles and that Sir Samuel and Lord Halifax remain intimates. But my role here, such as it is, is not connected to the embassy. I have only met the ambassador once, with the Duke, and he made it clear that he did not include me in his plans.'

'That is candid, at any rate.'

'I have no reason to lie. As I have always said, I am a friend of Spain.'

Serrano studied Bramall for a second down the length of his nose. Then he consulted his watch and rose fluidly to his feet, indicating that the interview was at an end. 'Your conversation has been most stimulating,' he said. 'I am sure we shall meet again.'

'Thank you, Minister. You are extremely generous.'

As if by magic, Serrano's secretary, Señorita Casares, appeared in the doorway. She looked as if she had just returned from the hairdresser's.

'Please show Señor Bramall out,' the Spaniard said. 'Arrange for a car to take him to his next destination. Oh, and before he leaves, could you find for him a copy of our outstanding claim to Gibraltar and North Africa. There must be one somewhere.'

'Of course, Minister. I will fetch it personally.'

'I think you will find it interesting reading, Señor Bramall.'

'I'm sure I shall, sir.'

Bramall and Casares retreated into the minister's outer office, leaving Serrano himself gazing into the quare below.

'If you would wait here, Señor Bramall,' Casares said, indicating a chair by the window. 'I will be two minutes.'

'Of course.'

As soon as the secretary had gone, leaving the door from her office into the corridor slightly ajar, Bramall began, somewhat hesitantly, to survey the contents of her desk. He didn't have the gall to try the filing cabinets. There was a sheet of paper in the typewriter. He bent over the machine. *Good God!* It was the first two paragraphs of a letter to the Italian Foreign Minister, Count Ciano. He scrolled it up, click by click, reminded of the time in Cambridge when he examined the personal correspondence of his head of college. Serrano (for who else could it be?), wished the Duce well in his continuing prosecution of the war, but then asked for a reaffirmation of Italy's support for Spanish claims in respect of North Africa, which were now, apparently, 'under review in Berlin.' Oran was mentioned specifically. There was also a reference to 'disorder' in French Morocco, whatever that meant, and to the possibility of Spanish 'intervention,' in the near future. Nothing more: Casares had obviously been interrupted in mid-stream. Carefully scrolling the typewriter carriage back to its original position, he switched his attention to the leather-bound desk diary. Over the next few days, it told him, Serrano would meet twice with Franco and once with Beigbeder. There were also meetings pencilled in with the editors of the newspapers Arriba and ABC, as well as the chief of police and various advisers. He turned the page. Now this was interesting. A scheduled appointment with Sir Samuel Hoare on Monday the 8th was crossed out and in its place was a new entry, in red ink, apparently written in Serrano's own hand: 'German Legation/10.30/ Beigbeder, Vigón to accompany.'

Next to the desk diary was an open notebook. He picked it up. It turned out to be full of ornate squiggles – shorthand, Bramall assumed – that meant nothing to him. But as he was replacing it, his hand knocked against the diary, causing it to slip off the desk. He caught it just before it hit the floor, but not in time to prevent two embossed invitation cards from calling out.

Christ! He could hear footsteps in the hall. Cassares was coming back. Bramall felt the blood boiling in his veins. Stuffing the cards into the diary at random, he replaced the heavy volume on the desktop, then retreated hastily to the chair by the window and stared fixedly into the square below. His heart was pounding. The second he sat down, the door to the outer office opened and Serrano's secretary walked into the room.

Bramall turned around, wondering if he looked as guilty as he felt. It had been a desperately close-run thing. 'A wonderful view, Señorita.'

'Yes, Señor Bramall. 'I have the statement of claim for you that the minister asked me to fetch. It's sure to be useful. There is also a car waiting for you outside the front door.'

'Thank you, Señorita. You are most kind. I enjoyed my visit, which was everything I could have wished for. Please convey to the minister my grateful thanks for his time.'

Mers-El-Kébir, French North Africa: July 3

The unthinkable happened at tea time. Out of a cloudless sky, the battlecruiser Hood, the largest British warship afloat, opened up on the French with its secondary armament of 8-inch guns. The intention was to provoke a surrender, or at least a fresh response from Gensoul. But no signal came. Soon after, from its position ten miles offshore, the Hood fired its primary guns, joined almost immediately by the Valiant and the Resolution. Each shell weighed three quarters of a ton and was the length of a small car. The projectiles rained down on the French, huddled together in harbour. The third salvo fired hit the main magazine of the battleship Bretagne, which exploded in a massive fireball, then capsized. Gensoul, rushing to the foredeck of the Dunkerque, saw a group of his sailors, their clothes and hair ablaze, jump from the side of their doomed vessel, only to be crushed when it collapsed on top of them. He would be told later that 977 of the Bretagne's crew had died in the inferno. Consumed by rage, he ordered immediate retaliation. The big guns of the French ships opened up, firing blind. Shore batteries, better positioned, quickly joined in. Crucially, the Strasbourg, newly commissioned but battle-ready, announced that it was ready for instant departure. Gensoul reckoned that his anti-submarine netting, stretched across the harbour mouth, could be used to sweep the British mines. He ordered the nets drawn in, then sent the Strasbourg and its escorts into the maelstrom.

Gensoul's own ship, the Dunkerque, had also got up steam and was ready to join the escape. But no sooner had the flagship shipped its moorings than it was struck by a salvo of British shells and driven off course into the shallows of the harbour, where it quickly ran aground. The Provence, sister ship of the Bretagne, was also damaged. The Mogador, a newly-commissioned 'super' destroyer, blazed in mid-harbour, having lost its stern to a direct hit from a 15-inch shell. Many of its crew had been blown to pieces; others were horribly burned.

Fifteen minutes after the bombardment started, Gensoul signalled a ceasefire. Somerville responded: 'Unless I see your ships sinking, I shall open fire again.' While he awaited a French reply, the British commander instructed his inner ring of ships, mainly destroyers, to withdraw from the harbour mouth, fearing that they could be damaged by the 7.7-inch guns of the coastal batteries. This turned out to be a mistake. At once, out of the smoke of battle, the French destroyers appeared, accelerating to full speed, followed by the prow of the 26,500 tonne Strasbourg.

Captain Holland, by now beating a hasty retreat from the action he had been unable to prevent, could scarcely believe his eyes. The Hood, far from the scene, was ordered to pursue and destroy the breakaway group. Other British guns opened up, hitting several of the runaways and cracking open the funnel of the Strasbourg. But they were too late. The French leviathan, pride of the fleet, moved smoothly through the ocean, en route to the safety of Toulon. For a while, Swordfish from Ark Royal took up the chase, but achieved little. Somerville almost willed the French to succeed. The action in which he had just engaged sickened him.

No British lives were lost, but more than 1,300 French sailors died. Churchill, masking his shame, portrayed the attack as a necessary evil, one that would convince both Hitler and Roosevelt of his ruthlessness in the pursuit of victory. De Gaulle, inconsolable in his grief, would never accept in his heart that the sacrifice had been inevitable. But he did not complain, impressing the prime minister with his dignity. Throughout France and its empire, anti-British feeling plumbed new depths of rancour. 'Remember Oran!' the cry went up. 'Remember Mers!'

Pétain ordered that the anomaly of diplomatic relations with London be broken off at once. From this point on, he announced, the empire would defend itself at all costs. It would become the shining light of French honour. As the Strasbourg and its surviving escorts sailed triumphantly into Toulon that night, Germans and Frenchmen cheered together.

England: Secret Intelligence Service, MI6, Hanslope Park, July 3

Strickland glanced out of his office window. It was one of

those unsettled days, so wearyingly characteristic of the English summer. If you looked carefully, some of the flowers in the park were in bloom, as if they had decided they might as well make the best of things. Others were tight shut. Sun and showers. It had been that way for weeks. Cold, too. He still needed a jumper. Shouldn't grumble, though. A break in the weather was apparently just around the corner. At any rate, that's what they said. He was just about to look up before leaving for home when a signals clerk knocked and handed him a secure cable from the embassy in Madrid. 'Bugger,' he said. 'Give it here.' After signing the chit, he took off his trilby and laid his brolly on the desk. From Bramall, it said. Well, about bloody time. Everything he'd heard about him so far was via Hoare or Croft. He'd been wondering when he'd make contact.

Most Confidential
To Strickland, Iberia & N. Africa Section MI6
From Bramall, Madrid, July 3

Spoke with Serrano today. Discussed British attitudes to Gibraltar and his thoughts on the war. Clear to me that Madrid ready to go along with any German plan that would enable Spain to recover Gibraltar and expand its colonial territory at expense of France. Franco will consider any counter-proposals from UK but sceptical of their value. Had sight of letter from Serrano to Ciano in Rome asking for Italian support for Spanish claims in Africa. Said these claims were 'under review' in Berlin. Serrano gave notice of possible Spanish 'intervention' in French Morocco to quell 'disorder'. Serrano and Beigbeder, plus Vigón, will meet German ambassador at Legation July 8, 10.30 am.

Embassy here confirms that a planned meeting between Serrano and Sir S. Hoare at that time was cancelled without explanation. Suspect Serrano wishes to enter auction. Other issues under control. Duke in Lisbon, Hasselfeldt undecided whether to use me or kill me. No immediate danger I think.

Strickland sat for a moment and blew out his cheeks. Talk about the bleeding obvious! He could have written that memo near as dammit himself. Then he folded the cable and locked it in a metal filing cabinet. Pocketing the key, he put his hat on again, adjusting the brim so that it pointed downwards over his forehead. He nearly forgot his umbrella, but remembered before he reached the front corridor, with its giant chessboard tiles and faintly antiseptic smell, like a hospital. By the time he stepped out onto the turning circle by the main door, it was raining heavily and he wondered if he'd make it to his car without getting soaked through.

Madrid: Ritz Hotel, July 3

Bramall had an uncomfortable feeling that he was getting in over his head. With the Duke now safely in Lisbon, it was time for him concentrate on his main mission. Yet here he was, against all good sense, getting involved with Isabel Ortega. Her motives in approaching him in his hotel were difficult for him to assess. It ought to have been he who was in control. He was nearly ten years older than her; he had been with a number of women in his time. He was an army officer, a diplomat. For

God's sake, he was a *spy*. And yet he had been putty in her hands. It was infuriating, yet strangely compelling.

He poured himself a whisky and read through a memo he had written shortly before Isabel's arrrival – his second that day. He had typed it, using two fingers, on an old Underwood supplied by the hotel. It was to Hasselfeldt and he planned to hand-deliver it next morning.

Sturmbannführer Hasselfeldt,
German Legation,
Madrid

July 3

As you know, the Duke of Windsor left Madrid today for Lisbon, accompanied by the Duchess and his staff. You expressed interest in his views re a possible negotiated peace with Germany.

When we first met in Madrid, at the Ritz hotel, the Duke (who was at the time engaged in conversation with Don Miguel Primo de Rivera), expressed interest in the fact that I had once associated with Sir Oswald Mosley. He said how much he thought that the present Government of Spain, in which he had every confidence, would meet with the Sir Oswald's approval.

The following day, in private, the Duke asked me what I thought about a negotiated peace. I said it would depend on someone's being found whom the British people felt they could trust. The Duke replied: 'I was very popular, you know, when I was Prince of Wales. The people felt then that I understood them. I still understand them and I know that this dreadful war must be ended. It is the worst mistake a British Government has made in a generation.'

At a subsequent lunch with among others foreign Minister Beigbeder, the Duke was as indiscreet as I have heard him in public. Beigbeder asked him at one point if there was a possibility that peace could be restored to Europe. The Duke replied that mutual, unthinking antagonisms were what had brought us to this point. 'Europe is bleeding,' he said. 'Even here, at this table, each of us is bleeding. We have known so much hurt. I don't know how to resolve it. But I tell you this much: someone must make an end.'

Given his sentiments and experience, it seems to me possible, even probable, that His Royal Highness favours talks negotiations between London and Berlin and that he sees himself as a possible bridge-builder. You should realise, however, that Churchill is aware of this tendency and will take steps to negate it. The Duke will be kept under close guard in Lisbon. It will also be made perfectly plain to him where his duty lies. I would not bet on his being persuaded to come into the open on this question.

You should know also that I had a meeting today with Minister Serrano Suñer, who expressed interest in the Duke's intentions but gave me the clear impression that he did not expect him to adopt an anti-Churchill stance. This, in my view, is the attitude of many on the Spanish side.

Steuermann

He had made the second quote up, knowing that the others could be checked, if necessary, with Primo de Rivera and Beigbeder. What it all amounted to, he wasn't sure, but he hoped it would be enough to keep Hasselfeldt off his back while adding nothing of substance to the known facts. If it didn't, then his personal future could be dark indeed. The Austrian was a ruthless bastard and he had made it clear that he didn't trust his latest acquisition. As he made his way to visit Romero in the *tasca*, Bramall could almost feel the noose tighten round his neck.

6

Madrid: Villa Ortega, Calle Beatriz Galindo, July 4, 1940

'What do you mean, Felipe is here?' Isabel was standing at the top of the front stairs when her mother delivered the news that Luder had arrived unexpectedly from Buenos Aires. 'He's not due for another week at least.'

Doña Vittoria rolled her eyes. 'I do not organise your fiancé's travel arrangements, Isabel.'

'And stop calling him my fiancé.'

'Really, darling, not that again.'

Isabel hurried down the stairs. 'Where is he now?'

'He arrived at the airport an hour ago. He has taken a villa next to the war ministry. He'll be round later on, once he's settled in and had a bath. I thought you'd be pleased.'

'Mother!'

'Well, if you're going to spend the rest of your life with him, you might as well get started.'

'You're mad. You and Father. You're both insane.'

'You'd need to talk to your father about that. Anyway, I'm going inside to check with cook on tonight's supper. I expect we'll have to lay an extra place.'

Isabel stamped off into the courtyard. The very idea of Luder disgusted her. She had been just sixteen years old when they first met. She was with her parents in Argentina, visiting her father's brother Rafael, who bred horses in Córdoba. Luder was already coming up on 30 and looked to her adolescent eyes like a combination of butcher and secret policeman. His father, a Bavarian-born adventurer, had opened a beef export business after the Great War that eventually included a small commercial bank. Felipe, an expert horseman and polo player, grew up to run the bank, and with the coming to power of Hitler in Germany presided over seven years of spectacular growth. He had joined the Nazi party in 1936 in Munich, where his father still kept a home. Contracts followed to supply the German armed forces with beef, making made him a wealthy figure in Buenos Aires society. Later, with war imminent, the bank, now with a branch in Zurich, proved useful to the Reich. Isabel had heard that he smuggled all kinds of things out of Latin America intended for the German war effort. In Spain, wolfram was his main interest. No wonder the Nazis loved him.

On the surface, he could be charming. He was attentive to the vanity of women and the egos of men. But Bramall was right about him. He possessed no redeeming qualities. Of this she was sure. In Córdoba, when she was still just a girl, he had run his huge, steak-like hands through her hair and commented on how attractive he found her. At the same time, his eyes bored into her, seeking dominance. It made her tremble with fear. One afternoon, in the trees next to the paddock, when there was no other adults around, he had held her head in an unbreakable grip and kissed, sticking his fat slug of a tongue down her throat so that she almost threw up.

She shuddered at the memory. After that, she made a point of never being alone with him When he came to stay at the stud farm for a weekend a month after her arrival, ostensibly to buy polo ponies, she clung to her aunt's skirts, refusing to go near him. Aunt Pilar understood perfectly. Even Uncle Rafael was careful not to let her out of his sight when Luder was around. Once, though, he succeeded in stealing up on her in the stables. He crept up on her from behind and cupped her right breast, running his tongue down her neck and forcing her hand to the front of his trousers. She slapped his face and ran off. But he only laughed.

Matters got worse when her father up turned up in Argentina on business. It was a time when the Condor Legion and the build-up of German ground troops were starting to make a real difference in the Civil War. It was also the point when it became clear for the first time that Hitler, not Mussolini, was to be the senior partner in Europe's New Order. Colonel Ortega, desperate to bring glory to his family name, was captivated. But of course Felipe could step out with his daughter. Of course they should have lunch together. And, in the end, despite her tears and angry protests, of course they should become engaged. The colonel and Doña Vittoria would be proud to have Felipe as their son-in-law.

That was three years ago. There had been no one since. Once, in Córdoba, there was a boy, the son of a local lawyer, who was very nice. But when Uncle Rafael had caught them kissing, he sent him packing. In the meantime, Isabel had returned to Spain and, to her surprise and relief, she had seen nothing of Luder. He was busy, apparently, with his various enterprises and spent much of his time in Germany. She was sure he had had any number of affairs. What else he got up to she could only guess. But at least he stayed out of Madrid.

Until today.

Now he had turned up, anxious to claim his bride. Isabel shuddered at the very thought of his touch. All her father could think about was the dowry and the connections he would make. Her mother, though not unkind, was preoccupied with rebuilding a 'normal' life after the war and refused to give credence to the concerns of her daughter. In any case, she said, Felipe was *encantador* – charming. Isabel knew now that she must be the architect of her own salvation. She would get through the morning, she decided, then take a taxi to the Ritz hotel, were she would thrown herself on Bramall's mercy. She hurried upstairs to pack.

Two hours later, after an awkward lunch with her mother, she was ready to go. Just as she was closing her suitcase, there was the sound of a car in the driveway. She looked out. A tall, heavily-built man in his mid-thirties was standing next to a taxi, paying off the driver. He wore a heavy brimmed hat and she couldn't see his face. But she would recognise that neck and those shoulders anywhere. Luder! She could feel herself start to panic. She was out of time before she began. How could he have got here so soon? Seconds later, there was a knock at her bedroom door.

'Ah, there you are, my dear,' Doña Vittoria said. 'Felipe is here. Come down and meet him. You two have a lot to catch up on.'

The Argentinean was standing in the hallway, still wearing his homburg hat. There was a swagger to him, even in repose. He looked up, smiling. He had perfect teeth.

'Isabellita! My angel! It has been too long. Come and let me greet you.'

The very sound of his voice made her cringe, though the smile that broke across Luder's features put her mother in mind of the film star Walter Pidgeon, one of her favourites. He seemed to her quite irrepressible.

Mierda! What was she to do? 'Felipe!' she said, trying to keep a quiver out of her voice. 'This is so unexpected. How did you get here so quickly?'

'Quickly? Not quick at all. It's been an age, my dear. But, please, don't stand all night up there on the stairs. Come down to me that I may embrace you.'

'Yes,' said her mother, prodding her daughter sharply in the small of her back with a podgy finger. 'Hurry down to greet your fiancé.'

Isabel descended the steps slowly, one at a time, as if drawn inescapably to her fate. As she approached the bottom tread, Luder bounded forward and threw his arms about her. She gasped. 'Let me look at you. Ah, yes, now I remember why I wanted to marry you.' Without warning, he planted his lips on her mouth and pressed her hard against him, causing memories of the afternoon in the barn to come flooding back. Then he withdrew, holding her by the shoulders, like a hangman steadying his victim before the drop. 'Isabel,' he whispered. 'For years I have dreamed of this moment.'

'The thought of you has invaded my sleep also,' she muttered.

A puzzled look crept over the visitor's sallow features. 'What was that? What did you say?'

'I said I never thought it would really happen.'

'Ah. Of course. Well, good things come to those who wait.'

Isabel looked away, unable to think of a riposte that would not sound like an accusation. Luder stared at her, saying nothing. It was as if he had acknowledged the barrier that still existed between them and was trying to work out a different, more lateral, approach. Mercifully, the silence that followed was broken by her father's voice echoing across the hall from the front door of the house. Colonel Ortega had set off from the Interior Ministry as soon as he heard about Luder's surprise visit and now stood in the door clutching an attaché case.

'Felipe!' he shouted. 'You've arrived. But this is wonderful!'

'Father!' said Isabel, pulling herself free of Luder's grasp. 'You told me Felipe would not get here for another week at least.'

Colonel Ortega smiled. 'Yes. You must be so pleased to see him?'

Isabel glared at her father before turning round to face Luder. 'Felipe,' she began. 'This has all been too much for me to take in. I've had no time in which to prepare. Would you excuse me? I shall be as quick as I can.'

'But of course,' he said. 'Though I can hardly bear to be parted from you.' Reaching out and grasping her hands, he spun her round like a dancer. 'We have the entire evening ahead of us. More than that, we have a lifetime.'

Isabel shivered and shrank back from his embrace. It was not only revulsion she felt. She was also aware of a deep-seated dread – a dread more visceral than anything she had experienced in her twenty-one years of life. It felt as if the threat was to her very soul.

She hurried upstairs, intending to fetch her bag and make her way down the servants' staircase to the rear door of the house. Her mother was standing in her room, unpacking her things and replacing them in her wardrobe and drawers. 'Please, my dear,' she said, 'you must learn to be grown up about your problems. Running away from home is juvenile. Besides – where would you go?'

Isabel looked for a moment as if she was about to say something, but then sat down on the bed, waiting for her heartbeat to return to something like normal. Her mother was right, she realised. Not in the way she intended, but right nonetheless. She was a big girl now – a woman – and she could not simply walk out on her problems, no matter how terrible they seemed. If she bolted, the police would be called. Her father would insist on a city-wide search. It could end up with her being linked not only to Romero, but to Bramall as well. After that, anything could happen. It was frightening to realise that she had stumbled into something so much larger than herself. But that was how people grew – by becoming involved in issues outside of their immediate concerns. What mattered now – what truly mattered – was that she should keep her word and play her part, however small, in the fight against Fascism. There were so many lives at stake; so many people depending on each other. When she realised how foolish she had almost been, and how cowardly, she felt ashamed.

'Are you all right, dear,' her mother asked. 'You're looking very pale.'

'I'll be fine, mama. I've had a bit of a shock, that's all.'

'Take it from me,' said her mother, 'it's the first step that's the hardest.'

Dinner was fixed for half-past nine. Isabel took a bath, hoping to ease some at least of the tensions bunching up in her body. She began to wonder if she might not get something out of the situation that had been forced on her. After all, Luder was a friend of the Germans, with contacts all over the place. Perhaps he knew the Nazi plans for Gibraltar. If he did, maybe she could persuade him to tell her. She lay back in the hot, soothing water, laced with fragrance, trying to imagine herself as a seductress. But then she shuddered and hid her face behind her hands. She sat up suddenly, spraying water all over the bathroom floor. She couldn't do that. Not with him. It was too horrible.

She needed to discover what exactly Luder had in mind for her. Whatever plans there were, she had to be in a position to counter them. There would be talk, presumably, of a wedding – which month, which church, even which country. She would be asked who she wanted to have as her principal bridesmaid and who would be maids of honour. Beyond that, arrangements would be out of her hands.

That was what was so incredible about it all – and so hateful. No one asked her what she wanted. Luder hadn't asked her for her hand in marriage, he asked her father. What century were they living in? Only four years before, the people of Spain had been offered their freedom. The Communists and the Anarchists joined with the Socialists and the liberals to map out a new future for the country in which the old ways would be swept away. Women were to have been among the chief beneficiaries, They would have the vote and they would be free to aspire to positions in society that up to then were the preserve of men. It was a golden moment, when everything seemed possible. No doubt that was why her father sent her away. He did not want his daughter to be contaminated by revolutionary ideals. But the moment vanished as quickly as it came. The ancien regime was once again the latest thing. The Army, the aristos and the priests were back in charge.

Well, she would not have it. Felipe Luder and her father might think that they could dispose of her life as if she were a farm animal in a market. But they were in for a rude awakening. Her independence was not a commodity, to be bought and sold. Bramall would help her. She was in no doubt of that. But tonight? Tonight she would be on her own. There was no point in arousing suspicion and setting everyone against her. No. She would stoop to conquer – offering honeyed words that would put them all at their ease. Only when she was ready to act decisively would she stand up and tell them exactly what she thought of them. That is when they would discover the real Isabel Ortega, and it would be a moment she would remember for the rest of her life.

At any rate, that was the plan.

She reached for the shampoo and lathered her hair. Still in the bath, she knelt with her head below the tap, running her fingers down the thick strands of her hair, rinsing out the suds. The water gushed over her head and shoulders. Just for a second, she felt clean and pure, as if she was reborn. Then she heard her mother's voice, telling her to hurry up and come downstairs.

Luder stood up when she walked into the courtyard twenty minutes later. She wore a black dress, black stockings and a short string of her grandmother's pearls around her neck. The delicately patterned *mantilla* she had chosen was of fine-spun silk, and the effect, as it fell from her still damp hair to settle around the naked expanse of her shoulders was devastating.

She spoke first. 'Good evening, Felipe – Mother, Father. I hope I didn't keep you waiting.'

'It was worth the wait just to look at you,' replied the

Argentinean, with a passable attempt at gallantry. He walked across to where she stood and kissed her three times on the cheeks, once on the left, twice on the right. Then he reached for her hand to guide her to a chair next to his.

Colonel Ortega looked on approvingly. His daughter looked beautiful. Just as important, she appeared to be making an effort not to spoil things by giving everyone the benefit of her opinions.

Over dinner, served in the main dining room, with the shutters and windows thrust open to the evening, Luder gave a virtuoso performance.

He had been to New York and gone shopping at Tiffany's. For Isabel's mother, he bought a gold bracelet, studded with sapphires. Doña Vittoria was almost overcome with gratitude. 'Felipe,' she began. 'You shouldn't have.' She held out her arm as the Argentinean deftly encircled her wrist with the heavy band and pressed the clasp ever so gently, yet firmly, until it clicked into place. 'Look, Raúl,' she said, extending her arm at full stretch towards her husband. 'Isn't it the most beautiful thing you ever saw?' Colonel Ortega nodded and smiled. One day, he thought, he too would be able to buy gifts such as these.

Luder turned next to Isabel, who was watching him guardedly, fearful of what was coming. Twisting off his chair, he descended to one knee, grasping her right hand between both of his. It was like a scene from Rossini. 'I have been away from your side for far too long,' he began. 'It has been three years since our engagement was agreed, and during all that time I have barely seen you. For that, I ask your forgiveness.'

Still holding on to her right hand with his left, he reached into the pocket of his dinner jacket and withdrew a tiny box, inscribed with the name of New York's most famous jeweller's. Opening it with his thumb, he held it up so that she could see the ring inside. It was fashioned, she could tell, from the finest white gold, set with emeralds to match those in the bracelet he had just given to her mother. She could not deny it. It was a triumph of timing and taste.

He let go of her hand, which she did not dare withdraw, and extracted the ring, which he then held up, as if it were the Host at mass. 'This ring,' he said, 'is the symbol of the love I bear for you. I would be proud if you would wear it as a sign that we are betrothed and will one day soon be married in the sight of God.'

Doña Vittoria purred with pleasure.

Luder slipped the ring onto the third finger of Isabel's right hand, in the Spanish manner. It fitted exactly. 'The stones match your eyes,' he said, 'though they are, of course, not half so bewitching. If it needs adjusting …'

'No, it's …'

' – perfect,' said her mother.

'Quite,' said Isabel. She felt as if she was about to be sick.

The dinner dragged on like a penance. Throughout, Isabel could feel the unfamiliar pressure of the ring on her finger. It felt as if it were burning her skin. She kept twisting at it beneath the table. Luder, mindless of her discomfiture, clearly felt the evening was going splendidly and was happy to regale his audience with his adventures. In New York, he had met the mayor, Fiorello LaGuardia, and one of the city's leading gangsters, Carlo Gambino. 'Both small men,' he said, indicating with his hand that neither came up to his shoulders. 'But like the city itself, bursting with energy.'

'Yes,' said the colonel, 'but what if Churchill persuades the United States to join the war?'

Luder shook his head. 'Don't worry about that. Isolationism is the new American creed. They want only to be left alone to expand their industry. Everyone I met assured me that Roosevelt would never go to war with Germany. He and his advisers – and practically the whole of Congress – consider that it is up to the Old World to sort out its problems.'

He beamed at the colonel, for whom this latest piece of intelligence was intended as the best of good news. The he moved on to his main topic of the evening. America, it turned out, didn't impress him nearly as much as the Reich. Berlin, he assured them, was awe-inspiring.

'It is the true city of the future. It puts poor Paris in the shade. There is not only wealth there but great culture. When you stand in the *Führer's* study in the new Chancellery, you feel as if you are at the epicentre of the world.'

Colonel Ortega gasped. 'You were in Hitler's study?'

'Why, yes! Heydrich took me there. The *Führer*, I regret to say, was elsewhere at the time, but I could feel his aura. It was incredible. Like nothing else I have experienced.'

The colonel understood. He had felt the same thing when informed once by the minister that the seat on which he was sitting had once been occupied by Mussolini.

'We have so much to learn from Berlin,' Luder was saying – as I'm sure the *Caudillo* would be the first to agree.'

Luder, thought Isabel, was like a malign Medici. His conversation moved adroitly from banking, to property, to farming, to plans for the construction of a new opera house in Córdoba and a new presidential palace in Buenos Aires, then on to world domination. Her parents were transfixed. He brought to their world the sweep and dynamism of the frontier, combined with an international experience of which, as yet, they could only dream. He seemed to them the perfect amalgam of the virtues of Spain and Germany. To Luder, whatever was undeSirable in life could be sloughed off, like the skin of a snake. Argentina would resolve its economic and political difficulties and assume its rightful place as the leading nation of Latin America. Spain, after the vicissitudes of recent years, would be restored to greatness at the head of a new world empire by the boldness and clear-headed vision of the *Generalísimo*. There could be no turning back. Fascism had to be grasped with both hands. 'I promise you,' he said, within two years, the New Order will be confirmed across our continent, from the Atlantic to the Urals. Bolshevism will be swept away, like the Moors, or the heresies of old, and the Jews, the eternal canker in our midst, will be cast out as Christ cast out the money lenders from the Temple. It will be glorious, and we, seated around this table, will be part of it.'

Isabel listened to all of this in silence, remembering what her father had said to her and her commitment to Bramall. She did not demur when the Argentinean raised his glass to the defeat of the 'world Zionist conspiracy,' merely substituting, beneath her breath 'Nazi' for 'Zionist.' When the colonel praised the progress being made by the Spanish government in repressing every form of dissent, she said nothing, twisting and twisting at her new ring, wishing she could wrench it off and fling it into the street beyond.

The empty dinner plates were removed, and while they waited for the cheese to be brought Doña Vittoria attempted to raise the subject of the wedding. Luder, to Isabel's surprise, did not respond. He would, he announced, be ready to discuss such matters later in the week, when he was better rested after his journey. It was enough, apparently, that he was now formally engaged. Colonel Ortega, conscious of the fact that this could have been more delicately put, leaned across the table to his daughter. 'Do not trouble yourself,' he said. 'Felipe and I, together with your mother, will ensure that it is the best day of your life.'

'Thank you, father,' she said, smiling demurely, 'I have every confidence in you.'

Ortega offered an embarrassed smile.

Later, as the colonel and Luder settled down to brandy and cigars, Isabel retreated with her mother to the courtyard, where it was still warm and the cicadas were in full voice. The sky was black and ablaze with stars.

'I have to say, darling,' Doña Vittoria announced, sipping from a glass of white wine she had brought with her from the table, 'you made quite an impression this evening. I could see that your father was extremely pleased – and relieved. So, now that we are alone, tell me ... what are you up to?'

'I don't know what you mean, mother.'

'I think you do. That performance in there might have fooled your Papa. He is, after all, only a man. But I could see right through it.'

'Oh yes? And what did you see?'

'I saw a young woman biding her time, trying very hard not to offend anyone. And it made me wonder who was fooling whom, and to what end.'

Isabel felt a flush of alarm course through her. 'You know

very well, Mama, that I do not love Felipe and would never choose him for my husband. But I have to face facts, do I not? Isn't that what you and papa are always telling me?'

'And what facts would those be, exactly.'

'That in Fascist Spain, as it is now constituted, woman have little control over their lives and can only make the best of what comes their way.'

'Is that why you have taken off your engagement ring?'

The ring lay on the armrest of her chair.

'I am not used to wearing it, that's all.'

Doña Vittoria raised her head and stared up into the star-filled night. It was as if some memory, long neglected, had reasserted itself and she was far away in a place where everything was possible. The moment passed. Abruptly, she lurched forward, tipping her wine glass onto the ground, where it broke into several jagged shards. She looked dazed and made no move to pick up the pieces. Instead, she sighed. 'There is so much you have to learn about society and our place in it. We do not make the rules, my darling. If we did, the world would be a very different place. What we do, if we have any sense, is to follow the rules in public and bend them in private.' She paused and looked her daughter straight in the eyes. 'Do you suppose that your father and I live in a master and servant relationship?'

'Of course not.'

'I obey him when the occasion demands. I offer him the respect required of his position. But here, in our household, it is I who make the decisions that matter. You and Felipe …'

' – are two very different people to you and Papa.'

'Yes. But the relationship is the same, is it not?'

'Oh, Mama. You don't know the half of it.' Isabel reached

out and squeezed her mother's hand, aware, amid her own pain and anxiety, that they might never again have such a conversation. 'Would you like me to fetch you a coffee or another glass of wine?'

Doña Vittoria shook her head. She looked suddenly tired, as if she too had an intimation of something ending. 'No, my dear, I think not. I think I should like to be alone, and I think you would also. Please say goodnight to Felipe for me. He and your father will probably carry on talking for hours yet.' She laughed quietly to herself, as if at some private joke, before turning serious once more. 'I know that what lies ahead for you is not the life you would have chosen, and I feel for you in this. But remember, things are rarely as bad as they seem.'

Isabel snorted. 'In this case they couldn't be, could they?'

'I shall take that as agreement.'

As her mother rose, somewhat unsteadily, from her chair, Isabel stood, too, and kissed her. 'I'm sorry for the trouble I've caused you,' she said. 'It hasn't been easy growing up like this.'

'I'm sure it hasn't. But when was it easy? It wasn't easy for your grandmother and it certainly wasn't easy for me. You are about to join a great tradition, Isabel – the tradition of the virtuous wife – and you must learn to accept it. It's the fate you were born to. It is the fate of all women.'

It will not be my fate, Isabel thought. Not so long as there is breath left in my body. The only thing that is fixed in my future is the strength of my resolve.

Alone in the courtyard, she pulled her legs up beneath her on her chair and looked up at the night sky, wondering what it was her mother had seen there. There was peace in the heavens, but none below. Spain was Hell on Earth: so many people with so much to offer, and most of them hungry, looking for work and a reason to live.

Through the open windows of the dining room, she could hear her father and Luder still discussing the war and the inevitability of German victory. It was the same rubbish she had heard many times before, and it disgusted her. But then her father said: 'The fact of the matter is, so long as Berlin continues to ignore our economic needs, we are bound to maintain trade links with Britain. After all, not only do the British see to it that we receive supplies of grain and gasoline, but they pay more than Germany for the wolfram they buy. What would you have us do? We have already bankrupted ourselves once. Must we do it a second time?'

The Argentinean knocked the ash from his cigar onto the dining room floor. 'I appreciate what you are saying, Don Raúl. Sometimes, it seems to me, Berlin cuts off its nose to spite its face. The German war machine cannot function without wolfram. Tungsten is vital to modern weaponry. England can easily get what it needs from the USA, Canada, Australia. But so long as the British navy maintains its continental blockade, Germany has no other source but Spain and Portugal. London knows this. It knows that every tonne it exports from Iberia is a tonne denied to Germany. That is the basis for the trade – and for their inflated price. But think of it this way. What if I were to help bring about a change of mind in Berlin? I know that Heydrich would welcome a better economic balance between Spain and Germany. It makes sense to him. Why beggar your clients? I can also tell you that there are those in the inner circles of the Party who would not object to making a little personal gain from any deal we might construct.'

Colonel Ortega looked around, as if someone might be listening. 'No more than we do here.'

A chilling laugh rose from the Argentinean's throat. 'Ah, Colonel – you are a man after my own heart. So let me spell it out. If you can arrange for Don Ramón to apply something of a brake on sales of Wolfram to England – nothing dramatic to begin with, simply a scaling back – I at the same time will attempt to persuade Heydrich that he should increase the scale of payments on the German side. He has funds, and access to more. He can make it happen. And in the give and take between the two sides, there is no reason why men of goodwill, such as ourselves, should not see an improvement in our personal situations. Who ever said that patriotism and profit could not co-exist?'

'Indeed,' said Ortega. 'And your bank in Switzerland, it could facilitate such arrangements?'

'It will stand ready. Listen to me. You and I have already benefited from our trade in platinum and industrial diamonds. Berlin knows of your role and appreciates it. Why should the same not be true of wolfram?'

Ortega puffed at his cigar. 'But what if the British and Americans were to retaliate by cutting back on exports of oil and cereals?'

'As part of a more 'flexible' arrangement with Germany, I do not see that being a problem. When Hitler invades Russia, as he is bound to do, the wheat fields of Ukraine will be open to us. Spain will have all the flour it needs. Central Asia's oil will at the same time become Axis oil. In the interim, so that the British do not cut off supplies too early, you must practice deception. You should tell Churchill that Spanish neutrality is assured. Hint at the pain this brings you – that way they will be more inclined to believe you. Meanwhile, continue to supply them with wolfram, only gradually cutting back on the amounts. There will be complaints. Angry words, I should imagine. But that is what diplomats are for. What you have to bear in mind is that once the *Caudillo* commits Spain to the war, all past agreements are void. Gibraltar will be seized, North Africa will become the new battleground. For Spain, as for Italy, it will be the dawn of a new golden age.'

As Isabel listened, horrified by the sheer audacity of the scheme of which her father was a part, Colonel Ortega grunted and said nothing. Isabel knew that silence. It meant he was arriving at a difficult decision. 'You are right,' he said at last. 'I was with the minister today. He briefed me on discussions that are even now taking place between our own general staff and the German High Command for the capture of Gibraltar.

Luder slapped his right fist hard into the palm of his left hand, so that Isabel in the courtyard beyond heard the impact. 'Operation Felix" is what they are calling it in Berlin. It would be a masterstroke. History, my friend, is unfolding in front of our eyes and there is no time to lose. When might this happen?'

'We don't know. It is early days. The plans are still being developed. It all depends on the *Caudillo*, who has said he will only grant permission for the insertion of German forces into Spain on condition that we are granted expansion of our empire in North Africa.'

'At the expense of the French, I suppose.'

'Who else? He was quite explicit on this point. The minister is to go to Berlin for talks. Later, the *Generalísimo* will meet Hitler on the border with France. What is important now is that I should talk to Don Ramón. It is likely that he will call on you in the next few days. You must appear ignorant. Make no mention of what I have told you.'

'Have no fear on that front. And don't worry about the Germans either. They will listen to me. I know them well and they know me. I am someone they do business with every week of the year. Heydrich will expect a consideration, naturally ...'

'Naturally,' said Ortega.

' – But if he says he will do it, then you can depend on it. He is one of the *Führer's* most valued lieutenants, and, as it happens, in ten days' time he and I meet for lunch in Berlin.'

'Excelente!' Ortega said, raising his glass. 'I give you a toast. To victory!'

'To victory. Heil Hitler!'

A lengthy pause ensued as the colonel wrestled with a separate issue he felt honour-bound to raise. 'And on the matter of my daughter?' he began.

Luder's voice dropped. 'She will be the seal to our bargain.'

'But you will be good to her? I wish only for her to be happy.'

'My dear colonel, you worry too much. Isabel is a wilful creature, who needs to be tamed. But she will be the wife of one of the richest and best connected businessmen in Europe, with a husband and a father who are pillars of the New World Order. She should be grateful.'

'True. And she will also provide me with grandchildren.'

Luder laughed again. 'Of that, my dear Colonel, you can be assured.'

These last words were like a dagger plunged into Isabel's heart. The very idea that she would have children by such a man! But her personal fears were not, she realised, what was truly important about the conversation she had just overheard. What mattered was this 'Operation Felix' Luder and her father were discussing. If it went ahead, it could cripple England in the Mediterranean and shift the balance of the war even further in Germany's favour.

She had to speak to Bramall. It was urgent. But it was also late. The risks at this hour were too great and she would leave it until first thing in the morning. In the meantime, she would go to her room and write down what she could remember of the conversation in the dining room. Slowly and silently, so as not to betray her presence, she walked back into the house and stole upstairs to her bedroom.

Half an hour later, after finishing what she hoped was a reasonably accurate transcription of what she had overheard, she began to undress. It was as she finished unbuttoning her dress that she heard footsteps on the landing and realised with a start that her bedroom door was unlocked. It didn't occur to her that Luder would simply burst in on her, and when he did she almost screamed.

'What's the matter?' he asked, leering at her, slightly drunk. 'Aren't you pleased to see me?'

Quickly, before he could notice, she pushed the note beneath the bolster of her turned-down bed and began to pull her dress back up over her body. 'What are you talking about?' she said. 'I hardly know you. It's been three years.'

'True,' Luder said, eying the exposed swell of her breasts. 'Three years, surely, of passionate anticipation.' He slumped down beside her on the bed. It was then that he noticed her hand. 'But wait a moment. Your engagement ring – where is it?'

'I ... I was showing it to mother. I must have left it downstairs.'

'That was careless of you.'

She stood up. 'You are right. I will go and fetch it.'

'First, let me hold you.'

'No,' she said.

'Why not?'

'It isn't right. You can't. You mustn't.'

"Can't?' 'Mustn't?' These are not words I am familiar with, my dear Isabel. In the New Order they have been replaced by the triumph of the will – or haven't you heard? Now give me your mouth. I need to taste you again after so long apart.'

He stretched out one of his muscled arms and drew her towards him. She felt his hot breath enveloping her as his free hand found its way to the hem of her dress and began to push up her thigh towards the tops of her stockings. My God! It was her nightmare come true. She felt the vomit rise in her throat. If it was only her honour that was at stake, she might have succumbed to his advances, loathsome thought they were. At least it would have got rid of him. But the note detailing the Germans' war plan was only inches from where he was sitting. Even if he were preoccupied now with making love to her, he could easily find the note afterwards. There was nothing else for it. She was still wearing her lace-up boots and, with a supreme effort, she kicked out, hard, at his shin.

He howled, letting go of her and reaching down to rub the bruise that was already forming on his leg. Then his brow furrowed into a scowl. 'Perra! You bitch!' he rasped. 'If you should ever do that when we are married, I will have you flogged and thrown into a sty with the other sows.'

She jumped up and threw open the door to the landing. 'Not if I kill you first. Do not presume to touch me in my father's house. If you have no respect for me, at least show some for him.'

Luder bared the points of his teeth. 'You are a spitfire now,' he said. 'In years to come, you will be spitting blood. That I promise you.'

'Shut the door on the way out,' she said. 'And next time, knock before you dare approach me.'

Madrid/Gibraltar: July 5

Bramall was travelling south to Gibraltar. Orders from Croft had arrived first thing by the usual method, an envelope stuffed under his door. Perhaps, he mused, there was an espionage postal department that distributed information and instructions to spies of all nations on a disinterested, professional basis. The contents of the note were not altogether unexpected. He was to meet with Strickland and others to discuss the nature and precise purpose of his mission. Serrano's office had come up with the necessary paperwork. His reason for going, he told a stone-faced official, was to inspect an American liner chosen to convey the Duke to his new post as Governor of the Bahamas. Serrano had raised no objection to his mission It seemed harmless enough.

Before leaving his hotel, Bramall spoke briefly to Buchanan-Smith, who didn't seem in the least put out that he would be left in charge of the Duke for the next few days , He also left a message at reception for Isabel asking her to meeting him in the Café Gijón on Monday morning at nine. He still wasn't sure what to make of her, but he was concerned that she should not feel abandoned. As for his personal feelings, these, he decided, must be put to one side until his return from Gibraltar.

Atocha station on the Friday morning was swarming with travellers and rank with sweat. Only a minority of Spaniards – and hardly any of the hundreds of thousands of former peasants who had flocked into the capital since 1939 – had access to soap. Most were dressed in clothes they must first have worn before the war. One baby, which stared at Bramall with unabashed curiosity, was trussed in a former flour sack, tied at the shoulders, with holes cut for her legs. The train to Algeciras, via Cordoba and Seville, was packed and tempers were short. Bramall pushed his way to his seat, mumbling a series of *perdóneme por favor's*. The middle-aged woman sat next to him was practically steaming and holding onto her handbag as if her life depended on it. When he bade her good day, she did not reply, for which, he realised, he was grateful.

He looked around. There was an argument going on involving a number of passengers. So far as he could tell, those who had brought nothing on board to eat were jealous of those with as much as a hunk of stale bread. One stocky-looking man in his forties, swigging from a bottle of beer and slicing pieces of salty manchego cheese with a clasp knife, appeared to be the main focus of resentment.

'Why don't you offer the rest of us some of your cheese?' a young man asked. He was thin and asthmatic – with a boil burning a hole in his cheek.

'There's only enough for one,' the man replied. 'It's a long journey. You should have brought your own.'

'Where would I get money for cheese? Where did you get it, come to that? And enough for beer as well.'

'Mind your own business.'

'*Cabrón!*'

'Bastard yourself,' the main with the cheese said, jerking the point of his knife at his tormentor. '*Vete al infierno!*'

The younger man turned away, muttering.

Smoke, laden with soot, flew in through the carriage's open windows, getting in everyone's eyes and clothes, causing the children to cough. The slatted wooden seats grew increasingly hard and unyielding. Outside, the barren flatness of La Mancha, shimmering in the heat, flew by like the surface of the moon.

Two hours after leaving Madrid, the train stopped at the provincial capital, Ciudad Real, belching smoke and smelling of burned lubrication. While a maintenance crew worked on the engine and several sets of wheels, the train was boarded by a contingent of secret police and *Guardia Civil* keen to add to the general misery of the passengers. A middle-aged man carrying a briefcase was arrested and taken off, followed by the cheese-eater, whose indignant departure was greeted with delight by the youth with the blemished cheek, who had coughed incessantly throughout their time together. The train started up again after half an hour before continuing fitfully as far as Córdoba, where a young married couple who had just joined were asked for their papers and travel permit. There must have been something wrong, for the documents were passed down the carriage to the officer in charge, an overweight sergeant with an improbable Hitler moustache, who indicated with a twist of his head towards the door that the pair should be held for questioning. The husband's plea that he and his wife had done nothing and were only trying to make their way home to their family provoked the arresting officer to drive the end of his baton hard into the man's kidneys, making him squeal in pain.

Bramall said nothing. Like everyone else in his compartment, he looked the other way, fanning himself with a copy of *Arriba*. When it came to his turn to show his papers, the British passport he displayed was picked over and examined with scrupulous dedication. Only the stamped laisser-passer from Serrano's office convinced the sergeant that the foreigner should not join the others in the back of the police wagon parked in the station yard. Bramall caught his eyes and fixed him with what he hoped was a chilling look.

The remainder of the journey, which included a change from the Malaga express to a local, took three long hours, during which the Andalucian heat continued to build. Bramall, seated next to the window, found it hard to keep awake. But the sleep he entered did not bring him rest. Minutes later, he was back on the banks of the Ebro. A group of dead soldiers, cut down by the German raider, stood gathered at the riverbank staring at the corpse of twenty-one-year-old Manuela Valdés. Manuela's left hand was pointing across to the Nationalist forces lined up in ranks on the far side. No one spoke. Suddenly, as if in response to a military command, the soldiers shifted their glare to Bramall. 'It's not my fault,' he told them. 'I loved her. I didn't want her to die.' But the words that came out of his mouth made no sense and they ignored him. He returned his gaze to Manuela. She was naked now – he felt shame for her – and he saw the trail of bullet holes that ran in a diagonal from her waist to her shoulder. He bent down, needing to touch her, needing to confirm that she was dead. As he placed his fingers to her wounds, she shuddered and, in an obscene parody of arousal, twisted over onto her back. Now he could see her breasts, which flowed with thick, arterial blood. He tried to look away, but couldn't. Slowly, deliberately, beneath his horrified gaze, the hand that had pointed across the river towards the Nationalist army rose up in an arc, shifting by degrees until – dear God! – it was pointing at *him*. He backed away hysterically, his boots scrabbling for purchase in the wet earth. This wasn't fair. It wasn't *right*. Then he looked at her again and it was her eyes that now caught his attention. There was nothing there, only empty sockets. He couldn't bear it. That was when he heard the sound of boots stamping in the mud. Manuela's dead comrades had formed up in a line and they, too, were pointing in his direction. It was as if he was the accused in a Greek classical drama, identified as the murderer by the omniscient chorus. Gibbering, he placed a hand to his mouth and burst into tears.

'*Tickets, please!*'

'What?'

It was the train conductor.

'Your ticket, Señor. I came aboard at Córdoba. This is a fresh check.'

'Oh, right. One moment, please.' He fished out his ticket from his inside pocket, then rummaged for a handkerchief and dabbed at his eyes, hoping that no one was looking at him.

Another hour went by. By the time the Mediterranean came into view, the atmosphere in the railway carriage was almost unbearably pungent. Just getting off this damned train had become a major objective. When, at last, they pulled into Algeciras, Bramall stumbled onto the platform like a drowning man swept unexpectedly onto the beach. A taxi, at least twenty years-old, was waiting for him. The driver picked him out at once from the crowd, but let him carry his own bag. He didn't object. The fact that there was a car at all was something. He'd supposed he'd have to walk. The taxi – some sort of Renault, painted canary yellow – was a mess, missing regularly on at least one cylinder, But it took him the five miles or so to the Gibraltar border crossing at La Linéa, where, after a further inspection of his travel documents by Spanish border guards, he was met in a Land Rover by a lieutenant with an eye patch.

The Neutral Zone between the two jurisdictions was appropriately bleak, For fifty yards, a windswept swathe of asphalt, baked to an almost liquid consistency, was all that marked the transition from Spanish to colonial territory. But once behind the British Lines – a newly constructed network of anti-tank defences, backed up by razor wire and machine gun nests – Bramall was in no doubt that he had entered a war zone. A battery of howitzers, their muzzles jutting out from ramparts first built by the Moors, guarded the 'Landport' approach. Larger, naval-style guns, anchored in embrasures in the Rock itself, hundreds of feet up, looked towards Algeciras and its hinterland.

The lieutenant, heading in the direction of an opening in the fortifications marked Landport Tunnel 1729, halted at a set of flashing lights. Immediately ahead was the colony's newly extended airstrip, running West to East across the littoral. An RAF Wellington bomber coming in from the Atlantic applied its brakes full-on upon landing to avoid getting its feet wet in the Mediterranean at the other side. While they waited for the Wellington to turn round and taxi back, Bramall shifted his gaze to the harbour. The ships of Force H, as well as a group of submarines and various supply vessels and freighters, rode at anchor in the lee of the Rock. He couldn't help thinking, in spite of the impressive defensive capability on display, how vulnerable they would be in the event of a concerted enemy assault. An attacking force, German or Spanish or both, might not take the colony straight away. But it would almost certainly render it unviable for shipping and aircraft. The British garrison, in that event, would be forced either to beat a retreat or else to hunker down with no other objective than mere survival. And the big question, the one that he had first asked of Strickland, re-entered his head with all the force of the bomber that had just touched down on the exposed tarmac: how in Hell's name was he supposed to prevent it?

In the *Abwehr* observation post overlooking the neutral zone, a camera, connected to a motor drive, focused on the Naval officer and his guest. The zoom lens caught his features quite precisely.

By now it was 6.30 in the evening and Bramall, after checking in to the Hotel Bristol on Cathedral Square, was invited to change and join the local SIS station chief, Alastair MacLeish, and Gibraltar's head of naval intelligence, Commander John Garfield, for dinner at Government House.

'They normally sit down at 7.30,' the lieutenant advised, 'but I expect they'll be in the bar some while before that. Try and not be late.'

Government House, formerly a Franciscan convent, was just around the corner from the Bristol. Beneath the lengthening shadows of the portico, Bramall showed his papers to the Marine guard and was taken directly to the bar. MacLeish, a ruddy-faced Scot, and Garfield, sporting a Navy-issue 'full set,' were standing by a window overlooking the garden. There was no sign of Strickland.

'Glad you could make it, laddie' said MacLeish in a restrained Highland brogue before introducing himself and his companion. 'We've a lot to talk about.'

'So I believe.'

'Aye. And there's someone I want you to meet …. But, speak of the devil, here he comes.'

A tall, portly figure, wearing horn-rimmed spectacles, aged somewhere in his late fifties, was shuffling towards them. MacLeish stepped forward and extended his hand. 'Charles Bramall, sir George Sharpe MP,' he announced. 'Sent by the PM to make sure we're all doing our jobs. Isn't that right, sir George?'

The reply was slightly breathless. 'I wouldn't put it quite like that.'

'No. That would be why you're the politician and I'm stuck in the back rooms.' Sharpe emitted a hoarse laugh, which caused his cheeks to wobble. He looked like a man who enjoyed a whisky and, sure enough, he immediately ordered a large Malt from the mess sergeant hovering discreetly in their midst.

'Where's Strickland?' Bramall asked, accepting a smaller version of the same.

'Oh, sorry,' said MacLeish. 'He sends his apologies. He only just got in. You probably saw his aircraft land. He's with the Governor and Admiral Cunningham at the moment. They've a lot to get through, as you can imagine. But he'll see you in the morning.'

'I look forward to it.'

The meal, eaten beneath the turning blades of a ceiling fan, was dull even by the standards of wartime Britain. Bramall wondered what damage the attack on the French at Oran had done to morale. Garfield forked an extra sliver of lamb onto his plate from the serving dish in the centre of the table and sucked in air through his teeth. 'You can't kill more than twelve hundred of your former allies one day and forget it the next,' he said, swamping the lamb in gravy. 'It's something we'll all have to live with for a long time.' Bramall nodded and sipped at a glass of rough red wine.

'Stupid buggers,' said Sharpe, running a knuckled finger back and forth across his upper lip. 'Should have sailed with us to Gib.' He turned to face Bramall, staring at him across the top of his glasses. His eyes were pink-rimmed, surmounted by brows like twin thickets. 'A bad business,' he growled. 'But what did they expect? That we'd just leave 'em to be press-ganged by Mussolini? 'Fraid that's not how things are done anymore – not since Winston. More to the point, what about Madrid? Things any better there now?' Bramall opened his mouth to speak, but Sharpe just ploughed on. 'I was there for three days in '37. Place had taken quite a battering, but the people looked as if they'd rather die than give in to Franco. Couldn't understand it m'self. Bloody Left had made a complete cock-up of everything. Along comes someone who at least knows his business, and what do they do? – man the barricades.'

Bramall took in the sleek, well-fed politician, who looked as if he hadn't gone hungry since the last time he'd thrown up at Oxford. 'Since you ask,' he said, 'I'd have to say that things are better now – but worse, too. A lot worse. Franco's restored order on the streets – no problems there, so long as you're on the right side, that is. The trams are running. Even the street lamps are coming back on, district by district. Trouble is, reconstruction is a painful business. Madrid won't be rebuilt in a day. Meantime, there's plenty of hungry people around, lots of beggars, women and children in rags. The way things are going, it'll be 1950 or after before the Spanish economy gets back into any kind of shape.'

Immediately, the MP's mood lightened. 'Excellent,' he said. 'So they'll not be voting to join the war, then?'

'They'll not be voting at all, sir George. They do what they're told.'

Sharpe thought about this, then snuffled and sneezed into a large linen handkerchief. He seemed to be having trouble with his nose. MacLeish took the opportunity to turn to Garfield, the naval man, who up to now had concentrated on his dinner. 'So what's your view, Commander? Think Franco's up to scratch?'

Garfield was sweating profusely and picked at his teeth with a fingernail, rolling the results between finger and thumb. 'You really want my opinion?.'

'That's why I asked?'

'Well, fact of the matter is, chap's not the devil incarnate. Wasn't for him, Spain would be locked tight in the grip of international communism. He put a stop to all that. We should be grateful.'

'True enough,' said MacLeish. 'And he's made sure the navy's run by its officers, not a bunch of mutineers.'

'Exactly.'

MacLeish's reference was to the murder of a large proportion of the Spanish Navy's officer class in the opening days of the civil war. Ratings opted, almost to a man, for the Republic, while their officers, from 'traditional' families, were sympathetic to the rebel cause. The mutiny horrified British naval officers in Gibraltar, most of them dyed-in-the-wool conservatives, confirming them in their belief that Franco's arrival on the scene hadn't come a moment too soon.

As the coffee and digestifs arrived, Sharpe, who had climbed aboard Churchill's band wagon the moment he was appointed First Lord of the Admiralty, returned to the fray. What sort of a cove was Franco? he wanted to know. What would it take to persuade him to stay out of the war? The PM isn't opposed to the fellow *per se*. Considers him a bit of a brute, but unavoidable in the current climate. He simply wants him to concentrate on the rebuilding of his country and avoid meddling in things that need not concern him.'

Bramall couldn't disagree with this. MacLeish asked matter-of-factly if the *Generalísimo* and his comrades might not simply be 'bought off.'

'You mean bribed?'

'Encouraged to do the right thing.'

Bramall thought for a moment. 'Who knows? Isn't that what economic warfare is all about? My guess is it'll work well enough so long as too much isn't expected from it. Most of Franco's inner circle have got access to as much power and show as they can handle right now. They eat well, they've commandeered the finest real estate and they have power of life and death over millions. As for Franco himself, I wouldn't want to be the one to offer him a bribe. Last time someone questioned his honour, he drew his revolver and shot him.'

MacLeish took a moment to absorb the significance of this brief character study, twisting his tumbler of Famous Grouse back and forth in his hands. 'It's just that Sir George here seems to feel that larger funds could be made available.'

Bramall turned to the portly parliamentarian. 'It's up to you how you spend taxpayers' money. That's your job. That's why were elected. All I'm saying is that there are issues at stake here which go far beyond money. Blood and honour, for a start.'

Sharpe's face creased into an amused contempt. 'I must say, Bramall,' he said, 'you take too lofty a view of our Spanish friends. Must be the Irish in you. Never forget, every man has his price – especially the dago.'

Bramall bristled. 'Wasn't it an English politician said that? And I think he was talking about the House of Commons. So what would your price be, Sir George? A thousand pounds? Ten thousand? Where would I have to start?'

The insult hit home like a slap in the face. The MP looked as if he might actually explode. 'Cheeky young pup. What are you implying? How dare you?'

'Well, you did say every man, Sir George. Wouldn't that include you?'

Sharpe's cheeks, which started out a pale pink, were now a vivid purple. His eyebrows, dripping with perspiration, congealed into the consistency of a small hedge. For a moment, Bramall feared that he might be about to have a heart attack. Instead, he picked up his table napkin and drew it slowly across his brow so that the linen changed at once from crisp white to dirty grey.

'It's the heat, Mr Bramall,' he said at last. 'Gets to all of us.

Something we need to watch. So incentives are out, is that it? And I thought power corrupted.' He blew his nose noisily into the napkin. 'I don't suppose you'd go along with assassination either.'

Previously, Bramall was surprised. Now he was bewildered. 'Is this a joke?'

'Just something someone mentioned the other day.'

'And who did this someone have in mind?'

'Who do you think? If you want to kill the snake, go for its head.'

Bramall looked around the table. Neither MacLeish not Garfield spoke, but both looked at him with interest. 'But even if you took Franco out of the picture,' he said, 'you'd still be left with a bunch of highly motivated Fascists – only now they'd be very angry Fascists, spoiling for a fight.'

Sharpe seemed suddenly to have tired of the exchange. 'Look,' he said, 'the two of us could probably carry on like this all night. But where would it get us?' He pushed his chair back from the table and rose slowly to his feet. 'Right now, what I need is a good night's sleep. I'll say goodnight to you, gentlemen. It has been a most instructive evening. And Mr Bramall, I shall look out for your reports.'

'Do that, Sir George. And safe journey.'

As soon as the dining room door closed behind the MP's retreating figure, MacLeish offered Bramall a cigarette. 'Well,' he said, reaching into his jacket pocket for his lighter, 'that certainly livened things up.'

Bramall looked sheepish. He tapped his cigarette on the table top before putting the end in his mouth. 'Yes,' he said, 'sorry about that. Got a bit carried away.'

The SIS station chief smiled and rubbed his thumb against the flint wheel of his Dunhill lighter. 'You don't have to apologise. Man's a windbag at the best of times. Did you know he commanded one of the firing squads in Dublin after 1916? '

Bramall sat up. 'Really?'

'Proud of it. For King and Country,' he said.

'Is that right? I hadn't realised he was that much of a shit. But then, Empire does that – gives third-rate people the chance to lead second-rate lives.'

'Aye, well I'll not argue with on that point. But he's not stupid. Not entirely. If it got through to him that we're on a hiding to nothing here, maybe we'll come through this crisis after all.'

'You don't sound too hopeful.'

The Scot looked at his younger companion, deadly serious. 'I'd like to tell you we don't rely on miracles. But, after Dunkirk, that would be naive. Gibraltar's on a war-footing like never before. There are guns on every street corner. The Rock itself is so honeycombed with tunnels, it's a wonder it's still standing. Whole damned place is an arsenal. If it comes to a fight, you can be damned sure the garrison will give as good as it gets. But we can't put the Navy underground. We can't stop ships at anchor from being blown out of the water by guns ten miles away. We saw that at Oran. And at the end of the day, if Britain loses Gib, she loses the war.'

'So everyone keeps telling me.'

'Well, they're right. Just because things are quiet now doesn't mean the threat isn't there.' Bramall merely nodded by way of reply. He'd had a long day and was obviously exhausted. MacLeish finished his scotch and called to the mess sergeant to fetch his bill. 'You must be shattered,' he said. 'Away and get your head down. In the morning, we'll talk about where we go from here.'

It was when he got outside, into the open air, that Bramall realised he was slightly drunk, and it may have been this fact that explained why he didn't hear the drone of aircraft approaching. The first he knew that Gibraltar was under attack was when the Sirens sounded and anti-aircraft guns began to fire from every possible location, including the various ships at anchor.

The noise was deafening. He began to run back towards the relative safety of the former Convent building, but, realising that the attack, whatever it was, was almost certainly directed against the fleet, changed his mind and made his way down a side street leading to the harbour. Ahead of him, as he reached the perimeter wall, he could see a couple of destroyers opening up, and then a heavy cruiser. None of the Ark Royal's aircraft was in the take-off position, so far as he could see, and there was no indication that any ground-based fighters had been scrambled. So much for being prepared.

But how the hell did the Germans get down this far? Their nearest airfields would be somewhere round Biarritz, 800 miles or so North. The distance was too great. Besides, the aircraft were coming in from the South. Germany had no bases in Africa. And then it hit him. Bloody Vichy! The Navy had destroyed the French fleet at Mers; this would be their attempt at revenge. He edged closer to the water's edge. The anti-aircraft fire had by now reached an ear-splitting peak of intensity, but there was still no sign of the enemy. Then he saw them, skimming the waves – a trio of twin-engine torpedo planes powering in from the direction of Algeciras. They would have to be crazy, he thought, to maintain such a course through this volume of flack, and sure enough, while they were still a thousand metres or more from the outermost of the concrete moles that guarded the harbour, they released their payload, banked sharply and turned for home. He watched, appalled, as the torpedoes sliced through the water in the direction of the Ark Royal and its escorts. Oh, my God! One of them was sure to get through. He waited for the explosion. Nothing happened. There was to be no triumph of French arms. Two of the torpedoes exploded harmlessly against the stone defences of the outer harbour; the third went completely off course and sank in the deep water off the southern approach.

Thirty seconds later, as the light began to fail, the ack-ack guns trailed off. The French aircraft were no more than smudges in the evening sky. Bramall stood up and took in the scene. Shouldn't there have been pursuit aircraft up there as soon as the alarm sounded? Shouldn't the warning have come five or even ten minutes earlier in any case? Was there no one up there on the Peak keeping an eye out? It was unbelievable. How was he expected to stop Franco teaming up with Hitler when this lot couldn't even stop three French mavericks drunk on Pastis winging in from Africa? *War footing, my arse!*

7

Gibraltar: Government House, July 6, 1940

The clock in the entrance hall of the old Convent building struck eight o'clock as Bramall strode into the building. It was still striking as he made his way into the breakfast room, where Strickland was waiting for him at a table by the window studying a copy of the previous day's Daily Telegraph.

The Yorkshireman looked up, his face greyer than Bramall remembered. 'Ah,' he said. 'There you are. Right on time. That's something at any rate.' He folded his paper, which was opened, Bramall noticed, at the Court and Social page, and placed it on the floor next to him.

'Take a pew. I'm told you were out in the open last night when the French dropped in to leave us their calling card.'

'Yes. I was. And we were bloody lucky, that's all I can say. If even one of those torpedoes had hit…'

'Slept through it myself,' the Yorkshireman said. 'The only thing to waken me once I get my head down will be the last trump. The first I knew about it was this morning when they brought me my tea. But you're not wrong. At least no one was hurt. All we can hope for is that lessons have been learned.'

The response of the bureaucrat down the ages. 'Seriously, though, what if last night's raid had been carried out by a squadron of Stukas?'

'From where, exactly?'

'How should I know? But I was down at the harbour. I saw what happened. Do you know, they didn't scramble a single fighter.'

'Hardly surprising,' said Strickland.

'Eh?'

'There aren't any. Oh, there's plans. They've a couple of fighter squadrons ready to be shipped out, if Hitler gives us a breathing space. But for the next few weeks, as far as air attacks are concerned, ack-ack guns are all we've got.'

'You're joking.'

'Something else you might have noticed: there aren't that many squaddies about either. Governor tells me he's got three battalions so far, shortly to be joined by your friends, the Black Watch. Not exactly an Army – but all there's room for.' The waiter shuffled across to refill his glass of orange juice. 'Still, who'd have thought the French would have had a go like that?'

Bramall drew in his chair closer in to the table across the tiled floor, sending a high-pitched squeak echoing across the dining room. 'Admiral Darlan, for a start,' he said. 'But there must have been talk ... I mean, it wasn't just their ships we sank, it was their pride. Who took account of that?'

Strickland looked away from Bramall to the seagull, still perched on the windowsill outside. This was not a discussion he wished to get into. 'We're working on it,' he said. 'Not my department.'

'Yes, well I would advise whosoever's department it is to assume that Darlan isn't exactly overjoyed about seeing his fleet destroyed by – what is it? – Force H. Can you imagine what it's like being French just now? Especially if you're in uniform.

Three months ago, they believed they could beat Germany on their own. Now their country's sliced in two, half of it occupied, their remaining forces harassed and humiliated by us.'

At this point, the waiter brought their eggs and bacon. He made a point of never eavesdropping on conversations. Habits like that only got you into trouble. 'Tea, is it, gents?' he inquired.

'Coffee for me,' Strickland replied. He turned back to Bramall. 'Haven't had a proper coffee in months. Apart from last night, of course. I don't know what the stuff is they offer us now back home. Hickory or something. Comes out of a bloody bottle.'

Bramall dabbed some margarine on a slice of toast and slid it beneath one of the eggs on his plate. He wasn't going to say to Strickland, but he, too, had been looking forward to a 'proper' breakfast. 'So what do you think?' he said.

'About what?' Strickland was busy with the salt.

'About France.'

'Oh, that. Well, I'm sorry for them, of course. A right bloody mess. But this is no time for sentiment. If we're not ruthless now, it'll be too late after.' He looked up, a slice of bacon speared on the end of his fork. 'Which brings us to the business in hand. How are you getting on? What's your assessment? Are you making progress or are you just pissing about?'

'Didn't you get my cable?'

Strickland scratched his eyebrow and grimaced 'Oh,' he said – 'that.'

'Yes, that. I thought you might have mentioned it.'

'Aye, well let me see, what did it contain? Something about Serrano writing a letter to Ciano, wasn't it? Asking Italy to support Spanish claims in North Africa. And then something about Serrano and his top brass going to meet the German ambassador.'

Bramall was aghast at this show of studied indifference to his efforts. 'Are you telling me that neither of the nuggets I uncovered was of any value to you?'

Strickland spread his elbows on the table and clasped his hands in front of him. His mouth opened and then closed again. It was as if he couldn't find the words to frame the thoughts that were in his head. After a second, he picked up the copy of the Daily Telegraph he had brought with him from England. 'Do you see this newspaper? It's full of things that interest me. Most of them are new to me. But they don't change what lies ahead. Your cable was a bit like that. If you want to know what I did with it, I mentioned it in a memo I sent to Lord Halifax. It was a couple of lines on page two. I should imagine he nodded as he read it, then turned the page.'

Bramall felt utterly deflated, but Strickland, rather like Croft in Lisbon, wasn't done. 'Let me explain. What you have to do with pieces of information like that is follow up on them. On their own, they're indicators, not evidence. I wouldn't expect you to race off to Rome to take a look at Count Ciano's Olivetti, but I would expect you to do your best to find out what happens at that meeting between Serrano and his colleagues and the German ambassador. Now that's what's really interesting. If you could bring me a transcript of that conversation, then we'd be getting somewhere.'

'And how in hell am I supposed to do that?'

'That's for you to work out, lad. It's why you're there. No one ever said it would be easy.'

Bramall sat back in his chair, feeling as if the stuffing had been knocked out of him.

It was Strickland's turn to frown. 'Look,' he said, 'don't take it personally. Let's be positive for a moment. You've made a start. You're on your way. You've added another small piece to the jigsaw and, with luck, the big picture will soon start forming in your head.'

Bramall wasn't convinced. 'You really believe that?'

'Why not? Tall oaks from little acorns grow. So stick at it and cheer up. Tell me about the Duke. You must be pleased to be shot of him.'

'Too bloody right. I'm just glad the Bahamas business worked out. Hoare seemed a bit sceptical about the idea, I thought. But I must have picked him up wrong.'

A look of puzzlement crept across Strickland's ruddy features. 'You've lost me. Are you saying that was your idea? Sending him to Timbuktu, I mean?'

'Well, yes – for what it's worth.'

'I see.' Strickland looked almost impressed.

'I was going to include it in my cable, but after the event, there didn't seem much point.'

'Crafty old sod.'

'Who?'

'Hoare. Never said. Claimed all the credit for himself. I'm glad you told me that. Well done.'

An unaccustomed warmth coursed through Bramall. It was as if he had just drunk a large restorative brandy. 'Thanks,' he said. 'I realise the Duke established my cover, and I'll not pretend that wasn't useful – not least with Serrano. But what a pain in the arse!'

'No argument here,' said Strickland, chewing contentedly. 'If I'd had my way, he'd have been put on the Army List and sent straight to Front Line.'

A blob of egg yolk dropped from Bramall's raised fork onto his plate. 'Which is where exactly?'

Strickland offered a wry smile, acknowledging the joke. Britain was at war, but apart from the occasional dogfight over the Channel, there hadn't been any fighting for weeks. 'Well,' he said, 'according to what we saw last night, it's right here in Gibraltar.'

'Except that the enemy turns out to be French.'

'True. Funny old world, isn't it?' He reached once more for the salt. 'Speaking of which, I heard from Croft the other day.'

'Oh yes?'

'Sent me a cable. A lot of it was about you.' The statement hung in the air for a moment before Strickland resumed with a request for the pot of marmalade on the table next to them.

Bramall pulled his chair back and stretched across to fetch the jam. Once again, a piercing screech rang through the room.'

'And do you mind not doing that? said Strickland. 'It sets my teeth on edge.'

'Sorry. But you were saying ...'

'He says you're still a bit green about the gills, but we should maybe persevere with you.'

'Well, that's very white of him.'

'Is he right, though? That's the thing. Are you just bedding in for the duration, hoping for a stroke of luck somewhere along the way, or do you honestly think you might make a difference? There's no room for passengers in this war. So what do you think? How do you assess things so far?'

Bramall took a deep breath. He felt like a slow boy at school who'd just been told he was being held back a year. 'Well,' he began, 'I've made headway with Serrano, which wasn't something I'd expected to happen. That has to count for something.'

Strickland harrumphed, but said nothing.

'He's in two minds about joining the war and I think my talk with him – that and the Mers-el-Kebir business – might just have convinced him to hang back before rushing into a course of action he might regret.'

'Oh aye? Trusts you, does he?'

'I'd say so. So far as I can tell, just about everybody in Spain thinks I'm batting for Hitler – or at least for Fascism.'

'I told you we'd get the word out. What about Beigbeder?'

'I had lunch with him last week – along with the Duke and Duchess, that is. Seemed friendly enough. Well disposed, even. But there's talk he might not last the distance.'

Croft had mentioned something similar over the phone and Strickland was disappointed to have the rumour confirmed. 'Who would replace him?' he asked.

'Who do you think?'

'Serrano?'

'That'd be my bet. With any luck, I'd be well in with the most powerful man in Spain Spain – apart from Franco, of course. Not bad for a beginner.'

Strickland digested Bramall's latest piece of conceit along with a slice of egg. 'And since you're a betting man, what odds do you put on Sir George Sharpe's nightmare of a second front coming true? I hear you and he had a bit of a barney last night.'

'We did. But nothing to frighten the horses. It all depends on Hitler. If Germany comes through with food and fuel – and plenty of both – and promises to back Madrid on North Africa as well as Gibraltar, then it's Plan B for us, I'm afraid. It all could hang on what assurances Canaris can give to Franco. But if we get in first with material assistance and convince him we're ready to fight to the end, with America behind us, I'd say we're in with a shout.'

'So what are you doing to convince Serrano that England means business?'

Bramall's brow furrowed. 'That's the problem,' he said at last. 'If there was only something I could use, some leverage I could apply, before Hitler commits himself to Spain, it might just tip the balance – always providing Downing Street and Hoare come up with the goods their end. Right now, though, I haven't got anything.'

Strickland nodded and stabbed at a piece of bacon. 'What else?'

'What do you mean?'

'Anything you haven't told me?'

'Well … '

'What?'

Bramall let out a sigh. 'There's this girl … '

Strickland was immediately suspicious. 'Go on.'

'Daughter of Serrano's principal aide, engaged to an Argentinean Nazi I met a couple of times in Buenos Aires who seems to be something of a go-between for the Germans in their dealings with Spain.'

'Really?' Now Strickland actually looked interested. 'And where precisely do you fit into her plans?'

Bramall stared hard at the wall opposite. 'Hard to say. But she came to see me at my hotel the other night and made it clear that she would do whatever she could to keep her country out of the war.'

'What made her come to you?'

'I'd met her at a reception at her parents' house a few days previously.'

'Must have made quite an impression.'

'I didn't think she liked me, actually. You could have knocked me down with Chamberlain's piece of paper when I opened the door and there she was.'

'I see.'

'The thing is, she hears things. She knows Serrano. Her father is his chief of staff. Just as important, she's horrified by the possibility that Franco might ally Spain to the Nazis.'

The Yorkshireman sniffed. 'Just be careful you're not being set up.'

'I really don't think … '

'And don't go falling for her. Good looking, is she? What's her name?'

'Isabel Ortega. And she's pretty enough, I suppose – not that I've really noticed.'

Strickland's expression on hearing this was that of a man who had listened to generations of young men protesting their immunity to female charms. 'Well,' he said wearily, 'I've warned you. Be on your guard. When women come into the bedroom, good sense usually goes out the window.'

'I'll try to remember that.'

In the silence that followed, a welcome Highland lilt could be heard wafting across the breakfast room. It was MacLeish. 'Morning, gentlemen,' he said, 'I trust you've enjoyed your breakfast. But now, if you don't mind, there's work to be done.'

For the next half hour, as the sunlight intensified and the overhead fans came on in the dining room, the three intelligence operatives compared notes and stratagems. Bramall was left in no doubt as to the vulnerability of Gibraltar and the urgency of his mission. He was told to build on his relationship with Serrano but, at the same time, to infiltrate the German Legation in search of the information they were sure was there that would reveal Berlin's intentions and provide London with vital leverage in its war of nerves with Franco.

'There has to be something,' said Strickland. There always is. If Berlin puts its forces into Spain and mounts an attack on Gib, with all that that entails, there has to be a price to pay and someone that loses out in the process. Find out what the price is and who would be the losers. France would be my guess. Give us something we can use.'

Bramall nodded, wondering how on Earth he was supposed to come up with the keys to the Legation's files. 'And in the meantime?'

'In the meantime,' said MacLeish, 'the armed forces will continue to build up their strength here on the Rock. We won't be caught napping again like last night.'

Strickland butted in. 'And we'll look to Hoare in Madrid to soft-soap Franco – a task for which he is peculiarly well adapted. You probably feel you're alone in this business. It's in the nature of espionage. But there's a team behind you. Never forget that. Feed us a decent ball and we'll go for the line.'

'I'll do my best,' said Bramall.

'Course you will,' said MacLeish. 'We never doubted you.'

Strickland began to fidget. His mind always seemed to be racing off in new directions. 'There is one other thing.

Hasselfeldt probably knows you're here. There are at least fifty Nazi agents in the area: *Abwehr, SD, Gestapo* – the lot. They'll have taken photographs. The pictures will go back to Madrid for analysis – probably on the same train you're taking. Hasselfeldt will have been wondering where you've got to. He'll be asking around. Chances are he'll want to talk to you when you get back.'

This didn't sound good. 'So what do I do?'

It was MacLeish who cut in this time. 'If I were you, I'd get in first.'

'You mean pay him a visit?'

'Exactly. Show willing. Make it look like your trip here was the most natural thing in the world.'

Strickland polished his glasses with his breakfast napkin as he took up the theme. 'Pre-empt the bastard. Tell him you've got some useful bits and pieces about Gib… nothing special, mind, don't get him all excited. Tell him we're flying in a fighter squadron next month – which is true – with others to follow, most probably Hurricanes … no, make it Spitfires. Tell him the Black Watch are on their way, and that we're training some of our bigger guns on Algeciras, just in case. Say we're bringing in heavy AA platforms and a dozen searchlight batteries to help with night firing. He'll check it out and more than likely find you've stayed on the level with him. As for morale, no harm letting him know not everyone here favours continuing the war. Let him think you've got allies – people it might pay to keep in touch with. Then, if we ever need to get you down here, we can always arrange for someone to come up with a suitable invitation. Do you see where I'm going with this?'

Bramall nodded. 'What if he asks for names?'

MacLeish produced a sheet of paper, with photographs attached. 'I took the liberty of getting three 'candidates' lined up, just in case. They're all serving officers, but leaving with Force H in the next week or so – and they won't be coming back. Study their names. Remember their faces. Chances are they'll have photographs to match the names. You don't have to make a song and dance about them. Just say that they're what our American cousins like to call 'flakey' on the war.'

'Got it.'

'The simpler the plan, the better it works.,' Strickland said, searching in his jacket pocket for his pipe. 'If we'd more time, and you had more experience, we might have come up with a little of what we like to call 'disinformation' – maybe volunteer a supposed weak spot in our defences – somewhere they might like to concentrate their attack. But if you don't mind my saying so, you're not quite ready for that. Nor is Gib, come to that. Top priority right now is to preserve your cover.'

Strickland's eyebrow arched. 'And don't go soft over that bloody girl! She's trouble.'

'All right, all right. You've made your point.'

'Good. Anything you want to add, MacLeish?'

'No,' the MI5 man said. 'Just to wish him luck. He'll need it.'

Madrid: Villa Ortega, July 6

Isabel dreaded the weekend. Luder was due to leave for Germany on Monday, but until then, for the next two days, she would be in his hands, almost literally, and she had no idea how she would deal with the situation. Her discovery that

Bramall was out of town and not due back before Sunday had been a blow. He wouldn'thave allowed her to be assaulted by the Argentinean, or anyone else. She would feel safe with him around. Now she would have to survive on her wits. There was no point in talking to her mother, who believed Fate and submission to be virtually identical. She would put her daughter's dilemma down to 'men' and advise her to lie back and think of the household budget she would one day control. Her father, preoccupied with advancing the family's wealth and standing, would consider any intervention from him to be both inappropriate and embarrassing and suggest she discuss outstanding issues with Luder or her mother.

More important even than her personal concerns was the 'intelligence' about this 'Operation Felix' that she now carried around with her tucked into her bra – along with the revelation that Hitler and Franco were negotiating Spanish membership of the Axis and the dismemberment of France's empire in North Africa. She was ready, she decided, to sacrifice anything, even herself, to ensure that this vital information reached London. It would be an action she could be proud of – something to set against the self-obsession and evasions of recent years. Only when she had completed the task that lay ahead, would she feel free to indulge in the luxury of revenge. It wasn't easy. Luder was like no one else she had ever met. Most men – most women, too – were a mixture of good and bad, and most of the bad was just weakness. But Felipe was entirely without redeeming virtues. There was no 'good side' to him. He was pure evil. As she contemplated, for the fourth or fifth time that morning, the hateful, shameful nature of the Argentinean – a man, she was sure, so ignoble as not to comprehend the very meaning of honour – the thought of the violence and humiliation he could unleash on her was almost more than she could bear. In the meantime, she had to steel herself. If it happened, it happened, and she would deal with it. But she prayed fervently that she would be spared. The politics of war was something else. As a Spaniard, she looked forward to the day when the British hauled down their flag in Gibraltar and the flag of Spain was raised in its place. Yet with Franco's regime busy plotting imperial aggression on its own account at the expense of the native peoples of North Africa, to say nothing of the French, what right did Madrid have to point a finger at anyone?

She had asked her father about the situation over breakfast. He had been surprised at first, then gratified by her interest. With France out of the war, he told her, and the Italian fleet, backed by Hitler, manoeuvring between Taranto and Libya, the only thing standing in the way of a Fascist takeover of North Africa and the Balkans was the Royal Navy.

'The British think they can intimidate us with their fleet, as if no time at all has passed since Trafalgar. Gibraltar is the key to everything, they say. But what will they do when they wake up one morning to find the key in the *Caudillo's* pocket.'

Lisbon: Praça das Cebolas district, July 7

Strickland's flight to Lisbon had been delayed due to fears of enemy action, and after an hour spent with The ambassador, sir Walford Selby, he took a taxi straight to the restaurant where he was due to meet Croft for lunch. It was just off the Praçadas Cebolas, next to the Santa Apolónia railway station, and was apparently celebrated for its native cuisine. Croft was there already, dressed as always in his crumpled linen suit. The two men greeted each other.

'Douglas,' good to see you.

'And you, Tom. Sit down. Take the weight off your feet.'

'I take it we're not alone.'

'Hell, no. Chap over there, with the newspaper, he works for the Legation. A Sudeten German, doesn't speak much English. I doubt he's even heard of you.'

Strickland tried not to turn around, feeling ever so slightly miffed. 'Anyone else?'

'The *Gestapo* head of station often entertains here. He'll probably be along in a minute. I'll let you know.'

'If you would.'

'Nice day.'

'Well, the real heat's still to come. But how were things in Gib?'

'Not too rosy, if you must know. Governor's doing a hell of a job, but it'll be another three months before they're fully ready to withstand an assault.'

Croft grimaced. 'So we'd better hope Jerry's timetable spins out even longer than ours.'

The Yorkshireman smiled. 'That's about the size of it. But I haven't got much time. The Sunderland takes off at six. How are things? How's the Duke?'

'Oh, still settling in. There've been a couple of dinner parties – and the Holy Ghost is, as you know, omnipresent.'

This reference to the Portuguese banker, Ricardo Espírito Santo Silva, the Duke's host at his palatial residence, the *Boca do Inferno* – the Hellmouth – was not lost on Strickland. 'Is he a threat?' he asked.

'Depends what you mean by threat. I'd say he's half in love with the sheer prestige of having the Duke to stay, half looking to the main chance, which could mean working with us, but more likely a deal with Jerry.'

'Slippery as ever, then?'

'Too right – a complete tosser. But I've got my eye on him. Speaking of which, any chance I can have that backup I talked about? We're outnumbered ten to one. It's not a fair fight.'

Strickland sighed. Budgets for MI6, which still had to prove its usefulness in wartime, were depressingly small. Most cash was going on the new Special Operations Executive, with its concentration on France and other parts of occupied Europe. 'There's a lad coming out from London in the next week or so. Name of Crowther. Speaks the lingo, studied here and he's a crack marksman. He'll be accompanied by a couple of Special Branch chaps who'll stay with you so long as the Duke's here. They'll be under your orders, so don't worry. Oh, and I've brought you a few extra escudos. I'll not hand them over to you here, if you don't mind, but they should enable you to add a couple at least to your Portuguese support crew.'

'And that's it?'

'I'm afraid so.'

'Well, it's something. Thanks, Tom.'

'I only wish it could have been more.'

The waiter stood poised. Croft ordered a bottle of red from the Dão region to go with the clams in olive oil, garlic and fresh coriander that turned out to be the speciality of the house. Strickland lobbied briefly for a white, but Croft said it wasn't worth it.

Once the waiter had gone, Croft asked how Bramall was doing.

Strickland pursed his lips. 'Not too bad,' he said. 'A pity he didn't have more time to settle in. He's having to make it up as he goes along. He won't have the luxury of learning from his mistakes.'

'But he's not screwing up?'

'Not so far.'

'That's something, I suppose. But we shouldn't expect too much of him. If Franco decides to go to war next month, I don't reckon Bramall will be the one to tell us. But if it's next year, who knows? He's an investment. We'll only know down the road how he performs.'

Strickland's eyes brightened so that Croft thought he could detect an almost paternal glint. 'In that event,' he said, 'I shall say he was always our best hope. And call me a sentimental old fool if you like, but I don't completely rule it out.' He paused, glancing across the square towards the blue of the ocean. 'Seriously, though, as far as Gibraltar is concerned, Hoare and Eccles are our best hope. With luck, they'll have half of Franco's generals on the payroll by end of the year.'

At this point, the wine arrived. Strickland too a sip, which clearly pleased him, before broaching the subject of Portugal and its relations with Germany. What Croft had to say on this point was alarming. The Spanish, it seemed, had launched a new diplomatic initiative, spearheaded by Serrano. 'What he wants is for Portugal to renounce its treaty of friendship with the British. But if you ask me, it's the incorporation of Portugal into a greater Spain that's his long-term goal. That and a whole lot more. We need to watch that. The *Reconquista* isn't finished yet. It's noticeable that the Germans have gone deathly quiet. I reckon they're hoping Serrano can do the business for them and bring Salazar into the war alongside Spain. Either that or they're planning some kind of stunt. Which brings us back to HR Bloody H.'

Strickland once more savoured his wine – a rare treat. 'In which case, the sooner we get him to the Bahamas the better. That was Bramall's idea, by the way, not Hoare's. He merely passed it on. But you're not seriously suggesting they'd kidnap him and fly him to Berlin? What as? A trophy?'

'More of an inducement, I'd say. A way of giving London an alternative strategy.'

Strickland made a face. 'Bit of a long shot.'

'Depends who's doing the calculations. Ribbentrop spent quite a while in London as ambassador. He knows the Duchess and he knows the power the Royal Family exerts on the popular imagination.'

'Yes, but does he appreciate the sea-change that occurred after the Abdication?'

'Almost certainly not,' said Croft. 'He'll be relying for his information and judgement on views that were out of date even before the attack on Poland.'

Strickland wasn't sure where this conversation was going, but it didn't sound good. 'So what you're telling me, if I understand you aright, is that Ribbentrop might be mad enough to seize the Duke and Duchess, with or without their approval, then use them as a rallying point for pro-German sympathies. Is that it?'

'That's exactly what I'm saying.' Croft looked up. Their starters had arrived. He was about to resume his speculation when a flurry of activity at a nearby table caused him to put up a warning hand. 'Don't look now,' he said, 'but the *Gestapo* gentleman I was telling you about has just sat down over in the far corner.'

'Oh yes?' said Strickland, intrigued. 'Who's with him? Anyone we know?'

The intelligence man adjusted his glasses. 'Bloody hell,' he said. 'It's Lourenço.'

'Who?'

'Head of the PVDE – the security police.'

'Oh, him! I thought he was on our side.'

'He is. At least I think he is – if he's on anyone's side, that is. But that's him, large as life – or, in his case, as small.'

'Don't suppose you can hear what they're saying?'

'No. And there's a couple of goons standing right behind. If I keep on staring, they're going to be over here in a minute.'

'And we don't want that.'

'No, we most certainly don't.'

Strickland tried his sardines. Excellent. Quite meaty, with a hint of spice. He wasn't looking forward to his return to wartime Britain, with its rationing. 'I suppose you're about to tell me this adds weight to your theory.'

Croft moved his spoon around in his bowl of fish soup. 'Well it doesn't exactly subtract from it, does it?'

'No. What it does, in fact, is leave it exactly where it was. So pray continue.'

'Okay. Let's just say Ribbentrop wants the Duke. Two possibilities then exist. One, that the Duke is agreeable and goes quietly, in which case we have to act fast. Two, the Duke doesn't go along, in which case the Germans have to act, and we have to move even faster. It doesn't matter how absurd the whole notion is of the British people rallying to their former King. What matters is that the sight of the Duke of Windsor in Berlin is not one we would wish to parade before the world in present circumstances. Am I right?'

The spymaster put down his knife and fork and thought for a moment. 'So let's review the situation. You've got Crowther and the two Special Branch bods coming in, and money for another two lookouts, maybe three. And that's on top of Millar, your existing legman, who, even if he's no genius, is a marksman who can hit an apple with a knife at thirty yards. Then there's the embassy security squad. How many are they? Four? Six? Plus, the Duke's own bodyguard, here from Spain, and whatever locals you've already got on the payroll. Not a bad haul, if I say so myself. So gather your forces and see to it he gets on that bloody boat. There's nothing more you can do. You might even say it's what we pay you for.'

Croft laughed. 'Oh yes? Growing rich, am I? Ready to retire to my Cotswolds mansion?'

Strickland returned to his sardines. 'When the time comes, you can move in with me, Douglas. You'll have the West Wing all to yourself.'

Madrid: Ritz Hotel, July 7

'I am sorry, Señor,' said the receptionist, 'but the embassy has closed your account and removed your clothes and other personal belongings to the Hotel Paris.'

'Brilliant!' said Bramall, exhausted after a return journey

from Algeciras that had proved even worse than the journey south. The Saturday morning local connecting with the Express at Córdoba had broken down completely north of Ronda and got taken out of service, forcing passengers to wait overnight for a replacement. He had spent the entire time on the platform, sat up against a brick wall being eaten alive by mosquitoes. Back at last in the Ritz, he now looked at the uniformed figure behind the desk, hoping to detect some quality of mercy in his eyes. There was none. 'So you're saying I can't go upstairs to my room and get some sleep?'

The reply was brisk and distinctly unaccommodating. 'I am afraid not, Señor. But your room at the Paris is waiting. Would you like me to call you a taxi?'

'Why not? Let's go for it. I'll be the one slumped over there on the sofa.'

'Of course, Señor, I understand. By the way, there was a message for you, from a young lady.'

'Oh yes?'

'She wanted you to know that she would meet you in the Gijón tomorrow morning, as agreed.'

'I see. You did, of course, inform her of my change of address?'

'I took the liberty, Señor. I am sure you will like the Paris. Lots of businessmen stay there, they tell me. From Germany and Italy and … other places.'

'Sounds fun.'

Twenty minutes later, the taxi pulled up at the main door of the Hotel Paris on the Calle Alcalá, just off the Puerta del Sol. As he paid the driver, he looked up at the Interior Ministry, whose brooding presence dominated the square.

His room, as he had feared, was a dreary single at the end

of a long corridor on the hotel's southern side, facing a ham emporium. His bags, neatly packed, sat on floor next to the wardrobe. They had even included his unopened bottle of champagne. But no gramophone. He sat on the edge of the bed. The springs squeaked.

The Interior Ministry clock in the Puerta del Sol showed 12.17 when he left the hotel and headed across the square towards the Calle de la Montera, then due north to Malasaña. He was too keyed-up to sleep, he realised, and hoped he might catch Romero in the *tasca*. Next to the massive Telefónica building on the Avenida Antonio, a sour-faced young *Guardia Civil* officer stopped him and asked to see his papers. He remembered the Telefónica being officially opened. It was 1929. He was on his year out from Cambridge, working in bars, occasionally turning up for tutorials at the University of Madrid. The *edificio*, with its up-to-date switchboards and miles of cable, had reminded him of a New York skyscraper, embellished with detail straight out of Spanish baroque. Alfonso XIII had used the occasion to proclaim his country's entry into the modern world, not realising that he himself would soon be consigned to the past. When the police officer saw the laisser passer signed by Serrano still folded inside his passport, he saluted and sent him on his way.

There were various stragglers about the city centre, but no obvious brigands. Perhaps they only acted under orders. He was lucky, too, when he got to the *tasca*. Romero was at something of a loose end and seemed glad of the company

The Dubliner indicated two chairs by the window. He filled a glass of wine for his guest, but stuck to water himself. He had to get in shape, he said, and drink just held him back.

'Not like O'Duffy, then.'

Romero laughed. 'O'Duffy? Jesus, I haven't thought about that prize bollox in years. Crazy fucker. What's happened him anyway?'

General Eoin O'Duffy was a hate figure for both men. A native of Monaghan, who rose through the ranks of the IRA to become chief adjutant to Michael Collins, he had pushed the 'gaelic Ireland' strategy that forced thousands of Protestants, including the Bramalls, off their land. Later, after falling foul of DeValera, he led a Blueshirts battalion in the Spanish war, humiliating himself and his men in a series of disastrous, drink-fuelled episodes until Franco lost patience and ordered him out of the country.

Bramall – who remembered how his father dismissed DeValera as a half-Spanish 'bastard' – eyed Romero, who sat slumped back in his chair. 'Last I heard, he was making pro-Nazi speeches in Dublin. But I can't see anyone taking him seriously after what happened here.

'It's the fact he's alive at all, not stuck through with a bayonet, that bothers me,' Romero said. He scowled, trying to exorcise the memory of the Irish Fascist, then relaxed his features. 'Just because I'm off the stuff, don't mean you can't have another glass.' He picked up the bottle of wine from the bar counter and planted it on a table next to the window. 'So where you been, anyway?' he asked. 'It's been a while.'

'Can't you guess?'

'I'm not psychic.'

Bramall began to assemble a cigarette and pushed the *Ideales* packet across the table towards Romero. 'I've been to Gibraltar.'

Romero ran a hand across his brow, which was glistening

with sweat. 'Learn anythin'?'

'Only that I'm on borrowed time and they're thinking of calling in the loan. To listen to them, you'd think all they have to do is dial up the problem and I come up with the intelligence to stop it from happening.' He laughed a hollow laugh. 'I mean, if it was that simple, we'd all be doing it.'

Romero shrugged and said nothing. Bramall stared into his glass as if looking for inspiration. 'The one good piece of news,' he said at last, 'is that we're not entirely on our own. There's someone I'd like you to meet.'

'One of your "chaps" from London, I take it.'

'Not at all. It's a she, and she's Spanish.'

'Really?'

'Really.'

'So where is she?'

'You can meet her tomorrow morning in the Gijón – nine o'clock.'

Romero took a sip of water. 'I can't wait,' he said.

Madrid: Villa of Dominique de Fourneau, July 7, 11.30pm

Beigbeder's eyes were growing heavy and he was drifting into a contented, post-coital slumber when Dominique suddenly said, 'You know, Juan, I saw your wife yesterday. She remembered me from Casablanca.'

The Foreign Minister was awake in an instant and his head twitched round. 'My wife?' he said. 'You *talked* to her?'

'But of course. I called round. She gets so little opportunity these days to speak French. I really think she was pleased to see me.'

Beigbeder scrabbled for his glasses, which had fallen onto the floor next to the bed, and pulled them on over his ears. 'You don't think she suspects anything, do you?'

Dominique ran the backs of her fingers lightly up her lover's cheek. 'No, *Cherie*, don't worry. Your secret is safe with me. You know that.'

'Because she's a terribly jealous woman.'

'How exhausting for you – and you such a pillar of rectitude.'

'Yes, well, I cannot help the way I am made.'

Dominique sat up in the bed. She needed the Spaniard in a relaxed mood. That was when his natural loquaciousness ran riot. He would tell her anything once he'd shot his bolt. Beigbeder groaned appreciatively and reached across, cupping each of her breasts in turn in his bony, olive-skinned hands. 'I don't have to go straightaway,' he said.

'Honestly, Juan, you're such a performer. Where *do* you get the energy?'

'It's my diet,' he said. 'Lots of fruit and nuts.'

'I see. You're such a busy man these days. But you're like a gymnast. You leave me gasping. Perhaps it's just as well that there are others to keep you occupied when I'm not around.'

'I don't know what you're talking about.'

'Oh come now. Your reputation proceeds you. My only question is, what can your various little trollopes possibly do for you that I can't do *so* much better? For example, do they do *this* for you?' She reached beneath the bedclothes.

As he stiffened, she could hear the catch in his breath. 'There is no one else ...'

Dominique brushed a strand of hair from her face, then half

closed her eyes and slowly ran her tongue along her top teeth beneath the swell of her upper lip. In her experience, which was considerable, this simplest of ploys invariably drove men to fresh heights of arousal. She turned towards him and lifted the sheets over her head. 'And they do *this*?'

Beigbeder's eyes grew wide. He threw off his spectacles and fell back on the pillow. 'Oh, Dominique,' he said. 'When I told you I missed you terribly after you left Morocco, I wasn't lying. You really ... are ... the most ... *Oh, God!*

The clock on the mantelpiece struck midnight.

Madrid: Café Gijón, next morning

From her corner table at the famous glass and marble café where she had been sitting for the last half hour, Isabel glanced up at the ornate clock on the opposite wall. Bramall had said he would be there at nine and it was already twenty-past. She had been to the Gijón only once before. It was famous for its *tertulias* – noisy get-togethers of artists and intellectuals, most of them opposed to whichever regime happened to be in power. But it was too early, especially on a Monday morning, for most of these rebels to be out of their beds. Apart from a dishevelled bootblack and an elderly woman reading Saturday's *ABC* with a magnifying glass, only the young Galician writer Camilo José Cela was there, a cigarette welded to his fingers. He was sipping from a café solo while continuing to work on his interminable manuscript, said to be a novel of bohemian life. From time to time he looked up to survey the other customers, snatching at his coffee, rubbing his eyes. Then he would mutter to himself and scribble another sentence. Isabel wondered whether she might occupy a line in his narrative. What would he say, she wondered? *'At a table beneath the clock, a proud-looking young woman – Castilian, with a father in a high government position – observed the author with an amused contempt, no doubt wondering what he would write about her.'* The double-take made Isabel laugh out loud, and Cela stared at her, his pen poised.

She called for another cup of chocolate, but rejected the waiter's offer of a second slice of doughnut. She had never cared for *churros* – probably something to do with her genteel upbringing. She would give him another ten minutes, no more. At nine thirty-three, just as she was placing a handful of coins on the table, she felt a tap on her shoulder. She looked up. It was Bramall, looking tired and careworn, as if he hadn't slept in a week. With him was a second man, who, to judge by his appearance, rarely slept at all. He put her in mind of a vampire, with pale white skin, black hair and piercing eyes that looked slightly dazzled in the light.

'Sorry I'm late,' he said, 'This is Eddy – Eddy Romero. He's a friend – another Irishman, I'm afraid – and he's going to help us. Eddy, this is Isabel.'

The stranger took the tips of her extended hand and planted the faintest kiss on her fingers. 'Good morning, Señorita. I hope you know what you're doing getting involved with this man.'

He spoke excellent Spanish – fluent. But there was an accent there. Had he Mexican blood, perhaps? Not Irish, surely. Not with that skin.

Bramall answered her unspoken question. 'Eddy's from Dublin. Fought in the IRA to make Ireland green, gaelic and free. But his father was from Badajoz. Back in '37, he joined

280

the International Brigades. Now he runs a *tasca* in Malasaña. A man of many accomplishments.'

Dublin? Isabel had read some of the poetry of Yeats and tried and failed to make sense of Joyce's Ulysses. She would love to visit the city some day. She pulled out a chair. 'Please sit down, Señor. You are most welcome. But I had no idea.'

'Charlie plays things by ear. He'd like you to think he plans everything three months in advance – you know, that upper-class Protestant prescience. The truth is, it was me found him, not the other way round.'

'*Charlie?* You call him Charlie. Oh, *Señor*, I think you and I are going to get along.'

'Eddy. Call me Eddy. If we're going to win this war for the British Empire, we ought to be on first-name terms.'

This made Isabel laugh. Bramall noticed this and felt a faint twinge of jealousy.

Over the course of the next ten minutes, Eddy and Bramall painted in their shared history in Spain. Isabel felt suddenly infused with confidence. Luder might still be a brooding presence, but with these two -men newly arrived in her life, she was sure she could handle him.

A waiter brought three *cafés solos*. When they were alone again, Isabel told them in a whisper that she had something important to say. Bramall motioned her to continue. She then recounted the conversation between her father and Luder and the looming threat to Gibraltar.

'It's called Operation Felix. Hitler wants to send in his special forces and his Luftwaffe. But first the plan is to smuggle in huge guns that will be positioned in the hills around Algeciras to pound the Rock and your navy. Spain will join in. We will get to plant our flag. But Gibraltar will be German."

Bramall was stunned. 'And I've only been away a couple of days.'

Romero tucked into the plateful of olives that had just been set down in front of them. 'I know.' He was talking English now, with an accent she had to work hard to follow. 'Makes you feel pretty useless, huh? But sure don't worry about it. Your role in all this is still there lookin' right at you.'

'You mean I'm the one has to stand all of this up?'

'Who else? If you don't it's just rumours and hearsay.'

'And the only way I can hope to do that is to get something from the Spanish or the Germans, preferably both, that spells the whole thing out in black and white, with official government seals and a photograph of the smoking gun.'

Romero sipped at his coffee. 'Sounds about right. Things are moving faster than you thought. But now we've got Isabel, sure it'll all be just fine.' He turned to the young woman sitting by his side. 'How's your English?'

'I try,' she said. She had a soft, honey-brown voice that was easy on the ears. 'I learned it at school and I spent a month one time in London. But I am – what is it you say? – not in practise.'

'Don't worry, it'll come.'

Bramall felt like he had once when he was a small boy playing with his lead soldiers and his father, in his general's uniform, had walked into the room. Reality was a bastard. Operation Felix was a nightmare. He would have to get back inside the German Legation to find the evidence he needed. There was no alternative.

'If I can prove that Franco has no intention of stopping at

Gibraltar, but intends to take over France's African empire, with Hitler's backing, then a whole new perspective opens up. Pétain would get straight on to Berlin and issue an ultimatum: either Germany says no to Franco and publicly guarantees the status quo in Africa, in which case Spain is out of the game and stays neutral – or else the French empire re-enters the war.'

He was warming to his theme. Romero let him talk on. He was intrigued to see how long Bramall's train of thought could travel before it hit the buffers.

'I know it sounds like a bit of an empty threat, but the French colonial forces could do serious damage. With the British, they'd control the southern Mediterranean and be in a position to take on the Italians in Libya. French ships out of Dakar would join the war against raiders and U-boats in the Atlantic. At the same time, the Germans would have to end the free zone and double the size of their army of occupation. That'd mean another 100,000 *Wehrmacht* removed from frontline duties. Is that what Hitler wants right now? I don't think so.'

Romero reached for tobacco and paper, then pushed them away. 'It's a high risk strategy all right, no question of that. You think it's possible?'

Bramall shrugged. 'The game is going to play itself out, whatever happens. I don't deal the cards. All I'd be doing is giving Vichy a sneak look at Franco's hand.'

The Dubliner couldn't fault the logic. 'And if Pétain played his own cards right, Franco could end up a busted flush. He'd have to leave the game, stick to Patience. And wouldn't that be nice? Wouldn't that be somethin' worth seein'?'

Madrid: German Legation, July 8, 1940

It was a fine, clear morning in downtown Madrid and Ambassador Von Stohrer was in an expansive mood. 'Operation Willi,' Schellenberg's codename for the kidnapping of the Duke of Windsor, had not so far been dropped, but at least the miserable affair had shifted to Lisbon and become the nightmare primarily of his esteemed colleague, Hoyningen-Huene. In Madrid, the previous Friday's diplomatic bag had brought Stohrer something much more interesting: a preliminary draft of the plan designed to tempt Franco into the war and deal a fatal blow to Britain's Mediterranean ambitions.

The draft of Operation Felix bore three signatures: Ribbentrop for the Foreign Service; Reichenau for the High Command; and Martin Bormann for the *Führer*. Stohrer never quite understood Bormann's role in the Party Establishment. He seemed to have a finger in every pie. Mention of the Saxon-born apparatchik always brought to his mind the image of Cerberus, guardian of the infernal regions. In an accompanying letter, from Ribbentrop, the ambassador was instructed to gather together Franco's top people – though not the *Generalísimo* himself – and discover from them what practical enthusiasm, if any, now existed for Spanish entry into the war. He was permitted to sketch an outline of the assault on

Gibraltar, but not to go into detail. The plan was still fluid, apparently, and subject to change. What was required of him was an exposition of the likely response and any conditions that might be attached.

Stohrer still marvelled at the irony. Only weeks before, intoxicated by Germany's defeat of France, Franco had pledged to join the fight. He had told Hoare – an opponent from the top drawer in Stohrer's opinion – that England should capitulate at once and spare itself further humiliation. He even rebuffed an offer of economic assistance from the United States, arguing that Spain's neutrality was not for sale. But in Berlin, State Secretary Weizsäcker had rejected a switch to 'belligerence,' arguing that, while welcome in tone, it came at too high a price – and his argument was the one that prevailed. The present war, however, was nothing if not fluid. Less than two months after rejecting Franco's offer, the omnipresent Plans and Contingencies department of the Reich (Stohrer was sure it had an office building somewhere, probably next to the Chancellery) came up with its own, quite separate verdict.

Though no soldier, Stohrer had made a significant contribution to the preparation of Felix. He knew a great deal not only about the mind-set of Spain's military and political hierarchies, but about the capacity of the Spanish state in the fifteen months since the Civil War ended to mount any kind of strategic operation. His view was that while the spirit was willing, the flesh was weak – and the infrastructure weaker still. Even with German help, the task was immense. The Spanish railway system was a joke. It wasn't even the same gauge as the rest of Europe and hadn't been properly maintained for years. The *Wehrmacht* would have to bring in the necessary heavy equipment by road.

The thousands of troops involved would then have to cross the entire length of Spain in secret and be supplied along the way. Crucially, an airstrip would have to be constructed in southern Andalucia capable of supporting both bombers and fighters. Just setting up batteries of guns in the hills behind Algeciras without the British suspecting what was happening would in itself be a major achievement.

The High Command, however, was nothing if not resourceful, and the proposal, while taking all – or most – of the known adverse factors into account, looked to have a genuine prospect of success. Stohrer and his chief military attaché, Colonel Walter Bruns, a former infantry commander and machine gun specialist, had spent the weekend reading through the documentation, comparing notes. Stohrer and Bruns, together with the three main service attachés, *Wehrmacht, Luftwaffe* and *Kriegsmarine*, had gutted the plan, summarising its principal features and military requirements. This morning, Interior Minister Serrano Suñer, Foreign Minister Beigbeder and Franco's Chief of Staff, General Juan Vigón – already privy to the goal and the necessary preparations – would be briefed by himself and Bruns. The hope was that, following a judicious presentation, the Spanish would come to the correct conclusion, and act accordingly.

One obvious weakness in relation to presentation was the fact that the assault would probably never happen. Reich Marshal Göring was building the pressure on England and would shortly begin what promised to be the greatest aerial assault in history. According to Berlin, the so-called Battle of Britain would be over within six weeks, preparing the way for an invasion and the final triumph of Hitler's western strategy. Could the British withstand such an onslaught? Stohrer had no idea. Fortunately, such matters were not his concern. What mattered was that the plan had all the mandatory stamps and signatures. It was essential for his own survival that its endorsement by Franco should be safely filed away. Stohrer was too experienced a diplomat to expect any immediate commitment. Approval in principal would be enough to satisfy his masters.

He pushed down one of the switches on his intercom. The voice of his ever-obliging private secretary, Franz Klausener, came on the line.

'*Herr Botschafter!*'

'Bring me a coffee, please, Franz. But also, put a bottle of good champagne on ice – one of those sent down to us from Biarritz – and five glasses. But do not, under any circumstances, serve the champagne until I call for it.'

'*Jawohl, Herr Botschafter.* Your coffee is on its way.'

Jawohl didn't seem right for a coffee. Was this what Germany had come to? Beverages as part of the order of battle? Stohrer shuddered.

In his office, two doors up, Hasselfeldt, just back from his daily workout in the embassy's fitness centre, congratulated himself on his foresight. Klausener was a long-time Party member, whose application to join the SS was turned down primarily because of his bad teeth. He didn't work for the ambassador, he worked for *him*. He had previously given him the names of those who would be attending this morning's encounter, as well as some indication of the topic for discussion. A successful conclusion to the meeting would, it seemed, be the cause of considerable celebration. Against that, should things go wrong, he, uniquely, would be in a position to reveal the culpable negativity of the ambassador, which if allowed to go unchecked could ruin an alliance potentially vital to the Reich. His vigilance had been rewarded. Promotion would surely follow, leading to a triumphant return to Berlin. Schellenberg – destined, surely, to be a general – would see to it.

He reached up to the shelf behind him and took down a shallow box containing a brand-new magnetic tape. He lifted the tape carefully from the box and spooled it through the mechanism of the *Magnetophon*, running it past the electronically charged recording heads. The machine was working precisely as specified. Whatever was said in the ambassador's office might be confidential, but it would not be a secret from the SD.

The Spanish delegation arrived precisely on time. Bruns was in his dress uniform, complete with Iron Cross and bar from the first war. Stohrer, as ambassador, wore his formal jacket and sash of office. Nothing would go wrong this time. General Vigón would be persuaded of the practicality of taking Gibraltar. Serrano would be persuaded of the glory that would accrue to Spain. Beigbeder would be happy to go along with both of them. After months of ill feeling, today would mark a new beginning.

'Good day, gentlemen,' Stohrer said, as Klausener ushered his guests into his office. Extra chairs were set out for the occasion. Bruns stood by a blackboard, draped with maps of Gibraltar and its region.

Serrano Suñer was the first to speak, his manner that of the principal of an exclusive boys' school greeting alumni whom he hoped would donate funds to their alma mater. 'It's good to see you again, Ambassador,' he said. 'You're looking well. I bring you greetings from the *Caudillo*. He and I look forward with confidence to the outcome of Operation Sealion and trust that the battle will be both short and decisive.'

'Have no fear, Minister,' said Stohrer, noting to himself the fact that a successful invasion of England would render all that he was about to say entirely academic. 'Germany leaves nothing to chance.'

Beigbeder looked like he could do with a coffee. If Serrano was a headmaster, the foreign minister was a jazz pianist surfacing after a night on the town. He shook hands with Stohrer, mumbling 'good day,' and glanced across at Bruns, standing with a pointer in his hand as if it were a billiard cue. The two men nodded. Bruns's military rank was the same as Beigbeder's, which always made things easier between them. He presumed – wrongly – that the colonel found it more awkward to deal with Vigón.

General Juan Vigón, the Spanish armed forces chief, was a remote, austere figure, who had fought with Franco throughout the civil war. Tall and lanky, with long ears and a prominent nose, he resembled an underweight bloodhound. He said nothing, merely exchanging glances with his hosts, not wishing to give anything away. He had been to Berlin just weeks before and spoken with Hitler. Hitler, he recalled, was unimpressed by the prospect of Spanish entry into the war. He was even less enthused with Franco's plans – dependent, of course, on German approval – to annex French Morocco, add Oran and set up an entirely new Spanish sphere in West Africa. If Berlin had changed its mind since, he would be interested to know. But he could not help thinking that this morning's presentation would prove little more than window-dressing.

Stohrer quickly confirmed the general's suspicions. 'Before

I yield the floor to Colonel Bruns,' he began, 'I must impress upon you the provisional nature of what we are about to disclose. You will be aware that the *Führer* wishes to bring England to the negotiating table as quickly as possible …'

' – After you have destroyed their air force and reduced their cities to ashes,' Serrano quipped. Beigbeder laughed nervously. Vigón, again, said nothing.

A look of mild exasperation crossed Stohrer's larger-than-life features. 'All I am authorised to tell you at this moment is that Reich Marshal Göring has been charged with preparing the ground for an invasion and will carry out his orders at the appropriate time. We are in no doubt that in the months ahead the Churchill clique will fall and Britain, under a more compliant leadership, will thereafter accept its role in the New Order.' He looked around at the anxious faces of his guests, hoping to find some compliance there at least.

'You already know the overall objective of the proposals for an armed intervention by the *Wehrmacht* in Spain, which have been discussed in detail by both sets of military experts for many months now, albeit without resolution. The immediate consequence would be the restoration to Spain of Gibraltar, bringing to an end an injustice that has persisted for far too long.'

Serrano's eyebrows shot up.

Stohrer continued. 'War, like politics, is influenced by many factors. Nothing is certain until it is achieved. The *Führer's* mind is filled with options that could take us, literally, in any direction, but I am here today to propose to you that the Spanish option, more specific in its application, but no less efficacious than an invasion, should be employed to knock

England out of the war.'

Now, he had their full attention.

'With Gibraltar seized, and returned to the lawful sovereignty of Spain, England would at once lose command of the seas. It would be separated from its empire and obliged to fight off German commercial raiders and U-Boats without a secure base off Africa. In short, it would be isolated and demoralised and forced to abandon its misplaced and foolhardy defiance of National Socialism.'

Beigbeder applauded. After his evening with Dominique Fourneau, he was exhausted but otherwise in excellent spirits. She always helped him clear his mind. Serrano pulled at his cuffs. Vigón, already appraised of the thinking behind the plan, chose the moment to polish his spectacles.

'That, then, is our goal,' Stohrer continued. 'The question is, how do we achieve it?' He looked steadily into each of the faces of his guests. 'Well, that is why we are here today. The German High Command, under General von Reichenau, has put together some ideas and opinions. There have also, as General Vigón will know, been contacts with the relevant military personnel in Spain. Colonel Bruns will now give a brief outline of the plan as it currently exists. Afterwards, we will be happy to take questions.'

Bruns's presentation, complete with maps and charts, was brief and to the point. He spoke in robust, but simple Spanish, in sharp contrast to the ambassador, whose orotund command of the language was a matter of some pride to him. He also stressed the importance of Spanish military participation. Protected by squadrons of Stuka dive-bombers and Bf109 fighters, flown south from France under cover of darkness, Spanish commandos would lead the assault, carrying the Spanish flag. Spanish artillery (provided by Germany) would pound the Rock from Algeciras, while German mountain troops would be dropped by parachute behind the enemy's first line of defence. Afterwards, when the British had surrendered, with their fleet dispersed to the four winds, *Wehrmacht* mechanised forces would take up positions on the Spanish coast and North Africa to forestall possible counter-attacks from the sea. The German colonel did his best to make it sound not only that the plan was irresistibly elegant, but that Spain, in supporting it, would be the architect of its own destiny. Yet, as he spoke, the impression that grew in the minds of his audience was of a German army of occupation taking up station not only in Gibraltar, but in large parts of Andalucia, Extremadura and, most alarmingly, Spanish Morocco.

Vigón could live with this. He was a realist and he believed that, once the war was over, the Germans would pull out – at least from mainland Spain. After all, why would they remain? Serrano, on the other hand, was disturbed. 'You ask a lot of us, Colonel,' he said. 'And you ask that we should take everything on trust.'

'My dear Minister,' Stohrer interrupted. 'I assure you …'

' – I know, I know. It will be a joint operation, jointly fought, and the most enduring beneficiary will be Spain. But' – and here he paused for effect – 'if we are to repose our faith in a German-led operation, what guarantees do you offer (a) that we will win and (b) that it will all have been worth it?'

Stohrer groaned, then made it appear that he was merely clearing his throat.

Serrano was not finished. 'I heard no mention of

French-occupied Morocco, save for the fact that German armoured divisions would proceed there as a garrison. Oran was not alluded to. Nor was Guinea. Tell me, Ambassador, aside from Gibraltar, a spit of largely uninhabitable land some three kilometres in length, what incentives are you offering? What, specifically, do you propose that would compensate Spain for joining the war?'

'And if I might,' Vigón interjected, 'This Operation Felix is one thing. But how exactly would we protect *Los Canarios* from a British counter-invasion? If the result of your campaign was a Spanish flag over Gibraltar and the Union Jack over Las Palmas, how would you assess the gain?'

The chief of staff looked inquiringly at Serrano, who nodded his approval.

Stohrer twisted the top off his fountain pen, then screwed it back on. It was early in the day to be dealing with such intractable matters. But Vigón should not have known the codeword, Felix. That was not yet official. Bruns had not mentioned it. But Berlin leaked like a sieve. What did the Spanish general knowing about it imply about access and security? He feared the worst.

'Gentlemen,' he began, putting on his most emollient face. 'In the first place, we would not embark on such an enterprise if the result was not assured. Germany is winning the war and it will go on winning. We are the masters of Europe. If you join us, Gibraltar will be taken. The British occupation, that has lasted centuries, will end in a matter of days. Second, I repeat that this is no more than a provisional plan. Admiral Canaris, our chief of military intelligence, has requested that he and General Vigón, at the head of a team of experts, should discuss the best way forward at a meeting later this month. With your permission, they would visit Algeciras and assess the situation for themselves. Then, with both sides working together, flesh would be put on the bare bones of our plan.'

Stohrer took out a large linen handkerchief and mopped his brow. 'As to the geopolitical context of all this,' he said, 'Berlin is aware – almost painfully so – of your territorial claims in Africa. The *Führer*, though unwilling to commit himself in advance of any Spanish participation in the war effort, is sympathetic to these claims and would undoubtedly view in a positive light any 'adjustments' that would benefit a proven ally of the Reich.'

Serrano clasped his hands in front of him. 'Does that mean he would back our title to a united Morocco and Oran?'

The ambassador could feel the ground shifting beneath his feet and chose his words carefully. 'The *Führer* does not forget his friends. He appreciates the wealth of sentiment and history that underpins your claim. Accordingly, he would consider it an honour if the *Caudillo* were to meet him in the autumn to resolve these matters face to face.'

'Who else would attend such talks?' Beigbeder piped up, running a bony finger round his collar. 'Would it be purely for the two leaders or would there be a delegation as well, led by the ministers for foreign affairs?'

'That,' said Stohrer, 'would be a matter for negotiation. But I would think a team from each side would be the best way forward.'

'Very good,' said Beigbeder.

Serrano simply nodded. He had heard enough. 'I will speak this evening with my brother-in-law. I anticipate no objection to the visit of the head of the *Abwehr*. From what I know of Admiral Canaris, he has no wish to drag Spain needlessly into the war, so a fact-finding mission led by him seems eminently sensible. Beyond that, I should be surprised if I was not despatched to Berlin in advance of any meeting between himself and the *Führer*.' On hearing this, Beigbeder looked as if he might explode with indignation, but a glance from the *cuñadísimo* silenced him.

'Spain,' Serrano continued, 'wishes to recover Gibraltar as a matter of national honour. To pretend otherwise would be ridiculous. We are also, as you know full well, committed partners in the Fascist alliance. Your fight is our fight. We share the same goals and are part of the same struggle. But you should understand that the problems of our nation after the civil war are severe and unresolved – exacerbated, if anything, by the continuing European conflict. I do not need to tell you this, Stohrer. You have been here long enough. We need supplies of food, we need guarantees of fuel, we need adequate weaponry with which to defend ourselves against retaliatory strikes. Above all, we need to know that Berlin will look with favour upon our territorial claims in North and West Africa, upon which our status as a European power will ultimately rest. Without the relevant assurances, we would be embarking on an adventure that could finally bankrupt our economy, starve our people and leave us with nothing to show for our efforts but a rock with a flag on top.'

'My dear Minister,' said Stohrer, 'an invitation to Berlin can of course be arranged – though I must caution that in the weeks ahead, for reasons that my soon become apparent, the *Führer's* time will be strictly rationed. For now, I urge you and

Spain to give most serious consideration to these matters. An opportunity such as this comes only once in a lifetime. Do not waste it, I beg of you.'

When the Spanish trio left, Stohrer collapsed into his chair. He was not a Nazi. He found most Party members coarse and infantile in their opinions, as did many of his older colleagues in the service. But Hitler, he had long ago realised, was an unstoppable force of nature, with mesmeric qualities. No one in Germany dared oppose him: certainly not Eberhard von Stohrer. Such qualms as the Bavarian had in Hitler's service took second place to his need to hold on to his job and stay as far away from Berlin as possible. How had he performed today? he wondered. He wasn't sure. All he knew was that the Spanish would not easily or quickly be sold on war.

Bruns, busy with his maps and charts, sought to reassure his boss. 'You worry too much,' he said. 'You did the best you could.'

'So did you,' said Stohrer. 'But they are not stupid. They know we are asking them to engage in an enterprise that could ruin them.'

Bruns looked mildly surprised. 'Are you suggesting, Ambassador, that the Reich could lose the war?'

'I am saying, colonel, that victory is rather further off than many imagine, especially those in Berlin. War is not only brutal, it is notoriously unpredictable. Ask Canaris. The Spanish people have known nothing but savagery, hunger and humiliation since 1936. They know exactly what cost to put on "national honour" and who will do the paying.'

Heaving himself once more to his feet, Stohrer strode across the expanse of his office to the oriel window overlooking the street. 'Serrano lusts for glory. He yearns to take the salute at the victory parade. But he knows the realities as well as I.' He pointed to the pavement below, along which bedraggled groups of Madrileños picked their way. 'Just look at them. It's pitiful, Bruns. Nothing short of pitiful. Half of them are wearing clothes that were not new when Hindenburg died. Can you imagine if such a thing happened in Berlin! That fellow over there – you can see his ribs. The woman down by the lamppost, with a child at her feet: every day I see her – her entire life consists of begging. My God, I even saw two fellows fighting the other day in the street over a crust of bread. If we are to persuade these people that the best thing they can do after fighting each other like animals for three years and destroying their economy is to go back to war, we have to be damned sure we know what we are talking about.'

Bruns grunted. Such things did not concern him. 'That is why you are a diplomat. All I know is that if we capture Gibraltar, the British are screwed.'

At that point, Klausener knocked and entered the office, reminding Stohrer for an instant of Jeeves, an invention of the English comic novelist, P.G. Wodehouse, one of his favourites before the war. He looked solicitously across the room, assessing the mood in an instant. 'I take it, Herr Ambassador, you will not be requiring the champagne.'

A wheezy laughed emerged from Stohrer's throat. 'No, Franz. I will not be requiring the champagne. Take it home. Drink it yourself. Better still, find a pretty *Señorita* and impress the hell out of her.'

In his room three doors down from the ambassador's office,

Hasselfeldt switched off the *Magnetophon* and once more congratulated himself on his initiative. He was now privy to one of the best-guarded secrets in the Reich. What he did with the information he acquired was entirely a matter for him. Diplomats worked through persuasion, soldiers with force. The SD worked any damned way it pleased. His next report to Schellenberg, with a copy to Heydrich perhaps, would contain more than an account of place settings for the Duke of Windsor's latest tea party; it would be a forceful critique of strategic thinking in the Spanish sphere and of the sorry limitations of those whose duty it was to achieve a positive result.

As it happened, a point of entry had just presented itself. The British aide, Bramall, was back in Madrid after a visit to Gibraltar – a visit of which he had not been forewarned. The reason he knew about it was that he had an informant in Serrano Suñer's private office. According to his source, Bramall had told Serrano that he wished to make contact with some conservatively inclined naval officers in the colony, but this seemed fanciful. Photographs of Bramall at the frontier in the company of a British naval commander with an eye patch had been sent to him by the *Abwehr* head of station in Algeciras. Hasselfeldt was still unsure what Bramall was up to. The Wilhelmstrasse was convinced he was a reliable contact and 'Friend of the Party.' His provenance had been checked out several times – even, via a sympathiser posing as a family member in London, with Oswald Mosley himself. It was also a fact that his father was a prominent pro-German sympathiser and that the son had been selected by the appeasement-minded Duke of Windsor as his Spanish liaison in Madrid.

But might it all not been a ruse? He remembered the

photograph of Bramall at the London riot: the shock and revulsion in his eyes. There was definitely something not right about him. Something in his eyes and bearing. It was maddening. Keeping track of the fellow was turning into a farce. He kept on disappearing. Yet Serrano Suñer obviously regarded him highly. Just the other day, he had even given him use of a government car. Hasselfeldt snorted. It might take time, but he would get to the truth in the end. All he had got out of him so far was a single memo telling him things he already knew about the Duke of Windsor. There was one good quotation, which he had immediately forwarded to Berlin, but nothing of real value.

It was as if he was playing for time. But Bramall would not get the better of him when it came to the main event. He would have him brought to the Legation for an in-depth debriefing. If he refused to cooperate, he would have him snatched from the street, and to hell with the Spanish! He looked forward to it. It hardly mattered whose side the fellow was on, he could provide key details of Gibraltar's defences and the readiness of its garrison. People under close questioning always gave away more than they knew. It was a fact of human nature. Afterwards, he would kill him – slowly – and have him buried beneath the floor of the embassy cellar, covered with quicklime. If nothing else, it would be an opportunity to refresh his techniques.

He felt like an athlete who had skipped training for too long. Regularity and repetition were what kept you sharp.

In the meantime, there was much to be done. He looked at his watch, which showed 11.36. There was an hour remaining before lunch, which gave him time to begin transcribing and translating into German the lengthy meeting between Stohrer and his Spanish guests. Ordinarily, he would have entrusted the job to an assistant or stenographer, but with material as sensitive as this he could take no chances. Have made sure his door was securely shut, he pushed the rewind switch on the *Magnetophon* and engaged the mechanism that took the spool of magnetic tape all the way back to the beginning. The dialogue replayed in reverse at high speed, reminded him of a group of hysterical chimpanzees he saw when he was a child in Vienna's zoological gardens. He had thrown stones at them through the bars so that they howled at him in impotent rage until his mother pulled him away. When the spool halted, with a heavy click, Hasselfeldt moved a chair next to the device, turned down the volume and took up a notebook and pencil.

Soon the booming baritone of the ambassador could be heard, speaking Spanish, followed by the higher-pitched responses of Serrano Suñer. What a windbag Stohrer was. He ought to have been on the stage at Bayreuth.

'Reich Marshal Göring has been charged with preparing the ground for an invasion and will carry out his orders at the appropriate time. We are in no doubt that in the months ahead the Churchill clique will fall and that Britain, under a more compliant leadership, will thereafter take its place, respectfully, in the New Order.' And then a pause – no doubt intended to bring his audience to the edge of their seats. *'You already know the overall objective of the proposals for an armed intervention by the Wehrmacht in Spain, which have been discussed in detail by both sets of military experts for many months now, albeit without resolution. The immediate consequence would be the restoration to Spain of Gibraltar, bringing to an end an injustice that has persisted for far too long.'*

Hasselfeldt wondered to what extent Stohrer was following

orders and how much he was extemporising, giving away more than was necessary. The young SD officer was adept at taking notes. He wrote fast and had an excellent memory. Even so, he rewound each passage several times before he was satisfied that he had got it right. He had just moved on to page four of his notebook, with Serrano declaring the centrality of Spain's African Empire to its national dignity, when the telephone rang on his desk.

Without pausing the *Magnetophon*, he reached for the receiver. 'Hasselfeldt. Who is it?'

The voice of the duty receptionist came on the line. 'There is someone to see you, Herr Major. He says his name is Bramall.'

'Bramall?'

'Yes, Herr Major.'

'Put him on.'

Downstairs, in the Legation's lobby, Bramall heard the line go dead for a second. When the connection was made, it sounded at first like a crossed line. He could have sworn he could hear Serrano Suñer asking someone if Germany was ready to back Spain's title to a united Morocco and Oran. The minister's voice was mellifluous and distinctive. He would have known it anywhere.

Abruptly, with a click, the voice ceased, to be replaced by Hasselfeldt, speaking in German. 'Bramall, what is going on? Where have you been?'

'I've been out of town for the last few days and thought I should report back.'

'*Na-ja*. Very well. Give me the reception clerk.' Bramall did so. 'Check that he is not armed,' Hasselfeldt ordered, 'and send him up.'

'At once, Herr Major.'

While he waited, Hasselfeldt began pacing back and forth between the door of his office and the window on the opposite side. He was unsettled and he didn't quite know why.

At the reception desk, a bespectacled SS corporal checked Bramall for weapons.

Satisfied that the visitor was not a threat, he then escorted him upstairs to the SD office on the first floor, where Hasselfeldt was standing, with his arms crossed, next to the window. He was alone. There was no sign of the Spanish interior minister.

'You are starting to irritate me, Bramall,' Hasselfeldt began.

'Really? And why would that be?'

'You have not reported to my office for several days. You provide me with no information on your movements. How am I to know what you are up to?'

Bramall offered a rueful smile. 'But you must have got my report. I brought it here myself.'

'You mean your memorandum on the Duke? Yes, I got that. It would have made an amusing diary item in the Daily Mail, but I must tell you it did not excite either me or my superiors in Berlin. However, that is not what is at issue here. I wish to know where you have been for the last three days.'

As the Austrian was speaking, out of the corner of his eye Bramall had noted the *Magnetophon*. He had no idea what it was, but it looked impressive. There were two large spools on either side, with a tape stretched between them by way of some kind of mechanism with lots of little wheels. There was a red light – presumably to show that it was working – and a background glow of valves. There was also a notebook on a small table next to the machine in which Hasselfeldt, in a curiously childlike hand, looked to have been writing just before he came in. If he squinted round, he could just about make out the letters 'RSS' followed by a lengthy paragraph that included the words 'Morocco,' and 'Oran,' each of them underlined, together with what looked like ... 'Operation Felix'. This was unreal. He felt his heart skip a beat.

By now, Hasselfeldt was looking at him exasperatedly, like a teacher, he thought, dealing with a recalcitrant child. 'Well?' he began. 'What is the matter with you? You look like you've seen a ghost.'

Bramall dropped his head. 'My apologies, *Herr Sturmbannführer*, I should have told you before, but I have just returned from two days in Gibraltar.'

'Gibraltar? *Ach so.* For what purpose?'

'As ever – following orders.

'Which were ... ?'

'As you will know, the Duke has been posted as Governor of the Bahamas – Churchill wants him kept out of trouble for the duration of the war – and London ordered me to check on arrangements being put in place to ensure his security and the safe passage of the American ship that will take him to Nassau. I was given a briefing on the current situation in the Atlantic sector and what sort of an escort his ship could expect. The vessel itself, the American steamship Excalibur, had berthed in Gibraltar en route to Lisbon, and part of my job was to inspect its accomodation to see if it was suitable. While there, I spoke to MI5, just to be sure. Their duty officer said it all looked pretty routine, no problems he knew of. American ship, safe as houses, he said. And I'm sure that's right.'

At this, Bramall looked up as if he had recovered his nerve. "I mean,' he said, 'the thing is, none of us would actually benefit if His Royal Highness was lost at sea, would we?'

To Hasselfeldt, this sounded eminently plausible, but he couldn't help wondering if Churchill might not have a torpedo in mind for the Excaliber. He could even have arranged for a bomb to be planted onbard, timed to go off in the middle of the Atlantic. It would get rid of the Duke, who was a millstone round his neck while arousing the English to new heights of patriotic fervour. At the same time, the ship's loss would outrage the Americans, many of whose citizens would be among the passengers. Wasn't that what happened with the Lusitania in 1915?

'I see,' was all he said. 'So what else did you get up to while you were in Gibraltar? And please do not try to – what is the expression? – pull the wool over my eyes.'

Bramall remembered what Macleish had told him about the value of disinformation laced with independently verifiable truth.

'I suppose that's where it gets interesting,' he said.

'I do hope so,' Hasselfeldt said.

'I met with some old contacts – party members, naval officers mostly, who don't see a war with the Reich as being necessarily in the best interests of their country.'

For a split second, Bramall glanced across once more at the *Magnetophon*, whose mechanism had begun to emit a loud hum. Hasselfeldt followed his gaze and, as if aware of something he had neglected, leaned across and switched the machine off, shutting the lid at the same time. He also grabbed the notebook he had been writing in and placed it in one of his desk drawers, from which he then took out an envelope containing a number of photographs. He selected one and threw it across the desk. Bramall picked it up. It showed him in the Land Rover with his naval escort. Paterson was right. The Germans didn't miss a trick.

'Ah,' he said. 'So you got there before me.'

A look of theatrical indignation greeted his response. 'I hope that you are not implying I have nothing better to do than to follow you around the country taking your photograph.'

'No, no. I just meant that you seem to know what I'm doing before I do.'

'Please to remember that. Now tell me about your visit. These officers you spoke with – who were they?'

Bramall stuck out his chin. 'I'd rather not give their names, if you don't mind.'

'Don't be ridiculous. We are not in high school now. I want to know who they are and what they said to you.'

'Is that absolutely necessary?'

'Their names, Bramall.'

'You're not going to …?'

'They will be for our records. Nothing will happen to them.'

'Well, if you insist. They're good chaps, all of them. There was a Lieutenant Harris – he was in the BUF at one point, but had to resign or else give up his career. He's on the cruiser Gloucester. Lieutenant Commander Brewer is flying out to Alexandria today to join the aircraft carrier Eagle. but he'll return with Force H. We had dinner two nights ago. He said Franco was the best thing to have happened to Spain in years. He was in Gibraltar in '36 when the crew of the battleship *Jaime Primero* mutinied and threw their officers overboard. He couldn't understand how radicals like that were allowed to get away with it.'

Hasselfeldt looked bored. 'Go on,' he said.

'Harris thought if the Army could just put on a decent show somewhere ... maybe in Africa, then we could sue for peace on honourable terms. Brewer agreed. Both of them wanted to see an end to a war they think England has no chance of winning.'

'And?'

'And that's about it,' Bramall added lamely. 'I was to meet up with another chap, name of Cardwell – an artillery officer I served with in Narvik. Last time we spoke, he told me he'd give anything to see a bit more German-style leadership in the government in London. But he turned out to be on duty the whole time I was there, so I didn't get to see him.'

'Which ship is he on?'

'He's not. Shore batteries are his specialty. He's been helping set up new emplacements.'

'What calibre?' Hasselfeldt was no military expert, but he liked to sound knowledgeable.

'Six-inch, I believe. That's 150 millimetres. But they've got 9.2-inch as well, and more on the way. Quite impressive, really.'

'I see. And that's it, is it?'

'I'm afraid so.'

'Very well.' Hasselfeldt examined his fingernails. 'How did you gain admission to the base in the first place?

'It wasn't easy. Problem was, I couldn't contact Gib directly. I had to go through the embassy or else the interior ministry in Spain.'

'And which did you use?'

'Both. I saw Minister Serrano Suñer the other day. Something else I should probably have mentioned. We got on famously, as a matter of fact. We had quite a chat. He's keen to know how serious London is about holding on to the Rock. The next day, I got his people to give me a *laisser-passer* as far as the frontier post at La Linéa. Then the embassy here cabled the Governor's office, telling them to expect me.'

'Anything else, or is that it?' The look Hasselfeldt directed at Bramall was one of pure contempt. He knew he had to keep the man he thought of as an *Engländer* in place, but it would have been so much satisfying to go to work on him with a pair of pliers.

'Well, I got to see the Governor for a couple of minutes. Nice chap. His job is to transform Gibraltar into a fortress, which he seems to be doing quite successfully. He wanted to know if Hoare was doing everything he could to ensure that Spain stayed neutral.'

'And you told him … ?'

'I told him that I didn't work with the ambassador but that I had no reason to think he favoured any other course.'

'Quite,' said Hasselfeldt. 'But let us step back a little. When you left Madrid, you did so without informing me. That is not how the game is played. Don't you remember our little talk?'

'How could I forget? But the Duke had moved on to Lisbon, leaving me as Spanish liaison with pretty well nothing to do. I'd spoken with Serrano, who impressed upon me his wish, and that of Franco, that Spain should be seen as a full partner in the Axis. After that, there didn't seem any pressing reason for me to hang around. Besides, they were turfing me out of my hotel. Did you know, I've been downgraded to the Paris?'

Hasselfeldt's patience was being stretched to the limit. 'When you were in Gibraltar, you must have witnessed the French air assault.'

'Saw the whole thing from the harbour. Now that was a surprise.'

'How was the response?'

Bramall leaned back and looked up at the ceiling. 'By our side? Pretty decent, I'd say. Considering the first fighter squadron won't arrive until next month at the earliest and the searchlights aren't due until about the same time. They managed to drive the French off before they got within 500 metres of the harbour. From what I can judge, they're a lot more worried about the Italians, who have naval and air forces ready and are a lot better prepared than the French.'

Hasselfeldt picked up a pen and began scribbling on a piece of paper – the same childlike hand, with large loops and heavily defined full stops.

'Tell me about troop strengths.'

'Hard to be sure. They're pretty hush-hush about that. I recognised a couple of battalions: the Somersets, the Devonshires – oh, and the King's Own. And I know the Black Watch are coming – crack regiment from Scotland. Some other unit as well – I've forgotten which. I've got it written down somewhere. Oh yes, and there's a battalion of anti-aircraft specialists arriving at the end of the month to handle the big Ack-Ack guns they're bringing in.'

'It sounds as if the British expect something might happen.'

'Certainly looks that way. Why, are you thinking of having a go?'

Hasselfeldt emitted a slightly forced laugh. 'I don't think the *Caudillo* would be too happy about that, ha! What do you think?'

'No, I suppose not. Not unless he's decided to join the war, of course.'

'Exactly. But now, before you go, there is one other matter we should discuss. What is your current relationship with the Ortega girl?'

'Isabel Ortega? Finished. Not that there was anything to begin with. She came to see me in my hotel, completely out of the blue. I told her I couldn't be seen with her.'

'How did she take it?'

'Well enough, I suppose. Like I say, we never actually ...' He let his voice trail off.

' – And you have stayed clear of her?'

'Of course. I don't believe in coincidence either, you see.'

Hasselfeldt grinned. 'That is more like it. You see, Herr Bramall, it is really very easy for we two to get along. All that is required is give and take.'

'You mean, I give and you take.'

'*Selbstverständlich*. Exactly. Now you are getting it. But the thing is, I have very much enjoyed our little talk. Indeed, I have enjoyed it so much that I wish to have it repeated to me in written form, as a memento.'

'What are you driving at?'

'Very simple. I want a full report, with your signature attached, of everything you saw in Gibraltar. Everything. From the shine on the regimental buttons of the resident battalions to the calibre of the guns being trained on Algeciras. Consider it a test. Pay particular attention to remarks people may have made and the mood they were in. Describe any newly built defences you may have observed and the extent of any gun emplacements inside as well as on the perimeter walls. And do it quickly. As I believe you say in Hong Kong, chop-chop. You have twenty-four hours. Unless, of course, you would like the photographs of you and me dining here in the Legation to turn up in the British Embassy.'

Bramall allowed his jaw to fall open. 'Listen,' he spluttered, 'I don't see what more I can possibly …'

Hasselfeldt allowed himself a pained expression. 'Must I always repeat myself? I said twenty-four hours. Is that clear?'

Bramall sighed. 'Very.'

'Excellent. Then get on with it. Oh, and should you hear anything further about the Duke, include that as well. I do so love your royal family.'

As soon as Bramall left, Hasselfeldt retrieved his notebook from his desk drawer and locked the *Magnetophon* with a key that he then placed in his pocket. It was time for lunch. The *Engländer's* spirit looked to have been broken. He was a fool, whose intelligence must have been affected by years of in-breeding. It was true that he had come forward with some interesting details about security in Gibraltar – information that would add a welcome new dimension to his planned cable to Berlin. He had also, apparently, broken with the Ortega girl, as instructed.

And yet … a nagging doubt persisted. What if he was playing him? What if he was a double-agent? He would wait until he received the report on his visit to Gibraltar, then decide what to do with him. In the end, it might be simpler just to eliminate him. It would be like cutting the Gordian knot – and it would be such a pleasure.

Madrid: Romero's bar, Malasaña, July 8

Bramall wasted no time. He had called an urgent meeting with Romero and Isabel and got down to business almost at once. 'I hate to sound like the chairman of the board,' he began, but something's come up and it could change everything.'

'Go ahead' said Romero, winking at Isabel. 'We're listening.'

'Okay. The way I read it, the key to Gibraltar, and its tie-up with France, is right there in the German Legation. All we have to do is get in there and take it. The problem is we have to do it now. We have no time to waste.'

He told them about hearing Serrano's voice in Hasselfeldt's office, only for it to be cut off in mid-sentence. 'It was like he was there, but not there, if you see what I mean.'

'I don't understand,' Isabel said. They were speaking in Spanish. 'Are you sure it was him?'

'Positive. Who else sounds like him? No one I know. And don't forget, I spent an hour with him just last Monday.'

'Could be some kind of recording device,' Romero said. 'I hear the Germans are ahead of pretty well everybody when it comes to that kind of thing.'

'Well, that's just it,' said Bramall, a definite glint coming into his eye. 'When I got to Hasselfeldt's office, there was this machine switched on in the corner. I'd seen it before, except that the lid was closed. I'd assumed it was a radio transmitter. This time, it was open and on full display. It was the size of a suitcase and, by the look of it, it weighs a ton. There were valves – you could see them glowing. There was what looked like an amplitude dial and a series of knobs that could be turned up from 1-10. But what really made it stand out for me was the fact that there were two reels, laid flat next to each other, with some kind of tape running between them by way of a slot with a series of little guide wheels. I'm no technician; still it was obvious to me it was pretty advanced stuff. I'd interrupted Hasselfeldt in the middle of something. He'd been sitting on a chair next to the machine, taking notes. The pages of his notebook were filled with direct speech – quotation marks, colons after names, that sort of thing. And here's the thing: from what I could see, the initials of the main person he was transcribing were 'RSS'.'

'Ramón Serrano-Suñer!'

'Exactly.'

Romero's yes opened wide. '*Coño!*' he exclaimed. Then, noting the shock on Isabel's face, he apologised for the crudity of his language. She blushed attractively and he went on: 'Well, there's your answer. There's your proof. You get hold of that notebook, and the tape goes with it, and you'll have all you need to convince the French.'

'Yes, but how do I get into Hasselfeldt's office, in the middle of the German Legation, break into a locked steel cabinet, take what I need and get out again with nobody the wiser?'

'That's why you're a spy,' Romero said, matter of factly. 'You're supposed to be good at that sort of thing. Didn't they send you to spy school?'

Bramall looked away. 'Yes, well, the less said about that, the better.'

It was Isabel who came up with the answer. 'Maybe we could help,' she said.

'What do you mean?'

'You could visit Hasselfeldt unannounced, in disguise

or something, while we created some kind of ... disturbance outside.'

Romero's eyes brightened. 'A diversion, you mean? Yes, that could work.'

'What sort of diversion?' Bramall asked.

'Something that would grab their attention. A bit of activity on the street. Maybe a grenade through the front door.'

'And while they're dealing with the emergency ...'

'You're upstairs saving the world.' He paused. 'If you think you're up to it.'

Isabel gave a nervous laugh.

'No, seriously,' said Romero, turning to Bramall. 'It could work – always supposing that the secret you're after is there in the first place. But then, I don't suppose you're in any doubt about that.'

'I'm convinced of it,' Bramall said.

'Well, there you are, then. No problem.'

It was Isabel who brought them back to earth. 'But what do you do afterwards? How will you get the material to London?'

'Whatever way I can,' said Bramall. 'The way I see it, once I find what I'm looking for and get out of the Legation, I need to get over the border into Portugal as quickly as possible. Croft will know what to do.'

Romero nodded approvingly. 'And Isabel can go with you.'

'Well, actually no.'

'What do you mean?' Isabel asked, her eyes wide open. 'You're going to leave me here?'

Bramall pulled at the knot of his tie. 'No, of course not. But it's a question of priorities. If I get hold of this tape and the notebook that goes with it, my overriding responsibility is to get them back to London. I don't want to exaggerate, but they could prove vital to the war effort.'

'Yes, but …'

'Yes, but nothing. For all we know, they're going to be looking out for you at the frontier. You're the daughter of a leading government official. My duty is clear.'

'But Charlie … '

Romero put a hand on Isabel's shoulder. 'He's right,' he said. 'He can't risk it. So I'll take you.'

Bramall closed his eyes in silent prayer. 'I was hoping you'd say that.'

Isabel shifted her gaze between the two men, settling in the end on Romero.

'You'll take me to Lisbon?'

'Sure, why not?'

Isabel looked relieved and pained at the same time. She turned to Bramall. 'So what will you be doing while we're risking our lives at the border? You'd have to make your choices, Charlie, and follow them through, no matter what. If you froze at any point, it'd be others that paid the price.'

Bramall decided to ignore the insult. 'That depends on the situation. If I've got the material, but no one knows it – which I suppose is just about possible – my best approach is to get to the nearest frontier post and flash my official credentials. Don't forget, I'm equerry to the Duke of Windsor, and right now the stupid bugger's in Portugal.'

Romero considered this. 'And if there's a general alert, then what?'

'Then I sneak over on my own and we meet up at an appropriate point.'

'Like the railway station at Elvas?'

'Good idea. Perfect.'

'Just be careful is my advice. Bad things happen in border country. It's easy to wind up dead.'

Bramall's eyes narrowed. 'Well you'd know, Eddy,' he said.

Isabel gave no sign that she detected the tension that had arisen between the two men. 'If you do this for us,' she said to Romero, 'what will you do afterwards? Will you not come with us to Lisbon?'

'What? And make my way over to England? Join the RAF or some such? I don't think so. I'd take a day or so to let things settle, then head back to Madrid. I'm feelin' better now – or maybe you hadn't noticed – and there's a few threads I wouldn't mind pickin' up.'

'I will miss you.'

'I'll miss you, too, sweetheart, but there's a war on, right?'

Bramall had turned away during the most recent exchange, as if suddenly preoccupied. Now he returned to the fray. 'I spoke to Croft today, told him I'd get to Lisbon as soon as I could.'

Romero nodded. 'What'd he say?'

'To watch my back.'

'Sounds about right.' Romero used a cocktail stick to pick at his teeth. 'He knows the route you're takin' – right?'

'He knows I'll be improvising. Hell, I don't even know if I'll get into the Legation, let alone walk out with their most closely guarded secret.'

'True enough, Charlie. Sure you're the boss.' The Irishman turned to Isabel, switching to Spanish. 'And what about you, Izzy? Heard anything from Luder?'

'He is due back tomorrow. If he met with Heydrich and won approval for the scheme he and Papa were hatching, he won't want to waste any time. He'll want to get on with it.'

Romero grimaced. But it was Bramall who voiced what they were all thinking. 'The way things are shaping up,' he said, 'we may have to consider the possibility of a permanent solution to the problem of Luder.'

'You mean kill him?' Isabel asked. The colour drained instantly from her face. *'Madre de Dios,* that seems so …'

'… permanent,' said Romero. 'I think you're right, Charlie. You want me to see to it?'

'It might be best,' Bramall said.

Isabel looked aghast. Her face turned pale.

'You're going to have to get used to it,' Romero said, his voice suddenly cold. 'If Luder lives, a lot of other people could die, including you.'

'Even so, I'm going to have to think about it. It's such a …'

Bramall shook his head. 'Eddy's right. This is no time for finer feeling. It's war: kill or be killed. If you ask me, Luder's had it coming for a long time.'

Madrid: Villa Ortega, July 9

Isabel sat on her bed, thinking about events of the past few days. She didn't like to admit it, but the truth was she was scared to death. Romero had given her a handgun – an Italian automatic – and yesterday, while Bramall worked on how best to gain entry to the German Legation, he'd shown her how to use it. It was 'just in case,' he said, but instead of making her feel more secure it only added to her growing sense of unease.

It was insane. She had always been the rebel; the one who stood up for fair play; the one who denounced the bullies; the one who, on one famous occasion, struck a particularly vicious nun with her hair brush. But teenage rebellion was one thing, taking a stand against Franco was something else. She was a patriot, she told herself, running her finger over the cold metal of the Beretta, not a revolutionary.

Not like Romero.

Bramall said he was the Scarlet Pimpernel of the *barrios*. But there was a terrible emptiness in his soul. In the short time she had known him, she had come to realise that he would never be at peace – not outside his kitchen, anyway. There would always be dragons to slay and windmills to tilt at. No form of government would satisfy him. His deepest passion was the struggle itself.

He reminded her of a Protestant pastor she had met in Argentina. He had been Irish, too, from Belfast. He preached the doctrine of Original Sin, which her local priest had always said was none of her business. The Pastor didn't see it that way. The way he saw it, everybody's life was a struggle to redeem themselves in the eyes of the Creator.

Bramall was different. He believed in comfort, tolerance and good living. She had asked him if these were the qualities most English people admired. He said yes, he rather thought they were, but not to confuse him with an Englishman. That made her smile. So where did the Empire fit in? she wanted to know. After all, one third of the world was pink on the maps. The English were forever sticking their noses in other country's affairs, telling them how to live and run their governments.

He looked at her and rolled his eyes. 'If you ask me,' he said, 'The English picked up the Empire in a fit of absence of mind and they'll live to regret it.'

'What about Spain?'

'Much more cold-blooded. It was gold you were after and you didn't mind how many millions died in the process.'

Isabel thought about the young men she knew, most of them Falange. They nearly all took the deaths of others in their stride, believing that only through war and conquest could Spain recover her national honour. Then she thought of her father and a shiver ran through her. You could change your friends, you couldn't change your family. What really upset Isabel about her father, whom she loved, was that he had strayed so far from his own, honourable beliefs and allowed the weaker traits of his character to take him over. Once he was a man of principal – an army officer who simply wanted to do his duty. She remembered when she was tiny and he was promoted to captain. That was immediately after the election of 1931, which confirmed the new Republic. He didn't object then to the reforms sweeping the country. According to her mother, he had even expressed doubts to her about the morality of opposing the workers' strike – though when ordered into action against militant anarchists he had followed his orders to the hilt.

Fascism had destroyed him, replacing his beliefs in an enlightened order with the harsh dogmas of the Falange. Personal greed and ambition had done the rest. She wondered if he could ever come back. Her mother, she was sure, could see through the ruin of man he was today, back to the bright young lieutenant who captured her heart. She made allowances for him, poking gentle fun at his pretensions. But whatever light it was that once burned bright within her, it was all but extinguished today.

Isabel didn't want that to happen to her. She wanted to live life in her own way. If that meant taking up arms, then that was how it would have to be. But the change was so sudden and she was frightened. She was afraid of what would happen to her if she was caught and taken to the Interior Ministry for interrogation. She had heard the stories. The secret police would say she was a traitor. Serrano would make an example of her. She was also worried about her mother's position, even that of her father. The thought that they might suffer for her wilfulness was hard for her to bear.

Luder had called her earlier from the airport to say that he had had a 'magnificent' visit to Berlin and was looking forward 'very much' to a walk with her that Saturday in the Retiro. He was extraordinary. It was as if the incident in her bedroom had not occurred. He had blocked it out. As far as he was concerned he remained a man of honour. At the weekend, once his important business affairs were settled, he would select a light summer suit and stroll through the park with his adoring fiancée, flicking at leaves with his cane, touching the brim of his hat at the other *damas y caballeros* as they passed.

She would not allow him to possess her. She thought of Estéban, whom she had not even had the chance to meet, cut down by a Francoist bullet. She thought of the sacrifice and idealism of Bramall and Romero. And then she thought again of Luder.

And her heart hardened.

9

Madrid: Hotel Paris, July 10, 1940

The insignia on the cuffs, four gold stripes surmounted by a single star, denoted a *Fregattenkapitän*, or Commander, in the German Navy. The accompanying papers, handed over to him fifteen minutes earlier in the lobby of the Paris Hotel, identified him as Gunter Rath, head of the *Abwehr* in La Linea. Apparently he was already an MI6 target. The request from head office had simply bumped up the timetable. Bramall was impressed. He unfolded the jacket and examined it carefully: blue serge; German Eagle emblem on the right breast pocket; two rows of silver buttons. It had no medal ribbons, but that was hardly surprising. Aside from the events of recent months, the German Navy hadn't fought an action since Jutland, in 1916. He held the material up to his nose. It didn't smell of the sea; it smelled of tobacco.

Strickland had been as good as his word. Bramall had put in an urgent request for such a uniform just thrity-six hours previously, via Burns at the embassy. Without it, he said, he would be forced to pass up a unique opportunity to fulfil his mission. And now, here it was.

He couldn't help wondering about the man who had previously worn the uniform – a man killed in cold blood for the clothes on his back. He had been waylaid by two of MacLeish's men on a train while on his way to Madrid to report to Colonel Bruns at the German Legation on the state of play of Britain's defences in Gibraltar. So it was a case of two birds with one stone. Bramall got the unfortunate Commander's uniform and ID, along with a appointment that would get him inside the legation; MI6 got the contents of his briefcase.

Sometimes, things were meant to be.

As for Rath himself, his body, dressed only in his underwear, had apparently been dumped from the train in a tunnel half-way to Córdoba. It was unlikely he would be missed for at least the next twenty-four hours – unless he failed to keep his rendezvous with Bruns. And that was not going to happen.

Inside the suitcase that had contained Rath's uniform and ID was a detailed description of the late *Fregattenkapitän*. He had been six feet one inch tall – almost the same height as Bramall – with black hair and grey eyes. He wore steel-rimmed spectacles and on his right cheek was a one inch scar pointing in the direction of his right shoulder. According to his military ID, he was from the Hanseatic city of Hanover, which, given his rank, suggested he would speak the German equivalent of Oxford English. Bramall took note. There could be no Viennese whine or throaty Berlin *schnauze*.

According to Rath's diary, his appointment with Bruns was for ten o'clock the following morning. That left Bramall hardly any time in which to refine his plan. He had to move quickly. Romero and Isabel were primed and ready to move at a moment's notice. What mattered now was that their actions be minutely coordinated. If they got their timing wrong, the entire plan would unravel, with potentially disastrous consequences for all of them.

Setting out on foot at two thirty the next morning from the side door of his hotel, he arrived at the *tasca* shortly before three. He hadn't been followed. One thing he had learned about eternal vigilance was that it tended to peter out after midnight. Romero, asleep in the room behind the bar, was already on standby, but he needed to know exactly when to move. Bramall briefed him, leaving it to the Dublin man to bring Isabel up to speed. She had agreed to join Romero at the *tasca* at eight-thirty in the morning – just enough time, if they were lucky, in which to spring the trap.

By the time Bramall arrived back at his hotel, it was four in the morning. 'Been visiting a friend,' he told the reception clerk, half asleep at his desk. The fellow shrugged. The sexual habits of the guests were no concern of his – not unless the *Guardia Civil* expressed an interest.

Three hours later, having had virtually no sleep, it was time to get ready. Fortunately, Rath's glasses were slightly tinted, and the prescription wasn't strong, which, if anything, improved Bramall's vision. Blackening his hair wasn't difficult. He used soot from the fireplace in his room, mixed with water. The scar was more problematic, and painful. With the blade of his cutthroat, he incised a line, a millimetre or so deep, diagonally into the skin of his right cheek, following the line of his shoulder. He cut first from one side, then the other, so that a triangular section of his skin's upper layer was removed without any significant loss of blood. The resulting impairment would heal over in a month, he thought, but for a couple of days, so long as it was not subjected to any unusual scrutiny, it would resemble a scar. There was nothing he could do about his eyes, which were blue, not grey. But the tinted glass of his spectacles helped even the score. With the brim of his officer's cap casting a shadow over his brow, it was likely no one would notice.

At twenty-past nine, he was ready to go. He looked in the mirror one last time and adjusted his cap. Then he shut his eyes and drew a deep breath. Romero and Isabel would play their part, he was in no doubt about that. The rest was up to him. He exited the hotel via the café on Calle Alcalá. Ten minutes later, he arrived at the side door of the Legation, where he calculated that the personnel on duty would be different from those working the front lobby.

The two SS guards on duty came to attention at his approach. He reminded himself that he was a German officer and saluted in the formal Nazi style. *'Heil Hitler!'*

A familiar voice came straight back at him. *'Heil Hitler! Entschuldigung, Herr Fregattenkapitän.'* Bramall swallowed. It was the same, bespectacled corporal who had frisked him during his previous visit. 'The main entrance to the Legation is round the corner. This is for commercial deliveries and junior staff.'

Strickland had told him that when things got rough, bluster was the only way forward. Always take charge. They should never suspect you're not on top of things. Bramall summoned up his best *Hochdeutsch*, or High German, in an approximation of the 'pure' Saxon of Hanover. 'Don't bother me with trivia, Corporal,' he said. 'I have an appointment with Colonel Walter Bruns, our military attaché, at ten o'clock.'

'Then you're early, sir. It's only nine-thirty.'

'What?' Bramall looked at his watch – actually Rath's watch, included with his uniform. *'Ach*, my watch must be fast.'

'Not a problem, sir. I trust your hotel was comfortable?'

'I wouldn't know. I arrived five hours late and got next to no sleep. These Spanish trains are unbelievable!'

'Indeed, sir. I heard one of our diplomats last week say just the same thing.'

'Let's go, then. Or are you proposing I wait out here until ten o'clock?'

'Of course, not, *Herr Fregattenkapitän*. If I could just see your *Ausweis* …'

'My pass? Good God, man, don't you know who I am?'

'I'm afraid we haven't met, sir.'

'Na-ja.' Bramall reached into the inside pocket of the jacket of his uniform and withdrew Rath's *Militärischausweis*. This was a delicate moment. He had stained the main ID section of his pass, with water, so that the photograph, with its embossed stamp, was slightly discoloured. Even so, anyone with a keen eye would see that he and Rath were less than twins. The only thing to do was bluff. He opened the pass and thrust it at the corporal, making sure that the open pages were no more than a couple of inches from his eyes. All the hapless NCO could see, squinting behind his glasses, was a stern, impassive face, with a scar down one cheek. He looked up at Bramall. The scar was practically glowing. The corporal drew back, blinking.

'Yes, sir. I'm sorry, sir. This way, if you please.'

Once inside, he was asked to take a seat. 'I'll telephone Colonel Bruns's office and let them know you're here. Perhaps he can see you now'

'That would be helpful.'

This was the second difficult moment. If Bruns happened to be at his desk, with nothing better to do, he would invite him straight up. He would then have to think of some way of putting off the encounter. Perhaps he could say he wanted to visit the washroom – or that he needed to make an urgent phone call to Berlin. Fortunately, the requirement did not arise.

'I'm afraid the colonel is with the ambassador right now. He will see you shortly, as agreed. I am to escort you to his office where no doubt his secretary will arrange a cup of coffee.'

Not there. That was a relief.

'Thank you, but there's no need to waste your time, Corporal. I know the way up.'

'If you say so, sir. Third floor, second on the right. The *Fahrstuhl* is straight ahead at the end of the passage.'

Bramall nodded and made his way down the narrow hallway. The German-made *Fahrstuhl*, or Lift, was like a never-ending sequence of dumb waiters. There were no doors, simply a rising series of square-cut floors that appeared one after the other and continued upwards on a never-ending loop that came down again on the opposite side. He stepped in. The Lift didn't pause and he had to be quick to step out on the first floor.

Bramall didn't know it, but at this second Hasselfeldt was struggling to contain his rage. Not only had he been forced the spend the entirety of the previous day compiling a report for Schellenberg on the Duke of Windsor's entourage and state of mind, but now, while he was in the middle of transcribing the second half of the meeting between Stohrer and Serrano, his *Gestapo* colleague, Paul Winzer, had chosen to make another of his impromptu morning visits. The suave, self-assured *kriminalkommissar* seemed to drop in all the time these days. It was as if, in a reverse of the normal order of things in Berlin, he regarded the activities of the SD as no more than an adjunct of his own operation. In fact, if Hasselfeldt only knew it, Winzer's concern was that it was his functions that were being usurped by the SD. The Duke, it seemed to him, had been allowed to slip away from Spain almost unnoticed while Hasselfeldt meddled in the embassy's broader, and much more important geopolitical remit. This wouldn't have mattered if nothing else were going on. The Duke and Duchess were, after all, inherently irrelevant and Ribbentrop was rapidly going the same way. But with Operation Felix in the offing, Winzer's job was to ensure that only those, German and Spanish, who needed to know what was going on were privy to its secrets.

He began his questioning with the usual pleasantries. *Wie geht's?* ... not quite as hot today as yesterday ... did you read that cinema attendances are up again in Berlin? Hasselfeldt was not fooled. He waited for the knife to go in and he was not to be disappointed. Winzer sat down on a swivel chair and clasped his hands in front of him. Then, lifting his elegantly shod right foot onto his left knee, he pushed himself with his other foot slowly right and left. 'Tell me,' he began, 'have you heard anything from Schellenberg?'

'The *obersturmbannführer* is in regular contact.'

'I am relieved to hear it. Anything I should know about?'

Hasselfeldt's expression tightened. He found these regular interrogations intrusive and impertinent. 'Shouldn't you be dealing with your own cases, *Herr Kriminalkommissar*? Has the *director general de seguridad* come up with nothing interesting lately? Is that why you keep coming in here asking questions about matters that need not concern you?'

Winzer, technically inferior in rank to Hasselfeldt but with the power of the *Gestapo* behind him, affected a mixture of injured innocence and indignation. 'Klaus! How can you say such things? We work for the same masters and I have by far the greater experience of Spain. Do you wonder that I like to see what you are up to with your ...what do you call it?' He indicated the *Magnetophon*, over which the SD officer had been bent as he entered his office.

'My *Magnetophon*, you mean? *Ach* ... so that's what this is all about. You want to know how it works and what information it may contain.'

'Not at all,' said Winzer. 'That is a matter for the protocol section and the ambassador, which no doubt they will resolve in their own time. But you should know, Klaus, that the Prinz Albrechtstrasse is not happy. Not happy at all. There is concern that your attention is not focused, as it should be, on ways and means of attracting the Duke and Duchess of Windsor back to Spain, and thereby to the Reich. I hope that you are not allowing any personal interests you may have in the political and diplomatic arenas to cloud your judgment in respect of this central priority.'

The two men glared at each other. Once again, Winzer felt he had scored a palpable hit.

'You may be assured, *Herr Kriminalkommissar*, 'that my concept of my duty is undiluted by personal considerations. I only hope that the same can be said of the *Gestapo*.'

Winzer rose up from his chair, knowing he was taller than Hasselfeldt by a good five centimetres. He looked for a moment as if he was about to deliver some further admonishment, but in the end he only smiled. The smile spoke volumes. 'I have given you good advice in good faith, *sturmbannführer*,' he said softly. 'When things go wrong, do not say that you were not warned.'

As soon as Winzer left, Hasselfeldt struck his fist against the door in rage and frustration. How dare he speak to him like that? On whose authority did Winzer, a jumped up *Kripo* officer who by rights should be back in his native Hamburg checking papers in the Reeperbahn, question his procedures and priorities? It would be a different story when he, on behalf of the SD, not the *Gestapo*, brought the Duke and Duchess back to Madrid and revealed to the Prinz Albrechtstrasse the strengths and weaknesses of Gibraltar's defences and the treasonable incompetence of those in the Legation charged with bringing Spain into the war.

With a grunt, he moved back to the *Magnetophon* and reached for the earphones. The mishandling of Operation Felix by the ambassador and his staff was what truly mattered. It would be his exposure of all that was wrong at the legation that would cement his reputation at the SD. He reached for his pen. He would not allow himself to be distracted again.

Proceeding down the corridor after leaving Hasselfeldt's office, Winzer was momentarily perplexed to come across a tall, rather intense-looking naval officer striding in his direction, checking the names on the doors, probably lost. The *Gestapo* chief prided himself on his memory for faces and was pretty sure the man wasn't a member of the Legation staff. Back in Berlin, he'd studied military ranks back across the various services. It was always useful to know who was what and who not to offend. In the Reich, the more brutal a man was, the more sensitive he was likely to be about his place in the hierarchy. But it was hard to keep track and all he could be sure of was that the stranger was a naval officer, which was unusual, but not unknown.

'Excuse me,' he said. 'Can I help you?'

Whoever the fellow was, he was clearly preoccupied. 'I'm sorry,' he replied. 'Did you say something?'

'I asked if I could help you. Only you seem to have lost your bearings.'

'Lost? Oh no, assuredly not. I am on my way to the office of Colonel Walter Bruns. It is along here, is it not?'

The man was a Saxon – from Hanover, by the sound of him. Hanoverians of a certain class spoke as if they were reciting from the dictionary.

'I'm afraid you're on the wrong floor. The colonel is one flight up. Would you like me to show you?'

'No, thank you. Most kind, but that will not be necessary.' Bramall wanted to get away from this fellow as quickly as possible. 'I can find my own way. But if you could direct me to the nearest … *Bedürfnisanstalt*.'

Winzer couldn't help smiling. He hadn't heard that word used in years. 'The gentlemen's lavatory is at the end of the corridor, just before the stairs.'

'I am most grateful. *Danke schön*.'

'*Bitte schön*. Winzer is the name – *Gestapo*.'

'Rath – *Abwehr*.'

Winzer's sense of puzzlement deepened. There was something about this stranger, but he couldn't quite put his finger on it. '*Abwehr?* I wasn't informed that someone from military intelligence was visiting the embassy.'

'Really?' the stranger replied, looking vaguely apologetic. 'That is most unfortunate. I am here to report to Bruns on the latest developments in Algeciras.'

'*Ach! Selbsverständlich.* Forgive me. Not exactly my area of expertise. But perhaps I will see you in the bar later?'

'An excellent suggestion. Give me an hour. Until then, *auf wiedersehen.*'

Winzer continued along the corridor, leaving Bramall to heave a sigh of relief and wipe a bead of sweat from his brow. He had thought the *Gestapo* man would place him from the party at the Villa Ortega, but apparently not. Even so, time was pressing. Romero and Isabel would be getting anxious.

He made his way to the washroom, suddenly aware of how tired he was, and how nervous. The facility overlooked a side street, but, as he knew from his previous visit, the end window provided a vew of the road a hundred metres down from the Legation, where Romero's team were waiting for his signal.

Just as he reached to release the handle on the window, he heard a noise behind him. He turned round. *Holy shit!* It was Hasselfeldt.

The Austrian, whom few details ever escaped, took in his naval insignia at a glance. '*Guten Tag, Herr Fregattenkapitän.*'

Bramall turned back to the window, hiding his face. This was turning into a mightmare. '*Guten Tag, Herr Sturmbannführer.* It is warm, is it not? I was just going to let some air in.'

'Let me help you. Those fasteners are tricky.'

Redoubling his efforts, Bramall wrenched open the window. He could feel the sweat gathering on his brow. 'No, no – thank you – it is done. And now, if you will excuse me ... ' He marched straight into the nearest cubicle, shut the door and locked it, hardly daring to breathe.

He waited two minutes, maybe three, listening as Hasselfeldt took a piss, which seemed to go on forever, and then moved to one of the wash-hand basins on the opposite wall. At last, he heard the plop of the stopper being released and the gurgle of water disappearing down the drain. This was followed by the rip of a paper towel, footsteps and, finally, the swish of the main door opening and shutting. Seconds later, Bramall peered out from the cubicle, heart pounding. As he did so, Hasselfeldt walked back in.

'I left my watch by the basin,' he began. Then their eyes met. 'But wait a moment, I know you. You're …'

For a split second, Bramall was rooted to the spot, unable to move. But then, from a place he hadn't acknowledged since the assault on Narvik, his soldier's resolve rose up and banished his fear. He walked briskly towards the German, a fixed smile on his face. 'Is there a problem, *Sturmbannführer?*'

Hasselfeldt tore at the flap on his holster, trying to release his Walther 9mm automatic. 'Stand back!' he ordered, 'or you are a dead man.'

Undeterred, Bramall hurled himself bodily at the Austrian, the force of the collision sending both men tumbling to the floor. Hasselfeldt recovered with surprising speed, twisting and turning where he lay, groping for his Walther. But his adversary, with the advantage of surprise, was fractionally quicker. As Hasselfeldt rose to his knees, the automatic in his hand, Bramall sprang up and kicked him in the side of the head with one of his steel-capped boots. The German fell back onto the tiles, groaning. Bramall followed up savagely, with kicks to the stomach, then once more, for luck, to his face, causing his nose to pour with blood. After a couple of seconds, he lay still.

Bramall stood over the unconscious figure, horrified by the effects of the violence he had inflicted. It was obvious he would be out for some considerable time. Grabbing the Walther, which had spun several metres across the floor, he contemplated for a moment letting him have it right in the chest. It would have been a deeply satisfying moment. But the shot would be heard. He couldn't risk it, and beating him to death in cold blood wasn't something he could contemplate. Instead, he dragged the limp body into the cubicle he had just vacated. Then he returned, breathing hard, to the window at the opposite side.

One hundred metres down the road, adjusting her lipstick beneath the shade of a newly planted plane tree, Isabel looked up to the Legation's first floor windows. The plan was that Bramall would wave a handkerchief out of a window as soon as he was in position. It was important that she shouldn't stand for too long on the *avenida*. Someone would grow suspicious. She checked her watch for the third time: 9.47. Then she glanced down the broad avenue, as if looking for a taxi. Thirty seconds later, she saw the handkerchief. Thank God for that! She had almost given up. It was time.

Trembling, with her heart rising to her mouth, she paused in front of the Protestant church next to the Legation. She was wearing a yellow dress, quite low cut, with a hem that finished only just beneath her knees. As she drew level with the embassy, guarded by a pair of SS riflemen, she turned to them and smiled. Each of the men smiled back. She was easily the prettiest thing they had seen all day. Then she stumbled. Her heel had apparently caught on a paving stone. The two guards motioned forwards, anxious to be of assistance. One of them reached for her elbow in order to help her back to her feet. That was when Romero, appearing from nowhere, shot each of them with a single bullet to the head. Neither cried out; they simply flopped over. Isabel averted her eyes as the Irishman wheeled round, checking that the coast was clear. 'Good job,' he told her. 'Now get out of here! Go!'

Shaking violently, fighting the urge to gag, she rose to her feet, took off both her shoes and began to run as fast as she could. Passers-by were screaming and shouting. One elderly man collapsed, clutching his chest. A dog barked furiously. A tram thundered past, its bell clanging, the passengers either crouching below the level of the windows or else staring out, transfixed.

As the electrically driven, bomb-proof inner doors of the embassy began to close, Julio Navarro, a veteran of the 1936 siege, rolled a grenade into the building's front hall. Three seconds later, it exploded. Romero meanwhile squeezed the barrel of his gun between the closing doors and directed an intense volley of shots towards the rear of the lobby. *'Viva la República!'* he shouted. 'Death to Fascism! Down with Franco! Down with Hitler!'

The steel doors finally closed. As the attackers turned away, a car, stolen from a side street twenty minutes earlier, screeched to a halt in front of them. It had been waiting two blocks away for the sound of shooting. Romero and Julio jumped in and sat back, breathless, as it roared away.

Inside the Legation, there was pandemonium. Alarm bells screeched; red lights flashed. Bramall, armed with Hasselfeldt's Walther, knew he had only a matter of minutes in which to complete his task before someone either attempted to arrest him or else ordered him to leave the building empty-handed. He pulled open the door of the washroom and checked there was no one about. The only person he could see was Winzer, standing with his back to him at the far end, Luger in hand, outside the ambassador's suite. He shifted his gaze across the passage. Hasselfeldt's door was open. Seizing his chance, he slid silently across, closing the door behind him, turning the key in the lock. Seconds later, he froze as someone in the corridor began to jiggle the handle. But then a voice shouted: *'Klar!'* Whoever it was evidently satisfied and moved on to the next door.

So far, so good. Taking a deep breath, Bramall shifted across to the *Magnetophon* in the corner and tried the lid. Fuck! It was locked. There must be a key. But where? He tried the top drawer of the desk. There was nothing, except the usual array of pens and pencils – and the Leica camera Hasselfeldt had used the other day to take his picture. He grabbed the camera and stuffed it in his pocket before moving on to the drawer below. Still nothing. But there, next to a paper knife and a stapler, was a screwdriver. He moved back to the recorder and applied the heavy steel blade to the catch. It was made of metal and did not give easily, but eventually, after a steady application of pressure, it snapped. Thank God for that. He raised the lid and pressed the on-switch. Outside, there was a rising clamour of voices and the sound of stampeding feet. Stay calm, he told himself. Everything's going to be fine. Then he had an inspiration. He pulled the Leica back out of his pocket and checked to see that it was loaded. It was. Not only that, the mid-summer sun was pouring in and the office was flooded with light. He photographed the *Magnetophon* from every possible angle, including a close-up of what he took to be the recording head. It would save him having to describe it back in London. An unexpected bonus.

The machine was powering up. It was warm to the touch, and glowing. He twisted one of the knobs, marked *Spiel*, to the right. It clicked and a voice came booming out, speaking Spanish. He recognised the voice. It was Beigbeder. He shut it off and the voice stopped. Now he tried a different switch. This one had three settings. He tried the setting on the left. The tape began to rewind, picking up speed, emitting a babble of high-pitched, high-speed nonsense, which he took to be speech in reverse. *Fuck!* Once again, he halted the operation, searching this time for a volume control. There it was: *Lautstärke*. He twisted it to zero, then resumed the rewind. In a little more than thirty seconds, it was done. Everything was now on the left-hand reel. He unscrewed a metal cap holding the reel onto the machine and carefully, so as not to spill it onto the floor, lifted it off. Why wasn't there a top to it? He glanced up to the shelves behind Hasselfeldt's desk. Stacked on one of the shelves was a set of shallow boxes that looked as if they might contain tapes. He seized hold of one of them. It rattled. He opened the box and took out the tape inside, replacing it with the one he had removed from the machine. Then, on an impulse, he took a second tape as well, still in its box. But where was the notebook? It had a black cover, he remembered, with silver lettering on the front: 'Property of the *Sicherheitsdienst* of the SS.' He shifted his gaze back to the desktop. There were three identical notepads sitting there. One of them had a pencil sitting on top of it. He checked it. His hands shook and it was difficult to turn the pages. But there they were: Serrano-Suñer, Beigbeder, Vigón, Stohrer, Bruns – the whole fucking lot of them.

He almost laughed out loud, then remembered where he

was and stuffed the entire collection, including the camera, into Rath's attaché case. Listening out for any movement in the corridor, he closed the case and made his way back to the door. Sirens were going off in the street outside. The *Guardia Civil* must be on the scene by now. Through the frosted glass, he could see that embassy personnel were being herded along the corridor, away from the front stairs. Someone was shouting orders. He turned the key and began to twist the handle.

For several seconds, he remained motionless, waiting for a suitable gap in the throng of people, most of them chattering nervously, others white-faced with shock. Choosing his moment, he stepped out the door and joined them, wondering how he might look alarmed and inconspicuous at the same time. Ahead of him, he realised, was Stohrer, the ambassador. The German appeared remarkably calm. The man giving orders wore the uniform of an army colonel. Bruns, perhaps, but best not to check. He hadn't a clue where they were headed, but there was obviously a recognised drill. The important thing now was to get back onto the street, and the best way to achieve that, he decided, was to allow himself to be evacuated along with everyone else.

'This way, hurry!' someone shouted. The colonel again. 'There will be no panic.'

The ambassador stepped forward. 'I don't want the Spanish police to enter the building,' he told Winzer, who still had his Luger in his hand. 'This is a German affair. The embassy is to be sealed.'

'Jawohl, Herr Botschafter.'

Bramall tried to brush past the colonel, still issuing orders, but as he drew abreast, Bruns caught him by the elbow.

'*Fregattenkapitän* Rath – it is you, is it not?'

'*Herr Oberst*. What the hell is going on?'

Bruns appeared to relish the new situation. 'There is no time to explain,' he said. 'The Legation has been attacked. We are sealing it off. You must accompany these people downstairs to the bunker, while I take charge up here. We will talk later.'

'If you say so.'

'I do. Now, please hurry.'

Bramall nodded and moved on, relieved to have survived the encounter. He didn't like the sound of the embassy being sealed. He must get out, and quickly. But how? Under SS direction, he found himself descending two flights of back stairs until he arrived in what appeared to be a sub-basement. There, the file of evacuees was being directed along a dark corridor towards a set of steel doors – probably the entrance to the bunker. It was now or never. To be trapped would be the end of everything. He looked about him. To his left, just slightly ahead, was an open door. Bramall stopped for a second, appearing to check his briefcase. When the group he was with had all filed past, he slipped inside, closing and locking the door behind him.

He was in some sort of storage facility. The sour smell of rubbish drifted in from the outside. Set into the opposite wall was a long, low window, with wire-mesh glass. It overlooked a narrow yard lined with bins. He heaved himself up onto the sill, unlocked the window and pushed it open. There was no one about. No time to lose. Squeezing lengthways through the gap, he dropped the four feet or so to the tarmac and made his way across the yard, looking for a means of access to the street. If there were bins, he reasoned, there had to be some means of getting them out. And, suddenly, there it was: a black metal gate, at least eight feet high. It was locked and a thick coil of razor wire ran across the top. How was he supposed to scale such a monster? That was when he noticed that a couple of the bins back in the yard were larger than the others, on wheels, about chest high. He doubled back and dragged the nearest one towards the gate. It was heavy, but he managed. If he stood on the bin, he might just be able to reach the top of the gate. But there was no room for error. The razor wire would slice through him like a knife.

Before starting the climb, he ripped back a section of wire grill from behind the gate's lower section and pushed the attaché case through the bars onto the ground outside. Now he returned his attention to the metal bin and clambered up. The next step was critical. He looked for a hand-hold. A security light was fastened to the wall above the gate. It was fixed to the brickwork with a metal bracket. He took off his jacket. Holding onto a bar of the gate with his left hand, he reached up with his right to spread the thick, serge material over the razor wire until it formed a pad about fifteen inches across. Then he twisted towards the wall and raised his right leg, inserting the tip of his boot into the gap between two bricks. With a grunt, he pushed off, rising some three feet into the air. His fingers scrabbled for the metal bracket, but only the tips made contact and he fell back. Don't give up, he told himself. You can do it. He selected a second gap, one brick higher up, which meant stretching his thigh almost vertical to his chest. Then he pushed off a second time. This time, though he felt his tendons stretched almost to breaking point, it worked. His fingers closed round the bracket. Now he was able to pull himself up until his left shoe slid onto the top surface of the gate. He brought up his right leg. For a moment, he balanced crazily on the edge. Feeling that he might easily topple backwards, he jack-knifed forwards, shifting his weight to the front. Then he jumped. As he plummeted earthwards, his left leg caught against something sharp and he could feel the shock of metal ripping into his flesh. He hit the ground hard, jarring his feet. He reached down. His calf was bleeding and his fingers came up smeared with blood. Half an inch of flesh had been torn out of his calf. The pain began coursing through him. He felt sick and almost wretched. But he forced himself to think positively. He would make it. He *had* to. Picking up the attaché case, he stumbled forward out of the shadows.

'*Halt!*' a man's voice said in Spanish.

Fuck! That was all he needed.

A tall, rangy officer of the *Guardia Civil* stood in front of him, a revolver in his hand. The sun was in his eyes and he was squinting. He was nervous, probably afraid he might be shot. 'Don't move. Raise your hands and step towards me. Who are you? What are you doing there?'

Bramall replied in German. 'You fool! I am a Commander in the *Abwehr*. Don't you know the Legation is under attack? You must get me to safety. At once, do you hear?'

The officer couldn't understand what was being said to him, but the fact it was being said in German made him instinctively uneasy.'

Bramall immediately followed up his comments in Spanish, employing a heavy German accent: '*Soy oficial alemán. ¡Ayúdeme!* – I am a German officer. Help me!'

'Ah!' Now the fellow understood. '*Sígame* - follow me,'

he said.

'*Ja, ja. Aber schnell!*'

The Spaniard turned to lead the way. As he did so, another voice rang out, in German this time. 'Halt! Don't move or I fire!'

Bramall glanced round and up. It was Bruns, leaning out of a first-floor window. He was aiming a Luger straight at him. 'Arrest that man!' he shouted.

Bramall lunged to the left, the briefcase in his right hand. The Spanish police officer, now thoroughly confused, attempted to cut him off. Two shots rang out from the upstairs window. The policeman fell, shot in the leg. Bramall staggered on and, after a further five seconds, ran into two of the Spaniard's colleagues, rushing to investigate this latest disturbance.

'There is a man shooting at me from the Legation,' he told the startled officers. 'He has killed a police officer. He has got to be stopped. The two men started forward, guns raised, leaving a by now breathless Bramall to continue onward out onto the street.

An ambulance sped past, its Siren screaming. His jacket was already gone. Now he tore off his *Kriegsmarine* cap and threw it over the Legation fence. Finally, gritting his teeth against the pain in his leg, he turned west and began hobbling away.

In the *tasca*, Romero and Julio had just made it back and were waiting anxiously for news. The Irishman had bloodstains on his shirt. He took it off and handed it to the barman, Francisco, who rinsed it under the tap before hanging it out to dry in the yard. They had dumped the stolen car a kilometre away, off the Avenida Vittoria, and left their weapons, including those taken from the SS guards, with the driver, Stefano, who hid them for future use beneath the rotting floorboards of a bombed out house. Having run, screaming, from the scene of the attack, Isabel made her way to the Café Gijón, where she ordered a glass of white wine and took a seat at a table from which she could see the writer Cela, who continued to smoke and work on his manuscript as if he hadn't a care in the world. At one point, he looked up and gave her a brief nod, then scratched another entry.

She was still trembling. The two German guards had died together in less than a second. Blood and bits of their brains had spattered onto the pavement. Fortunately, there was no blood on her dress. Romero had been careful. After that came the ear-splitting crack of the grenade and the rattle of automatic fire, but by then she was already fifty metres down the road, losing herself in the crowd of terrified onlookers.

She could only guess what had happened to Bramall. He could have been arrested; he could have been killed or wounded; or he could have succeeded in his mission. She prayed fervently that he had found the tape and got safely away.

Was this the new life she was looking for? She could only guess how many people had lost their lives this afternoon because of her. Did they all deserve to die, and if they did, was she any better? Who was entitled to make the judgement? She remembered her argument with her father about how his values had become those of the regime and wondered what he would say to her now if he knew what she had done. She sipped nervously at the wine, wishing it was brandy, and glanced over at Cela. He looked up and for a split second their eyes met.

At five-fifteen, she paid her bill and left the café by a side door. There was a lot of police activity, she realised. Twice she was asked for her papers, which were perfectly in order. She tried to reassure herself that was no reason for the police to suspect a pretty Señorita of anything, especially one whose father was chief of staff to the minister of the Interior.

She arrived at the *tasca* just before six and went immediately to the counter. The barman was polishing glasses. 'Where's Eddy?' she demanded.

'Out the back with Julio. They're cleaning themselves off. They will be here in a minute. Are you hungry? Would you like something to eat? I've got some ham.'

'No thank you. I don't think I could eat a thing. But I would like a brandy.'

Francisco nodded, as if he understood entirely.

She sat down with her brandy at the corner table. There were no writers here, only a couple of old men playing draughts. Bramall ought to turn up soon, assuming he wasn't dead or in custody. She looked out the window, hoping to see his tall, slightly stooped figure, but the only people in view were two elderly women dressed in black and a gypsy sat on a stool on the street's shaded side sharpening knives on a portable grinder.

Suddenly, the image of the two Germans spilling their brains on to the street re-entered her mind and she shuddered with a mixture of fear and distaste. Bile rose in her throat and she fought to keep it down. She didn't want to show herself up by being sick.

The bead curtains parted and Romero strode into the bar. 'There you are,' he said, talking to her in Spanish. 'I was worried about you. How are you? You did a great job there – *maravilloso!*'

At this, she burst into tears. 'It was awful, Eddy,' she said.

342

'It was the ugliest thing I ever saw. How can you live like this?'

He took her hands and gave them a gentle squeeze. 'Practice,' he said.

'But …'

'You have to tell yourself that these are people who made their choices. They lived by the gun, and that's how they died. In the long run, what we did was right. You'll see. It takes time, that's all.'

She looked up at him. He let go of her hands and wiped the tears from her eyes with the tips of his fingers. 'Let's hope Charlie made it,' he said. 'Face it, he had the hardest deal.'

'Do you think he'll be all right?'

'Can't say. He'll have done his best, that's for sure. But look, have you two talked about where you go from here? I seriously wouldn't advise hanging around Madrid. Even if Charlie made it out, someone's bound to have spotted him at the Legation. There'll be questions asked and the Brits won't want to know. That leaves you. What did you tell your parents? Didn't anyone think it odd when you walked out of the house with a suitcase?'

'I told my mother I was going to visit my Aunt Elena, in San Sebastián. Uncle Adolfo is an architect. He was sent there last month to work on the rebuilding of the Government quarter and they have taken a villa for the summer, next to the sea.'

'Won't they check?'

'The phone won't be installed at the villa for another week. Bomb damage in the area was severe and a lot of lines are still down. Mama would have to phone Uncle Adolfo at his office, which she doesn't like to do. Anyway, it takes a day to get there. So far, she has no reason to worry.'

'If you say so. Just remember, I can get you to the other side of the frontier. After that you're on your own.'

Isabel nodded, then resumed staring into the street, scanning it from end to end. It was three or four minutes after that she thought she could make out someone hobbling towards them in the distance. She looked again, screwing up her eyes. It had to be, it was Bramall. There was something wrong, though. He was limping. 'There he is,' she cried excitedly. 'Over that way. But he's hurt.'

The two draughts players looked out at the street, then resumed their game. They had seen worse and knew better than to get involved in other people's business.

'Okay,' Romero said, turning to the barman. 'Time to get the first aid box out, Francisco. Looks like we've got a patient.'

The barman disappeared behind the bead curtains.

Bramall walked in seconds later. There was sweat on his brow. He looked ready to collapse.

Isabel rushed up to him. 'Are you all right? What's happened to your leg?'

'It's okay. It's a tear, not a bullet wound. But it hurts like Hell.'

Romero motioned him behind the bar. 'Let's go out back,' he said, in English. 'How'd it go, anyhow? Did you get it?'

Bramall held up the attaché case. 'God knows how, but I got it.'

'Good job! What about Hasselfeldt, though? What happened with him?'

'He got to me before there was any chance to hide. Bastard pulled a gun. But I got lucky. Managed to smack him before he got a chance to shoot. I gave him a good kicking after he went down to make sure he stayed out of it.' He looked at Romero. 'Your little diversion worked just fine, by the way …

and yours, Isabel. I'm very grateful.'

Romero was incredulous. 'You mean you didn't finish him? Jesus! Typical bloody Protestant.'

'How could I? There was a crowd of people outside in the corridor. The security people were in charge. If I'd shot him, they'd have heard.'

'You could've smashed his skull. Been doin' a lot of people a favour if you had.'

'I didn't think,' Bramall said, refusing to meet his friend's eye. 'Fact is, I was making it up as I went.'

Romero nodded. 'Okay, so you put him out of action. Then what?'

'I got the tape, I got the notebook and I took pictures of the machine – I think. We did it, Eddy. I just hope it was worth it.'

'That's for others to work out. Truth to tell, I didn't think you had it in you. But fair play to you.'

Isabel looked puzzled. Much of the English had gone over her head. 'Please,' she said, 'I should wash that wound for you. It looks deep.'

Francisco handed her the first aid kit. Inside was some antiseptic, a bottle of pain killers and various bandages. She took off his shoes and socks, then asked him to remove his trousers, which he did, looking slightly embarrassed, she thought. She bathed the wound in hot water provided by Francisco and dabbed on some antiseptic with a cotton pad. When she was satisfied the cut was clean, she unwound about half a metre of bandage round his ankle.

'You should really have stitches in that,' she said. 'But I think you'll do. A bit stiff, that's all. But what about your trousers? You can't go out with them torn at the bottom like that.'

'Francisco's taking care of it,' Romero said. Isabel looked across to a small table, where the barman was sitting with a needle and thread. He had already steeped the trousers in cold water to remove the worst of the blood. Once he had finished mending the torn material, he would wash them in hot, soapy water and dry them off under the sun in the back yard.

'I take it,' Romero said,' that you didn't get a chance to play the tape.'

'Just enough to check I had the right one. I couldn't risk being heard. But the notebook's there. There must be half a dozen pages at least of transcription.'

'Mind if I have a look?'

'Be my guest.'

As Romero glanced through Hasselfeldt's notes, Bramall held his hands out in front of him. They were shaking. He had thought that after his experiences in the Civil War, and later at Narvik, that he would be used to danger. But you never got used to it – not unless you were a brute or a fanatic. But at least it was over. He'd got the tapes and the notebook. These had to be got to London without delay.

Romero closed the notebook and placed it back in the attaché case. 'Definitely a result,' he said. 'My German's not up to much, but Gibraltar, Morocco, Oran: it's all there, chapter and verse. Franco's bloody map. You were right, Charlie. If the French don't act after this, they're more stupid than we thought.'

Madrid: British embassy, July 11

Hoare would never have thought it possible. That morning, emerging from his official residence and making his way out to his car, he had been confronted by his neighbour, the German ambassador. It was a superb irony, he had always thought, that he and Stohrer should have ended up living next door to one another – a hang-over from happier times, which neither side had bothered to correct. They never spoke to each other, of course – that would never have done – though just occasionally, if they happened to coincide on the pavement, they would nod curtly. This morning, however, Stohrer had blundered towards him, waving a copy of that morning's *Arriba*, in which the attack on his Legation, under the screaming headline ¡Traición!'– Treachery! – was the front-page lead.

'You may think,' the German growled, in his excellent English, 'that this business has worked out very well for you. But you will soon discover that the Reich knows how to protect its secrets. You are being watched, Mr Ambassador. Everyone around you is being watched. If your man – or whomever you employed to engage in this despicable piece of daylight robbery – should attempt to go anywhere near your embassy – he will be picked up and taken away at once for interrogation, after which he will be handed over in chains to the official executioner. This is not diplomacy, Hoare – it is theft! And we know how to deal with thieves in the Third Reich!'

At the conclusion of his outburst, the like of which the Englishman had never thought to witness, Stohrer thrust his newspaper at Hoare's feet as if it were a gauntlet and he was challenging him to a duel. Then he turned on this heels and stalked off to his car, his face suffused with fury.

After he had gone, Hoare bent down and picked up the discarded newspaper, planning to have it framed as a keepsake. It was then that he noted a message, in English, scrawled above the masthead.

'You have been warned!'

Sat now at his desk in the British embassy, Hoare tried desperately to make sense of the incident. Was Stohrer simply expressing his rage and indignation, which is what his smirking chauffeur appeared to think, or was he trying to tell him something? He knew, of course, that Stohrer was no Nazi. He was Old School, simply doing his duty. But to risk everything like this – if that is what he had done. It was bizarre. Was it possible, was it conceivable, that something so out of the ordinary had happened that he was prepared to risk his career – even his life – to help ensure a deSirable outcome?

The more he thought about it, the more certain he was that Stohrer's flare-up was an elaborate, and coded, piece of pantomime. The scrawled message in *Arriba* only confirmed it. The break-in at the German Legation, of which he had been given just one hour's advance notice by Croft in Lisbon, had obviously succeeded beyond Bramall's wildest dreams, and for his pains the young man was to be hunted down by both Spain and Germany.

Hoare grunted. Life was full of surprises. What was important now was to let Bramall know that Madrid was not safe for him and his only hope was to get out as quickly as possible.

Extremadura: July 13

They had travelled to a farm close by the Portuguese border owned by friends of Romero's family in Badajoz. Carlo Robles, whose son had been killed by the Fascists during the Civil War, could be trusted not to betray them and his land gave directly onto the frontier. Romero took the main road out of the city, figuring that this would seem less suspicious. He was travelling as a small-time building contractor, using false papers provided by contacts in Madrid. Bramall and Isabel were concealed in two hidden compartments in the van's rear, covered by sacks of cement and lengths of rusting scaffolding. They were stopped twice, once just beyond the city centre, the second time a few miles further out, where a security perimeter had been established. Both times, officers crawled inside and poked around. On the second occasion, as Bramall and Isabel quite literally held their breaths, a dog was sent in. They could hear its claws skittering on the metal floor. But the rancid smell of the cement, plus a vat of strong glue, newly made from the boiled-down bones of a mule, disguised their human scent. For a second, as Romero looked on, the dog looked to have detected something. It stopped, and its muzzle darted about in tiny circles directly over Bramall's head. But then the stench of the glue took over and the animal shifted its attention towards the fetid pot until its handler, disgusted, dragged it off.

After that, apart from a routine halt at Mérida, they weren't bothered. It was as if the authorities were concentrating their effort on the capital. Just before Badajoz, less than a mile from the international frontier, they bore north some fifteen kilometres following a narrow, one-track road that twisted between two fast-flowing rivers until it was time to turn off to the farm.

It was a typical Sunday evening, less humid than usual for the time of year. After the intensity of Madrid, the freshness of the upland air, filled with pine, came as a relief to Isabel. The peaks of the Serra de São Mamede rose up ahead. There were wild flowers everywhere. Flocks of newly shorn sheep grazed the rough fields, while a pair of tethered goats stared out at them from a paddock next to the barn.

Bramall felt almost light-headed. He had brought the tape and the notebook with him, as well as the undeveloped photographic film of the *Magnetophon*. They were in the attaché case, lying by his feet. The important thing now was to see his task through to completion. He would get the material to Croft, who would put it on a flying boat to London, after which it would be up to the Special Operations Executive to present it to Vichy as the genuine article.

Madrid was in uproar after what had happened. People had been rounded up all over the city – not just the usual suspects, but anyone who knew them. The interrogators were working overtime. Some of those who were arrested had already been shot. That was the word on the street. The search for those responsible for the raid was turning out to be relentless, and it couldn't be long before Bramall rose to the top of the Wanted List – if he wasn't there already.

Hasselfeldt had recognised him. That much was certain. He might be out cold now – in hospital most likely – but the moment he recovered he was bound to reveal what he knew. Winzer, meanwhile, would be on the case, putting two and two together, working out who could possibly have known about the *Magnetophon* and who most stood to gain from getting hold of the tape.

An immediate exfiltration to Lisbon (that's what Croft had called it) remained the only realistic option. Channels to London from the Portuguese capital were more secure, and more reliable, than from Madrid. Just as important, though the Nazis were tolerated in Lisbon, so were the British. Among Portuguese officials and ordinary people there remained a fund of goodwill for their oldest ally.

Romero, who had been driving for the last five hours, yanked the van's big steering wheel hard left and began bumping up the lane to the farmhouse and its surrounding corral. 'Nearly there,' he said, turning round and tapping the metal floor behind his seat. 'Time to get up, children.'

Protected by a palliasse from the worst of the buffeting, Bramall yawned. He had been catching up on lost sleep ever since they started the long back roads climb over the Sierra de Guadalupe, fifty miles back.

'Are you going to get me out of this thing any time soon?' he called out, his voice both muffled and tinny. 'I feel like I'm the passenger in a hearse.'

'Almost there,' Romero replied. 'Hold your horses.'

The van stopped and Bramall could hear the ratchet of the handbrake locking home. Romero threw open the rear doors and began hauling out the sacks of cement. Once he cleared sufficient space, he stuck the heavy blade of a screwdriver under the lid of Bramall's compartment and levered it up.

'Welcome to paradise,' he said, beaming.

Isabel's compartment was opened a moment later. 'Is this it?' she asked, wiping the sleep from her eyes. 'Have we arrived?'

'What do you think?' Romero said.

Robles and his wife, in their sixties, came bustling out to greet them. There were chickens at their feet. Nothing had happened, they assured Romero. No one had called. The nearest police – apart from the occasional border patrol – were back in Badajoz. He should relax. There was nothing to worry about. Romero thanked them and pressed a small wad of banknotes into the farmer's hand.

'No, no, it is not necessary,' the old man said. 'It has been an honour.'

'Yes,' said Romero, but these are hard times. If anyone deserves a little bit extra right now, it's you and your wife. Take it, please.'

The farmer nodded and put the notes in his pocket. He had a cataract in one eye and could barely see out of it anymore. 'Come, come,' he said, pressing the Irishman's hand. 'Your rooms are waiting.'

A goose hissed at a dog that had wandered up from the backyard, anxious to meet the new arrivals. Romero bent down to pet the dog, which rubbed its muzzle against his leg. Then he followed Robles into the house. The walls were two feet thick. The floor was made of earth and in one corner was a black metal stove on which the evening meal was cooking. Whatever it was, it smelled delicious. This was the hidden secret of the countryside. If you were far enough away from a major road and you kept out of harm's way, most of the time you had enough to eat. There was no school, no electricity or running water, no medical care and no political freedom, and the police were mostly murderers and thieves. But you didn't starve.

Leaving Isabel to wash off the grime from their journey, Romero and Bramall made their way behind the farmhouse to the fields leading down to the river and the border beyond.

'How far is it?' Bramall wanted to know.

'To the border? A mile. Less maybe. After that, another couple of miles to Campo Maior.'

Bramall took in the terrain. 'Have you worked out your route?'

Romero sat down on the grass and leaned his back against the trunk of a Spanish oak – one of a row planted as a windbreak by the farmer's grandfather. The valley lay open before them, its colours, formerly vibrant, starting to fade as the sun began its long descent over Portugal. The crickets and cicadas were starting up, answered by the frogs on the river bank. 'There's only one route – straight across,' he said. 'It's an easy descent, not much water in the river this time of year. The only risk would come if they've stepped up border patrols or installed mines or somethin'. We'll just have to see how we get along.'

'Simple but direct, Eddy. You deserve both our thanks.'

The Dublin man shook his head. When he spoke, the words came out without any hint of his characteristic bravado or irony.

' No need for thanks,' he said. 'Sure I'm only repayin' what I owe you.'

'How do you work that out?'

Romero indicated the stump of a cork tree. 'Take a seat. There's something I've been wanting to tell you, only I wasn't sure how to start or how you'd react. It's not easy.'

Bramall did as he was asked. 'Go on,' he said. 'I'm all ears.'

The sun was turning crimson. A little way off to their right, a heron rose, a silver fish wriggling desperately in its bill.

'You remember I told you my mother was from Monaghan?'

'Clones, I think you said.'

'Right. Well, the thing is, after my father died, I spent a lot of time up there. I was a Dub – a city boy – and we're not supposed to like culchies. But my family was there and I always found Monaghan people good to be with. When the sun shone there was nowhere better.'

'True enough,' Bramall said, wondering where this was going.

'When the Troubles came and the Tans were on the rampage, there was a lot of resentment towards Protestants. Some of it was fair, most of it wasn't. Once it was clear that we were winning – before partition, I mean – the feeling was that it was time to get shot of them.'

'Literally, as I recall.'

'That's what I'm coming to.'

Bramall decided not to interrupt him further. He wasn't going to like what came next. He could feel it in his bones.

Romero continued. 'I'd joined the IRA back in Dublin. Because of my Monaghan connection, I was sent north. The plan was that if the Brits set up border posts Dev would gave the order to go over and take the fight to the Prods. Except the order never came. The odd raid, a few guns smuggled, that was all.'

He mopped the sweat from his brow. Bramall didn't need to be filled in on the background. DeValera was a classic Republican, who had no truck with partition. But in 1922, he had his hands full with the new national government, which having endorsed the division of Ireland was determined to enforce its will, even at the expense of all-out war against former comrades-in-arms. For more than a year, as the battle raged beween the two sides, the IRA and its fellow-travellers went out of its way to even the score with the old Ascendancy class – *his* class, his people.

'The thing is,' said Romero, extracting his tobacco tin from his pocket and rolling a cigarette on his thigh, 'I didn't exactly emerge from the whole affair with clean hands.'

Bramall drew in a breath and tried to empty his mind. He sensed what was coming. He'd known for days that something hidden was about to emerge.

'It was you,' he said quietly.

There was a pause. Romero lit his cigarette and inhaled a lungful of smoke. 'I was only seventeen. Wet behind the ears. I hardly knew what I was doing. One afternoon, the head of our local unit called round and said we were going to 'do' a Big House in the area.'

'Dreenagh,' said Bramall, still in a whisper. 'Built by my great, great grandfather. Our family had worked the land for centuries. It was where I grew up. The only home I knew. Until one afternoon, June 17, 1922 – I remember how bright and sunny it was – a group of "volunteers" turned up with revolvers and a couple of cans of petrol, claiming they were there in the name of the Irish people. Two of them made my mother and me stand out on the lawn while the others went inside with the petrol and set fire to the place. I was 12 at the time, home from school. I watched as the windows blew out and the flames raced up the walls. We lost everything. My mother couldn't stop crying. Can you imagine how that made me feel? Can you imagine how scared and angry it made me?'

Romero didn't say a word.

'But it didn't end there, did it? Go on, Eddy. Finish it. Finish your story.'

There was a long silence, and when Romero spoke again his

355

words were barely audible. 'The oul' fella with the shotgun. I never knew his name.'

Bramall nodded, making fists of his hands. 'Billy McKenna. Our gamekeeper ever since he came back from fighting the Boers. Taught me how to fish, how to swim, the names of the different birds and animals. He'd seen the flames and come running up from the river. When he saw the house burning and my mother and me surrounded by armed men, he acted on instinct.'

Romero shut his eyes tight as the memory came flooding back. 'He shouted out to us: "Get the hell away from herself and the boy!" We looked at him like he was mad. Then he lifted the gun. "Don't make me tell you again, you ignorant bastards!" That's what he said.'

'That's right. Those were his words.'

'And Sean Maguire shot him.'

'In the belly. He was fifty-six years-old. A grandfather, never done anyone any harm. He died in my mother's arms. Her dress was covered in his blood.'

Romero had gone deadly pale. 'And I said …'

'And you turned to me and you said, "Aren't you goin' to call the Fire Brigade, son? Much good it'll do you." And then you laughed at me. Billy McKenna was bleeding all over my mother; our home was blazing – and you laughed.'

'I remember. Jesus, Charlie, I'm sorry. But God forgive me, I was little more than a boy.'

Bramall stood up and faced towards the farm, where he could see Isabel bending down to pick a lettuce in the vegetable garden. She looked happy. Then he turned back to Romero.

'I'm glad you came clean with me, Eddy. It must have been

hard for you. Do you know what I always planned to do if I met the men attacked our home? I planned to shoot each one of them in the belly, just like Billy got shot. It would have been appropriate, wouldn't you say? Natural justice But I'm not going to do that. Not now. Maybe it's just that a lot of time has passed. Or maybe it's the realisation that it was all inevitable, brought on by centuries of occupation. War lets people get away with things that in the ordinary way they'd be locked up for, or worse. Look at the Irish government today. How much blood do they have on their hands? Anyway, like you say, you weren't much more than a boy when it happened. The ones that led you into it are the ones that bear the real responsibility.'

He drew in a long breath, struggling to keep his emotions in check. The episode had scarred his mother most of all. She never truly recovered. From that day on, she kept her thoughts and feelings to herself, communicating with her family from inside an invisible shell. His father, outraged by the audacity of the IRA but surprised as well that people he'd known all their lives were capable of such hatred, had lurched to the right, giving rise, years later, to Bramall's own flirtation with the BUF and, ultimately, to his presence here today on a remote farm in western Spain. *Only Connect* – that's what E.M.Forster said. And he was right. Nothing was an accident. Disparate events, 'accidental' encounters: for good or ill they came together in ways that had implications that extended far beyond him and his small life, governed by rules that he could never hope to understand. Gunther Rath getting murdered just when his uniform and ID were needed was one more example. The only wisdom lay in recognising the significance of chance and the possibilities it offered.

He lifted his head and looked across to Romero, who was clutching a hand to his chest and emitting a series of low coughs, and what he felt was not any kind of loathing but, to his surprise, something akin to sympathy and understanding – even love.

He glanced up at the farmhouse where a crow sat perched on the gable end. 'I want you to promise me something, Eddy,' he said. 'I want you to promise me that you'll get Isabel to Elvas railway station safe and well at the appointed time. I want no slip-ups. Her life is in your hands. You owe me.'

In reply, Romero's voice barely rose above a whisper. 'She'll get there, Charlie. You can depend on it.'

Bramall nodded.

But Romero wasn't finished. 'But since we're in the Confessional, isn't there somethin' you need to get off your chest as well? I mean, you're the one got Isabel into this in the first place. Shouldn't you be sure you're up to the task?'

Bramall felt the hairs rise on the back of his neck. 'What are you on about?'

'I'm talking about Manuela Valdés.'

Bramall stiffened. 'What about her?'

'I was at the Ebro – the International Brigade's last hurrah. It was where I met you, remember?'

'I remember.'

'Manuela was some girl, right enough. Fiery, committed … passionate, I'd say. You and she were quite a number.'

Bramall's mouth had gone dry. 'What's your point?'

'My point is, Charlie, she was a bit of a pin-up girl for the troops. But more than that. They worshipped her – the younger ones especially. The word was that if she was with them they couldn't fail. All bollox, of course, but you know how fightin' men are – superstitious as bedamned. Anyway, after she was killed I spoke to a young Army captain that saw it happen. He'd got shot in the neck and was taken to the same hospital where I landed up a couple of days later.'

Bramall felt a lump rise in his throat.

Romero took a final drag from his cigarette before nipping the end between his finger and thumb and flicking the butt into the long grass. 'He told me that Manuela had been carrying on an affair with a British journalist and that she'd saved his life when a 109 launched an attack. At the cost of her own, he said.'

'That's not how I remember it.'

'Isn't it, though?'

'No. We were standing together at the time. The Jerry came out of nowhere. I looked up. Manuela shouted a warning. Then we both dived for cover. When it was over, I was still alive, but she was … '

'*Dead*, Charlie. The word is dead. Only the thing is, according to the captain, that's not how it happened. He said you were petrified with shock, like a rabbit caught in the headlights. You didn't know what to do. I'm not blaming you, you understand. You were taken by surprise; you had no weapon; it looked like you were a goner.'

'It all happened in a split second.'

'Sure isn't that often the way? It's what happened next that you'd do to recall.'

Bramall jumped up. 'For Christ's sake, Eddy!'

'Hear me out. The captain said that while you stood rooted to the spot, Manuela – who'd dived clear – got up again and ran back to where you were standin'.'

It was Bramall's turn to shut his eyes. He couldn't speak. The memory locked inside him for the past two years had come flooding back.

'She was shoutin' out your name, except you couldn't hear for the roar of the engines and the crash of the guns. By the time she reached you, all she could do was shove you into the trees, leavin' her stood in the open with her back to the 109.'

By now Bramall had collapsed onto his knees. 'And the bullets nearly cut her in two ... while I finished up behind a tree, unharmed.'

'Not unharmed, Charlie ... *traumatised*. There's a word for that as well.'

'I swear to God, Eddy, I didn't know. For the last two years, she's been in my head, invading my sleep, making it impossible for me to believe in myself. And I've never known why.'

'You'll have told yourself it was just one of those things – the fortunes of war and all that.'

' ... so that I didn't have to face up to what I'd done.'

Tears began to course down Bramall's face and Romero's voice dropped once more to a whisper. 'We've all done things we shouldn't, Charlie. You and me more than most. It's the life we were born to, God help us. But some of us get a chance to make up for it. Absolution isn't just somethin' the priests talk about – it's what we grant ourselves when we make things right. I'm going to do whatever I have to to get Isabel into Portugal. For you, your mother, yer man McKenna and my own self-respect. So that I can live with myself again. Then it's back to Madrid to sort out that bastard Luder. Your job, in memory of Manuela Valdes and all those that went down under Franco's terror, is to make sure Isabel makes it over to England, where she'll be safe, and after that to keep Spain out of the war. If we both do what we have to, we're all square. Wouldn't you say?'

Bramall drew a deep breath, remembering how Strickland had laughed when he'd asked him how he was supposed to keep Spain from joining the Axis. *'They told me you were a particular sort of chap, but they didn't say you were a card.'* Now, here, three months later, he couldn't stop his hands trembling 'I don't know about all square, Eddy,' he said. 'Nothing can bring Manuela back, or Billy McKenna. But at least we can do our best to make things right.'

Romero placed a hand on his friend's shoulder. 'Or die tryin'.'

Guadalajara Military hospital: July 14

Sometimes his dreams would last long after waking. Hasselfeldt opened his eyes in the darkness and sat bolt upright in the bed. The SS trainers in charge of the academy in Bad Tölz were bullies, obsessed with Jews and Communists. They bullied the new arrivals. They were 'March violets,' they said, latecomers to the party. They would rouse them from their beds in the middle of the night, forcing them to present themselves in ranks, stripped naked, for immediate inspection. Questions would be screamed into their ears. Anyone who got an answer wrong got a punch to the kidneys that caused him to piss blood all of the next day. Hasselfeldt was teased because he was short and didn't have blond hair and didn't appear to the staff sergeant to be obviously Nordic. The fact that he was circumcised meant they would ask over and over if he was sure he did not have Jewish blood. Even his Catholicism was mocked. He would kiss his bishop's ring; would he also kiss his arse? Was he a homosexual? they wanted to know. A *warmbruder*. Was that his dirty little secret? And what about his half-sister, Gilda, from his father's first marriage? Was it true her grandmother was a Jew?

Shaking his head, mumbling his denials, Hasselfeldt realised that the only way forward was to accept abnegation of self as a Jesuit embraced the rigours of his cell. He would not give in. He would deny the Old Guard their easy triumph.

He could recall each of the high points of his training after that as if they had been yesterday: November 8, the date of the beer hall putsch, when he was allowed to wear uniform for the first time. The time – deeply satisfying – when he had beaten the staff sergeant senseless in the boxing ring. January 30, the anniversary of the Party's seizure of power, when he was admitted as a cadet. April 20, Hitler's birthday, when he received his collar patches and swore his oath of allegiance to the Führer.

> *I vow to thee, Adolf Hitler,*
> *As Führer and Chancellor of the German Reich,*
> *Loyalty and Courage.*
> *I vow to thee*
> *and to the superiors whom thou shalt appoint*
> *Obedience unto death*
> *So help me, God.*

The veterans scoffed. But he had had the last laugh. His tormentors now snapped to attention when he entered a room. The staff sergeant had been stripped of his rank for sexual misconduct and exiled to guard duty in the forests of Poland. When the war came with Russia, he would be among the first to die. It was the new intake, like Schellenberg, with brains and academic standing, who had risen to the top of the movement, alongside aristocrats like Graf von der Schulenburg and Prinz von Hohenzollern-Emden, brought in by Himmler to give the movement a veneer of class.

But now, waking up, disoriented, in the middle of the night, all that he had gained was lost. He was back in Bad Tölz in 1934, listening for footsteps on the stairs. He lay still and prayed under his breath that the klaxon would not sound and there would be no 'impromptu' inspection. Then, as the night nurse did her rounds between the beds, he drifted back into sleep, muttering to himself, not wishing to be paraded naked in the corridor.

The second time he awoke, everything was different. The sun was shining. A young woman, wearing a starched linen headdress folded like a kite, stood over him saying something in what sounded like Spanish, which he couldn't follow. Who was she? A nun? That would mean he was in a convent. But why? And why did his head feel like it had been run over by a tank? It took him several seconds to adjust. He shut his eyes and a newsreel began to play on the screen inside his skull.

There had been someone in the washroom – a naval officer. The fellow had run at him and knocked him to the floor, kicking him viciously in the head. So long as the newsreel continued to unwind, he could see and hear everything. He had tried to draw his gun. He had tried to regain his feet. But the stranger was too quick, too strong. There was nothing he could do.

He gasped as the memory exploded in his head, raising his hands to protect his face. The action switched off the projector.

His eyes opened. The image flickered and died. He looked about him. The walls and ceiling were white and there was a faint smell of disinfectant. He could hear the echo of feet on a marble corridor and the squeak of wheels and the crump of a trolley hitting against a door, making plates jump. He twisted round, feeling a sudden twitch of pain. His hand went automatically to his temple. There was a bandage wound tightly about his head. So he was in a hospital and the woman with the winged headdress beaming down at him must be a nurse.

What was she saying? His head was swimming, but he concentrated and her voice came slowly into focus.

'... gentleman from your embassy here to see you. But only if you feel well enough. The doctor will be along immediately afterwards. Can you hear me? Do you understand?'

He looked up at her and nodded. 'Where am I?' he asked.

'Don't you remember?' she said kindly. She was speaking Spanish. 'It's the military hospital in Guadalajara.'

Ah! Yes, yes. They had told him that earlier, when they had brought him in. When was that? Mother of God! He raised his head from the pillow, and instantly regretted doing so as the pain in his skull rose to a crescendo. Bramall! It was Bramall! Bramall in the uniform of an officer in the *Kriegsmarine*. It was the *Engländer* who had attacked him.

He fell back on the pillow. His head was starting to clear. It was as if the sun was burning away the mist that clouded his brain. What was Bramall doing there? What did he want? Sending him those ridiculous notes, full of obvious statements and tittle-tattle; parading the Duke as an ally of the Reich, but doing nothing to prevent his departure from Spain. He was after something. But what?

Then it hit him. The *Magnetophon*! The tape! His transcription of everything that was said. Bramall must have them. He raised his fingers to his mouth. That was his plan all along – to learn the details of Germany's plans for Gibraltar. Of course! Now the entire project to bring Spain into the war would be compromised. And he would get the blame. Nothing was more certain. His career would be finished. He would be finished. The SD would launch an investigation and present the findings to *Reichsführer* Himmler, who would declare him a dangerous liability to both SS and Party. After that, it would be either the Russian front or the guillotine.

Something was happening. Someone was coming. He heard the curtains round his bed swish back and Paul Winzer entered and sat down on the chair next to him. The *Gestapo* chief was wearing a plain, dark suit. He had brought some oranges with him and what looked like a copy of *Das Reich*, which he left, without comment, on the bedside table.

'How are you, Klaus?' he asked.

Hasselfeldt shrank down in the bed, his eyes swivelling in their sockets. 'I'm not sure.'

'Hmm. Well, according to the doctor, you will live ... for now. Do you know what happened?'

'Someone ... someone attacked me. He struck me from behind. I didn't get to see his face.'

Already he felt like a suspect.

Winzer pulled up a chair next to the bed. 'There was an armed raid. Two, maybe three men. They shot the guards at the front entrance and threw in a grenade. Then they sprayed the lobby with automatic fire. Five of our people were killed. If you know anything about any of this, you should tell me – now!'

Hasselfeldt furrowed his brow. 'I went to the washroom. I left my watch. I went back to retrieve it. There was someone there – a naval officer. But there was something about him that wasn't right. I asked him who he was, he attacked me. I tried to draw my gun, but he was too quick. That is all I know.'

The *Gestapo* officer nodded and pressed the ends of his fingers together beneath his chin. A naval officer – the fellow he had directed to the toilets. Now that he thought about it, he had looked familiar. But who? Winzer peered closely at Hasselfeldt's injured face, with its vivid red and blue bruising and broken nose. Fortunately, there was no witness to his own brief encounter. 'A naval officer, you say? And yet not one of our own.'

The Austrian could feel the police officer's eyes boring into him. He felt trapped.

Winzer continued. 'Strange, don't you think, that the only person hurt, other than the victims of the terrorists on the ground floor, was you, *sturmbannführer*? Not the ambassador, not the military attachés, not I – even though I am well known for my work in setting up the Spanish secret police. Just you. You were the target. Have you any idea why that might be?'

'None!' His denial, he realised, had shot out too quickly, like a bullet fired in his defence. He must be more careful.

'Was there something in your office that an enemy agent might especially want?'

'I am the head of the SD in Madrid. Everything I do would be of interest to an enemy agent.'

Winzer pressed the flats of his hands together in an attitude of prayer. He reminded Hasselfeldt of a portrait of Savonarola his mother gave him when he was a child. He had the same full nose and fleshy lips, the same small, darting eyes. 'Quite so,' he said. 'Quite so. We examined your office. It wasn't ransacked. Your filing cabinet wasn't tampered with. Your books were on your shelves. Your desk looked undisturbed. Everything, in fact, appeared to be in place.'

'That's good news, surely.' Again, too quick. He must slow down.

'Yes ... except for one small detail.'

Hasselfeldt tried not to sound alarmed. 'What do you mean?' he asked.

'The lid of your recording device, the *Magnetophon*, had been forced. You apparently locked it before visiting the washroom. An intruder used a screwdriver to break the lock.'

'I see.' Please God, don't let him follow this line of questioning.

'We found it on the carpet, next to the machine. So here is my question, *sturmbannführer*. What was on your *Magnetophon* that would have interested an enemy of the Reich?'

'I have no idea.'

'The machine had been on for some considerable time. Its valves were overheating. Why should that be?'

'I don't know.'

'Were you using it? If so, what was on the tape?'

'I can't think.'

'Then think harder.'

'I can't. My head. It's ...'

Winzer stood up. His eyes, it seemed to Hasselfeldt, had taken on a cold, reptilian quality. 'Of course,' he said. 'My apologies. You are not well. But you will be out of here in the next twenty-four hours, yes? We will talk then. Depend on it. In the meantime, I shall pursue my investigations in the

Legation itself. Naturally, I will have to go through your files and personal effects. You will raise no objection, I am sure – not when what is being done is in the interest of Reich security.'

Hasselfeldt swallowed. His headache was growing worse by the second. 'No,' he said, weakly, 'Of course not.'

Winzer smiled grimly. 'It is logical. And now, if you will excuse me, I will leave you to make a full recovery.' He looked down at the figure on the bed, and as he did so his eyebrows rose up his forehead. 'If you could report to my office tomorrow afternoon, around four, that would be perfect.'

'Yes, yes. I'll do that.'

'Enjoy the oranges.'

The moment Winzer left, Hasselfeldt broke into a cold sweat. The *Gestapo* man had always suspected he was up to something. Now he would be hell-bent on proving it. If it came come out that he had secretly taped Stohrer and Bruns in their negotiations with the Spanish, and then lost the tape and the transcript to a British agent – an agent whom he had recruited as a spy for the Reich – he would immediately be arrested and judged by the insanely strict SS Code of Conduct.

There would be no second chance. It would be an open and shut case. He had encouraged Bramall, who in turn had organised a murderous attack on the building by armed thugs. He had lunched with the fellow in the embassy dining room – even placed his photograph on the wall. He had allowed him to visit his office, not once, but three times, until, on his third visit, he had knocked him senseless and stolen the Legation's most closely guarded secret. Worst of all, he had disobeyed specific instructions from Schellenberg to leave the issue of Spanish participation in the war to others and to concentrate instead on apprehending the Duke. The Duke! Who was now in Lisbon!

I vow to thee and to the superiors whom thou shalt appoint, Obedience unto death.

God protect him! He had even allowed Bramall to visit Gibraltar, the objective of Operation Felix, where he would have spoken at length with his MI6 Control. Now he would be interrogated until he told them everything he knew. After that, he would be left alone in a cell with a revolver, loaded with a single round, which he would be expected to use to expiate his crime. If he didn't, he would be denounced as a coward and a disgrace to the Order. His Death's Head ring would be removed, his dagger taken from him and his shoulder flashes stripped away. He would be sent to the guillotine like a common criminal or Jew. He looked at his hands. They were trembling. He had to find Bramall and take back what was his. He might not be able to prevent the information itself from being forwarded to London, but he could still eliminate the one man who could point to him as the source.

One thing he knew for sure: he dared not fail.

10

Spanish-Portuguese frontier, July 14, 1940

The light was fading when Romero set out with Isabel down the rough, sloping fields from the farmhouse to the valley floor. The conditions were perfect. There were light clouds only. A three-quarters moon hung overhead, promising sufficient illumination to enable them to see the way ahead, not enough to highlight them as targets.

Isabel had said her goodbyes to Bramall outside the house. 'Eddy will look after you,' he told her. 'I've asked him to take special care. Do what he says. We'll meet up again at Elvas.'

The border proper began fifteen minutes down the hillside where the river twisted through the valley. Romero had a torch with him, but was loath to use it. According to village gossip, an extra squad of border guards was active in the area and there was no way of knowing how they would deploy, or when.

A badly-maintained barbed wire fence and occasional warning notices were all that marked the dividing line between the two Iberian neighbours. Romero squinted into darkness and cut through the rusting strands of the fence on the Spanish side with a pair of wire cutters. Ahead of them, across no-man's land, lay a dried-up stream that marked the actual frontier and then, past olive groves and cork trees, the uneasy sanctuary of Portugal.

The distance couldn't have been much more than a mile, he reckoned, but it was slow going. At one point, he thought he heard twigs snapping and signalled to Isabel to stand still. But it was only a small animal, probably a Genet, scurrying through the leaves in search of prey.

Isabel was dressed in a light summer frock. She had a pair of town shoes in a strung across her shoulders, but wore stout walking shoes for the crossing.

'Almost there,' Romero whispered. They spoke in Spanish. 'The river's mostly dried up at this time of year, but there could still be pools, so you should pick up your skirts.'

It was hard to see clearly, especially beneath the trees, but she did her best, picking her way carefully among the rocks. But then, just as they were about to ascend on to the farther bank, her foot slid into a deep pool and she almost fell over into the mud. Stumbling forward, she cried out. Romero immediately put his hand over her mouth, stifling most of the noise. Isabel could feel her heart thumping. She stood stock still for a second to recover her nerve, then nodded to indicate that she was ready to continue. Romero was first on to the bank. He extended his arm and took hold of her hand.

It was at that moment that a torch beam caught him full in the face and a voice shouted out.

'¡Alto! No se mueva. Policía español de la frontera.'

'Get down!' Romero hissed. 'Lie flat. Don't say a word. Leave this to me.'

The two-man border patrol, thirty metres upstream, had been on duty for less than an hour when their dog became excited and began dragging its handler south along the riverbed. All the second officer saw in the torch beam was a man, who looked startled and immediately ran off. While his colleague drew his gun, the dog handler slipped the leash of his animal and encouraged it to give chase. Romero could hear it barking as he made his way up and away from the river in the direction of Portugal. His first and only thought was to draw the patrol away from Isabel. He didn't think they'd seen her and if he could lose them in the trees up ahead, there was still a chance that she could make good her escape.

He drew his own gun, a black-barrelled revolver, and ran, panting, into the cover of the trees. Behind him, he could hear the dog gaining ground on him. When he reached the trunk of a large and particularly gnarled cork tree, he stopped. The dog was almost on him now, its savage bark filling the night. He waited. It sprang. In the split second before it reached him, he managed to swing the barrel of his gun upwards in a long arc. He pulled the trigger. The bullet caught the slavering beast in mid-air, in the softest part of its throat, and as it fell on him, knocking him headlong into the roots of the tree, it was already dead.

Pushing the dog off him, ignoring the blood that clung to his shirt, he stumbled to his feet. He was breathing heavily now. His chest was not up to this. From the valley floor, he could hear the two police officers shouting to each to be careful, the man was armed. Then he saw a muzzle flash and heard the zing of a bullet as it whistled past him and lodged in the soft bark of a cork tree.

He stood still, hardly daring to breathe.

The two men were coming at him from separate directions. Pressing his back against a tree, he quietly flicked open the switchblade that he always carried on such occasions. He heard footsteps squelching in the undergrowth. Another gun went off, some distance away. The bullet came nowhere near him. Five seconds later, the man nearest came into view.

Romero's knife flashed. In the pale moonlight, his victim's face looked startled as it registered the horror of what happened. The man's hands flew to his throat. But his windpipe had been severed and he made no sound. Romero grabbed his head and thrust him backwards. He fell with only a slight crump into the leaf mould.

Isabel had done what she was told and lay still on the river bank. The shooting had alarmed her, bringing back memories of the embassy business, but the dog was even more disturbing. She wondered why it wasn't barking any more. One of the two border guards had rushed up the hill behind his dog. The other was somewhere to her left and had fired several shots in Romero's direction.

What should she do? Should she stay put or should she get up and create a distraction? Maybe that was what Eddy needed. She didn't know. But then she heard the Irishman's voice calling out in Spanish to the officer nearest her, daring him to come and get him. That must mean that the first officer and the dog had been dealt with. My God! What sort of a man was Eddy? And what would he expect from her now?

Another shot rang out. She could see the flash from the barrel less than ten metres from where she lay. The Spaniard was obviously afraid to venture any closer. He didn't know, any more than she did, what had happened to his comrade or the dog.

It was stalemate. They could remain like this all night. After a moment, the surviving border guard called out in a nervous voice that reinforcements were coming and whoever was up there should give himself up or be killed. The fellow didn't want to die, she decided, but he wasn't going to run away either. 'Give up, Señor,' he shouted. 'There is no escape.'

A cloud passed over the moon, making it impossible to see more than a metre in front of her face. When it passed, Isabel was surprised to see the officer standing with his back to her no more than three metres ahead. He was obviously trying to circle round. Romero, meanwhile, was making his way down the hill, causing the officer to strain his eyes and move the barrel of his gun from right to left and back again.

Seizing the moment, Isabel reached down and picked up a dead branch, about a metre in length. She waited a moment until she was certain that the man hadn't detected her presence, then leapt forward, screaming. The officer swung round, also screaming, and tried to focus his weapon on his mystery attacker. But he was too late. The branch crashed into his skull, pitching him sideways into the mulch. With a grunt, he rolled over and lay still.

Romero arrived seconds later. 'Good work,' he said, reaching for his knife.

'No,' she said. 'Don't kill him. There's been enough killing tonight.'

The Irishman looked down at the prone figure of the border guard. 'Maybe you're right,' he said. 'He doesn't look like he's going anywhere.' He reached into the man's jacket and pulled out a pair of handcuffs. Placing the unconscious figure's wrists either side of a sturdy-looking sapling, he then fastened the cuffs shut and stood up. 'They'll find him sometime tomorrow,' he said. 'But by then you'll be halfway to Lisbon.'

He looked at her. Her eyes were filled with tears. 'Does it always have to be this way?' she asked him.

'I don't make the rules,' he said.

By the time they arrived on the Portuguese side, a light rain was falling and they collapsed in exhaustion beneath the spread of a cork tree. Isabel passed Romero a small flask of brandy old Robles had given her. He said no at first, then gave way. As he leaned against the soft bark of the tree, listening to an owl hoot, he could feel the hot, burning liquid trickle down his throat.

He felt exultant.

Next morning, Romero waited until the first warmth of the day took the dew from the grass before he wakened Isabel and escorted her the remaining two miles to Campo Maior. 'Time to change your shoes,' he said, as they approached the town boundary. 'We can't have you looking like some kind of peasant.'

Isabel grinned and removed her boots, throwing them into a ditch and replacing them with the town shoes from her bag.

'Now take my arm,' Romero said. 'We need to look like any other couple, not a pair of desperados on the run.'

As they walked along the road into Campo Maior's commercial centre, Isabel couldn't help wondering what would become of the mercurial Irishman after she and Bramall left for London. He would be one of the most wanted men in Spain.

When they arrived in the centre of town, Romero bought coffee in the Café Delta and arranged for a taxi to take Isabel on to the railway station at Elvas. The driver, a lean, ugly man with a preposterously oversized moustache, assumed immediately that they were fugitives from Franco's Spain, but appeared sublimely unconcerned. His only comment was, 'I don't suppose you've got dollars.'

Romero opened the cab door and ushered Isabel inside. Then he leaned in and kissed her on both cheeks. 'Good luck,' he said, reverting finally to English. Tell Charlie I did my part. Tell him I kept my word.'

'Of course you did, Eddy. Who could ever have doubted it?'

'Well, that's just it, you see. He worries about you. My job was to see to it that you're safe. If he could have done the job himself, he would, believe me. Only right now he doesn't have a whole lot of choice. You need to understand that.'

'But what about you, Eddy?'

'Me? Now you're askin'.'

At this, she reached out and squeezed his hand. 'You've come as far as Portugal, why not all the way? Take the train to Lisbon. You could come with us to London, or even make it home to Ireland. You don't have to go back to Madrid.'

He looked at her. 'I don't think so, sweetheart – more's the pity. I've got to be headin' back.'

'Back to what?'

'Back to what I do. Don't get me wrong, England has to win this war, though God knows how they'll do it. By winning the last battle most likely. Isn't that always the way of it? But I have my own war to fight, even if it's a losing cause. Do you know what I heard the other day? Up in Ucles, in Cuenca, there's an old monastery surrounded by vineyards that were abandoned during the war. Hundreds of ex-soldiers from our side were held there, beaten and starved and made to work every hour God sends. But in the end, word came through to make an end to it, and the Fascists and their lackeys had them dig a trench a hundred metres long and two metres deep. When the work was done, they were made line up around the edges and shot until they fell into the trench that was to be their grave. Afterwards, they threw lime into the pit and levelled the soil, declaring it government land, out of bounds to civilians.

'I can't forget that, Izzy, and I certainly won't forgive. One day, and I have to believe it will come, their bodies will be exhumed and the souls of the dead will rise up to condemn their persecutors. Until then, they will be remembered in my prayers and the prayers of others who won't allow Franco and his hounds to spread the lie that these men and these women, whose very children were taken from them and given to the victors, never drew breath, never believed in their cause, never fought and never died.'

'I wish you God's protection,' was all Isabel could say. 'The war you're going back to will last for years. This is only the beginning.'

'I know it,' Romero said. But meanwhile I have unfinished business to attend to.'

'Felipe, you mean?'

'For starters.'

'He deserves it. I know that. But it shouldn't have to be this way.'

Romero shrugged but said nothing. Then he withdrew his head, closed the cab door and banged twice on the roof as a signal to the driver to pull away. Isabel craned her head out the open window and watched with infinite sadness as the Irishman grew smaller and smaller until he disappeared entirely.

The cab turned onto the road that led south to Elvas. Half an hour later, she was on the station platform waiting for the midday express.

Bramall's border crossing had gone without a hitch – so much so that he wished now that he had invited Isabel to join him. But better safe than sorry. The car that had brought him from Spain, arranged by Romero, was a big old limousine normally used for weddings and funerals and was well known on both sides of the frontier. The driver, who arrived complete with peaked cap, took a sequence of back roads that led an hour or so later to the frontier post at Valencia de Alcantara, where the official on duty, seeing the be-suited *caballero* reading his copy of *Arriba* in the back of his car, carried out only a cursory inspection of the vehicle before stamping his passport and raising the barrier. A hundred metres further on, at the two-man Portuguese post, all Bramall did was brandish his embassy papers while invoking the magic words, *O Duque de Windsor*. His driver dropped him at Elvas railway station in plenty of time to locate Isabel, who greeted him with a kiss on the lips that, so far as he was concerned, made the entire experience worthwhile.

Back at the frontier, the local *Guardia Civil* checking that day's comings and goings did not report to Badajoz until lunchtime. Badajoz in turn did not report to Madrid until four in the afternoon, which was when the alarm bells began to ring.

In the meantime, the regional express from Badajoz had pulled in to Elvas station just one hour and fifteen minutes behind schedule, arriving in Lisbon seven hours later, where Croft was waiting. The station chief had brought with him in the embassy car a bottle of Veuve Cliquot.

Madrid: German Legation, July 16

Winzer's manner was so cold and clinical he could have been a pathologist dissecting a corpse. Even so, Hasselfeldt felt that he had done well against him. Though his face was a mess, the two days he had spent in hospital had set him well on the road to recovery. His mind was free of the fog that had gripped it and he was convinced that his situation, though bad, was not irrecoverable. The former *Kripo* investigator had gone through Hasselfeldt's files and personal papers and put together a dossier on anything that might have been of interest to an intruder. What he lacked, however – and he knew it! – was evidence of what had been removed.

Bramall had taken the tape, plus his unfinished transcript, as well as two other notebooks that were sitting on his desk – one of them containing details of his spy network in Madrid. Hasselfeldt admitted only to the loss of his address book. He denied there was any missing tape. What tape? And if there was no missing tape, there was no missing transcript either. No. It must have been his address book that the intruder was after. The terrorists attacked the guards on the ground floor. At the same time, an accomplice, dressed as a *Kriegsmarine* officer, made his way to the first floor and attacked him when he attempted to make an arrest. The whole affair, he suggested, was the work of Spanish Communists, or anarchists, trying to find out which of their countrymen were employed by Berlin.

'I very much regret that I was unable to protect my contacts, *Herr kriminalkommissar*. But I did what I could in the middle of an extremely chaotic situation. The raiders must have known that I would be the one with the important contacts, not the

Gestapo. Otherwise, the attack might have focused on you, instead of me.'

It was a shrewd ploy and appeared to have some impact on Winzer, who smiled softly and offered Hasselfeldt a coffee. 'So you have no idea who the intruder might have been?'

'None whatsoever.' How dearly he would have liked to spend five minutes with Winzer in the boxing ring.

As Hasselfeldt rose to leave, Winzer threw out one last question. 'Tell me, Klaus, do you know anyone by the name of *Steuermann*?'

The SD man froze. '*Steuermann?*' he repeated. 'No, I don't think so.'

'It's just that we found a letter in your files, dated June 28, appointing a Mr Charles Bramall, equerry to the Duke of Windsor, to be an agent of the Reich, with the codename, *Steuermann*.'

'Oh, *Es tut mir leid* – I'm sorry. Yes, of course. It was in connection with my primary mission, which, as you know, is to assist Foreign Minister Ribbentrop and *Obersturmbannführer* Schellenberg in their pursuit of the Duke and Duchess.'

'Except that you'd forgotten his name.'

'Only his cover name. I remember now.'

'But you didn't see him on the day of the attack?'

'Not at all.'

'You didn't, for example, meet him in the washroom?'

'In the washroom? Not that I know of. But if he had visited the Legation, Reception would know all about it. Why don't you ask downstairs?'

'I would, naturally, were it not for the fact that all of those on duty at the time are dead.'

'Ah yes. How tragic.'

'Except for one, a corporal, who was on duty at the side entrance.'

'The side entrance?'

'Exactly. This fellow informs me that *Fregattenkapitän* Gunter Rath, head of the *Abwehr* in Algeciras, presented himself at the side door of the Legation at 9.30 on the morning of the attack, half an hour early for an appointment with Colonel Bruns.'

'Was the identity of this officer confirmed?'

'The corporal insists he saw Rath's naval ID and checked his face against the stamped photograph. Rath was tall, black haired, in his thirties, with a scar on his cheek. All of this corresponded with the visitor's appearance. Furthermore, he spoke with a pronounced Hanover accent, which would certainly fit the facts. Given that the appointment was valid, there seemed no reason to detain him.'

'What has happened to the corporal?'

'He has been arrested, naturally, and will face the charge of dereliction of duty. If found guilty, he will be sent to the Eastern front.'

Hasselfeldt shivered. 'Well,' he said, 'if you have concluded your questions, I should resume my duties. It was good to speak with you, *Kriminalkommissar*.'

'I am sure we will do it again soon.'

Winzer smiled. He and his staff had already checked the ambassador's suite and discovered Hasselfeldt's eavesdropping device, which they quickly traced back to the SD office. He hadn't mentioned it to Stohrer in case he needed to use it himself at a later stage. Before Hasselfeldt came to see him, he had placed a call to SD headquarters in Berlin. How many recording tapes had been allocated for use with the *sturmbannführer's Magnetophon*? The answer came back in a matter of minutes. Six. He had signed for six. There should have been six tapes in the locked cupboard next to the device. In fact, there were only four. He wondered how his SD colleague would account for the missing two. Perhaps they were in his apartment. Perhaps he had sent them back to Berlin in connection with a research project. And perhaps they were even now in the hands of a British double-agent, tall, early thirties, with a talent for impersonating German officers, codename *Steuermann*.

Back in his office, a space surrounded by a neat perimeter of dust indicated where Hasselfeldt's *Magnetophon* should have been. The Austrian groaned and sat down heavily at his desk. Winzer would not relent, he knew it. He could not remain here in Madrid while this investigation hung over him. Sooner or later, the *Gestapo* chief would piece his case together and the guards would come for him. His only hope lay in retrieval and redemption, and the place to start was Lisbon. He reached across to his desk to pick up his phone. As he did so, it rang.

'Buenos Dias, Señor. My name is Villalobos. I work for the Ministry of the Interior in Badajoz. My job is to liaise with the Portuguese authorities along the central border region.'

The man's reed-like voice reflected what the German felt would be his seedy appearance. 'Go on,' he said.

'Si, Señor. I spoke a short while ago to my superiors in Madrid, who informed me that I should report to you. Two hours ago, an Englishman crossed the frontier into Portugal some kilometres north of Badajoz. It seems he was a diplomat working for the Duke of Windsor.'

Hasselfeldt could feel his chest tighten, so that his ribs started to hurt. When he spoke again, his voice came out almost as a surprise. 'What was his name? What was the Englishman's name?'

'Bramall, Señor – Charles Bramall.'

It was unbelievable. He had him. Maybe God and his Holy Mother had not deserted him after all.

'Where is he now?'

'Impossible to say. But there was a train to Lisbon at midday, which stopped nearby at Elvas.'

'Damnation!'

'Si, Señor.'

Madrid: Villa Ortega, July 17

'I tell you, Raúl, she is not here. She is gone!'

Colonel Ortega yawned, pushing his elbows out either side of his head. Then he wiped the sleep from his eyes with his knuckles and groped for the switch of his bedside lamp. 'What are you talking about, woman? Gone? Gone where?'

Doña Vittoria was beside herself with grief. She was crying. 'I don't know. She was supposed to be spending a few days with my sister Elena in San Sebastián. Remember?'

Her husband, aching in every muscle after a day's hunting, nodded.

'She should have been home tonight. But she still hadn't arrived when I went to bed. I thought maybe she had caught the late train and would take a taxi back from the station. But when I got up just now to check, her room was empty.'

Ortega hauled himself up in the bed and ran a reflective hand across his brow. The vein in his forehead had begun to throb. 'She will be with Felipe,' he said quietly, his tone that of a father explaining to an innocent the facts of life. 'It is not something of which we can be expected to approve, my dear, but Felipe is, well, that kind of a man.'

'I know the kind of man Felipe is,' Doña Vittoria said, her voice dripping with contempt. 'But she is not with him. It is because of him that she is gone. Read for yourself. I found this letter on her pillow when I went to turn down the bed.'

Ortega grabbed his spectacles off the bedside table and squinted at the sheet of notepaper his wife handed him, fearing what he would find there.

Dearest Mama,

These have been difficult times for all of us. But the moment has come for me to make choices of my own. I cannot marry Felipe. I do not love him and I despise everything he stands for. I also oppose with every fibre of my being the direction in which Spain has moved under the Caudillo and cannot bear to remain in the country so long as he stays in the Pardo.

I ask you to find it in your heart to forgive me for the action I have decided to take, and also to know that I wish that I could have been a better daughter to you. When I get to where I am going, I will try to contact you. It is my dearest wish that the situation will change so that I can return home and live my life as a free and loyal Spaniard.

Please tell Papa that, in spite of all our differences, I continue to love him. He should inform anyone who asks that he has sent me back to Argentina.

Pray for me, as I shall for you,
Your loving daughter,

Isabel

Ortega scanned the letter twice, then threw it down in a rage. *'¡A pequeña hembra!'* he shouted – the little bitch! 'She will ruin us.'

Doña Vittoria could not believe what she was hearing. 'Husband,' she said, 'have you become so hard and so ambitious that you no longer care about your family? Our daughter has left us. Do you not care what has happened to her?'

The vein in Ortega's forehead was pulsing. A single high-pitched note was playing inside his skull. He made a fist, then thought better of it and sat back heavily on the bed. It was so unfair. Isabel had betrayed him. When Luder found out, he would be beside himself with fury. But then he looked at his wife, standing distraught above him, and his heart began to melt.

'Where has she gone?' he asked. 'Have you any idea?'

'None. I knew she was unhappy, but I never dreamed it would come to this. Oh, Raúl, these are such dangerous times. There are so many mad and wicked people around.' She sat down on the edge of the bed so that her husband could place his arms about her. After a moment, she said: 'But do you know? I think she is right. Felipe is a pig, and Spain is a nightmare. Wherever she has gone, it has to be better than this.'

Colonel Ortega said nothing. He felt drained of all resolve.

His mind was numb.

Madrid: Interior Ministry, July 17

Serrano Suñer's ears were burning. He had just taken a call from Stohrer in which the ambassador had expressed Berlin's fury over lack of progress by the Spanish police concerning the attack on the German Legation. Accordingly, he was in a foul and vindictive mood. He buzzed through to his secretary.

'Contact the chief of police, the head of the *Guardia Civil* and the governor of Madrid. Tell them I expect them here, in my office, in one hour.'

'Yes, Minister.'

'And then put me through to the British embassy. I wish to speak with Sir Samuel Hoare.'

'Of course, sir.'

Colonel Ortega was fluttering in the background, nervously batting one of the shutters of the minister's office window backwards and forwards between his hands. 'And stop that wretched noise, Raúl – it's driving me mad.'

'Yes, Minister, My apologies.'

'What's the matter with you? As if I didn't have enough on my plate already, I have to put up with you mooning around my office like a lovesick boy.'

The comparison stung Ortega, who had not been lovesick for many years. 'I am sorry, sir. It is nothing. Just a few personal worries. Family concerns, that is all.'

'Then worry about them at home. We have work to do and I require your full attention.'

Ortega nodded and swallowed hard. The lines around his throat and jaw were growing taut – a sure sign that he was losing his grip. Isabel, he was convinced, had run off with Bramall. Luder had told him earlier that morning that she and the aide were seeing one another behind his back and that Bramall was now suspected by the *Gestapo* of being behind the armed raid on the German Legation. If that was true, then his daughter might shortly be declared a fugitive from justice, with a price on her head. It was monstrous. Luder had already upbraided him in no uncertain manner for letting Isabel run wild; now the minister was about to involve the police and the *Guardia Civil*. Running his finger nervously round the edge of his shirt collar, he could almost feel the garrotte tightening.

The phone rang on Serrano's desk.

'Get that,' the minister said, gesturing towards the still shrieking instrument. 'Unless it's the British ambassador, tell whoever it is that I am too busy to speak to them.'

'It was the Pardo,' Ortega announced a minute or so later. 'His Excellency says he is most concerned about the situation and expects it to be resolved as quickly as possible. He has asked for a report.'

This actually made Serrano laugh – a rare event. He whinnied for a second, reminding his subordinate of a thoroughbred with a cough. Then his scowl returned. 'You will tell the Pardo that we are going to find who was responsible for this attack, who planned it and for what purpose. You will say that we are going to arrest those responsible and everybody who has ever met them or spoken with them – and their families. And when we have done that and completed our investigation, we are going to keep the city executioner busy for the next three months.'

It was unbearable. Ortega could feel the hairs on the backs of his hands stand on end. 'Everybody who has ever met them or spoken with them?' he repeated.

Serrano glanced up over his shoulder, already thinking ahead. 'And their families,' he added.

Lisbon: British Embassy, July 17

Croft could hardly believe what he was hearing. Bramall's description of the operation he had mounted at the German Legation had filled him with admiration – and envy. He held the tape up to the light as if it were a strip of cine film; he took note of the Leica and the pictures of the *Magnetophon* he was told it contained. Most of all, he read through Hasselfeldt's notebook, containing its comprehensive revelation of Germany's plans for Gibraltar and North Africa.

At length, he sat back, with the notebook still opened on his knee, and slowly shook his head. 'It's brilliant,' he said. 'First class. Congratulations. I never thought you'd do it. What matters now is that we should get this stuff back to Strickland first thing.'

'What about me?'

'What about you?'

'Well, shouldn't I go with it?'

A look of sympathy mixed with triumph crept across the Londoner's features. 'Listen, Sunshine,' he began, 'you might think you're off the hook far as the Duke's concerned, but you're not. He doesn't leave for the Bahamas until August 1. That leaves us the best part of two weeks to get through. My guess is that if the *Abwehr*, or the SD, really do decide to make a play, they'll wait till the last few days, when the opportunity's greatest. Then, God help me, I'm going to need you here.'

'I see.'

'Far as the tape's concerned, there's a plane in the harbour. I'll speak to the ambassador, see what's what. I suggest you write a memo to Strickland setting out everything that isn't immediately obvious. The Ortega girl can go with it, help fill in some of the blanks.' He paused. 'Of course, you probably think you should go to France and deliver the material personally.'

'It did occur to me.'

'Ordinarily, I'd say that made sense …'

'But on this occasion …?'

'On this occasion, I think the SOE will demand the right to carry things forward. We have to face it, France is their patch.'

Croft was referring to the Special Operations Executive, newly set up by Churchill to operate within the occupied territories. France was the SOE's main focus and it was unlikely its chiefs would willingly consent to an act of piracy by 'Six.'

'And in the meantime,' the Yorkshireman continued, 'we still have the small problem of your friend Hasselfeldt. What if he manages to put two and two together?'

'Romero will take care of him.'

Strickland frowned. 'Let's hope so,' he said.

London: SIS, Baker Street, July 18

Strickland looked up in mild surprise as Isabel knocked and walked into his London office. He wasn't wearing the jacket of his brown suit; in its place was a bright yellow waistcoat. 'Good God,' he said, struggling to his feet. 'Miss Ortega, isn't it? That were fast. I wasn't expecting you until tomorrow.'

Isabel had heard a lot about Strickland from Bramall but had no idea what he would be like in the flesh. He reminded her of her Uncle Adolfo.

'The RAF brought me. Mr Croft told them that what I have is important for the war effort.'

'Ah! Well, we'll see about that.' Strickland had been wary at first about inviting the young Spanish woman into his office. He had fancied a pub round the corner might be more appropriate. He smiled at her, slightly embarrassed, as he usually was with women under forty. 'Sit down. How are you, anyway? Recovered from your ordeal?'

'I am sorry?'

'Your ordeal. I am aware that since meeting Mr Bramall your life has change markedly, and not necessarily for the better.'

'Oh, I see. But I'm fine – really. And I think my life now is not worse than before, it is better … much better.'

Strickland pushed his glasses back up the bridge of his nose. 'Even so, I'm very grateful to you for the work you've done and the, er, sacrifice you've made. It can't have been easy.'

Isabel thought of the pain and anger she had caused both her parents and the shock of seeing the two SS guards die in front of her. 'No,' she said. 'It was not easy.'

'Well you're safe now. So what have you got for me? Let's have a look.'

Isabel handed over the metal box in which the embassy in Lisbon had placed the tapes, Hasselfeldt's transcript and the Leica camera.

Strickland undid the clasps on the front of the container. Then he adjusted his glasses again and opened the shallow box inside that contained the primary tape, marked 'Felix.' He held it up to the light, examining it in gingerly fashion. 'So this is it, then. Doesn't look like much, I have to say.'

'You must be careful!' Isabel warned. 'Charles says if it unravels, it is very hard to get it back on to the reel.'

'Why didn't they just put a top on it?'

Isabel looked puzzled.

'It's got a bottom, but no top. Daft that. But you're saying that if we can only work out how to play this, we can hear Serrano and Co. negotiating with Stohrer to enter the war, is that it?'

'Yes. But there is also information concerning Morocco and Oran and how they are to be given to Spain. Charles says it will drive the French ... what did he say? ... *barmy*.'

Strickland smiled. 'Bit late for that, if you ask me. But okay, let's get the boffins in.' He pressed a switch on the telephone console on his desk. 'Strickland here. Could you send Mr Caxton up, quick as you like, please? We've got something for him.'

He took out the transcript while they waited.

'Charles has the original,' Isabel said, in case you want him to go with it to France. He copied out the German and added a translation.'

Strickland grunted and began leafing through the document. After a couple of minutes, he put it down. 'Bloody hell!' he said, 'Croft was right.'

'Actually,' said Isabel, ' Charles was right. He went into the embassy, he obtained the tapes and the transcript. And, if I may say so, I was of some help as well.'

Strickland pursed his lips. 'You've made your point, Miss Ortega. Don't push it.' He reached back into the metal box and brought out Hasselfeldt's SD notebooks. ' So what are these?'

'I do not read German, but Charlie says ...'

'Charlie?' Strickland was looking at her quizzically.

'I am sorry. *Mr Bramall* says the entries are appointments for Hasselfeldt in recent weeks. He gives his opinion on the reliability of the ambassador; his assessment of, er, Mr Bramall, and – oh yes – there is a list of SD agents in Madrid.'

'I see. Not bad, not bad at all A good week's work.'

It was clear that the older man had offered as much praise as he was likely to dispense this side of Christmas, so Isabel sat back and waited for him to take the conversation forward.

'Always assuming,' Strickland began, 'that the tape is up to snuff ... kosher, that is ... ' He could see the puzzlement on her face. 'I mean, if it's the real thing. Then how do you think we should proceed? What does "Charlie" think?'

Isabel reached into a cheap handbag she had been given by one of the secretaries at the Lisbon embassy. 'He gave me this letter for you.'

'Aah, right.'

'But I know that he thinks he and I should go to France.'

'Does he now?'

'Yes. It is obvious why he should go. But I, too, speak French, my father works for Serrano and I have met many of the current Government, including the *Caudillo*. If the French in Vichy don't believe what Mr Bramall is telling them, maybe they are believing me.'

The Yorkshireman sniffed. 'Aye,' he said, 'an interesting

idea. But I'll need time to think.' He leaned forward, his eyes narrowing to slits. He looked as if he was about to say something particularly caustic when he was interrupted by a knock at the door.

'Enter!'

A man of about fifty, no more than five-feet-eight, with wire-rimmed glasses and a fringe of black hair surrounding a domed head, walked into the office. He wore a white lab coat over a wrinkled grey suit, like a doctor.

'So, Mr Strickland, what have you got for us this time?' he said. His accent was soft, but his eyes were hard. He didn't look the sort of man who would be easily impressed.

'This,' said Strickland, pushing the tape towards him.

The boffin's eyes lit up. 'Oh, well now, that *is* interesting.'

'Recognise it, do you?'

'I haven't seen one of those since, when would it have been? ... 1935, Berlin Radio Fair, if I'm not mistaken. AEG made the recorder; I.G. Farben and BASF came up with the tape to go with it. An amazing breakthrough. Quite extraordinary. Plastic tape, light as a feather and easy to use – reproduction like nothing you'd find this side of the Channel. Wait a minute ... don't tell me. The *Magnetophon* – that was the name of the machine. Am I right?'

Isabel nodded. She had taken an instant dislike to Caxton.

'Oh yes, I remember it now. We were keen to get hold of one. I mean, you can imagine. But then bloody Himmler stepped in and halted exports. No more than two or three ever got out. And, if you're wondering – no, I don't have one. I doubt there's one anywhere in the UK.'

Shifting his glasses up to the top of his head, he picked up the reel and unspooled a length of the tape. He was like a wine buff with a rare and ancient vintage. 'Oh Lord, yes,' he said, running his finger and thumb lovingly along the sides, 'this is the genuine article. I read somewhere – *Rundfunk Magazine*, it must've been – they'd got high frequency biasing now. But of course you couldn't tell just by looking.' He sniffed at it. 'Ferric oxide coating. That'd give you a better dynamic width. Tape no more than – what? – three millimetres? I have to tell you, Mr B, I never thought I'd see the like of this again – not until Jerry came marching down Whitehall.'

'Yes,' said Strickland, doing his best to be patient. Boffins tended to get his goat. 'No doubt. The thing is, can you play it?'

Caxton shot him a puzzled look. 'Play it?'

'Yes.'

'On what?'

The Yorkshireman sighed. 'You seem to know all about it. You're our top man in the field. Is it really beyond your wit to come up with something that will enable us to hear what's on this tape and maybe go on to win the bloody war?'

Caxton grimaced, revealing several blackened teeth. 'Mr B,' he said. 'I think maybe you should come downstairs with me. Your friend, too, if she'd like. You never know, you might learn something – and that'd be a first.'

Once again, Strickland ignored the barb.

As they made their way down the lino-covered back steps, smelling of disinfectant and tobacco, Isabel thought about Bramall, still up against the Germans, only this time in Lisbon, and wondered what was going to happen to him. He had been relieved when Croft said she should go to London on the next flying boat, leaving just hours after her arrival. It got her out of danger, he said, which was the most important thing. Then he had hugged her and kissed her on the forehead before turning away, embarrassed. When she got to London she should go to the pub, he called out to her, and try a glass of English beer.

The steps took them all the way down to the basement. A warehouse and research lab, on two floors, had been built out the back. Caxton pressed a buzzer on a large metal door and a military policeman peered out through the thick glass. He nodded and turned a key. 'Your ID, please, gentlemen ... and lady'

Strickland showed his top-level pass. 'And I can vouch for Miss Ortega here,' he said.

'Very good, sir. If you'd care to step through.'

The room into which they moved was about forty feet across and maybe a hundred feet long. There were benches down one side, at which men in white coats – the 'backroom boys' – were busy with various complicated bits of machinery. Desks occupied the middle space. A separate group of men, and two women, were bent over adding machines and slide rules, next to a contraption contained in what looked like an oil drum that Caxton identified as a 'computation machine.' He waited a second, like a sideshow impresario, then said, 'And over here is what we've come to see.'

Isabel stared. Near the end of the room where they were standing, fixed to spools set into the wall, were two enormous metal reels, each nearly a metre across. Between them, via a series of wheels and springs, ran a ribbon of shiny metal foil, maybe five centimetres-wide. A technician, wearing goggles, was welding two lengths of foil together. The sparks were flying.

'What is it?' Isabel asked.

Caxton grinned. 'The Marconi-Stille recorder. Britain's answer to the *Magnetophon*.'

Isabel blinked in astonishment; Strickland stared at it with suspicion.

'See those reels?' said Caxton with relish. 'A full one weighs thirty-five kilograms. It's got over three kilometres of steel foil wound onto it, enough for half an hour's recording – and it takes two men just to mount it. The foil moves past the recording and reproduction heads at one and a half metres a second. Bloody dangerous, take it from me. Like having a cutthroat razor blade flashing past your wrist. If it's not loaded right, or it snaps, it can take your hand off.'

'Bang up to date, then,' said Strickland. 'Just what we're looking for.' He inclined his head in the direction of the welder, who looked as if he had just stepped out of a shipyard. 'So what's he up to, then? Broken, is it?'

'Broken? Lord, no. It's working perfectly. He's the editor.'

'What? You mean if you want to add something, or take something out, you need protective clothing?'

'Now you're getting it. If he gets the weld wrong, it'll ruin the heads. And you want me to play your little bit of plastic tape on this? You might as well ask me to build a radar scanner small enough to fit on an aircraft.'

The seeming impossibility of the task seemed to gratify the little man.

Isabel remembered Charles's description of the *Magnetophon* sitting snugly in the corner of Hasselfeldt's office. It seemed like something from another world. Caxton, at the same time, reminded her of Dr Frankenstein's assistant in an old Boris Karloff monster movie she had seen in Buenos Aires. She almost expected him to wind back an opening in the ceiling and wait for an electrical storm to breath life into his equipment.

Back upstairs, the boffin accepted a cup of tea, sweetened with a spoonful of sugar from the Yorkshireman's secret supply, obviously brought with him from Hanslope.

'Now listen to me, Caxton,' Strickland said, 'what's on this tape isn't magic, it's technical. Bloody Germans were able to invent it; you can at least fathom how it works. If it's money you need – more space, more people – just say. But whatever happens, a week from now – two at most – I want to know what's on this tape, and no nonsense about welders neither.'

The little man made a face. 'You're asking a hell of a lot, Mr B,' he said. 'I'm going to have to find if there's anyone else around went to Berlin and what they picked up, if anything.'

'Maybe I can help,' said Isabel.

'*You?*' said Caxton, his vice dripping contempt. 'And what would you know?'

'More than you, I think.' She had had enough of Caxton and reached for the Leica, which she had earlier placed on Strickland's desk. 'Charles has already given you the tape. But he has pictures also – detailed photographs All you have to do is develop the film that is here in the camera and make prints. But he told me that the machine he saw was approximately one metre in length, about ninety centimetres across and maybe sixty deep. It has valves – big ones – and the tape runs through a central slot with guide wheels the size of a ... *dedal* ... Oh, what is that?'

'A thimble,' Strickland volunteered.

'Yes, a thimble. Thank you. These thimbles, they are made of rubber or some kind of plastic. They stretch the tape, but not too tight, Charles says. Not too much tension. It moved a lot slower – spooled was the word he used – than one and a half metres a second. Charles says more like three or four centimetres. So what do you think, Mr Caxton. Is that of use to you, or are you preferring to wait five years and read about it in *Rundfunk Magazine*?'

As she finished speaking, she looked round and caught Strickland's eye. The old man was actually smiling. 'There is something else I should tell you,' she said, reaching into the metal box. 'There is a spare tape which Charles took also. He does not know what is on it, but he says maybe you can use it to practise with.'

Strickland accepted the spare tape and handed it to Caxton still in its casing. It was clear that he had taken note of everything Isabel said, but he refused to acknowledge as much, turning instead to Strickland, once again baring his teeth. 'I think you'd better leave this with me,' he said. 'I'm not promising anything, but I'll do my best. Thing is, though, I think I'll have to pay a visit to Bletchley. Maybe there's someone there who could help.'

Bletchley was the Government's top-secret code-breaking, communications and high technology information centre, not far from Hanslope. 'Be my guest,' said Strickland. He jerked his index finger repeatedly against the scientist's stomach, tap-tap-tap, like a woodpecker's beak. 'Only don't, for Christ's sake, fuck up. Do you hear me? Don't let me down. What you've got there is precious material. Gold dust. Look after it.'

Caxton looked disapprovingly at the tape. 'For starters,' he said, 'we should get this onto a new reel. This one doesn't even have a top to it. It could all come off in my hand and then were would I be?'

'Fired,' said Strickland.

That evening, after she had eaten – fish and chips, with dried peas – Isabel went to a pub not far from her hotel, where she played a game of Shuv Ha'penny with an ambulance driver who told her, 'England'll never be beat, love, don't you fear.' A little later, a blonde woman in her sixties stood next to a battered piano and belted out 'We'll Meet Again,' a song made popular by a singer who was apparently the 'Forces Sweetheart,' Vera Lynn.

> *So will you please say hello*
> *To the folks that I know*
> *Tell them I won't be long.*
>
> *They'll be happy to know*
> *That as you saw me go*
> *I was sing—ing this song.*

It was funny, Isabel thought, the way a musical hall number like that, sung in a pub by some grandma whose husband had probably died in the Great War, or whose son was at the bottom of the North Sea, sent there by a U-Boat, could have the power and poignancy of art. It depended on whether your heart was in it, and hers obviously was.

On the way out, coming up to closing time, she gave the woman a hug.

'Home on leave, are you, ducks? You look like you're in the forces.' The old girl's perfume was overpowering.

'Something like that,' Isabel replied.

'Well, you come back safe next time an' all. We can't afford to lose too many like you.'

'I will do my best,' she said.

She'd heard about the Sirens over London and the tension that rose when they sounded. Fear like that, she thought, used to be confined to the battlefield. Not any more. Hitler had changed that, as he had changed so much else. Tonight, though, there was nothing, only silence. She could hear her feet echoing in the street behind her as she walked back to her hotel. At one point, a car passed her, with black tape over its headlights, so that only a slit of light got through. A cat, racing across the road, was lucky not to be run over. Turning the corner into what she hoped was the Bayswater Road, she said goodnight to an old man out walking his dog, using the walls and hedges to help guide himself as he shuffled along. There was a full moon, she realised, but it was hidden in cloud for much of the time and with the street lighting turned off it was hard to read the street signs. At one point, a middle-aged man on a bicycle, wearing a tin helmet and a white sash, came dimly into view. As he drifted past, something caught his attention and he blew a whistle and bellowed.

'Put that light out!'

Isabel didn't know what he meant until she saw one of the curtains in an upstairs window twitch and the room go dark. She called after the whistleblower, asking if this was the Bayswater Road, but he didn't even turn round.

She found her hotel just a minute later. She had been on the right road all the time. London seemed to her to be turned in on itself, like a widow in mourning. Madrid, she realised, must have been like this during the siege.

An image of Teresa Alvarez swam into her head. She could see her friend's matted hair and her sunken eyes, dull with fatigue. Then she heard the old man in the alleyway coughing. 'The dead and the dying are beyond our help,' he said. 'It's the living you have to watch out for.' She prayed for both of them and for Colonel and Señora Alvarez. She prayed for her mother and for Romero. She even prayed for her father. Finally, she offered a special prayer for Bramall. Then she got undressed and lay naked beneath the thin sheets. As she stared into the darkness, a sheet of lightning billowed briefly across the sky, throwing the window frames behind the cheap curtains into sharp relief. The clap of thunder that followed a few seconds later indicated that the storm, forming out over the Channel, was still some way off.

Next morning, with the rain trickling down the windowpanes of her hotel room, she called in to Baker Street and spoke with Strickland.

'Has anything happened? she wanted to know.

'Give it time,' Strickland said. 'It hasn't been twenty-four hours yet. We'll get there. Meanwhile, if it's all the same to you, we're thinking of sending you up to our training centre in Buckinghamshire.'

'Buck-ing … ? '

'North of London. Not far.'

'Does that mean … ?'

'It means, Miss Ortega, we're keeping our options open. And it'll give you something to do instead of just hanging about.'

'So I might go to France? Is that what you are telling me?'

'Let's just see, shall we?'

'When do I start? How soon?'

'Tomorrow. I'll have the details send round to you at your hotel.'

And she had had to be content with that.

Portugal: Boca do Inferno, July 19

The Duke of Windsor stared out the window of the home that he was convinced was now his prison. Far below, the sea crashed against the cliffs and he was reminded of the Count of Monte Cristo, stretching up to the bars of his cell in the Chateau d'If to catch the merest glimpse of freedom.

The Duke was an Anglican and had gone to Church that morning. He believed that the Almighty meant well on the whole. He couldn't help observing, even so, a connection between his present, dire predicament and the Catholic doctrine of purgatory. He had given up his throne for the woman he loved. He had abandoned the country of his birth – if not his ancestry – in deference to the finer feelings of his family. Most recently, he had denied his true political leanings lest the country and family that had abandoned him were offended, and agreed to remain in exile.

When would it be enough? He endured humiliation on a daily basis. Having fled from Paris, which had fallen to the Germans as a direct result of the ridiculous policies of the French and British governments, he had been told that he mustn't stay in Madrid – this in spite of the fact that Spain was neutral and the Spanish were obviously keen to have him. Portugal, too, was to be denied to him. Instead, each day, surrounded by Churchill's army of secret agents, he found himself hounded from pillar to post, awaiting the arrival of the ship that would taken him 3,000 miles out of harm's way to wear a plumed hat and wave to the natives. Were it not for the enduring love and daily ministrations of the Duchess, he would have been forced to conclude that God, too, had turned against him.

At least Churchill had now recalled Piper Fletcher from front line service to resume his duties as royal batman. That he'd been removed from his household in the first place was an outrage, typical of the spitefulness and small-mindedness of the present Palace establishment and their Whitehall collaborators. Progress, then. But still a long way to go. What of the Duchess's personal maid and *lingère*, Mlle Moulichon, despatched to Paris from Madrid to collect some personal things for onward passage to Nassau? Where was she? Who was preventing her return and why? It really was a wretched business. The British Government may have declared war on Germany, but it made sure that among those hardest hit were himself and the Duchess. It was typical and short-sighted. But he would not be deterred. *Ich dien*, I serve: that was his motto as Prince of Wales, and it was as true today as it was then.

Behind him the door opened to admit an American voice. 'Oh, there you are, darling. I thought you were in town.'

The Duke spun round. The Duchess was entering the drawing room with their host, the banker Ricardo Espírito Santo Silva. They both looked flushed, he noticed, as if returning from vigorous exercise.

'You seem to be miles away,' the Duchess said, hurriedly separating her arm from that of her companion.

'Soon we *shall* be miles away,' the Duke replied, 'and no knowing when we shall return.'

The Duchess allowed her features to crease into the semblance of a smile. She loved her husband, but sometimes his portentousness made her want to scream. 'Don't give it another thought. I'm sure we'll both be just fine. There's a new home waiting to be organised, parties to arrange – and New York is only four hours away by airplane. We'll have a ball.'

'Let's hope so. But how are you, anyway? I haven't seen you since breakfast. What have you been up to?'

'I've been out riding with Ricardo.'

'Really?'

'Yes. It was wonderful. I really am most grateful to him.' She smiled across at the banker, who immediately averted his eyes.

'I apologise to Your Royal Highness for having detained the Duchess for so long,' he said. 'And now, with your permission, I shall withdraw. I'm sure you have much to discuss.'

The second they were alone, the Duke resumed the litany of complaints that had taken up practically their entire breakfast together. The Duchess groaned inwardly. He complained about the servants, he complained about Espirito Santo Silva ('fellow doesn't know his place' ... 'well, actually, my dear, it *is* his place'). Most of all, he complained about the growing army of police and secret agents who dogged his every step.

'You'll never guess who's back,' he said.

The former Mrs Simpson, born and raised in Baltimore, was not a one for word games. 'I don't suppose I will, so why don't you tell me?'

'Bloody Bramall.'

'Mr Bramall? Oh, that's nice. Such a charming young man.

Such a breadth of shoulder.'

'Chap's an arse.'

The Duchess wandered over to a small table by the window and picked out a stem from a bouquet of red roses placed there earlier by one of the servants. She held it under her nose and drew in its scent.

'Those came for you this morning,' the Duke said. 'German embassy again. Don't know what their game is.'

'They're being polite, that's all. Just because we're enemies doesn't mean we can't be friends.'

'Bramall says from now on, until we're on the boat, surveillance will be at 100 per cent. Damned cheek, if you ask me.'

The Duchess looked faintly alarmed. 'We'll just have to grin and bear it,' she said.

'At least they can't spoil dinner.'

'No. Tiger still coming?'

'Absolutely. The Tigress, too. And Primo de Rivera says he's bringing the Comtesse de Fourneau.'

'Dominique? How marvellous. Haven't seen her in an absolute age.'

'Yes. Lives in Madrid now. Husband got shot, don't you know. Some Jew in Berne. But according to Tiger, she's bearing up. Been seeing Beigbeder, apparently.'

'The cunning old dog. And are we hosts or guests?'

'Hosts, I think – courtesy of the embassy. The ambassador will be there … oh, and Nicholas Franco, the *Caudillo's* brother. Did you know he was Spain's man in Lisbon? I'd no idea.'

'Fascinating. I must make sure I've got something decent to wear. I don't suppose there's been any word of Moulichon.'

'Not a sausage.'

'A sad commentary on the state of Europe today.'

'Couldn't agree with you more, my dear. Sometimes I think the Fascists and the Socialists got Europe into this mess just to make our lives a misery.'

Lisbon: Praça das Celbolas district, July 20

Hasselfeldt sat at the bar of the restaurant, chewing at a cheese straw, waiting anxiously for the arrival of his contact in Salazar's security service, the PVDE. Earlier, he had spoken at length with the SD resident in the city, but the briefing he was given, on the Duke and Duchess's movements over the previous forty-eight hours, was of only marginal interest to him. His real purpose was to find and eliminate Bramall. But to reach his quarry, he must move crabwise, trusting to the tide of events to cover his tracks.

The officer he had arranged to meet at the bar had been on a retainer from the SD for the last eighteen months. He knew that Germany was interested in obtaining the cooperation of the Duke and whether or not this offended the British was none of his concern..

Hasselfeldt ordered a glass of port, into which he dipped another cheese straw. He liked the climate and general way of life in Iberia, but the casual attitude towards time frequently enraged him.

Twenty minutes after the appointed time, the Portuguese officer finally showed up. Inspector Amándio Mateus apologised. It was a Sunday – normally his day off. But he had brought with him a surprisingly voluminous file about the modus operandi of the British Secret Service in Lisbon.

Hasselfeldt was careful about the way he phrased his questions. He didn't want to give the impression that he was obsessed with Bramall – something that would inevitably get back to Winzer. Yet he needed to know where the *Engländer* was living and who he associated with.

Mateus began working his way through a bowl of olives, chewing the flesh and spitting out the pits in one continuous action. "Bramall,' you say. 'Yes we know him.'

Hasselfeldt bit his lip. 'As I understand it,' he said, 'Bramall is the Duke's right-hand man, in charge of his day-to-day activities. I can hardly question him directly, but there must be someone who works closely with him, a housekeeper possibly, something like that. I need a way in, if you see what I mean.'

Mateus popped another olive into his mouth and slurped a mouthful of cold beer as he considered the problem. 'There was a girl came over with him from Spain if I am not mistaken.' He started leafing through the documents on his lap, licking the ends of his thumb and index finger and twisting back the corners of each page. 'Ah yes. Here she is. Maria Rodriguez – at least, that's the name she gave us. Last time I looked, she was staying with Bramall at the apartment of – who else? – *Senhor* Douglas Croft, the MI6 resident in Lisbon.'

Hasselfeldt could feel the hairs rise on the back of his neck.

Mateus continued: 'But then she left for England.'

'Ach!' The Austrian clenched his fists. 'But Bramall – he is still staying with Croft, yes?'

'As far as I know. Close by. I can show you. But first, I'm famished. I haven't eaten anything since lunch. Why don't we we have something here? It's really very good, you know.'

Hasselfeldt was dismayed to learn that the Ortega woman had fled to England. Luder would be beside himself with rage. But the important thing was that he now knew where Bramall was staying. He felt alive again, as if God had first issued him a terrible warning, then offered the possibility of deliverance. He would not fail a second time. And if he got the chance, he would beat Bramall to death with his bare fists. He turned to Mateus, already signalling to the waiter. 'Yes,' he said, 'My colleague tells me that the fish here is *prima*.'

Madrid: Villa of Felipe Luder, July 20

Partly to take his mind off the humiliation of his rejection by Isabel, Luder had thrown himself into his joint project with Heydrich, aimed at doubling German purchases of wolfram from Spain. He hadn't made much progress so far. The British had anticipated his actions and taken steps accordingly, and Ortega's heart didn't seem to be in it, so that his line to Serrano was less sure than he had hoped. But he was not someone who gave up easily and he had arranged a dinner that night with leading bankers and trade officials at which he planned to lay his proposal right on the line.

He hadn't given up on Isabel either. There was still no concrete evidence that she was with Bramall in Lisbon. But the Argentinean was in little doubt. Hasselfeldt had assured him that he would go to Lisbon personally and bring her back, kicking and screaming if need be. Luder would then take his pleasure with her exactly as he always intended. She was nothing but a prick-teaser after all. Afterwards, when he was done with her, he would strangle her with his bare hands and take her body back to her parents as evidence of England's perfidy. In the meantime, Hasselfeldt, who would also attend the dinner, representing Heydrich, was bringing a couple of Moroccan whores for their pre-prandial entertainment. He had said he would turn up around eight, which was just about right. The little *putas* would help them relax in advance of their business engagement.

It had been a stressful day – and a hot one. Luder decided there was time for him to have a bath before Hasselfeldt's arrival. He would need a shower afterwards, of course, but that was something else. Stretching his arms and rolling his shoulders, he waited until he heard the bones in his back click. Then he grunted and began to unbutton his shirt.

Downstairs on the terrace, which he reached by way of the courtyard wall, Romero was catching his breath. The Argentinean's refusal to give up on the wolfram front was starting to irritate the British. Croft had earlier informed the Irishman, via Burns, of Bramall's safe arrival in Lisbon, along with Isabel. Now, as a matter of urgency, he had requested that Luder be removed from the picture.

Romero needed no encouragement. Not only had Luder bullied and threatened Isabel, he was a Nazi, who didn't even wear uniform but made himself rich from the suffering of others. He hated everything the Italian stood for. Killing him would be a righteous act. He felt good – almost back to his old self. His plan was straightforward. The simpler the better in his experience. That afternoon, he had picked up Luder's trail at the Ministry of Mines and followed him home. He would kill him, then return to Malasaña to take a shift running the bar. He had his revolver in his waistband but his intention was to use his switchblade, which was quieter and just as certain. Making his way into the house, he first checked out the kitchen. A housemaid was standing with her back to him carrying a pile of newly washed clothes. Romero came up behind her and grabbed her with one hand round her waist, stopping her scream with his other hand.

'Don't make a sound,' he warned her. 'Say nothing and you will be all right. Nod your head if you understand me.'

Terrified, the woman nodded. He twisted her round to face him. 'I am going to tie you up,' he told her, reaching into the side pocket of his linen jacket for a length of cord. 'I am also going to gag you. But you will be safe.'

Two minutes later, with the servant securely locked in the laundry room, he made his way into the passage outside and the main hallway beyond. He climbed the marble stairs, flooded with light from an overhead lantern, and began a systematic search of the first floor rooms. As he entered Luder's bedroom, he thought he could hear the noise of someone in the bath.

Perfect, he thought.

A man's voice called out to him – hard-edged and unpleasant. 'Klaus! Is that you? Did you remember to bring the little *putas*?'

Romero walked silently across the bedroom and pushed open the bathroom door.

'Reach me a towel,' Luder called out, reaching out blindly. 'I've got soap in my eyes.'

Romero didn't speak German but took a towel off the rack to the side of the tub and handed it across. The Argentinean sat up and wiped his eyes. Seeing Romero standing in front of him holding a switchblade, he gasped in shock and fell back heavily into the water.

What happened next was like a scene from opera bouffe. Luder flicked at the intruder with the towel, using it like a whip. At the same time, he began to scream out for someone to help him. The bathroom window was open and passers-by were bound to hear.

The Irishman shook his head, amused. His blade slid like a scalpel across Luder's extended arm 'You're not a nice fellow, Felipe,' he announced in Spanish, 'and some friends of mine have asked me to take care of you – do you follow?' The banker stared down at his wrist, from which purple blood was erupting from a severed artery. For a moment he fell silent. Then he started to scream again in the direction of the open window.

The blade above his head flashed again, this time across his throat. 'The first was for the people of Spain,' Luder said. 'That was for Isabel Ortega!'

Luder reached up to a gash that had opened beneath his chin. He felt the hot blood bubbling through his fingers. Fear gripped him. He tried once more to scream, but failed. Looking up at the face of his killer, he was consumed not by rage, but by terror. He stretched once more for the towel, hoping to staunch the flow of blood. It was too far away, beyond his reach. As his vision faded, he slipped down, gurgling, into the bathwater, which immediately flushed scarlet. His last breath caused tiny bubbles to form on the surface of the water.

Romero ran the blade of his knife beneath the bath tap before folding it back into its enamelled shaft. Time to get out of here. He turned around. A man in SS uniform, his face like a bruised tomato, was standing in the doorway. He held a Luger in his hand.

Hasselfeldt!

'I do not know who you are, *amigo*,' the Austrian said in heavily accented English. 'But I do know where you are going. You have an urgent appointment with my colleagues in the Puerta del Sol. Really most urgent. Now drop the knife. Quickly. At once.'

Romero weighed his options. Letting go of the switchblade, he kicked it, obligingly, towards the SD man. As Hasselfeldt bent his eyes fractionally towards the knife arriving at his feet, Romero wheeled round and reached with his right hand for the revolver in his waistband. He swung it up away from his body and squeezed the trigger.

Before the hammer could land, a shot from Hasselfeldt's Luger cut through his stomach. He felt to his knees, gasping, but still managed to get off a single round, which whistled past the Austrian's cheek, taking off the lower section of his right ear. Hasselfeldt let out a high-pitched roar, consumed with pain and rage. Holding one hand to his ear to stop the bleeding, he lashed out with his right foot at the stricken figure in front of him.

Romero's head began to fill with images of his childhood. He could see his dog, Pablo, that used to come with him to hurling practise in the Phoenix Park. Then he heard his mother calling him in from the street to come in out of that and have his tea, and his own voice replying (so high – it hadn't broken yet): 'I'll be right there, Mammy!' But then, as if a door had shut, the past faded from view and he felt his mouth fill with blood.

Madrid: Villa Ortega, July 21

Doña Vittoria was not, if the truth were told, overly upset by the news that her future son-in-law had been shot dead. But for her husband, it was a shock. 'What did the minister say?' she asked him.

Colonel Ortega took his wife's hand. Her face, normally so open, was lined with worry. 'If you must know, he didn't seem particularly bothered. The fact of the matter is, he didn't like Felipe at the best of times.'

'He wasn't alone in that. Isabel hated him – and with good reason.'

Ortega looked away. 'That may be. The fact is, I doubt the case will ever be solved. He had too many enemies and his assassin was almost killed in his turn by a German agent. The fellow is in hospital and so far has revealed nothing.'

'So what happens now? What about our daughter, Raúl?'

Ortega ran a hand across his brow. He had been dreading this moment. 'I don't know, my dear. I'm only guessing. But it's starting to look as if this Bramall may have had a hand in the attack on the German Legation. He has been spotted since in Lisbon ... in the company of a young Spanish woman.'

Doña Vittoria grabbed her husband's sleeve. 'Was it Isabel?'

'I can't say. She gave a different name, but she had green eyes.'

'It must be her, Raúl. She was determined to do something to keep Franco from joining the war, and now, when I think of it, I'm sure there was a spark between her and Señor Bramall.'

Ortega was thinking the same thing.

'You know better than I, Raúl,' his wife continued. 'You know what she is like. She is so ... wilful. And it is obvious she could not abide Felipe. But if it is true that they are together, you are to do nothing. You will make no inquiries; you won't mention anything to Serrano. We must just wait until we hear from her.'

'Very well. But Vittoria, what if the Germans get to her?'

'She is being protected by the British, is she not?'

'I assume so. Bramall is obviously much more than he appeared.'

'Then thank God and His Holy Mother!' Doña Vittoria turned away and sat down on a hard chair by the dining room table. There were tears in her eyes. 'Hear me now, Raúl,' she said. 'I don't mind you checking the file. We need to know that Isabel is safe. But I want you to leave her alone. Promise me you won't interfere. If you have never listened to me before, listen to me now. For all our sakes.'

Colonel Ortega drew in a deep breath, then let it out again before sinking down in the chair next to his wife. The truth was he was tired of conspiracy and ambition. The sheer awfulness of Luder's attitudes and the threat behind Serrano's practised smile: he could take no more of it. Yes, he would do nothing. He would wait for news of his child. And in the meantime, he would spend more time with his wife.

Maybe he could make a clean break and return to his regiment. Postings came up every month. He would talk to Serrano, see what could be arranged. San Sebastián was nice at this time of year, and Vittoria's sister was there. Maybe he could take charge of the garrison at Irún.

'Don't worry, my dear,' he said, glancing fondly over the top of his glasses. 'I am not a complete fool and I know when to let sleeping dogs lie.'

11

Lisbon: Boca do Inferno, July 22, 1940

'Mr Bramall! Is that you?' The Duchess was waving from the breakfast room, where she was seated in front of a sliced grapefruit and a bowl of imported Swiss muesli.

Bramall, on his way through the front hall, fixed a smile on his face and waved back. 'Yes, indeed, Ma'am. Always at your service.'

'In that case, come inside, won't you? There's somebody I'd like you to meet.'

Bramall felt his spirits sink. The previous day, at the ambassador's request, he had moved out of Croft's apartment into the main household, and since then the Duchess's trivia had plumbed new depths. Who was it this time?

'Delighted, Ma'am. If you could just give me a second.'

Inside the breakfast room, the Duchess had moved to her place at the head of the table. She wore a soft, embroidered hat of some kind, covered with sequins, and a Chinese dressing gown over silk pyjamas. Her face looked heavily lined, as if she had been up all night, which she might well have been, for all Bramall knew.

There was no sign of the Duke. Not a man for the early morning, he had discovered. Like his grandfather, Edward VII, he liked the day to be well aired before he consented to grace it with his presence.

To the left of the former Mrs Simpson sat Espírito Santo Silva, wearing what looked like golfing clothes, helping himself to a surprisingly large portion of scrambled eggs. But it was the woman seated on the Duchess's right that most interested Bramall. She was the most exquisite creature, aged perhaps thirty, with a flawless complexion and lips like chillies. Even at this hour of the morning, and it was not yet nine, she wore a low-cut blouse that showed off to perfection the pale, yet assertive swell of her breasts.

He wondered what Isabel would make of her, banishing the thought in an instant.

'Mr Bramall,' said the Duchess, slicing into her grapefruit, 'I'd like you to meet my friend, the Comtesse Dominique de Fourneau, visiting from Madrid.'

She spoke in French, with an excellent accent, he noticed.

Dominique extended her hand. Her nails looked sharp. Bramall took just the ends of her fingers and bent down to implant the faintest kiss. '*Enchanté, Comtesse*, I'm surprised we haven't met before.'

'I also, monsieur. But I have only been in Spain two weeks. You live there, I think?'

'Alas, no. I was there in the service of the Duke and Duchess. Now I have been transferred to Lisbon. Another week or so and I shall be back in London.'

'That is a pity. But I hear that you have been quite active during your time in Madrid.'

'Really?'

'But yes, of course. The rumour is that the Germans are not too enamoured of you just now. They think you are quite the man of action.'

The Duchess put down her knife and fork with a clatter. Her eyes seemed to catch fire.

Bramall stared at her for a second, puzzled, before turning back to her companion. 'I'm sure I don't know what you mean.'

Dominique offered him a dazzling smile. 'Please forgive me,' she said. 'Just my little joke.'

'And most entertaining, I'm sure.' Bramall switched his attention to the Duchess. 'But now, if you will excuse me, Ma'am, I have many duties to attend to.'

The former king's consort still looked animated, as if she had been subjected to a mild electric shock. 'Of course, Mr Bramall,' she told him, 'I wouldn't dream of separating you from your duty. His Royal Highness and I are depending on you.'

He bowed. 'Your Grace, Comtesse … *Senhor*.'

As he left the breakfast room, Bramall was convinced that de Fourneau had seen right through him. She knew something, he could tell. She was serene and self-possessed, but calculating. And attractive. Definitely attractive. She would make just the perfect spy. As for the Duchess, he had no idea what on earth had got into her. The Comtesse's characterisation of him as a man of action almost caused her to jump out of her chair. Right now, however, it was time to find Crowther, the new hotshot marksman, sent over by Strickland, and see what he was doing. One thing about eternal vigilance: it never let up – at least not while the Sun shone.

Madrid: German Legation, July 22

For one delicious moment, Winzer entertained the thought that Hasselfeldt had gone mad and shot Luder himself. Sadly, just the most cursory glance at the crime scene in the Villa Luder – to say nothing of the mystery assassin and Hasselfeldt's missing ear – had forced him to a quite different conclusion.

Whoever he was, Luder's killer was not Spanish. He had begun rambling in English, with what he was assured was a pronounced Dublin accent, at the military hospital in Madrid, But the fools taking care of him, instead of calling a detective to take notes, had sedated him and whisked him off to theatre for emergency surgery on his stomach.

As soon as the bullet was removed and his life was no longer in danger, his interrogation, supervised by Winzer, was brief, but bloody. He said nothing at first, then blurted out that he hated all Fascists and their Nazi agents. A personal crusade. then? It was possible. At one point, when Hasselfeldt had bent over him and taunted him in English, he had cursed at him and spat in his face. The Austrian was furious, punching him so hard in the face that his right retina had detached, rendering him partially blind. It was as Winzer had always suspected. Under pressure, the Austrian had no sense of what was appropriate. It was as if he was a wild beast. Winzer and a Spanish officer had dragged the SD man off, amid his protests, and continued the procedure alone. One by one, the detainee's fingernails were removed – the screams were heart-rending. Then electrodes were attached to his genitals. Normally, electrodes loosened the tongues of even the most determined villains. Not this one. The Irishman had screamed and roared and told them all they were the sons of bitches, but he had not broken. It was another man, a barman arrested forty-eight hours hours later, who had given up the missing name. Apparently, the fellow was no more than a frustrated *brigadista* – a Dublin-born Communist, with Spanish blood, by name of Romero – striking out against Fascism the only way he knew how.

Winzer hadn't made up his mind if the man being questioned knew more than he admitted. But the Spanish examining magistrate, acting on orders from Serrano, had taken the matter out of his hands and ruled that Romero should be put to death for his crimes. The minister, normally a stickler for detail, was not prepared, apparently, to devote the resources of the state to one out of the hundreds of homicides that happened each day in post Civil War Spain. As a result, Romero, his body broken, but his spirit intact, had been transferred to the prison of Cárcel de Carabanchel, where he would remain until a date was fixed for his execution.

Winzer's principal concern had been to satisfy himself that Romero – if that was his name – had acted alone, which he rather thought was the case. Luder was a brute, with enemies in at least three countries. It was easy enough to imagine how his death might have come about in more normal times. He would have insulted or humiliated someone; raped someone's wife or daughter. His fiancée, it transpired – the daughter of the same Colonel Ortega – had disappeared recently without explanation. It was possible Luder had murdered her and incurred the enmity of a rival for her affections, or of Ortega himself. That would not surprise him in the least. Or perhaps he had defaulted on a business deal, or said the wrong thing to the wrong man at the wrong time. Spaniards were so … volatile.

Ordinary criminal behaviour, as Winzer had good reason to know, had not been suspended while the *Führer* sorted out the evils of the world. Whatever the reason for Luder's demise, an assassin had been deployed as the instrument of justice – an assassin who was now already in the middle of a countdown to his own appointment with the executioner. Case closed.

The real pity was that the fellow hadn't managed to shoot straight. If Hasselfeldt had only ended up next to Luder on the bathroom floor, it would all have been quite perfect.

As it was, his SD colleague had been handed a reprieve when he most needed it. He was the man of the hour, praised by Serrano and by Heydrich for his decisive intervention. Winzer's muttered comment that it would have been helpful if Luder had in fact survived or it the assassin were still available for questioning, was lost in the general hubbub of approval.

He was not taken in for a second by the Austrian's sudden determination to return the Duke and Duchess of Windsor to Madrid. He was convinced that Hasselfeldt, who only the week before was trying to project himself into the heart of German diplomacy at the expense of those best capable of running it, was now seeking, rather desperately, to cover up his culpability in the attack on the Legation. It was clear to him that Bramall was behind the attack. Far from being a stooge, the man was a skilled and determined double agent.

The inquiry had all the makings of a classic dead end. You couldn't interrogate a corpse and, besides, some mysteries were destined to remain exactly that – mysteries.

What truly engaged the *Gestapo* man was the fact that Hasselfeldt had chosen Lisbon as his bolthole. It might simply be that he wanted to be wherever Schellenberg was. He was like a moth to a flame where power was concerned and the *obersturmbannführer* was Heydrich's favourite. But Winzer would put money on the fact that the real reason was proximity to Bramall, who had recently turned up in Lisbon. Did he want want revenge for what had happened to him in the washroom, or was there something more? He had no idea.

He would talk to Stohrer tonight. Heydrich had insisted that as head of the *Gestapo* he should remain in Madrid, where the Luder murder had been added to the attack on the Legation in his file of unsolved cases. But a good detective always followed the trail of evidence, and right now the trail led straight to Lisbon.

Boca do Inferno: July 22

Bramall was working at a small Italian desk in his first-floor bedroom in Espírito Santo Silva's seaside mansion. He was composing a cable to Strickland about the proposed mission to France, but finding it difficult to concentrate because he kept thinking about Isabel. Ever since his 'confessional' with Romero, he had been obsessed with keeping her safe. That was why he had agreed to let her go to London even when she had begged him to let her stay. But what if, in spite of everything, she were to fall in love with him? Stranger things had happened and she had already made it clear to him, not least on the train from Elvas, that she wanted their relationship to develop. If that happened, she would want to be with him in spite of all dangers – and he would certainly wish to be with her. What was vital was that he should always be there for her when danger threatened. That was the promise he had made to Romero and it was one promise he intended to keep.

In the meantime, he still had to decide what to recommend about Operation Felix and Spain's plan to usurp the French empire in Africa.

It wouldn't be right, he had decided, for him to approach Pétain directly, even if Strickland approved, which was far from certain. The Frenchman liked to observe the minutiae of diplomatic protocol and was, after all, eighty-four years-old. No. Laval would be the better bet. He was younger, and a career politician. He would be concerned with present realities, not eternal verities. If he could only play the stolen tape to the former Foreign Minister – a former colleague, after all, of Sir Samuel Hoare – then an accommodation would surely be reached.

He was just about to complete his draft when he became aware of someone standing beside him. He looked up in mild panic. It was the Comtesse de Fourneau. He hadn't heard her come in.

'Comtesse!' he spluttered, hastily turning his communication over and shoving it in the top drawer of the desk, which he promptly closed, wishing it had a key. 'I didn't know you were there.'

She smiled down at him. 'I'm sorry,' she said. 'Am I disturbing you?'

Bramall returned the smile. 'Not at all. You startled me, that's all.'

'Of course. But do women always startle you, Monsieur?'

'Less so if I know they are there.'

'It's just that I was wondering … '

'Yes?'

'I was wondering if you might be free to take a short walk with me in the garden. It's such a beautiful day and it seems a shame to spend it all indoors.'

Bramall thought of Isabel. 'I don't know …' he began.

'Please,' Dominique said, looking straight into his eyes. 'We'll walk just as far as the cliff and take in some of that marvellous sea air.'

Her eyes were quite hypnotic. 'Well,' he heard himself say, 'I suppose I could …'

'But of course.' She held out her arm.

On the way downstairs, they ran into the Duke.

'Ah, there you are,' he said, sounding almost jaunty. 'Thought you were working on something. But off to check on the local flora and fauna, I see.'

Bramall offered a smile that he fancied might be interpreted as a grin. 'Your Royal Highness. Just showing the Comtesse the gardens. I shall be back at work in a jiffy.'

'Take as long as you like. You too, my dear. Life is not all thrust and parry, Mr Bramall. Even Clausewitz, I expect, liked to take time off to smell the roses.'

'As you say, sir. You're most kind.'

Without warning, Dominique leaned across and planted a kiss on the Duke's cheek. He brightened instantly. 'You'd better be off,' he said, smiling at Bramall ' or you may have some competition.'

A minute or so later, as they stood at the top end of the garden, looking out over the Atlantic, Dominique said: 'I shouldn't have thought you were the nervous type. But then I wouldn't ever picture you as an equerry either.'

'What do you mean?'

'All that bowing and scraping.'

'A means to an end. If you have royalty, you have to set them apart. Otherwise, what's the point?'

'I don't know. What *is* the point?'

'You're a countess, you should know.'

'*Touché*. But you strike me as more of a doer than an organiser.'

'I do what I have to. That doesn't mean I have to like it.'

'And did you do what you had to in Madrid?'

Bramall could hear his own sudden intake of breath. 'That depends on what you mean.'

'I mean, Monsieur Bramall, that I think you may be a wolf in sheep's clothing – is that not what you say? For example, were you to run this second into *Sturmbannführer* Hasselfeldt of the SD, I doubt that you and he would exchange luncheon invitations.'

Bramall was almost as disconcerted by this as he had been on the occasion in which he and the Austrian actually collided. 'You know Hasselfeldt?' he asked.

'I have heard of him. We have not actually met. But I happen to know that he is in Lisbon at the moment. He arrived yesterday afternoon, in the foulest of tempers – or so I was informed. Someone, it seems, shot off part of his ear.'

'His ear?'

'So they tell me. Some dreadful murder he stumbled across. I don't have the details. But, of course, you wouldn't know anything about that, would you?'

'Not a thing, I'm afraid. I've been in Portugal for the last week.'

'So there's no reason he'd be pursuing you?'

'Hasselfeldt? None that I can think of. But tell me, Countess, would I be right in thinking that you are not in Lisbon for the good of your health?'

'No more than you, Mr Bramall.'

'The reason I ask is that I suspect you are not exactly unknown to the French authorities.'

'I am known to a great many people in positions of power.'

Bramall considered this for a moment. It was possible he had found an ally – someone who might provide him with entrée to the obscure world of Vichy. But with so much at stake he had to be sure. A single misjudgement could ruin everything.

'Your complexion is exceptionally clear,' he began. 'I assume, *citoyenne*, that from time to time you take the waters.'

'I'm sorry …?'

'Vichy. I'm told it's lovely this time of year. When the, em, bougainvillea is in bloom.'

'Is that so? Then perhaps we could meet there sometime.'

'Perhaps. You will understand, of course, that I am sworn to preserve and protect British interests. That calls for discretion. I could never discuss my business in public, even with someone as … engaging as you.'

'But in other circumstances, in other company, that might change?'

'It might. It would depend on how ready those in command were to endorse an honest appraisal of their circumstances.'

'Fascinating.' Dominique flipped open her clutch bag and withdrew a simple card inscribed with her address and telephone number in Madrid. 'Should such a situation arise,' she said, 'you will know where to find me.'

Bramall took the card. 'Absolutely' he said, 'but now I've really got to be getting back. It's not that I wouldn't much rather stay here with you, it's just that …'

'I understand. You have business to attend to.'

'Exactly. May I escort you back to the house?'

She kissed the tips of her fingers, then reached up and placed them lightly against his lips. 'No thank you, you go on. I think I'll stay here a little longer and enjoy the … bougainvillea.'

'Ah yes. I'll bid you good day, then. *Enchantée.*'

'Au revoir, Monsieur.'

As he walked back to the house, Bramall's imagination raced. Pictures of Hasselfeldt with his ear shot off chased images of Dominique unbuttoning her blouse. My God! He thought. A woman like that could have more impact on the course of a war than an entire division of troops.

Again, he wondered what Isabel would have thought.

Back in the house, lost in surmise, he made his way distractedly up the stairs instead of taking them two at a time as he normally did. It was when he reached the corridor leading to the spare bedroom he was using as an office that he sensed something was wrong.

At the end of the passage, he saw just the heel of a red shoe disappear around the corner in the direction of the back stairs. Hadn't the Duchess been wearing red shoes? He had seen her on her way to lunch and he was sure she had worn red shoes. But what would she be doing hanging round his office?

Panicking, he broke into a run, throwing open his door and making straight for the writing desk. He pulled open the top drawer and almost sighed with relief when he saw that the cable he had drafted to Strickland, outlining his thoughts on

Gibraltar, was there where he had left it. But then he noticed that it was the right way up. He remembered distinctly that he had turned the note over when he had placed it hurriedly in the drawer.

Christ Almighty! Someone had read his note to Strickland. *The Duchess!*

For a split second, he thought of summoning Crowther and heading up to the Duke's suite, gun in hand. Then he realised that was stupid. But he couldn't let the moment pass. She could do anything with that information. She could give it to Franco's brother – he was coming to dinner. Or she could give it to some of her French friends – or she could just cut the crap and go all the way to Berlin.

There was no time to lose. Stuffing the unsent cable into his inside pocket, he headed back out into the corridor. The back stairs led up to the second floor, but a service passage next to it gave access to the main guest suite. The security team checked it out several times a day. If the Duchess really had read his cable, she would presumably have gone straight back to her room while she decided what to do next.

It took him less than a minute to reach the royal suite. The Duke wasn't there, which was just as well. He had gone to the embassy for talks with Selby and Eccles. A Special Branch detective was on duty by the door but recognised Bramall and stood aside.

'Has the Duchess been here?' he demanded.

'Yes, sir. Went in a couple of minutes ago.'

'Alone?'

The man looked shocked. 'Yes, sir.'

'Right. Keep a careful eye out. Make sure no comes in that

you don't trust.'

Closing the outer door silently behind him, Bramall made his way through the suite's living area as far as the door to the royal bedroom. It was slightly ajar and he could see clearly all the way to the desk by the window, at which the Duchess sat writing. She had her back to him and paused every few seconds, as if trying to get her words exactly right. He did nothing, but looked on in silence, waiting for her to complete her task.

Three minutes went by before she put down her pen and began to read through what she had written, which was contained on a single sheet of notepaper. Apparently satisfied, she folded the letter twice and placed it in an envelope, which she addressed and sealed.

This was the moment at which Bramall knocked and entered the room.

The Duchess, a study in concentration, still had her back to him. 'Ricardo!' she called out. ' thank God you're here. I need you to do me the most urgent favour.'

'I should think not, Ma'am,' Bramall said. 'Treachery is often a matter of timing, wouldn't you say?'

She wheeled round, the incriminating envelope in her hand. The shock registered in her face was total.

'Mr Bramall! I don't know what you're talking about, but would you mind leaving? I was expecting someone else and ...'

Before she could do anything, he strode across and ripped the envelope from her grasp. She turned away, horrified. The address on it read: H.E. the German ambassador. In the top left hand corner she had written: 'Most Urgent! Strictly Personal.'

By now, the Duchess was on her feet and screaming at him to give her back the letter.

'How dare you come in here like this? How dare you invade my privacy?'

When he refused to hand it back, she kicked him with the point of one of her red shoes, bruising his left shin. He fended her off and told her to be quiet. She began to whimper, but stood obediently by the window, looking out at the Atlantic, where something of a storm was brewing.

For several seconds, he stared straight at her, not speaking, willing her into submission. Only when he was satisfied that she had collected herself and wasn't going to attempt anything stupid did he rip the phone cord from the wall next to the bed and make his way back out to the main door. The Special Branch constable was standing there, his automatic in his hand.

'What's going on, sir? I could hear the Duchess.'

'I'm sure you could, constable. She's going to be just fine, but until you hear from me or Mr Croft, I don't want anyone else going in that door – and that includes the Duke. The Duchess is to remain exactly where she is. It is a matter of the utmost importance. Is that understood?'

'Yes, sir. But...?'

'Just do it. It doesn't matter what instructions she may give you, she is to speak to no one, not even the Duke. And she is not – I repeat not – to use the telephone.'

'What if His Highness demands to be admitted ... ?'

'You have your orders. I'm depending on you. Do your duty. Mr Crowther will be in charge while I'm gone.'

The entire house was unnaturally quiet, as if anticipating the crisis. Back in his room, Bramall sat down at his desk and, very carefully, peeled back the flap of the envelope. The glue was not yet dry and it came away quite easily. Steeling himself for the worst, he began to read.

My Dear Ambassador,

In haste. I have most important news. British Intelligence was, as you feared, behind the recent attack on the German Legation in Madrid. I have since learned that my husband's equerry Mr Charles Bramall was the man chiefly responsible. He appears to have stolen a recording of some kind of a conversation, or negotiation, between the German and Spanish governments concerning the future of Gibraltar and tensions between the French and Spanish empires. Please inform Berlin in the person of the minister that he must act quickly or it may be too late.

WS

When he had finished reading, Bramall folded the letter and replaced it with care in its envelope. Then he ran downstairs, shouting for Crowther, who had raced in from the garden.

'What the hell's going on,' the bodyguard demanded. 'I could hear screams.'

'No time to explain. I've got to go and see Croft – and it can't wait. While I'm gone, you're to keep the house sealed as tight as a drum. No one in or out – and that includes the Duchess. She is to remain in her room, *incommunicado.*'

And then he left. Crowther stared after him in bewilderment. A car and driver were waiting outside the front entrance to the house. The driver was smoking, but immediately threw down his cigarette.

'Take me to the embassy,' Bramall ordered, 'and don't stop for anything.'

Lisbon: British embassy, Jul 22

Ambassador Walford Selby had known the Duke of Windsor for many years and had never approved of his marriage to the former Mrs Wallis Simpson. But the revelation that the Duchess was in league with the Germans shocked him to the core.

Croft was decidedly more sanguine. 'I told you there were things about her would make your hair curl,' he told Bramall.

'Yes,' Bramall shot back, 'but you neglected to mention the fact that she kept up a private correspondence with the German ambassador.'

'– Which we only know because you let her get hold of a piece of vital information!'

'– Which wouldn't have happened if I hadn't been interrupted in my office by the arrival of a Vichy spy whom you allowed to stay for the weekend!'

David Eccles, of the economic warfare department, had heard enough. 'Gentlemen,' he began, raising his hand in front of him as if trying to ward off the evil eye, 'this isn't getting us anywhere. And has it occurred to either of you that if you both hadn't made the mistakes you did, we'd still be in the dark? It's only because you both fucked up that we've chanced upon a key piece of intelligence.' He turned to the ambassador. 'Is the Duke still in the building?'

'I believe so,' said Selby, shocked by Eccles's expletive. 'He said something about making some telephone calls to London.'

'Well, shouldn't we should talk to him?'

Selby blanched. 'What on earth could we possibly say?'

'We could start with the truth,' said Croft – 'that his wife is working for the Germans.'

'Oh Lord.' The ambassador rose gloomily from his chair. 'I'll see what I can do.'

'Meanwhile,' said Croft, 'someone should check with Crowther that everything is as it should be in the Hell Mouth.'

'I'll do it,' Bramall volunteered, recognising the English translation of the Boca do Inferno. He reached for the telephone receiver on Selby's desk. A minute later, after a brief conversation with Crowther, he replaced it on its rest.

Croft and Eccles stared at him expectantly. 'It's all right,' he told them, 'she's calmed down. As soon as I left, she tried to order Crowther to bring her car round. She was going out, she said. But he wasn't having it. Now she's sitting in her room refusing to talk to anyone.'

'That's something ,' said Eccles.

At this, the door opened and Selby re-entered the room and held open the door for the Duke, who looked as if the sky had fallen on his head. They all rose.

'I've filled His Royal Highness in on the basic situation,' said Selby, 'and he's understandably upset. He wishes to talk with the Duchess.'

Eccles stepped forward, head bowed, as if offering his condolences after a death in the family. 'I think that would be wise, sir. But I think the ambassador and Mr Croft should be with you when you do. The Duchess has got to understand the position into which she has got herself – and you. And you must both realise that this is a matter which has gone far beyond the competence of the embassy. The prime minister will have to be informed, and also, I'm sorry to say, the King.'

Everyone waited for the Duke's response. When it came, it

was in a small, quiet voice that was as painful for his audience as it plainly was for him. 'I'm not sure what I should say,' he began. 'I am no traitor to my country. It is true that I have sympathies with the politics of Berlin and have opposed this war from the start. But I have never sought to undermine the efforts of the Government to prosecute matters as they felt they should best be ordered.'

No one said anything at this. They just waited for the Duke to continue.

'As for my wife, it is a fact that she has for some time been … enamoured of the Third Reich – and too damn close to that charlatan Ribbentrop, if you ask me. But I am shocked. I had no idea she would go this far. I can only assume that she has taken leave of her senses and needs urgent medical assistance. To that end, what is clearly most important is that she and I should embark as quickly as possible for Nassau, where, upon her arrival in Government House, I will see to it that no effort is spared in the recovery of her health.

He paused, realising that everyone in the room was staring at him. Nobody spoke. The Duke cleared his throat before resuming his peroration in a more forceful tone of voice. 'The Duchess, you may rest assured, will be prevailed upon most earnestly to behave in a manner more befitting her role as consort to a senior member of the Royal Household.'

A further silence greeted this latest essay into the world of the absurd.

It was Selby who finally spoke. 'We all appreciate your position, Your Royal Highness, and our sympathies are with you. But I'm afraid this cannot simply be swept under the carpet. There will be repercussions. Downing Street and the Palace will have to decide what to do. In the meantime, I suggest that you and I speak with the Duchess and impress upon her the gravity of her situation. Mr Eccles will contact London. Croft and Bramall will see to it that there are no further breaches of security. I can only pray that something can be worked out that will allow you to proceed with your appointment to the Bahamas and conceal from the British people, and the world, the shame and embarrassment of what has happened here today.'

The veteran envoy had spoken for all of them. There was no more to be said. Selby and the Duke, who looked mortified, made their way out to the official car, where an escort was waiting. Croft and Bramall looked blankly at each other. Eccles shook his head and reached for The ambassador's phone.

London: MI6 offices, July 24

Caxton didn't knock before entering Strickland's office. He just threw open the door and stood there, grinning. Behind him, an elderly porter in a brown coat was breathing heavily under the weight of what looked to be a gramophone.

'Hope we're not disturbing you,' Caxton said.

'That depends,' said Strickland, continuing to sip his tea. There were pictures of the late King George V and Queen Mary on the side of the mug dating from their fortieth wedding anniversary in 1933. News of the Duchess's treachery had hit him hard. 'What have you got for me?'

'It's a gramophone.'

'Well, I can see that.'

'Music to your ears, if you know what I mean.'

Strickland raised a sceptical eyebrow. 'Are you trying to tell me that you've actually made progress?'

Caxton couldn't conceal his satisfaction as he held open the door for the porter.

'About bloody time,' the MI6 man spluttered.

'I knew you'd be pleased,' Caxton rejoined, motioning to the porter in the direction of a small table next to the wall. 'Set it up, Jimmy. Let the dog see the rabbit.' Then he turned back to Strickland. 'It wasn't easy, I can tell you. I've had four of our chaps, plus a woman from Imperial College, working on the problem non-stop for a week.'

'I should damned well hope so. So don't muck about, what have you got?'

'Hold your horses.' The porter had plugged in the gramophone and opened the lid. Now he turned it on and let it warm up. He nodded to Caxton. 'Okay, Jimmy, that'll do.' The old man ran his finger under his nose as he left and Caxton shut the door behind him with his foot.

Strickland adjusted his glasses. 'I take it from this performance that you've put the taped material onto those gramophone records you've got under your arm.'

'Seemed the best way. Just playing the thing was enough of a challenge, I can tell you. We thought we'd got it right a few days ago, but all that came out was a squawk – and then the tape started to shear. We had to have new guide wheels fashioned, made from rubber this time. The other problem was, we had to install a motor drive that worked around a quarter of our normal speed, with no drag; and a pickup head tuned to the sort of dynamic range and frequency bias of the German tape.'

Strickland did his best to be patient.

'I don't mind admitting,' Caxton went on, 'it took a while to get it right – but we used the spare tape for the initial run, so we lost nothing in the end.'

'Bramall's observations weren't entirely useless, then?'

'Not entirely, no.' The scientist sped on. 'What you have here on these two records is everything relating to Spain and North Africa. I didn't bring the stuff on capturing Gibraltar, except for where they talk about it at the start. That's the big central section and you said you didn't want the French to hear the detail. We're working on that separately. It should be along first thing in the morning.'

'Makes sense,' said Strickland. 'I take it the Imperial College woman was vetted first.'

'Of course, Mr S. What do you think I am?'

The Yorkshireman grunted, as if judgement on that particular point had been suspended. 'Well, go on, then, put me out of my misery.'

Caxton had a lot of time for the old MI6 man, even if they didn't always see eye to eye on technology. But he wasn't always the easiest chap to work for. He started the turntable, checked the needle and placed it in the groove at the start of the first of the two discs.

After a moment, the rich baritone of Eberhard von Stohrer could be heard, talking in heavy, slightly ponderous Spanish. He welcomed his guests. Then a second, self-assured, rather haughty voice cut in.

'I bring you greetings from the *Caudillo*. He and I look forward with confidence to the outcome of Operation Sealion and trust that the battle will be both short and decisive.'

That was Serrano. Cheeky sod!

Strickland had already seen Hasselfeldt's transcription into German of the early part of the meeting in Spain. But his Spanish was better than his German and hearing the principals actually speak lent a powerful verisimilitude to the episode. He was mesmerised by the quality of the recording, as much as by its content. There was an underlying crackle, resulting presumably from the transfer from plastic tape to shellac. Other than that, it was as if Serrano was in the room with them. Bramall was right. The French were bound to be impressed.

He could hear people shuffling about and the sound of chairs moving on a hard wooden floor. Next to speak was Stohrer again.

'You will be aware that the *Führer* wishes to bring England to the negotiating table as quickly as possible …'

' – After you have destroyed their air force and reduced their cities to ashes.' Serrano again.

A strange definition of neutrality, Strickland mused. But not necessarily wrong. First reports he had seen only a quarter of an hour ago indicated more than a hundred enemy aircraft were massed over the Channel, striking at RAF stations and the harbour at Dover. The day before, at least fifty raiders had clashed with three squadrons of Spitfires over Kent, losing ten of their number against two defenders. Bombs had fallen throughout the Thames area and Dover approaches.

And this was only the beginning.

The talk on the record now turned to Gibraltar. Strickland listened, scarcely able to believe his ears, as the dialogue in the German Legation unfolded. Stohrer spoke at length of Hitler's plan for a 'joint assault' on Gibraltar. London, he said, would be left 'isolated and demoralised … forced to abandon its misplaced and foolhardy defiance of the Reich.'

Applause greeted his remark. And then the disk finished. This was almost as far as Hasselfeldt's version ran. Strickland could hear the click-click of the needle at the end.

'Put the next one on,' he said. This was extraordinary.

Caxton turned the record over.

'As to the geopolitical context of all this,' Stohrer continued, 'Berlin is aware – almost painfully so – of your territorial claims in Africa. The *Führer*, though unwilling to commit himself in advance of any Spanish participation in the war effort, is sympathetic to these claims and would undoubtedly view in a positive light any "adjustments" that would benefit a proven ally of the Reich.'

Serrano jumped in at once. 'Does that mean he would back our title to a united Morocco and Oran?'

This was sensational stuff. Listening to the exchange, Strickland clapped his hands together like a child with a new toy.

'The *Führer*,' Stohrer continued, 'does not forget his friends. He appreciates the wealth of sentiment and history that underpins your claim.'

Once again, the record ended.

Strickland sat back, exhausted. He felt like a man who had just seduced Mae West and wondered how he'd survived the experience..

'Ready for the next one?' Caxton asked, fiddling with his apparatus. He looked pleased as Punch.

By way of reply, Strickland could only wave his fingers at the gramophone.

The A-side of the second disc opened with a detailed exchange concerning food and fuel supplies. İranco had no shame. His shopping list was considerable. Then Serrano chipped in again.

'Above all,' he said, 'we need to know that Berlin will look with favour upon our territorial claims in North and West Africa, upon which our status as a European power will ultimately rest.'

'Dynamite! Absolute bloody dynamite.' Suddenly, all Strickland's fatigue left him. He jumped up from his chair and grabbed Caxton by his shoulders, so that for one horrific moment the scientist feared he was going to kiss him. Then he stepped back, breathless. 'It pains me to say it, but you've earned your pay this month – you and your team. This is exactly what we need. You've done us proud.' He paused, mainly to gather his thoughts. 'I'll need this stuff typed up. But now it's time for you to get back to your lab. There's more to be done. I'm going to need whatever you can get on Gibraltar. Let me know the second it's ready. The very second, do you hear?'

'Loud and clear. You should have it in 36 hours – two days at the most.'

After the boffin had gone, Strickland hunched forward in his chair for several seconds, holding his hand to his brow. Then he reached for the red telephone on his desk and picked up the receiver.

'I need to speak to 'C', he growled.

A prim voice came back, 'I'm sorry, Mr Strickland, but the admiral is extremely busy and cannot be distrubed.'

'Is he, by Jove? Well tell him to cancel everything, I'm on my way up.'

Vichy, capital of Unoccupied France: July 24

Delacroix didn't know what to think. Shortly after nine, he had received a telephone call from Madrid. Dominique, it turned out, had spent a couple of days at the residence of the Spanish ambassador to Portugal and wanted her boss to know that the British were up to something.

'Up to what?' he demanded.

'I can't say for certain. But you will have heard there was an armed raid on the German Legation the other day. The thinking here is that a British agent was behind it. Papers were stolen; the *Gestapo* are up in arms. Something to do with Gibraltar is my best guess.'

'Oh come now, Defarge. It's never guesswork with you.'

'Let me say, then, that I have reason to believe – from a usually reliable source – that plans are going ahead, involving Germany and Spain, that could force Britain to look to a future without Gibraltar.'

Delacroix felt instantly cheered. 'But that is marvellous,' he said.

'Yes, Alain, I knew you'd be happy. But what of the *quid pro quo*?'

'What do you mean?'

Dealing with her childhood companion was frequently wearisome. You had to spell things out. And yet, when he finally got there, he was like a dog with a bone. 'What would Franco want in return for letting the *Wehrmacht* into Spain?'

'Gibraltar, of course.'

'*Bien sûr*, Alain. But what else?'

'The empire.'

'Exactly: eternal and indivisible. You must tell Laval his worst nightmare may yet come true.'

Delacroix pulled at the tiny flap of skin beneath his chin. Just days before, Abetz had reassured Laval that Hitler understood the importance of a strong French empire and wished to promote Vichy in a new role as a partner of the Reich. The Deputy Prime Minister had been reassured by what the German envoy had told him, insisting to his subordinate that, by way of solidarity and partnership, France would once again hold its head high in the comity of nations. There could be no division of the spoils. That would be like pouring petrol on a fire that had only just been brought under control.

'Have you proof of any of this?' he demanded.

Dominique hid the mild exasperation she felt. 'None, Cherie. None at all. At this stage, it is all conjecture. But I was in Lisbon over the weekend, staying with the Duke and Duchess of Windsor. Did you know they were friends of ours, from Paris? Anyway, while I was there, I spoke to Franco's brother, Nicolás. He refused to say anything about Morocco and Oran – clammed up completely. It was what he didn't say – the silences – that confirmed my suspicions. Pétain and Laval should, I think, be prepared for a shock.'

'For myself, I am always ready to be shocked,' said Delacroix, which was perfectly true. 'But so long as Laval and the *Maréchal* are in charge, I refuse to believe that Hitler would stoop to such treachery. What else do you have?'

'Nothing – unless, of course, you want to hear the latest gossip about the Duke. *La toute Lisbonne* is talking about him.'

'Oh, please, Defarge. The man is a fool.'

'If you say so, Alain. You're the expert. But there is maybe one other thing.'

'Go on.'

'In Portugal, I met a British diplomat. His name is Bramall. He works for the Duke. The Germans believe that he may have been involved in the attack on their Legation. When I was speaking to him, I just happened to observe that he was writing a cable to London, in which he mentioned Pétain and Laval.'

'Interesting. What did he say?'

'I'm afraid he covered it up before I could get a proper look, but there was something about not bothering with Pétain, who was old and formal, but going instead to Laval, who was a politician, more concerned with present realities than eternal values.'

'What does that mean?'

Dominique ignored the interruption. 'Later, he indicated to me that he knew who I was working for and that, at a later date, he might wish to use my services as an intermediary. He did not say why, but my impression was that he had come into possession of information that would be of interest to France.'

'And that's it?'

'I'm sorry it couldn't be more, Alain, but you will appreciate that in our trade it is not always possible to proceed in a straight line.'

'I understand, of course. But what am I to make of what you are telling me? How concerned should I be?'

'Not so much concerned as intrigued, I would have thought.'

There was a long pause. After five seconds or so went by, Dominique enquired: 'Alain, are you still there?'

'Oh, I am sorry, I was thinking. You raise issues that cannot properly be discussed over the telephone – issues that, I must tell you, could go to the very heart of France's survival as an independent state within the New Order. I am asking myself if it might make sense for us to review your mission, and your assessment of how things stand, face to face. Do you think you might be able to pay a visit to Vichy sometime soon?'

Dominique thought about this. The truth was, she had been hoping to return home for a few days anyway attend to some legal matters arising from the death of her husband and the state of their properties. It was just that there was so much going on in Madrid.

'Good idea. Why not check with Laval and see if we can fix a date. I could attend to some personal business and drop in to Vichy on the way back.'

'Splendid. I will get back to you. In the meantime, please find out whatever else you can about this Bramall fellow. I will do the same from here.'

Delacroix replaced the receiver, wondering whether to approach Laval with what he had learned. He decided against it. The minister, after all, had appointed him in charge of policy relating to Spain. He did not expect to be burdened with every morsel of information that came in, especially when it had not been checked out. But he would talk to the chargé in Madrid and ask his opinion. When the good name and dignity of France were at stake, no stone could be left unturned.

Cascais: Boca do Inferno, July 26

'Look here, Bramall, I'm not a one to complain. You know that. But this has gone far enough.'

'I don't know what you mean, sir.'

The Duke had been in a foul temper all day. 'I won't be treated like a half-wit,' he said, his voice high and shrill, as it usually was when he didn't get his own way. 'I was going to play golf this morning, but you said no. I was going to take a swim nearby. We're living by the sea, for God's sake, and the temperature's in the nineties. But no, you wouldn't allow it.'

'It's for your own good, sir.'

'Don't give me that. I'm not a child.'

For once, Bramall gave way to his irritation. 'Your Royal Highness,' he began, 'I apologise for any inconvenience, but there are at least a hundred German agents in the vicinity and I have only a dozen men assigned to look after you. We're doing our best. Besides, after everything that's happened, you should perhaps be grateful that the Duchess isn't being transported back to the Tower of London. Do you ever think of it that way?'

'How dare you?'

'With respect, how dare *you*, sir? Had it not been for the prime minister's personal loyalty and the charity of your brother, the King – not shared, as I understand it, by Queen Elizabeth – you and the Duchess would be in disgrace and awaiting trial. You might get off. A jury could very well conclude that you had no idea what your wife was up to. But the Duchess's position would be as grave as it could possibly be.'

Listening to this, the Duke appeared to shrivel. He fell back slightly, steadying himself again the back of a chair. 'Very well, Bramall, I suppose you're entitled to your pound of flesh. But I have to say, you know how to kick a man when he's down.'

'I was raised in Ireland, Your Royal Highness. We were always told it was the best time.'

'So what happens now?'

'As I understand it, you and the Duchess begin a lifetime of decent obscurity and rehabilitation. More immediately, I am told that Walter Schellenberg himself, the head of the SD, is in town. I have no idea what he is up to, but I am determined he should not succeed.'

This seemed to get through to the Duke, who suddenly went quiet and grew deathly pale. 'Do you mean to say,' he began, 'that we really are in danger?'

'It's entirely possible, sir. That is why you and the Duchess must remain indoors. I'm sorry, but I don't see the alternative.'

A hunted look crept over the Duke's features. His eyes darted about and he looked suddenly like a frightened little boy. 'How do I know it's not you that plans to harm me?'

'Oh, come, come, sir. That's absurd. You must know that.'

'Must I? I've heard rumours. You're not the only one with contacts. I've been told that Churchill wants me gone – with the connivance of the Palace, I shouldn't wonder. What better way to do away with me than here in the obscurity of Portugal, and then blame it on the Germans?'

This was impossible. 'Please don't think me rude or disrespectful,' Bramall said, 'but there's a word for that kind of thinking.'

'Eh?'

'It's called paranoia. It's when you can't distinguish friend from foe and you think they're all coming for you.'

'You just said there were Germans everywhere.'

'Yes, but they're the enemy. England is at war with Germany. We're your friends.'

'Fine friends,' the Duke spat. 'I was your king – your

monarch. Now you treat me as if I were some kind of criminal.'

'Your Royal Highness, I give you my word ...'

'I don't know what I'm supposed to think. I hear shots – noises in the night. Rumours fly all around me. I've been gagged; barred from ever going home; forbidden to speak out. Just because I dared to think differently. I am to be the new Prisoner of Zenda, confined to a desert island while my brother plays the king. Next, it'll be an iron mask.'

Bramall wondered if all the Duke's childhood reading had been royalist hokum. 'You may be assured, sir, that if it ever comes to that, I shall at once assume the role of D'Artagnan and come riding to your rescue.'

Even the Duke laughed a little at that. 'Yes, well things have reached a pretty pass,' he said, 'when I lose my freedom and find myself locked up under armed guard – and all in the name of liberty.'

Bramall sighed. 'I quite agree, sir. It's bloody. But I must ask you to be patient. Only a few more days and you'll be off.'

'I suppose I should be grateful.' Bramall waited to see where this might lead. There was nothing. Instead, the Duke grunted and turned around to face the window. 'That will be all,' he said. 'Leave me alone. I need to think.'

Bramall backed off. He was as anxious as the Duke to bring the present encounter to an end. 'As you wish, sir. Dinner will be at eight.'

The harbour, Cascais, west of Lisbon: July 27

As he awaited the arrival of the passengers from that morning's flight from Southampton, Bramall felt more than a twinge of impatience. He knew how crucial it was that the Duke and Duchess should embark safely for the Bahamas, but the threat to Gibraltar was once more exerting a powerful pull on his imagination. It wasn't every day that an individual, other than a general or top political figure, had a chance to alter the course of a war.

A coded cable had arrived for him less than an hour ago from Strickland in London. 'Finish what you're doing, then get back here, ready for the mission to France. All approved. The game's afoot.' Caxton and his team, according to Croft, had finally constructed a device to play the tape, and the content was even better than predicted. The head of the service and the Foreign Secretary had spoken to Churchill, and the prime minister had officially backed the mission.

Just a few more days, Bramall told himself. He owed that much to Croft – and to the Duke, for that matter. Then he would proceed to what Croft had come to refer to as his 'rendezvous with history'.

At least Isabel was safe in England.

His brush with Dominique de Fourneau in the Boca do Inferno, though charged with sufficient electricity to power a small city, had only served to reinforce the strength of his feeling for the woman who had risked everything in his cause. In one sense, this was dismaying, even downright annoying. He had managed to get hold of himself in recent days. That's what his father would have said. He had managed to get his nerves under control. The business at the embassy had done that much for him. But that didn't mean he couldn't be distracted. There were moments when all he could think of was Isabel's glossy hair, her green eyes, her lips so impossibly inviting and that habit of hers of tucking her legs up beneath her when she sat down, so that he was able to observe close up the fine bones of her knees. If she hadn't been so sharp, so self-assured and so brave, he could have dealt with her more obvious appeal. The combination, however, was devastating.

But Isabel was not his problem today. He would put her out of his mind. Hasselfeldt was out there somewhere with an agenda all of his own. The bastard was up to something. And then there was Dominique. He had spoken to Croft about her. He said he'd never heard of her beyond her acquaintance with the Duke and Duchess, but undertook to make inquiries. If it turned out that she could be a conduit to Laval, a large part of their future difficulties would be removed at a stroke. But if she was anti-British, bent on revenge for Mers-El-Kébir, then she could equally be an invitation to disaster.

Bloody Hell!

Finally, there was the Duchess. Until the gangway was pulled back from the Excalibur and the American liner disappeared over the horizon, Bramall was part of a deadly game that required his undivided attention. He drew in a deep breath and let it out again. At no stage could he underestimate his enemy. The Germans had four times his manpower. If he and his team let their guard down just once, the Duke and Duchess could be seized, with God knows what consequences. Bramall was not going to let that happen. There had been more than enough setbacks already in this particular mission: from now on he was going to be on the winning side.

Beyond the harbour, the door of the British flying boat had

been pulled back and sealed. A launch was on its way in. *Obersturmbannführer* Walter Schellenberg, sent to Lisbon by Ribbentrop to personally oversee Operation Willi, surveyed the scene from the top window of a crumbling villa overlooking the harbour. The putt-putt of the launch's engine could be heard above the faint slap of the waves against the stones of the jetty. The SD chief had no reason to think that those arriving were of any particular significance, but it made sense to check.

He passed the Zeiss field glasses he had been using to Hasselfeldt, who removed his spectacles and adjusted the focus of the binoculars, which he then trained on the tall, broad-shouldered figure standing at the top of the harbour steps. A younger man, who looked as if he could handle himself, stood a few paces back. A few metres beyond that again were two more men and a couple of cars and drivers. The British were taking no chances. It wasn't as if the Duke was around. They just wanted to show they meant business.

'Recognise the one by the steps?' Schellenberg asked.

'No, *obersturmbannführer*. He must be new.' In fact, he had recognised him at once. Bramall! It might be too late to get back what had been stolen, but he would make sure the Englishman didn't live to implicate him in the fiasco.

'*Na-ja,*' said the SD chief. 'Make a note, though. He appears to be their leader. What matters for now is that they should suspect nothing. We will strike only if and when the right moment comes.'

Schellenberg, a tall, elegant figure, who could have been an artist or a priest had he not been a leading figure in the SS, reached into his jacket pocket and pulled out a packet of cigarettes. His subordinate immediately produced a lighter and

Schellenberg leaned into the flame.

'It occurs to me, *obersturmbannführer*,' said Hasselfeldt, 'that I could most usefully focus on the fellow at the dock. He looks, as you say, to be in charge of the security arrangements and we should know what he is up to.'

Schellenberg nodded. In the harbour below, the launch from the flying boat had drawn in to the steps. There appeared to be just five passengers. He didn't recognise any of them. The tall fellow on the jetty greeted each of the new arrivals in turn, but didn't seem especially impressed. He looked like he had other matters on his mind. Less than a minute later, both cars pulled away, leaving the launch and its pilot, plus a yawning customs officer, bobbing gently in the swell.

The SD chief turned back to Hasselfeldt. Such a shame Winzer wasn't his backup. But the Gestapo chief had barely made it to Lisbon, full of ideas, before Heydrich had ordered him back to Madrid. 'I want a complete rundown on all of those who arrived this morning. If you can't do it, find someone who can. Surveillance? Yes, I suppose so. See to it. But don't do anything rash. And keep me informed, you understand?'

Hasselfeldt jumped to attention. '*Jawohl*.'

Bramall stretched his legs in the front seat of the car as it made its way back to the Boca do Inferno. He had borrowed the Duke's Buick, from Paris, with its leather seats and brightly polished walnut dashboard. Behind, occupying the rear passenger seats, sat Sir Walter Monkton, a Whitehall mandarin, former legal adviser to the Duke as Edward VIII, come to explain the duties of a governor in wartime; and Major Grey Phillips, responsible for relations with Downing Street. None of them, so far as he knew, were aware of the Duchess's treachery, which Churchill, with the backing of a horrified Royal Family, had decided should be kept under wraps. Following behind in the second car, a Riley, were Piper Alistair Fletcher, the Duke's newly reinstated batman, and two more Special Branch heavies. Everything that he had asked for was now in place.

Lisbon: German Legation, July 30

Schellenberg found it truly tragic that he had been suborned into taking part in such a doomed and desperate venture. His spies had reported to him that there was absolutely no chance now that the Duke could be persuaded to return to Spain. Lourenço, the number two at the PVDE, said that everything had been done to create the suspicion in the Duke's mind that British agents planned to murder him – but to no effect. Not even the clandestine efforts of the Duchess, about which Hoyningen-Huene had expatiated at length over lunch, had persuaded him to abandon his protectors. The whole thing had become a fool's errand, and as if to prove the truth of this, he had just received an hysterical cable from Ribbentrop, ending: 'The *Führer* orders that an abduction is to be carried out at once.'

It was crazy. Everybody knew it – everybody except Ribbentrop. The former champagne salesman was a menace.

Yet for all that, a *Führer Befehl* remained a royal command. No one refused a direct order from Hitler. He telephoned Winzer and ordered him to prepare the ground at Badajoz. Hasselfeldt was not working out as he had thought. There was something distracted about him, something destructive. It was as if a piece of his brain had gone missing. He had been beaten up recently. Perhaps that was the reason. Whatever the truth of the matter, he could not depend on him in a crisis.

As for the rest, his hastily recruited team of Portuguese agents, several of them gypsies from the South, had been instructed to step up their efforts to frighten the Duke. At the last minute, Lourenço – would issue a bomb threat to the vessel, hopefully forcing an emergency evacuation.

Hasselfeldt's task was to try to divert Bramall and his principal agents from their key task of protecting the Duke. It remained to be seen how he would fare with that. As for Schellenberg himself, he and his chosen SS henchmen, Heineke and Böcker, would wait in a fast car. Their job would be to seize the Duke and Duchess at the optimum moment and then drive hell for leather to the frontier, where Winzer had arranged a reception committee, Spanish as well as German.

Would it work? It seemed unlikely. It was more a spin of the roulette wheel than a plan. But at least it might convince Ribbentrop – and the *Führer* – that he had done his best.

Cascais: Boca do Inferno, August 1

The previous days had been bizarre, even by the standards of recent weeks. Shots had been fired at the house, stones hurled at the windows in the middle of the night. The captain of the Excalibur had telephoned just that morning to report a possible bomb on board, which, fortunately, turned out to be a hoax. Immediately following lunch, the German ambassador, breaking with all precedent, had rung personally and asked to speak to the Duchess. 'I'm sorry, Ambassador,' Croft had told him, 'but our two countries are at war – or did you think Germany was neutral, too?' He passed the phone to Espírito Santo Silva, who turned pale and said he would call back the following day. Listening in on the hall extension, Croft wondered if the next surprise would be an invitation to the Mad Hatter's tea party.

The Excalibur, under constant guard, was scheduled to sail in mid-afternoon, as soon as the royal party was on board. Predictably, the Duchess was obsessed to the very end with the non-appearance of her personal maid, Mlle Moulichon, who had apparently been held up by the Germans in Paris. 'I asked her to fetch as much soap as she could fit into a suitcase,' she told Croft. 'Now what do we do?'

'The soap and towels will be sent on, ma'am,' Croft said ... 'together with your headed notepaper.'

When he was sure that everything was ready, the MI6 station chief left for the docks. Bramall was left to take charge of the actual journey from the Boca, through Lisbon city centre.

The Duke and Duchess would be in a bullet-proof Daimler, lent by the prime minister himself. The driver was an expert assigned by MI6. Inside, as well as the future Governor of the Bahamas and his bride, were the couple's two terrier dogs, plus Bramall and Crowther, both of them armed. The big Buick would take the lead, with a Special Branch officer at the wheel and two colleagues as lookouts. The assigned passengers in this instance were the Windsors' neighbours from Antibes, George and Rosa Woods, and the Duke's comptroller, Major Phillips. Finally, bringing up the rear was the Riley, driven by a member of the embassy security squad, with the redoubtable Piper Fletcher and a Special Branch officer to provide the necessary armed deterrence.

At three p.m. precisely, having bid farewell to the ambassador, the former king and his American wife stepped into their limousine and gave a last wave to their Portuguese host. The banker looked as if good riddance was not far from his mind.

Half a mile away, from his vantage point on the cliffs near Cascais, Klaus Hasselfeldt checked his weapons. He had a Luger and a Walther, both fully loaded, as well as a German stick grenade. So far, his plan to plan to assassinate both Britons had so far come to nothing. But he wasn't done yet. There was still a chance. As soon as it was clear that the British were on the move, he turned to Schultz, sitting on the running board of the commercial attaché's Volkswagen smoking a cigarette.

'Let's go, you idiot,' he said. 'I will drive.' Schultz just shrugged and threw away his cigarette.

Schellenberg's plan, outlined two hours before, was for him and his men, backed by a group of mercenaries, to shadow the British convoy and then, 200 metres ahead of the harbour entrance, stage an ambush and seize the Duke and Duchess. The *obersturmbannführer* considered the likelihood of success at less than 50:50. His resources were few and he had no faith in anyone other than Heineke and Böcker.

Following a parallel course, Hasselfeldt's VW was at this point one street below the convoy, undetected by Bramall and his team. Schellenberg, accompanied by his two henchmen, was waiting close to the intended point of contact, with his vehicle's engine running. The six hired gypsies responsible for the actual ambush were concealed inside a warehouse adjacent to the port. Lookouts would tell them when to strike.

Ahead in the British party, the mood was tense. 'Is everything all right, Mr Bramall?' the Duchess asked as they dropped down from Cascais into Lisbon's western suburbs. 'You look like you've just seen a ghost.'

'If you don't mind, ma'am, I'm trying to concentrate. All that matters to me now is that His Royal Highness should arrive safely on board the Excalibur.'

The Duchess turned away, glowering. She was not used to being spoken to like this.

It was Crowther who first suspected something was wrong. 'Hold on,' he said, as they drove past an intersection about half a mile from the turnoff. 'What's that down there? I'm sure I saw a car, moving at speed. It was that VW I spotted yesterday, near the Boca. It's like it's keeping level with us, one street down.'

'Right,' said Bramall. 'We're taking no chances. We'll use the emergency gate.' He turned to the driver. 'Turn left at the next major intersection. Flash the lead car. I'll indicate to the one behind.'

He pushed forward out of the jump seat and dived between the startled Duke and Duchess, using a torch to signal to the car behind to be ready to turn off. Up ahead, the Buick had got the message. At the next set of lights, it swung south.

By chance, the alternative route, leading to a second, barred-off harbour entrance, took the Royal convoy past the street in which Schellenberg and his men were now waiting – though facing in the opposite direction. It was Böcker, keeping watch out of the rear window, who spotted the convoy at the 'wrong' end of the street. Schellenberg shouted to Heineke to turn the car around. At the same time, he called the leader of the

Portuguese mercenaries on a two-way radio, ordering them to split into two groups and search out the British column.

The Daimler and its escorts were now less than half a mile from their destination, weaving in and out of the thin afternoon traffic at speeds in excess of sixty miles per hour. The pursuing Mercedes, with Schellenberg and Böcker poised to open fire, was nevertheless closing the gap, keeping one 'civilian' vehicle at a time between itself and its quarry. The SD chief could not be certain that the gypsies would get a chance to stage their ambush, but if they did, he had to be prepared.

Time was running out. The Mercedes swept out from behind its civilian cover. It was 200 metres, now a hundred metres, behind the third car of the convoy. In the Riley, the Special Branch marksman saw what was happening and released the safety catch on his revolver.

Schellenberg heard a crackle on his radio receiver. The leader of the Portuguese ambush party was on the line. 'I see them, *cheffe*,' he announced. 'But I have only two men with me. What do you want me to do?'

Schellenberg's mind raced. The odds were narrowing, but with the gypsies' help, he and his team could still get the job done. All it took was cool heads and steady hands.

'Fire into the air when the Duke's car gets to within a hundred metres of you. Make sure they know you mean business. And take care of anyone who gets in our way.'

He turned towards Heineke and ordered him to pull out and head straight for the Daimler. But it was at that moment, as turned to open fire on the Riley, that a Volkswagen hurtled out of a side street at seventy miles per hour and came straight at them. Schellenberg watched, aghast, as the car slammed into the rear end of the Mercedes, sending it spinning off the road into a parked car, throwing him hard against the windscreen. Blood spurted spurt from his forehead. At the same moment, Heineke's mouth and chin struck the steering column. The hefty Germany grunted and spat out a front tooth.

Hasselfeldt's Volkswagen, meanwhile, had ricocheted off the larger Mercedes and ended up jammed against a lamppost, its front bonnet pointing up at an angle of thirty degrees.

Schultz was unhurt but the SD man had injured his foot. Soon, he thought, ruefully, he would have no working parts left. There was a long silence before he got out and hobbled over to Schellenberg's car.

The *obersturmbannführer* was holding a bloody handkerchief to his head. His carefully devised plan – conceived in spite of the idiocy of his masters – had been reduced to a shambles by this idiot. 'You imbecile!' he said. 'Now the Duke and his party have got clean away and we – or, rather, you – are the one who will have to explain this mess.'

Hasselfeldt was devastated. These had been the worst two weeks of his life. 'We were trying to get ahead of the Duke's car, except that Schultz here chose the wrong street.'

'I am not going to discuss this with you,' said Schellenberg, examining the blood on his handkerchief. 'We will talk about it later, at the Legation.' He turned to his driver, who was sitting staring into the rear-view mirror at the sudden gap in his teeth. 'Heineke, listen to me. Does the car still drive?'

A small crowd had gathered. A Siren could be heard in the distance. The police would be on the scene within minutes. Heineke took a deep breath and tried the ignition. The engine started with a roar. Everyone, including Hasselfeldt, jumped back.

'Then get us out of here.'

The Mercedes, its rear mudguard bent hopelessly out of shape, pulled back with a scream of metal from the rumpled side of the parked car. As soon as it was clear, Heineke slammed it into forward gear and powered away, smoke belching from the engine, the broken mudguard trailing in its wake.

Half a mile ahead, at the side entrance to the harbour, the Duke's small convoy passed through the gates without further incident and drew up next to the gangway leading onto the Excalibur.

'Now, would you mind telling me what all that was about?' the Duke demanded. 'The Duchess and I were thrown about back there like nobody's business.'

'I'm terribly sorry, sir,' Bramall said, 'but I think you may just have escaped a Nazi kidnap attempt.'

'What?'

'Only it looks as if they weren't up to the job.'

'My God!' said the Duchess. 'Is that the best you can come up with, Mr Bramall?'

'My wife has a point,' said the Duke. 'Couldn't the whole thing could have been – what was the word? – paranoia on your part?'

The two men stared at each other. 'That is possible, sir,' Bramall said. 'But sometimes it pays to think the worst – wouldn't you say? Either way, we've got you and the Duchess to the ship unharmed.'

By now, the Portuguese foreign minister, standing alongside David Eccles of the Department of Economic Warfare and the captain of the Excalibur, were lined up to greet the former king. Croft was also on hand, trying to pretend that nothing had happened.'

The minister stepped forward, as if conducting a funeral. 'Your Royal Highness,' he began. 'We live in troubled times. Yet it is my Government's most earnest hope that you and the Duchess managed to enjoy your brief stay in our country. As you leave Europe to embark upon another glorious chapter in your career, may I wish you a safe, and comfortable, onward journey.'

'Thank you, *senhor* …' The Duke's voice trailed off, for he had no idea what the fellow's name was. 'The Duchess and I are most grateful for the hospitality that has been extended to us during our stay and hope that we may return to Lisbon in the not too distant future.'

The minister bowed.

'And now, sir,' said Eccles, 'If you don't mind, I think it would be best if you boarded the ship. Your stateroom is ready and cocktails will be served in half an hour.'

'Oh, excellent. Well, that's it, then, Croft. You too, Bramall. Let us hope that if we do meet again, it is in happier circumstances.'

Croft and Bramall looked at the Duchess, who stared blankly back at them, after which they turned to the Duke, dropping their heads just a fraction. 'Your Royal Highness,' they said in perfect unison.

The Excalibur did not meet its scheduled departure time of four pm. There were further security checks and problems with the Duchess's luggage, some of which, along with the Duchess's maid, had gone missing. When it did finally put out to sea at a quarter-to-six in the evening, Walter Schellenberg watched its progress down the Tagus waterfront from the tower room of the German Legation.

Things had not worked out as planned. Ribbentrop was sure to register his displeasure. How Canaris would laugh when he learned what had happened. On the other hand, he had a perfect scapegoat. Hasselfeldt, it turned out, was already under investigation by Winzer for gross negligence arising from the assault on the Legation in Madrid. The unfortunate *sturmbannführer's* latest performance, impeding a direct order of the *Führer*, would surely put paid to his career. Watching through his field glasses as the Excalibur turned west into the Atlantic, Himmler's head of foreign intelligence ran his free hand over the wound to his forehead, which the embassy doctor had managed to close with stitches. His temple throbbed. There would be a scar, he had been warned Could he call it a war wound? That would be stretching it. But an injury sustained in the line of duty? Why not? Others, as he knew, had been awarded the Iron Cross for a great deal less.

12

England: one week later

Isabel stood inside the open door of the Lysander, hearing the headlong rush of air, watching the landscape drift slowly past two kilometres beneath her feet. Hills and fields stretched out in all directions, like an illustration from a children's book. For once it was sunny, and the sun, she had discovered, transformed England instantly into a magic kingdom. The colours of earth and sky were no longer dull and lifeless, but intense and vivid.

But she was terrified.

'I can't do it,' she shouted to the RAF sergeant standing at her shoulder.

''Course you can, love,' he bellowed back. 'Don't think about it, that's all. Then it's easy as falling off a log. Just remember, count to ten and pull the ripcord. Oh, and don't forget to bend your knees when you land. Piece of cake.' With that, he gave her a shove. For a moment, she lost her footing, catching the tip of her boot on the doorframe, then she felt herself fall forwards into the abyss. Her scream was lost in the roar from the Lysander's engine.

The air accelerating past her was so sharp it hurt her eyes. She knew she should have worn goggles. She looked down, squinting. *Madre de Dios!* She was dropping like a stone. Count, they said. But how many was it now? *Cinco, seis, siete* ... Oh, to hell with it! She tugged hard on the cord.

The chute opened like an enormous bedsheet. One moment she was hurtling down, the next she was shooting straight up. At least that's what if felt like. For a moment, all the remaining breath was knocked out of her body

She was afraid she would be sick. Her stomach was in her mouth. She closed her eyes and waited a moment before re-opening them. But then, as suddenly as it came, her fear vanished and the sensation ceased to terrify her and became instead almost sublime. She looked up. The aircraft was tiny. It was impossible to believe she was ever inside it. Below her was the patchwork of the land: small, compact fields separated by hedgerows and trees. Earlier, it had rained; now the sun was shining.

So many colours. Over there was corn ripening: yellow, almost golden. Next to it, the dark green of some kind of vegetable. Cabbage perhaps (didn't the English eat cabbage?) And an unfolding expanse of pasture – so unlike Spain – with copses of trees, hedgerows and streams. The land was parcelled into small farms, each with its neat farmhouse and barn. She could see Hanslope with its thatched roofs and church tower. And over there was her hotel. It was so peaceful, so tranquil, so … untroubled. To bring war to such a landscape, she felt, would be nothing less than a crime.

It was a rare moment of detachment. They hadn't told her about this. She was floating. Alone in the sky, it seemed as if nothing in the world could touch her. Love was different. It was like a predator. It stole up on you unawares and consumed you. She hadn't expected to fall in love with Bramall. She thought they would have at most a brief affair, like in a French novel, and in a pragmatic way she had looked forward to that. It would be her first time and the final part of growing up. Instead, he had come to occupy the centre of her life.

The act of love had been everything she had hoped. It was raw, exhilarating and tender all at the same time – both a promise and a promise fulfilled. What would her mother think of her now? she wondered. She would be cross, of course, but a little bit jealous, too. The thought made her giggle.

There had been others before her. She knew that. Well, he was thirty-one years old. But why should she mind about that? If anything, she rather approved. His past was his own business. What mattered from this point on was that they should live each day as if it were the first one. Who knew what would happen to them anyway? Charles was a soldier, a spy. She was a refugee. Their very existence was uncertain. Soon they would be parachuted together into France and there was no guarantee they would make it out alive.

A bird flew past, causing her to catch her breath. *O Dios mio!* The treetops were not far beneath her. They were rising to meet her. She shouldn't have let her mind wander. What was it they said she should do? Wasn't she supposed to pull on the ropes or something? She grabbed at two of the lines connecting her to the billowing fabric above her head and yanked violently. Oh dear Lord! She felt herself lurch violently to the right. It worked. She had done it. Now the trees weren't below her any more. But the ground was. A field of some kind. It was close. Really close. Oh dear God, here it comes! As she fell to Earth, all thoughts of Bramall vanished. This was reality. She drew her tongue inside her mouth so that she wouldn't bite it, and bent her knees. Then she prayed. *Whoosh! Oomph!* Her feet touched down, her body toppled forwards, she twisted to one side, and in a tumble of limbs crashed headlong into the soft summer soil of England.

She lay still for several seconds, hardly daring to move. Her heart was thumping. She could hear a bee buzzing and birds singing. Then the canopy collapsed on top of her. She crawled sideways for a second until she could lift the silk material up, away from her face. A cow was staring at her, its nostrils looking unnaturally large. It had brown eyes and it seemed friendly. *'Hola!'* she said. She felt her legs. They were all right. And her head? No cuts. She was in one piece. She started to laugh. It was wonderful. Not bad for a little Spanish girl on her first time out, she thought.

Madrid: Office of Kriminalkommissar Winzer, August 9

Operation Willi had interrupted Winzer's investigation of the embassy raid. Now, with Hasselfeldt's return in disgrace from Lisbon, it was back on course and the evidence, though circumstantial, was damning. Intelligence material, as yet unknown, had been compromised. Once he had had a chance to discuss with the ambassador what exactly was missing and how best to present the loss to Berlin, a damage limitation exercise would be instituted. That way, the value to England of whatever Bramall had seized would be reduced and its impact minimised. The attack on the Legation would fade into legend: the work of Spanish diehards, nothing more.

A close-run thing just the same. It was the ambassador, lingering over a glass of brandy, who first noticed the unauthorised photograph on his dining room wall showing Hitler in apparent conversation with Charles Bramall, a key suspect in the case. Exactly as he would have expected, it was Hasselfeldt who had placed the picture. One of the waiters remembered him positioning it on the wall and checking to see that it wasn't crooked. So convinced was the Austrian that Bramall could be trusted, and so mindless of his duty, that he was prepared not only to frustrate Schellenberg's plan and the direct orders of the *Führer*, but to play stupid mind-games with his lunch guests.

Easy to blame the Austrian, then.

If only it were that simple.

Once alerted, the Winzer realised, with a start, where he had last seen Bramall. It was he who had impersonated the late *Fregattenkapitän* Gunter Rath of the *Kriegsmarine*, whose battered body had been found two days ago in a railway tunnel in Andalucia. He should have spotted him at once. He had spent time, after all, observing him at the Ortega garden party – even reported him to Hasselfeldt as a suspicious character. But he had failed to make the connection. As head of embassy security, he had in fact volunteered assistance to this determined enemy of his country and suspected ... *nothing*. That was the simple fact of the matter, and even now the knowledge of what he had done sent a shiver down his spine.

It was fortunate that the only person privy to this disquieting piece of information was Winzer himself. It was Hasselfeldt who recruited Bramall, not realising he was a 'double.' It was Hasselfeldt who apparently recorded Stohrer's confidential meetings. It was Hasselfeldt who had failed to account for two missing tapes from his *Magnetophon*, and it was Hasselfeldt whose office was broken into by an assailant whose accomplices had committed mass murder in the foyer of the Legation. Now, it transpired, it was Hasselfeldt whose incompetence and inability to follow the instructions of a superior officer had led to the collapse of a scheme initiated by Foreign Minister Ribbentrop and approved by Hitler.

Winzer's relief was unqualified. There could be only one possible response to such behaviour.

'Are we ready, gentlemen?' he asked.

They nodded.

'Very well. Let's go.'

Accompanied by two SS guards, Winzer descended the steps from the second floor of the Legation to the first and walked in step with his men along the corridor leading to the SD office. Von Stohrer and Colonel Bruns stood at the far end, looking on. The ambassador nodded, willing the unpleasantness to be over as quickly as possible.

Winzer called out: 'It's over, Klaus. Time for you to answer for your mistakes.'

The voice that answered was both defiant and anxious. He would not go easily. 'Stay back. You have no right.'

Winzer paused. Was Klaus about to make a heroic last stand? He nodded to SS corporal Frans Müller, who released the safety cap on his weapon and pushed open the door.

Hasselfeldt was standing by his desk. Seeing the SS man's outline through the frosted glass, with his machine pistol extended, he reached for the brand new Walther P-38 in his holster. His head filled with an image of him being dragged, gagged and bound, toward a waiting hangman's noose or, worse, the guillotine. He would not endure such humiliation. As Müller advanced, pushing the door open with the muzzle of his gun, took a deep breath and fired two shots in quick succession through the glass. Müller collapsed, hissing like a wet log on a campfire. Winzer, still in the corridor, dropped to a crouch and took out his Luger. The second SS guard meanwhile fired a burst through the open door with his machine pistol. There was a low cry, followed by a gurgle. Winzer stepped forward. Hasselfeldt was on his knees, clutching his hand to his chest.

Winzer's contempt was total. 'Too bad, Klaus, I would have enjoyed your trial.' As the Austrian looked up, his face registering all the agony of chronic disappointment, the *Kripo* officer shot him once through the head.

Stohrer stood outside the office, accompanied by Bruns. 'Is it safe to go in?'

Bruns nodded.

The ambassador observed the tableau in front of him with unambiguous distaste. 'The fellow had talent,' he pronounced gravely. 'Such a pity he was a fool.'

Winzer nodded. *But not the only one. What will they think of you, Herr Botschafter, when they find out what has gone missing from your embassy?*

Colonel Bruns wandered over to Hasselfeldt's desk. He felt no pity for Hasselfeldt, but just a twinge of regret. There was a note, next to what looked like a cyanide capsule. It read simply: *'I was at all times a true servant of the Reich and a devoted follower of the Führer. I regret my errors. Heil Hitler!'*

Bruns handed the note to Winzer, who read it, then crumpled it up and threw it in the wastepaper basket. The *Gestapo* officer could not conceal a bitter smile. 'Do you know?' he said. 'At the academy it was always suspected he had Jewish blood.'

Madrid: August 9

Dominique had just stepped out of her bath when the telephone rang in her bedroom. According to Beigbeder – whose garrulousness after sex was so blatant it was almost charming – her number was not among those being tapped by the secret police, but she was aware that as much as ten per cent of the 'regular' telephone traffic of Madrid was listened in to by someone or other.

She reached for the receiver. '*Bonjour!* Who is speaking, please?'

'*Citoyenne?*' A pause followed. 'We are in luck. I think the bougainvillea is in bloom.'

'*Comment?*'

The caller, whoever he was, was speaking in French. He sounded familiar – English, perhaps. But she couldn't quite place him.

There was a sigh at the other end. 'I was hoping to take the waters. These things are important, don't you think? And I was wondering if you might care to join me.'

And then it hit her. Of course. *Bramall!* He was talking about Vichy. 'The *waters*, you say? That sounds delightful.'

'I'm glad you approve. It would help, however, if you were to make the necessary reservations. You know the people who run the place so much better than I.'

'When did you have in mind?'

'Next week. Monday, I hope. It's all rather urgent and I should hate anything to go wrong. I'll have to fly in and, as you know, these things can be so complicated to organise.'

'I understand. So is it the *directeur-en-chef* you wish to see?'

'His deputy might be better.'

'I think so. You can rely on me, Monsieur … *Monsieur?*'

' … Le Duc. To be accompanied by a Mademoiselle La Roche.'

'Ah! Very well. I look forward to it.'

'Splendid. Au revoir, Citoyenne.'

Hanslope: August 10, midday

When Isabel got back to her room, Bramall was waiting for her, sat on her bed smoking a cigarette. He put it out as soon as she came in. It was cold and damp inside the Nissen hut, and he was dressed in his Army great coat. The other bunk in the room belonged, he'd been informed, to the girl who was on her way to Prague. Her English clothes were neatly folded on top of the bed; on the wall, to the right of her pillow, were the photographs she had pinned up of her fiancé, dressed in naval uniform, and her parents, smiling sheepishly for the camera.

'*Hola!*' Isabel said, still not quite recovered from the surprise. Her hair was up and she wore some kind of flying jacket, with a fur collar. 'I didn't know you were coming.'

Bramall stood up. 'Nor did I. But I needed to talk to you.'

She stood stock still for second, just looking, then ran toward him and threw her arms round his neck. 'I'm just so glad you're here,' she began.

'I gather we're alone,' he said, looking round.

'Yes. She left this morning. Her name is Angela. I didn't get talk to her, but they tell me, it is a very dangerous mission. She may not come back.'

Bramall bent down and joined his lips to hers. They kissed,

at first tenderly, then with increasing passion, until suddenly he pulled away.

'What's wrong?' she said. She looked faintly alarmed.

'Well, that's just it, you see. Your room-mate – what's her name, Angela? She's off on a dangerous mission and she might not come back. And I can't stop thinking, what if *you* don't come back? What if you don't make it?'

Reaching up to stroke his hair, Isabel, drew his mouth back down to hers. 'I will come back,' she said, between kisses. 'We will both come back. We have a lot of time ahead of us. This is only the beginning.'

'I could always go alone.'

Isabel's eyes narrowed. 'No! I won't hear of it.'

'It's not your fight. You don't have to do this.'

She pushed back his head. 'Yes I do. And it *is* my fight. I helped get us into this, and I will see it through to the end. We are together. We are a team.'

'I don't think you quite understand. You could be arrested. You could be thrown in jail. They could *torture* you.'

'Do you think I don't know that? I have thought about it, and I am ready.'

'I don't want anything to happen to you, Isabel,' he said.

'Then keep me by your side.'

'Very well.' He wiped her tears from her cheeks with his fingers and threw his arms around her. They kissed once more and he drew her tightly to him so that he could feel her breasts against his chest. Moments after, they fell back on the bed.

Half an hour later, as they lay naked, there was a knock at the door and a young brunette from the Intelligence section of the Women's Royal Army Corps stepped in. Immediately, Isabel drew the blanket up to cover herself. When the girl saw Bramall, who was once more smoking a cigarette, she pulled up short, not knowing where to look.

'Erm ... sorry to barge in like this, Miss' she stammered, 'but it's just been confirmed that you're to fly out to France tomorrow. There should be an aircraft available sometime after nine in the evening. You'll be travelling with Captain ...'

' – Captain Charles Bramall reporting for duty,' Bramall said, saluting smartly.

'Oh,' said the WRAC girl, returning the salute. 'Right, sir. I assume you've got the news already. Well in that case, I'll leave you alone. I expect you've got things to, erm, organise'

'We'll get right on it, Private,' said Bramall.

As soon as the unfortunate messenger left, they both burst out laughing. Then they stopped, as if forewarned at the same instant of something terrible to come, and they held each other, and for nearly a minute neither of them spoke.

RAF Newmarket: August 11

Strickland rang through to Bramall with the news of Romero's death a couple of hours before he and Isabel set off for the airfield at Newmarket. He had spoken with Croft, who the previous evening had met with Hoare in Madrid. Bramall was shocked. Isabel went white. She turned away as tears began to trickle down her cheeks.

Bramall put his arms about her shoulders. 'It all happened a couple of weeks back. He killed Luder, but got shot himself by that bastard Hasselfeldt. He ended up in the hands of the *Gestapo*. The Spanish only released his name yesterday.'

Isabel gasped for breath, placing both hands to her chest. 'Poor Eddy,' she said. He was a crazy man, like no one else I ever met. He did many things during his life that bothered him. But he believed they were necessary. Most of all, I think he valued friendship. You were his friend.'

She paused. 'Do you know what he told me, after we escaped from the border police?'

Bramall shook his head.

'He said, "Tell Charlie I did my part. Tell him I kept my word."'

'I never doubted it,' Bramall said, avoiding her eyes.

'He called you Charlie.'

'Yes.'

'I think *I* shall call you Charlie.'

'If you like.'

She remembered how Romero spared the life of the second border guard. No one had spared *him*. 'Hasselfeldt is a pig,' she said, 'and I hope he is punished for his sins. But I'm not sorry Luder's dead. He was truly evil. Not even a real Nazi, just a thug. He twisted my father round his little finger.'

Bramall drew her towards him and kissed her forehead.

'Do you think we'll ever be able to go back?' she asked him.

'I doubt it. Not for years anyway. But you did the right thing. Eddy was proud of you.'

'Yes,' she said, drying her eyes. 'I think maybe he was. And that is something.' She paused, looking up into the trees and the sky beyond. 'Is there a chapel here – somewhere I could pray?'

'I'm sure there is,' Bramall said, taking her hand. 'Would you like me to ask?'

'Please. He died without absolution. Someone should beg forgiveness for his sins. Then we need time to prepare ourselves for what is coming. Eddy wouldn't like it if we – what is it he would say? – *fucked up.*'

'No,' said Bramall, remembering Romero's unsparing dissection of every plan he laid before him. 'You're not wrong there.'

The aircraft that would take them to Vichy was a twin-engine Whitley of 138 Special Duties Squadron. It could fly high, up to 26,000 feet, and, in steady flight, made little noise. Without its usual payload, it had a range of almost 2,000 miles. It was just about the only aircraft available that could make it to Vichy and back without refuelling.

They mounted the steps and clambered inside. Jump seats set against the bulkhead were the only accommodation, but an RAF corporal was waiting for them with sandwiches and a flask of coffee.

'It's a good night for it,' he said, handing each of them a plastic cup. 'There's not much of a moon and quite a bit of cloud cover. 'Long as the lieutenant can work out where we're going, we should have you over the target in less than three hours.' He turned to Bramall. 'The material you're delivering is in this 'ere box that you strap to your chest before you leave.'

'I see.'

The two 78 rpm records, Bramall was amused to discover, had been given labels identifying them as Maurice Chevalier's *Ça sent si bon la France* and *On Ira Pendre Notre Linge sur la Ligne Siegfried* by Ray Ventura. Someone obviously had a sense of humour. He looked up. A discreet cough had interrupted his train of thought. The corporal was still standing there. The fellow looked embarrassed.

'What is it, man?'

'I'm sorry, sir, but I've been told to give you these.'

He held out two small glass ampoules.

Cyanide.

'They fit into specially made pouches in your lapels,' he said. 'If the Germans capture you, or you're handed over, you might just want them.'

Bramall took Isabel's hand. She had gone white. 'Thank you, corporal,' he said. 'Let's hope it doesn't come to that.'

The Whitley took off in a steady drizzle at ten-fifteen and headed southwest toward Sussex, then over the Channel to Normandy, where it veered inland on a heading for Vichy. The drop site was a farm outside the village of Chantelle, ten kilometres north of the city. A newly formed resistance group, alerted by the SOE, would be waiting, with torches and a car. With luck, they would be in Vichy before breakfast.

It was difficult to talk over the steady drone of the Whitney. They were both in any case thinking about Romero. Isabel remembered him in the church, telling her to keep her voice down. She couldn't help thinking that Eddy had maybe been a little in love with her. That was sad. Bramall wondered if his friend had derived any real satisfaction from the life he led, or whether he simply followed an impulse, believing it to be right. He also wondered if he had been in love with Izzy – as he called her – and rather thought he was.

Isabel had fallen silent. Children. Eddy would have liked children. He would have been a good father – though a strange one. But that wouldn't happen now. She tried hard not to think of his last minutes. The Spanish garrotte was a particularly gruesome form of execution and she could not bear to think of the horror he must have endured. She wondered what thoughts had occupied his last moments. She wondered if he had thought of her.

It was a little after one o'clock – two a.m. French time – when word came through that they were over the jump zone. Bramall strapped the package to his chest. Inside, in addition to the two records and Hasselfeldt's notebook, was a note from Churchill to Pétain that he hadn't read and didn't plan to. The corporal checked the parachutes and made sure they were in order. Then he opened the aircraft door.

Cold air rushed in at 150 miles an hour. Isabel felt her teeth chatter.

'I've only done this twice before,' she shouted into Bramall's ear, 'and that was in daylight.'

'Me, too,' Bramall roared back. 'But we'll be fine.'

The corporal was looking up at a light above the door, waiting for it to go green. 'Okay,' he shouted, tapping Bramall on the shoulder. 'That's it. Good luck!'

Bramall went first, then Isabel. Fifteen seconds later, they pulled their ripcords. The chutes billowed up and, after the initial 'upwards' lurch, they began to float gently down. The lack of moonlight, combined with the cloudy conditions and steady rainfall, meant that they lost sight of each other during the descent. It also meant that it was hard to judge how high they were and when they should brace for impact with the ground. Bramall squinted into the inky blackness, looking for any trace of what lay below. At length, he saw three thin beams of light – hopefully from the welcoming party. It must mean he was almost down. He bent his knees and tried his best to relax his body. After a further five seconds, he thought he could make out some trees. *Holy fuck!!* He pulled on the lines, but it was too late. The canopy of his chute caught on a low branch and he came to a dramatic, breathless halt some six feet from the ground. The torch beams grew in intensity. He could hear footsteps in the undergrowth. Unbuckling his harness, he drew his revolver and fell the rest of the way to Earth.

Isabel landed a hundred metres or so to the east in the middle of a field of maize. Suddenly, it was hot and sticky, and the tall cereal plants were sharp and brittle. The husk of one of them grazed her cheek. Other than that, she was safe. She undid her harness and stood up. She could see fireflies. The sound of crickets filled the air. But then, abruptly, she was aware of footsteps moving in her direction and of the flash of a torchlight .

She waited, fumbling for her revolver.

'Bonjour!' a man's voice said. *'Bienvenue en France.'*

She almost fainted with relief.

The leader of the resistance group, who said his name was Thierry, took them to the home of the farmer in whose fields they had landed. As part of the deal worked out with SOE, the Whitley had also dropped a consignment of arms and explosives, with detonators and timers, which Thierry's comrades were now gathering in. Once the leader was satisfied that his deal with the British was honoured, he told Bramall and Isabel they should get some sleep.

'We leave for Vichy at eight. There is no point in going in advance. The offices will only be closed.'

He directed them up a ladder, rather like the one in Bótoa, to a loft in which a mattress and blankets were laid out. He then pulled down the hatch. 'I will wake you at seven,' he called. 'Dormez bien.'

They did not make love that night. It was too hot and clammy and they were nervous as well as exhausted. Instead, they curled up in each other's arms and fell at once into a deep and dreamless sleep.

Next morning, at exactly seven, the hatch flew up and Thierry's head appeared in the opening. 'I hope I am not disturbing you,' he said. 'There is coffee below. After that, we must go.'

Vichy, until the middle of the nineteenth century an unexceptional provincial town in the north of the Auvergne, had been transformed by the re-discovery of its thermal waters. During the reign of Napoléon III, it was the most fashionable spa resort in Europe, acquiring hotels, parks, an opera house and concert hall, as well as hundreds of chalets and villas, noted for their ornate architecture and trademark ironwork.

The new Government of France, with Pétain as a post-constitutional monarch and Laval as his enforcer, dominated the local scene. Hotels and other public buildings were now home to twenty-two ministries. The *Maréchal* himself had newly taken over the immense Hotel du Parc, which also contained the offices of Pierre Laval and his assistant, Alain Delacroix.

It was just after eight-thirty when Thierry, dressed as the schoolteacher he in fact was, dropped Bramall and Isabel in the centre of the town, some 500 metres from the Park. 'When you are finished, if all is well, I will meet you in the Hall des Sources. I will be there from three o'clock until five. If you do not come or you are not alone, I will not hesitate to leave without you, so please be careful.

'Understood,' said Bramall.

They walked down the street towards the hotel. Bramall carried the two 78s, in their paper sleeves, plus Hasselfeldt's transcription, in a bag under his arm. The original recording, less the material relating to the assault on Gibraltar, had been re-spooled onto two doubled-sided reels hidden in slots built into the heels of his boots. These were backup, nothing more, designed to impress the French should they demand to know the provenance of the recordings.

Everything looked normal. People were on their way to work, buses were running, cafés were serving breakfast. The new flag of France flew from the many public buildings. It was the same red, white and blue tricolour, but in the middle, in the white section was the Francisque, a Frankish axe, chosen by Pétain to symbolise the resolve and patriotism of the new Republic.

Two Gendarmes stood outside the front entrance of the Hotel du Parc wearing short waterproof capes against the rain which hadn't stopped since their arrival. Bramall and Isabel produced their identity papers, freshly made in London three days before, showing them to be natives of Clermont-Ferrand.

'You must go to reception,' one of the officers said. He looked vaguely bored.

The woman behind the front desk was bright and chirpy. 'Whom shall I say is calling?' she asked.

'Monsieur Le Duc and Mademoiselle La Roche, come to take the waters.'

There was a flicker of recognition. 'Wait here, please.'

While the receptionist made a telephone call, a gendarme examined the contents of Bramall's bag and frisked him for weapons. A white-haired woman in her sixties, wearing a uniform dating back to the building's days as an actual hotel, examined Isabel.

Two minutes later, a uniformed huissier arrived to escort them not to Laval's office, but to that of Delacroix, on the first floor, overlooking the gardens. The former Army captain was smartly dressed but had about him a strangely hunted look. He was obviously wary of his visitors. His eyes darted about, taking them in.

'I am Delacroix, principal assistant to Deputy Prime Minister Laval.'

'Good of you to see us,' Bramall said. They spoke in French.

Delacroix cast his eye up and down Isabel's trim form. She was dressed in a simple white blouse and pencil skirt. He then turned back to Bramall. 'You are English, I believe,' he said. The description came out laced with contempt.

'That is correct. My name is Bramall ...Charles Bramall.'

'And you, Mademoiselle, are from Spain.'

Isabel smiled sweetly. 'I am, Monsieur.'

Delacroix sniffed. 'I must tell you, your origins do not exactly imbue me with confidence. For the moment, I shall indulge you, but do not take me for a fool. Should the situation warrant it, I shall not hesitate to have you deported under guard to the Occupied Zone, where you will be handed over to the German authorities. Two Gendarmes are at this moment standing outside my door. Try to bear that in mind when you talk to me.'

'Charmant, monsieur,' Isabel said. 'May we sit down?'

Delacroix gestured vaguely towards some chairs. 'If you think you will be more than two minutes.'

'Before we begin,' Bramall said, 'I have a letter here for

Maréchal Pétain, written by the British prime minister Winston Churchill. Perhaps you would be good enough to see that he gets it.'

Delacroix's eyes opened wide as Bramall handed over the letter. 'How do I know that it is genuine?'

'Don't ask me. I haven't read it. If you think it's a forgery, you can always throw it away. But you would then have to answer for your actions to Pétain.'

'We shall see,' said Delacroix, placing the letter, with its Downing Street seal, in pride of place in the centre of his desk, next to a paperweight based on the Arc de Triomphe. On the opposite wall was a photograph of Pétain, taken after Verdun, in which his moustache was particularly luxuriant. He was in his late middle-age even then. The Frenchman narrowed his eyes. 'Now, why are you here? Proceed.'

Bramall felt like a second-rate actor. 'Until two weeks ago,' he began, 'I worked for the British Government in Spain. While there, I came into the possession of some remarkable information.' He paused. 'As you know, Franco considers the whole of Morocco, plus the western portion of Algeria, centred on Oran, to be a natural part of the Spanish empire. You may be less aware of his desire to expand the enclave of Spanish Equatorial Africa at the expense of the French colony of Gabon. At any rate, in the context of the present war, in which Spanish membership of the Axis is even now being negotiated, these claims have risen to the very top of the Spanish agenda.'

Delacroix's eyes were darting about quite feverishly now. This was exactly what Dominique had suggested – though without proof of any kind. If true, it could spell ruin for France. But Laval had assured him there was nothing to worry about.

'I am aware of these developments,' he said. 'France, too, has its sources of information. What do you bring me that is new? And why is the young lady here?'

'I am here,' said Isabel, 'because several times in recent months I have met personally with Minister Serrano-Suñer, who, under orders from his brother-in-law, is preparing a challenge to the French empire. I am also here because I can corroborate what M. Bramall is about to tell you. I can provide details of Serrano's recent conversations with my father, a senior government aide, that confirm the hostile intent of the Government in Madrid towards France.'

Delacroix's palms were now sticky with sweat. 'All this is very interesting,' he said. 'But what proof do you have? I do not deal in speculation.'

'The proof is right here,' said Bramall, trying to sound more confident than he felt. He opened the bag at his feet and took out the two records. 'I suggest you ask one of your aides to fetch a gramophone and then listen carefully to the two records I am now handing to you. You do speak Spanish, I take it.'

'Of course I speak Spanish,' Delacroix sniffed. He rose slightly out of his chair and took the records from Bramall's grasp. He looked at the first one, still in its sleeve, a hole cut out to expose the label. 'Maurice Chevalier – not one of his best, if you ask me.' He turned to the second. 'And this – what is it?' He squinted at the label. 'Ray Ventura, *'On Ira Pendre Notre Linge sur La Ligne Siegfried.'* Is this some kind of joke?'

'Not at all,' said Bramall, 'though it is, arguably, in poor taste. The two records you have there in your hand are proof positive of a high-level conversation – a negotiation, really – between Berlin and Madrid. The purpose of the negotiation, from Germany's standpoint, is the capture of Gibraltar. That explains my interest in the matter. From Spain's point of view, the objective is somewhat different.' He glanced at Isabel.

'Obviously,' she said, 'the Government of General Franco would like to retake Gibraltar. I do not need to explain this to you, I think. It is a matter of national honour. But the real reason for Spanish interest – indeed the only reason they are prepared to join the war – is, that, in return, Hitler grants them the whole of Morocco, plus Oran, as well as a large section of French Africa, at the close of hostilities.'

'Don't take our word for it.' Bramall resumed. 'Listen for yourself. On the German side, is Baron Eberhard von Stohrer, ambassador to Madrid, and Colonel Walter Bruns, the embassy's chief military attaché. For Spain, Interior Minister Serrano Suñer, Foreign Minister Beigbeder, and Army Chief of Staff General Vigón. They are speaking in Spanish, but I am told that will not be a problem for M. Laval.'

'No problem at all. He learned it, I believe, as a student in Bayonne. But how did you get hold of such a thing?'

'I told you. I work as an agent for the British Government. It's my job.'

'But wait! I remember. There was an attack recently on the German Legation. Were you responsible for that?'

'I'd rather not say.'

'And you, Mlle La Roche. What do you know of this?'

'I alerted M. Bramall to the existence of the meeting and the names of those taking part.'

Despite himself, Delacroix looked palpably excited. 'I see. Well, I do not have a gramophone in my office. It is not a nightclub.' He picked up the receiver of his telephone and dialled a number. 'Bring me a gramophone,' he ordered. 'Yes, a gramophone. At once.' He replaced the receiver and shot out a finger in Bramall's direction.

'How did you record this alleged conversation? You cannot expect me to believe that you set up microphones and equipment in the German Legation.'

'No, M. Delacroix, it was originally recorded by the SD – the *Sicherheitsdienst* – on a device known as a *Magnetophon*. I managed to obtain the recording. As no one outside of Germany possesses a *Magnetophon*, our technicians – with considerable ingenuity – transferred the original onto gramophone records. Should you be interested, I also have the SD transcription into German of part of the original Spanish.' He smiled. 'Apparently the fellow was interrupted before he could finish.'

Delacroix sat back. This was a real coup. He had already been given an intimation of what might be happening from Dominique, who had presumably obtained her information in flagrante from the Spanish Foreign Minister. But that was only hearsay. There was no proof. Laval had dismissed it. Now, however, came the confirmation.

Bramall was studying the Frenchman. A thousand different thoughts seemed to be running through the fellow's mind. 'Might I suggest something?' he asked finally. Delacroix shrugged. 'It's just that we were specifically instructed to speak with Deputy Prime Minister Laval. Do you think you could possibly let him know what's happening so that he too can hear the recording?'

Delacroix sniffed. 'Once I am satisfied that the information you bring us is real, I will bring it to the attention of Minister Laval. Then, and only then.'

Bramall opened his mouth to respond, but before he could speak there was a knock at the door. 'I regret, Monsieur,' said a uniformed huissier, but there does not appear to be a gramophone in the building. One of my assistants has one at his apartment and has gone to fetch it, but that could take some time.'

Bramall and Isabel exchanged glances. Delacroix pushed back on his chair, not quite knowing what to say.

It was Bramall who broke the silence. 'Respectfully, could I again suggest that we transfer to the office of Monsieur Laval? We can fill in the background and discuss the issues arising while we wait for your man to return with his gramophone. It makes sense, does it not?'

Delacroix considered this for a moment. He had hoped to attend the meeting with Laval in possession of all of the facts. ' I shall raise the matter with the minister personally. Wait here. And do not touch anything. I will leave the door open and there is an armed officer outside. Do you understand?'

'Perfectly.'

Two minutes later, Bramall and Isabel found themselves standing in the office of Vichy France's deputy prime minister.

Pierre Laval, once his country's foreign minister and for several months its prime minister, was talking on the phone, but broke off the conversation with a curt instruction to 'get it done' as Delacroix ushered Bramall and Isabel into the room. 'Sit down,' he said, indicating two metal chairs. 'I hope you are not here to make a fool of me. My aide tells me you have information suggesting possible collusion between Germany and Spain to the detriment of France and its empire. Is that true?'

'Yes, Monsieur, it is,' said Bramall.

Laval ran a podgy hand down his languorous moustache. 'Well,' he said, 'If that is the case, we must do something about it. But first I need to hear the evidence. Where is it?'

Delacroix leapt in. 'It is on two gramophone records.'

'On gramophone records! That is certainly a novelty. Then fetch them, Alain – the gramophone, too, while you're at it.'

'Yes, Minister.' Delacrois jumped up and sped out the door.

Isabel could see that the Frenchman was staring at her. He looked as if he had forgotten to brush his teeth that morning. He scratched the back of his neck and snorted. 'Is it correct,' he asked her in Spanish, that your father is an aide to the *cuñadísimo*?'

'Yes, Señor. His chef de cabinet.'

'How bizarre. And does it not bother you that in talking to me, you are betraying your father as well as your country?'

'Yes, monsieur, it bothers me very much.'

'So why do you do it?'

Isabel stiffled the urge to point out that Laval himself was widely regarded as a traitor. 'My principal concern is with peace in Europe. In modern war, millions die, and in my country too many have died already. I do not see how peace can be recovered if the British lose Gibraltar and seize the Canaries, and then the Germans move into Morocco and end up confronting the French.'

'Your logic is impeccable,' said Laval, reverting to French. 'But affairs such as these, involving national pride and conflicting ambition are intricate, like a minuet.' His thick eyebrows rose dramatically, as if on springs. 'Do you dance, Mlle La Roche?'

'The waltz, the tango.'

'Aah. Sheer frivolity. What of flamenco?'

'As a child.'

'Now there is passion. I love to watch gypsies dance.'

Isabel stared at him in silence. There was no obvious response to such a remark.

'In a few more moments,' Laval began. 'we shall get to the truth of this matter. 'And I must tell you that … ' But at this point the minister's words were interrupted by a loud crash, indicating that his aide's life had once more lurched into crisis. The flex of the gramophone, trailing down as he made his way the ten metres or so from his own office to that of his boss, had caught in one of the metal handles of an antique armoire. Just days before, the ornate piece of furniture, once owned by a sister of the Grand Duke of Luxembourg, had been removed from Laval's office, a former guest suite, to make way for a set of filing cabinets. As the chunky bakelite plug lodged in the handle, the gramophone jerked to a halt in Delacroix's nerveless grasp Caxton's records, balanced on the top, slewed forwards, hitting the hard parquet floor half a second before the gramophone.'

The Frenchman let out an involuntary cry. Laval sprang up, Bramall rushed to the door. Delacroix looked thunderstruck. He was staring at the floor, where both records, spilled from their sleeves, lay shattered into a hundred pieces.

'Oh, for fuck's sake!' Bramall called out, in English.

Delacroix, his face crimson with embarrassment, placed the gramophone on the ground next to the armoire, then got down on his hands and knees to gather up the fragments.

Laval glared at him icily. 'Alain, Alain! Is it any wonder your soldiers deserted you? What am I going to do with you?'

486

Humiliated, Delacroix averted his eyes. He began to mumble to himself, picking up two pieces of one of the recordings and pressing them together. 'Perhaps it can be repaired,' he ventured.

Laval dismissed the spectacle of his aide and turned back to Bramall and Isabel, whose dismay was written all over their faces. He shrugged. '*Désolé, mes enfants*. So much for your evidence! But you present me with a dilemma. Did you come to me in good faith? Was this all part of a trick? Have I missed out on the opportunity of a lifetime or been blessed by Fate? It is impossible to say. You burden me with concerns, but you do not provide me with any proof of the collusion you suggest. I will talk to Ambassador Abetz. I will seek the opinion of our own man in Madrid. What I will not do, on the basis of British hearsay, is put at risk a relationship between my Government and the Third Reich that has only recently been constructed and on which the success of France's future standing in the world depends.'

Isabel's face fell visibly at this. Laval observed her for a second before turning to Bramall. 'Have you nothing to say, monsieur?'

By way of reply, Bramall sat down, lifted his left foot up so that it rested on his right knee and pressed a concealed stud in the heel of his boot. There was a discernible click. Isabel gasped in alarm.

Delacroix, who had regained his feet and was now standing in the doorway, started back, as if Bramall had produced a grenade. Laval, however, looked on, intrigued, as the stranger twisted the heel to one side to reveal a small metal spool.

'I see that your ingenuity has not entirely deserted you,' he said. 'So what do you have there?'

'This, Monsieur, is part of the original magnetic tape,

recorded by the SD in the German Legation in Madrid. Everything, and more, that was on the gramophone records is contained on this reel. I appreciate that the necessary technology to play it does not yet exist in France, but if you will only bear with me, I feel sure that your scientists …'

' – Ah, but that is where you are wrong!' Laval slammed the door in Delacroix's face, leaving the aide stranded in the hallway. 'If I am not mistaken, the tape you have in your hand is meant to be played on a *Magnetophon*.'

The shock Bramall experienced on hearing this was total. Laval's casual reference to a technology for which the British would have given their eye teeth had come completely out of the blue. 'Yes,' he stammered. But you're not going to tell me that …?'

' It arrived two days ago. It is not even out of its box. A gift from Ambassador Abetz. He thought it would be useful for the *Maréchal* and I when we are recording our speeches for the wireless.'

The Frenchman walked purposefully over to a large crate in the corner of his office and drew open the flaps. Dipping inside, he rummaged through piles of wood shavings and shredded newspaper until he reached what he was looking for. There, inside, was a large metal casing. On the top were the letters AEG and the legend, '*Magnetophon*.'

Bramall was overwhelmed. The irony was stunning. 'I won't say that I'm speechless, but it is hard to know which words to apply to this situation.' He turned to Isabel. 'I can't believe that we went to all that trouble, and then here, in the middle of occupied France …'

' – Free France,' interrupted Laval.

'Yes. In the heart of free France, in the office of the man we were most trying to reach, is exactly the machine we needed.'

Laval struck a heroic pose. 'So now,' he said, 'if you will only help me to get this machine out of its box, we will discover what exactly it is that is so overwhelmingly important to my country.'

A plaintiff knock could be heard at the door. Laval called out over his shoulder: 'Yes, yes, Alain, you may come in. Everything is all right now. I have the situation in hand.'

Playing back the tape was simplicity itself. Laval had been taught how to use a *Magnetophon* during his last visit to Paris and proved surprisingly adroit with both tapes and recorder. Caxton had also done a good job. The tape, though more compressed than on its original reel, unwound without a flaw.

He pressed the button marked 'Play'.

'Good day, gentlemen.' The guttural Spanish of Eberhard von Stohrer filled the room.

Fifteen minutes later, the second most important man in France stubbed out a Gauloise in the ashtray on his desk and turned to his guests. He looked almost disappointed. 'My apologies,' he began. 'I underestimated you. You have brought me information that could prove vital to us in our continuing negotiations with Berlin. You may even, dare I say it, have saved the French Empire.'

Bramall smiled modestly.

'But,' Laval went on, 'regrettably, you have also left me with a most serious headache. How do I explain to the Germans that I suddenly know everything about their plans? They will be suspicious, no?'

'You can live with that, surely' Bramall volunteered. Isabel shifted in her chair.

'Possibly,' said Laval. 'It is true that we have our own agent in Madrid, who I may tell you has already divulged to us her view that Spain is conspiring against French interests.'

'You mean the Comtesse?'

'Who else? Even as we speak, she is on her way to Vichy. I expect her any minute/'

'Then we should wait.'

The Frenchman shrugged and wore a sad smile, as if he hated to be the bearer of sad tidings. As Bramall opened his mouth to speak, Laval lifted his hand, indicating that he had not yet concluded what he wanted to say. 'How am I to resolve the dilemma in which you place me?' he asked, looking from Bramall to Isabel, then back again. 'For we have reached an impasse, have we not?' He examined his fingernails, which were black, and quickly withdrew them beneath the parapet of his desk.

Isabel looked uneasily between the two men. The tension in the air was unbearable.

Laval pressed a red button on his desk. 'You leave me with no choice,' he said. At once, two gendarmes entered the office. Both had their guns drawn. 'Arrest these two,' Laval said. 'They are foreign agents. Search them and take them to the cells.'

Bramall and Isabel stared at each other. Delacroix's face lit up with unexpected joy.

'What did you expect?' Laval continued, baring his teeth. 'That I would take you to Pétain so that he could award you with the *Legion d'honneur?*' That was never going to happen. Thanks to you, I have learned what Berlin has in mind for the French and Spanish empires. This information will be greatly to our advantage in the weeks and months ahead. We can tailor our demands and responses in the light of what you have told us. But prudence dictates that I should also inform the Germans that we have shot two British agents who parachuted into Vichy and tried to foment rebellion among our young men. They will be pleased. They will know that we do not tolerate outside interference in our affairs.'

Isabel struggled to take in what was happening. They had risked their lives, overcome all kinds of obstacles, presented, against the odds, a flawless, unanswerable case, and now this ill-kempt buffoon, concerned only for his own position, was dismissing them as of no account. 'How dare you?' she began. 'You can't possibly ... have you no sense of honour?'

Keeping his hands hidden from view, Laval picked at his fingernails.

Bramall wondered what chance there was that he could get to the Frenchman before the gendarmes opened fire or beat him senseless with their truncheons. One stride, a metre at most, he reckoned. Pulling up short, he glared at Laval, as if engraving his image on his brain for future reference. 'You really are a bastard,' he said.

'And you, mon vieux, are now a prisoner of the lawful government of France, in Vichy to incite murder and rebellion, a course of action for which the punishment, I fear, is death. Forgive me, for, truly, I am desolée.' He turned to the senior of the two gendarmes. 'Take them away.'

The sun was still shining in the garden outside. The rain had stopped and the sky was a brilliant blue.

'This way,' one of the gendarmes said, jabbing the point of his gun barrel into Bramall's back. 'I'm glad I'm not in your shoes.'

A metal door, down the hall and round the corner from Laval's office, provided access to the newly built cellblock of the Hotel du Parc. But the door was locked and the gendarmes didn't have the key. A messenger was summoned and, after several minutes' delay, a sergeant appeared, somewhat out of breath. As one of the two gendarmes kept his gun on the prisoners, the sergeant tried first one key, then another. There were several, on a heavy metal ring, and it was going to take him a second or two to locate the right one.

'Who are these two anyway?' he wanted to know. 'Do I need to get a firing party together?'

Isabel looked questioningly at Bramall, who nodded, indicating with the movement of his eyes the officer standing next to her. Drawing a deep breath, she kicked out viciously, catching him square on his kneecap. He swore and dropped his automatic, which clattered to the floor.

Bramall immediately swooped down to pick up the weapon, which he then aimed at the two officers. 'Bit of a change of plan,' he told them. 'Looks like you won't be needing the firing party after all.'

'Not so fast, Monsieur!'

Bramall and Isabel's heads whipped round in unison. Delacroix was standing some 20 feet away, pointing a Mauser machine pistol straight at them. 'Put down the gun,' he said. 'I warn you, monsieur, if you do not give yourself up immediately, I shall shoot both of you, starting with Mlle. Ortega.' He was trembling as he spoke, but there was no doubting his seriousness.

The sergeant was smiling now, reaching for his sidearm. Bramall was out of time, and he knew it. Jinking first to right, then to left, he raised the automatic and ran at Delacroix. He had just managed to raise the barrel in the Frenchman's direction when the Mauser went off. Three of the oncoming stream of bullets thudded into his chest and left shoulder, sending a shock wave of pain straight to his heart. Five more tore into the head and body of the sergeant.

Isabel screamed.

Delacroix raced towards his victims, howling with rage, almost tripping over the dead officer as he ran. 'Imbecile!' he roared. 'Look what you m-made me do! But you won't get away with it.'

For a moment, there was total confusion. Isabel struggled to get to Bramall, who lay, bleeding profusely, on the floor. The second Gendarme held her back.

Delacroix had meanwhile moved beyond all reason. Hands shaking, he lifted the machine pistol and aimed it at Bramall's head.

'Put it down, Alain!' The voice, from the opposite end of the corridor, was steely and uncompromising.

Delacroix froze.

It was Dominique.

She stood three-quarters on to the Frenchman, her feet apart, holding a silver automatic in a classic, two-handed grip. 'I said, put it down.'

'No!' Delacroix replied, twisting his head in the direction of his boyhood companion. He had been tormented enough for one day. 'You m-may think you are in charge,' he stammered. 'But you do n-not g-give me orders. I g-give *you* orders.'

Dominique fixed her eyes on his hands and maintained a steady hold on her automatic. She had no wish to kill Delacroix, but she knew that in this mood he was capable of anything. 'I have spoken to Laval. If you force me, I will not hesitate to shoot you. You must know that I am a much better shot than you. For once in your life don't be a fool and allow us to work this out without further loss of life.'

It was more than Delacroix could stand. How dare she speak to him like this? And in front of the Gendarmerie! Who took the decisions round here? Was it him, with his years of service to his country, or Dominique de Fourneau, the child of privilege, who all of her life had enjoyed the natural advantages that were denied to him? He struggled to keep a hold of himself but knew he was in danger of losing control. He was sweating and trembling at the same time. He turned round, spitting with rage, determined to assert himself.

But then he saw her. She was looking at him down her nose, as she always did. And her hands were steady and she seemed entirely calm. He knew then that if he attempted to open fire, she would kill him, and, God help him, Delacroix did not want to die. He looked down. He could feel a knot in his throat and the shaking in his hands was getting worse. Sweat poured down his face. Uttering a strangled oath that was more of a drawn out admission of his defeat, he threw down his weapon and watched in despair as it skittered across the marble floor.

Dominique waited a moment before lowering her automatic. With the slightest inclination of her head, she signalled to a second duo of Gendarmes approaching from the opposite side of the corridor, accompanied by Laval. Immediately, they grabbed hold of Delacroix, who had begun literally to shake with rage.

There was a brief moment of silence, then Isabel broke free

of her captors and ran towards Bramall, fear gripping her heart. He lay still, face-down, not even twitching. A pool of blood was spreading out from his chest and leaching into the parquet. Dropping to her knees by his side, she lifted his head and turned it towards her. The eyes were pale and sightless, the irises contracted to mere points of black, like full stops on a page.

She bent lower and began to turn him over to check if he was breathing. As she did so, Dominique reached down and gripped her by the shoulders, pulling her back. Isabel's head shook violently. 'No,' she screamed, seizing hold of the Frenchwoman's wrists, desperate to free herself. 'Let me go! Don't you see what has happened? And it's all my fault. First Teresa, then Eddy. Now Charlie. Everyone I have loved is dead!'

It was one hour later that Sir Samuel Hoare in Madrid received a telephone call from Laval, in Vichy, routed via Lisbon. The two men had once been close and each could easily gauge the other's thoughts.

'You should know,' Laval said, 'that your message, as well as the letter to Pétain from Churchill, has been received loud and clear and that the appropriate steps will be taken in the months ahead. France will always defend its interests. However, I must inform you that your principal messenger in this affair has been shot during a most unfortunate altercation involving one of my subordinates whose existing anti-English fixation was reinforced by what took place recently in Mers-el-Kébir. Your compatriot is not expected to last the night.'

'That is most unfortunate,' Hoare said. 'As were the events in Mers to which you have just referred. The young man in question is a friend to France as well as Spain and regarded the information of which you are now in possession to be of the utmost importance. What, may I ask, of his companion?'

'The Spanish girl? She is unharmed, but grieving for her companion.'

'Of course. Please convey to her my best wishes. In the meantime, I shall inform Mr Churchill that you and Marshal Pétain will do whatever is necessary to safeguard the integrity of your country and its empire.'

'On that you may depend.'

Four hours later, a French Army surgeon emerged from the operating theatre at Vichy's *centre hospitalier*, to talk to Isabel, who had been pacing up and down in the corridor, desperate for news. A neat, spare figure, he was studiously polite, yet clinical in his explanation. He looked exhausted. One bullet had been removed from the patient's shoulder, he told her. A second had passed clean through his body, collapsing his left lung and inducing an immediate cardiac arrest. Fortunately, medical staff stationed in the building had managed to re-start the heart. The damaged lung had since been reinflated and was functioning almost normally. The third bullet had snapped the patient's left clavicle before lodging in the muscle between his neck and shoulder, narrowly missing an artery. With luck, the surgeon said, the wounds would heal within a year, but for the next month at least he would require lots of bed rest and regular medication.

'May I talk to him?' Isabel asked.

The doctor frowned. He looked exhausted. 'Your friend has undergone a most traumatic afternoon, mademoiselle. You must be careful not to tire him.'

'I understand,' Isabel said, offering the Frenchman an equally exhausted smile. 'Thank you for everything you have done. I am extremely grateful to you, and to your team.'

The doctor patted her hand. *'De rien,'* he said. *'À votre service.'*

Bramall was asleep in the intensive care ward when Isabel appeared at his side. He was dreaming about Manuela Valdés. Once more, he stood with the Catalan fighter on the bank of the River Ebro, her left arm hooked around his neck, his right hand raised a little above her head so that the lighter he held there could illuminate her face. As he gazed into her eyes, she told him she had to go to rejoin her unit. *'Te amo* – I love you – he told her, which for that split second was true. In reply, she had smiled at him and told him she loved him, too.

What happened next changed everything. As her arm slid from round his neck, the low roar of the incoming Messerschmitt switched to a high-pitched whine. Bramall looked up. The aircraft, silhouetted in grey against the old moon, was approaching low and fast across the waterway, targeting the assault boats pulling away from the river's eastern bank. The moment it came into effective range, the guns on its wings opened up, their muzzles flaring yellow and orange. On the boats, the effect was instantaneous. The Republican troops, packed tightly together, rifles by their sides, fell in serried ranks, their screams unheard. Bramall tried to get out of the raider's path. But his legs wouldn't respond. All he could do was look on as if he and the German pilot were bound together in a single destiny.

That was when Manuela re-appeared. What happened next happened very fast. Placing her hands squarely on his shoulders, she swung her right leg into the backs of his knees, causing him to topple over and tumble down the incline into the safety of a group of trees. He didn't see the bullets from the 109 that cut into her back, but he did hear her scream. Her body ended up next to the water, one hand pointing across to the Ebro's eastern flank.

For the first time since the night she died, he remembered everything. For the first time, he saw her sacrifice for what it was, a selfless act of providence that had given him a second chance at life. An intense sense of grief, and gratitude, flooded over him.

His eyes opened. At first, there were only shapes and shades of grey. But then colours began to break through and he was able to focus. Where was he? Something had happened to him. What was it? Then he remembered. He remembered charging at Delacroix and the Frenchman's machine pistol going off. He remembered thrusting the sergeant who had boasted of arranging a firing party in front of Isabel so that any bullets that came her way would have to go through him first. There had been a rattle of automatic fire, muzzle flash and someone screaming. After that … nothing.

He felt a hand on his face. He looked up.

Isabel.

He tried to speak, but his voice only came out in a whisper. 'Is it really you?'

'Yes,' she said. 'It's me.' And then she bent down and kissed him lightly on the lips.

'Thank God! What happened? Are you all right? Are you safe?'

He was sweating and she dipped a flannel into a bowl of cold water placed on the table beside the bed before gently mopping his brow.

'I'm fine,' she said. ' You saved my life.'

The relief that coursed through him when she said this was like no feeling he had experienced before. He raised one hand off the bed, wanting to reach out to her. 'I was so frightened that he was going to shoot you. I couldn't let that happen.'

'Hush now,' she said.

His mind raced. 'But how are you here? Where am I, anyway? And why aren't you in jail?'

'They let me go. You're in a hospital in Vichy. The doctors have removed bullets from your chest and shoulder and you're going to be fine. It will take time, that's all – but it turns out we have plenty of that.'

'How?' he mouthed.

'Churchill's letter,' she replied, smiling. 'It called on Pétain, on a point of honour, not to 'shoot the messenger,' and begged him to ensure our safe return to England. He personally guaranteed the genuineness of the tapes. There was more, apparently, but for Pétain alone. Laval took him the letter soon after you were shot – Delacroix had left it sitting on his desk – and asked if he thought it was a forgery. Pétain said no. He had seen Churchill's writing before, after the evacuation from Dunkirk. No one else, he felt sure, wrote in such execrable French.'

She paused. 'Anyway, the point is that we are to be kept hidden and sent back to London as soon as you are strong enough to travel.'

Bramall nodded. 'What about Delacroix?'

'Under arrest. He was going to kill you, Charlie, but Dominique stopped him. It was she who found the Churchill letter. She arrived from Spain and went straight to his office, and there it was. She took it to Laval, who opened it – well, he is that sort of man – and that was when the shooting broke out in the corridor. He ordered that you be given emergency medical treatment while he went to see Pétain.'

'The citoyenne is an extraordinary woman.'

'Yes, she is.'

Bramall closed his eyes. For a moment he thought he saw Manuela and Romero looking down at him nodding their approval. But then the image faded. The anaesthetic was continuing to dull the pain, but his breathing remained shallow. 'It looks like I warned you of the dangers, when I should have been warning myself.'

'We both knew the risks,' she said.

'How will they get us back to England?'

'By way of Lisbon.'

'Ah! Croft will be thrilled.

'He sends his best wishes and hopes to see us soon. He asked me to tell you that Mr Churchill is delighted.'

'That's something, I suppose.'

Isabel pulled a chair up against the bed and sat down, bending her face towards him so that he did not have to strain to make himself understood. 'Strickland spoke to your mother,' she said. 'He told her you'd been shot but that you were recovering and would be home before too long. She didn't ask any questions, apparently, but Strickland thinks he heard a catch in her voice. She may have been crying.'

'But what about *your* family? Your parents. Were you able to contact them?'

'Yes. I telephoned my mother in Madrid. I didn't tell her what happened to me. You never know who is listening in. I just said I was well and would be living in England until the end of the war. She understood completely. I am sure of it. She said my father has gone back to the Army and they will be stationed in Irún.'

'Irún? Then if the Germans enter Spain, he will be the first to salute.'

'I doubt that very much. I believe he has learned his lesson. Besides, after all that's happened, the Germans will not be coming.' She brushed his hair away from his eyes. 'Franco will soon discover that the French know all about his schemes and have moved to block them.'

'So Gibraltar stays British?'

'For now,' she said.

'And the Duke?'

'In Nassau. Mr Strickland plans to visit him there and explain the reality of his situation.'

'Really? I'd like to be there for that.'

She took his hand. 'Charlie. I know you have no faith, but when you are better I want you to come to church with me? I should like to arrange a mass for Eddy.'

Bramall thought for a moment. 'We should do it in Ireland. There must be a priest somewhere who isn't a Fascist. And I can show you where he and I began. The pair of us came out of the same earth, neither of us entirely belonging.'

'I'd like that.'

A nurse put her head round the curtains. Isabel nodded. 'I have to go now,' she said. 'You need to rest.'

'Will you be here when I wake up?'

She laid a hand on his brow. 'Always,' she said.

HISTORICAL NOTE

Spain, in spite of continuing pressure from Berlin, did not join the Axis. On October 22, 1940, the day before his summit with Franco in the French border town of Hendaye, Hitler met with Pierre Laval in Montoire sur-le-Loir, north of Tours. Laval warned that if Spain was rewarded with French colonial assets, most obviously Morocco and Oran, in return for joining the Axis, then the French empire and fleet, already tempted by De Gaulle, would rise against Germany. The *Führer*, aware of the prospect but shocked by its emphatic nature, took the message to heart. At Hendaye, he informed Franco that, in spite of assurances to the contrary given by Ribbentrop to Serrano Suñer just six weeks before, Spain would have to await the defeat of Britain and the re-allocation of its colonies before there could be any additions to its imperial map. Franco was outraged and demanded what he had been promised. Though he yearned to recover Gibraltar and win for himself a seat at the New Order's high table, he refused to give in to Hitler's bullying and maintained his neutrality, confirming the German leader in his view that his next big campaign should be the invasion of Russia.

Göring, who had come to realise the impossibility of invading England, considered Hitler's failure to go for the Mediterranean option the worst strategic mistake of the war.

Gibraltar remained in British hands. Vichy attacks petered out in the autumn of 1940, though the Italian air force and navy staged a number of attacks between 1940 and 1943, sinking several ships and forcing the British to remain on constant alert. In November, 1940, in response to the Axis threat, it was the ships and aircraft of the Gibraltar squadron that destroyed Italy's much-touted *Regia Marina* at the Battle of Taranto. Later, the same ships, together with the Alexandria squadron, supplied Montgomery's Eighth Army in its long, ultimately triumphant struggle with Rommel's Afrika Korps. Throughout the war, the Rock served as a base for anti-submarine warfare in the Battle of the Atlantic and, in 1942, as the key staging post in the Anglo-American occupation of French North Africa during Operation Torch.

Churchill's view of Franco's contribution to the War was surprisingly tolerant ('in victory, magnanimity'). In his History of the Second World War, he wrote: 'Spain held the key to all British enterprises in the Mediterranean, and never in the darkest hours did she turn the lock against us.' His true opinion of Franco, once he knew that victory in Europe was in the bag, is better echoed in a letter, delivered to the Pardo Palace in January, 1945, in which he reminded the Spanish dictator that he had on many occasions declared the defeat of the allies by Hitler to be both 'deSirable and unavoidable,' and in which the British leader unequivocally ruled out the admission of Fascist Spain into any future world body.

A note on the major (real life) players:
- Francisco Franco lived on as *Caudillo* of Spain until 1975, dying of natural causes just short of his eighty-third birthday. He continued to hunt and shoot almost to the end, but as death approached he was often to be found in tears.

- Marshal Philippe Pétain was sentenced to death as a traitor after the war, but had his sentence commuted to solitary confinement for life and died in 1951, at the age of ninety-five.

- Sir Winston Churchill ended his days a hero in 1965, aged ninety-one. He refused a dukedom and remained a member of the House of Commons until 1964.

- Ramón Serrano Suñer was dismissed from the Spanish Government in September, 1941 after Franco came to believe his brother-in-law was after his job. Trading on the fact that he and Hitler had fallen out at the end of 1940, Serrano successfully rehabilitated himself as an international lawyer and wrote a famous political memoir, *Between Hendaye and Gibraltar*, in which he was the star performer. But his true voice reasserted itself from time to time. In 1961, he boasted to a group of German journalists visiting Madrid that the press during his time as Minister for Information was unreservedly pro-Nazi. A lifelong hypochondriac, he died in September 2003, eleven days before his 102nd birthday.

- Joachim von Ribbentrop was convicted of war crimes at Nuremberg and hanged on October 16, 1946. 'I always did what I thought was right,' he wrote to his wife two days before he was due to die, 'although Adolf Hitler would not accept much advice about foreign policy.' His execution was bungled and he took ten minutes to die.

- Pierre Laval, revived after attempting suicide, was shot in the courtyard of Fresnes prison in October, 1945, strapped to a chair, without shoes, shouting out his defiance. All of France, including many judges and Public Prosecutors whom he had appointed, had demanded his blood. De Gaulle, who had denied him clemency, noted in his diary that the arch-collaborator had died well.

- Sir Samuel Hoare, tango and ice dancer extraordinaire, served as ambassador in Spain until 1944, when he was raised to the peerage as Viscount Templewood. His memoirs, *Nine Troubled Years* and *Ambassador on Special Mission*, sold well. During World War One, Hoare had served as a British Intelligence agent in Moscow and, some say, shot dead the debauched mystic, Rasputin. He died in 1959, aged seventy-nine.

- Eberhard von Stohrer was removed as German ambassador to Madrid in December, 1942 amid suggestions that he had always opposed the false prospectus of Hitler and Fascism. Proceedings against him, charging him with treason, were mooted in Berlin, but he survived the war and lived on in retirement until 1953.

- Walter Schellenberg (later promoted to *Brigadeführer*) continued to thrive in the SS, enjoying a particularly close relationship with Himmler, but eventually threw in his lot with the doomed 1944 conspiracy against Hitler. Most of those who took part in the attempt on Hitler's life died a horrible death, strung from meat hooks on piano wire. Not Schellenberg. *The Labyrinth*, his memoir of a life in espionage, was published with some success after the war. In 1952, having served six years imprisonment for his part in crimes committed by the SS, he died in Italy of cancer.

- Admiral Wilhelm Canaris. The wily head of the *Abwehr* was never in favour of Operation Felix. He had privately warned Franco – and Stohrer – that Germany was bound to lose the war eventually and that Spanish entry into the conflict would be ill-advised. By 1944, the admiral was a fully-fledged member of the German Resistance who hoped to arrest Hitler and open negotiations with the allies. He was shot as a traitor on April 9, 1945.

- The Duke of Windsor served as Governor-General of the Bahamas for the remainder of the War, after which he and the Duchess returned to Paris, where they lived lives of sublime idleness until their deaths. Shortly after arriving in Nassau, he sent a coded message to the Portuguese banker Ricardo Espírito Santo-Silva – a leading Nazi sympathiser, with links to Ribbentrop – in which he proclaimed his readiness to return to Europe to help end the war in Germany's favour. As he remarked unabashedly to a Bahamian acquaintance: 'After the war is over and Hitler crushes the Americans ... we'll take over. They [the British] don't want me as their king, but I'll be back as their leader.'

On 13th September 1940, an FBI officer sent a memo to his boss, J. Edgar Hoover, in which he claimed that the Duchess had conducted an affair with Ribbentrop and continued to communicate with him. The Duchess, he wrote, had obtained extensive information concerning the British and French official positions that she was passing on to the Germans.

The FBI kept an open file on the Duchess throughout the War. Later, the agency monitored the fact that she had a bizarre affair with Jimmy Donahue, the gay playboy grandson of stores mogul, J.W. Woolworth.

The Duke died in 1972, aged seventy-seven; the Duchess lingered on, in splendid isolation, until 1986.